EMBRACE
The Darkness

THE MAURA QUINN SERIES BOOK ONE

ASHLEY N. ROSTEK

Embrace the Darkness

Copyright © 2020 Ashley N. Rostek

Edited by Alexandra Fresch of To the Letter Services

Cover design by The Dirty Tease

Formatting by Dark Ink Designs

BOOKS BY ASHLEY N. ROSTEK

Maura Quinn Series
Embrace the Darkness
Endure the Pain
Endurance
Escape the Reaper

WITSEC Series
Find Me
Save Me
Love Me
Free Me

This book is dedicated to Alan—the love of my life. Without your sacrifice, constant support, and encouragement to keep writing, this dream would have never come true.

BEFORE YOU READ

The content in this book may be triggering to some. The trigger warnings below will contain spoilers. If you don't want anything spoiled and you're comfortable reading triggering content, stop reading this page, flip to chapter one, and happy reading <3

Embrace the Darkness contains descriptive violence, killing, drugs, alcohol, and sexual content. There's a lot of foul language. The main character was raped years prior to this story taking place. However, there are flash back scenes to the rape, and her injuries and trauma from it are talked about.

After reading the previous trigger warnings and you still wish to continue reading, welcome to the world of Maura Quinn. It's going to be a crazy ride :)

CHAPTER ONE

"Shit! Shit! Shit!"

Attempting to calm myself, I relaxed my white-knuckled grasp on the car's steering wheel and I took a deep breath. When that didn't work, I pulled at one of the many rubber bands around my wrist. *Snap!* The slight sting always anchored me, temporarily pulling my focus.

I was mentally kicking myself for forgetting my flash drive—the one thing I'd needed to make sure I'd had before I'd walked out the door this morning. It held my slide presentation for my afternoon psychology class, which was going to start in thirty minutes. The majority of my grade was depending on that damn presentation, and of course, the professor had to be a stickler when it came to punctuality and liked to lock the door as soon as class started.

Stressed and pissed off were the worst kind of combination. It made it harder to keep what I called my *darkness* at bay. *Just breathe, Maura. Reel it in.* Easier said than done. *Snap! Snap!* My poor wrist was going to be sore by the end of the day.

Driving more than ten miles per hour over the speed limit, I pulled up to the little townhouse community, located thirty minutes outside of Trinity College, which I'd managed to cut down to twenty. I whipped my black Audi into my reserved spot like a bad stunt driver and paused when I noticed my boyfriend's Jeep parked in the spot next to mine.

He was supposed to be at work.

Tom, my boyfriend of just a little over a year, had started working at a law firm downtown. Things had been moving along great for him there. His boss had assigned him his first case, one that'd been demanding a lot of his time, especially his nights and weekends. I'd never admit it out loud, but I was kind of relieved he was so busy.

Tom had graduated last May. The summer off together had been nice. When I'd had to return to school this fall, he'd been bored at home, still looking for a job. Our relationship had become... strained. My first three weeks back in class, all we'd done was fight. He'd wanted attention and thrown fits when I couldn't give it to him. I was working on my master's in behavioral psychology and the workload was atrocious. Tom had not been understanding of that. Instead, he'd made a point to make me feel guilty that my every waking minute of every day hadn't been dedicated to him.

Sighing, exhausted by the memory, I tried to remind myself it had been a difficult time for us both. The universe had decided to grant us a reprieve when he'd been offered his dream job. He was busy. I was busy. Things were better.

Despite his faults, Tom could be sweet and charming, and had that sexy intelligent appeal. He was kind of nerdy, with his goofy thick-rimmed glasses and mud-brown hair parted down the side. He loved to research old court cases as a hobby and watch Law and Order just to point out the mistakes. It was adorable. The good outweighed the bad. That was how things were supposed to be. Nobody was perfect... right?

The best of all his attributes: he was normal. He came from a normal family. He lived a normal life with normal thoughts and aspirations. Just being around him made me feel normal, which was something I'd wanted for a long time.

Was I getting tired of saying the word *normal*? Yes. I honestly hated the stupid word more days than not lately, but it was what I needed. It was what I'd dedicated the last six years of my life to maintaining. *There's no going back.*

I jumped out of my car with my house key at the ready. In my pursuit of the flash drive, I rushed through the front door and dropped my purse on the coffee table in the living room before dashing up the stairs and heading down the hall straight to our room. I was so focused on grabbing my flash drive and leaving as fast as I could, I didn't really pay attention to my surroundings, or else I would have noticed right away something wasn't right.

I beelined for my nightstand, where I'd put my flash drive the night before. From the bathroom connected to our room, I heard the shower running. *Tom must be in the shower*, I mused as I shoved the small black drive into the front pocket of my jeans. Because I was in such a rush, I debated whether I should just leave without saying a word to him or poke my head into the bathroom to say a quick *hi* before rushing back out the door. I decided on the latter. If he found out I'd come and gone without caring to see him, I'd never hear the end of it.

Be more caring and understanding, Maura.

Tom was a sensitive man. Not saying I wasn't. It was just, lately... I'd been trying very hard to ignore the fact it sometimes felt like a chore to have to be understanding toward his feelings. For the hundredth time, I reminded myself Tom was different. He was a good man, a normal man, even if he could be a big man-baby sometimes. He was extremely different than the men I'd grown up with, that was for sure.

Stop thinking about them. They're your past, not your future. Tom is your future. I had to stop comparing my life now to what it had been before.

I shook my head to clear the unwanted thoughts before heading toward the bathroom door to get my, "Hi, sweetie! Bye, sweetie!" over with so I could drive like a madwoman back to campus.

Reaching out to push open the door, I paused. *What the fuck?* The sound of a feminine giggle slammed into me like a semi-truck. Standing a few feet from the door that was slightly ajar, I was close enough to hear what exactly was going down in my bathroom.

When I heard the woman moan, my stomach plummeted. I backed up, stepping on something in the process. My unblinking eyes dropped from the door, finding my feet surrounded by clothes that had obviously been thrown askew. A sleazy red bra and matching lacy thong that were definitely not mine, along with the suit I saw Tom wearing this morning before he supposedly left for work. *What the fuck?* I mentally repeated.

"Oh, Tom! Right there!" the woman cried out.

I know that voice!

The knife of betrayal sunk a little deeper into my back. I was almost certain it was my friend Tina's voice. We'd been friends for five years, ever since we were dorm-mates sophomore year. Sure, she was a bit of a wild card and objectified men like they existed for her enjoyment alone, but I'd always liked that about her. She was fun and had always been a good friend to me. In the beginning of our friendship, she'd patiently coaxed me out of my shell, helped me adjust to a normal way of life, which in turn had prepared me for Tom. Hell, she'd encouraged me to date him!

I never would have thought she'd... We'd just had lunch yesterday. The entire time I'd vented about mine and Tom's problems and the bitch had just sat there pretending to be my friend while giving me advice.

I took another step back, trying to mentally remove myself from what was happening. I needed a moment to process everything. My emotions were threatening to take over and letting that happen was never wise.

My father's voice echoed in my head, warning me not to chase the rabbit. Stay in control.

I took a deep breath to collect myself. Once I had most of my pressing emotions locked up, I tried to think of how I was going to handle this.

Should I barge in there and watch them flounder at being caught? Should I go downstairs and wait for them to finish? Or should I go to class and pretend I didn't see anything? Pretending seemed like the easiest and most appealing option, but what did that say about me? Could I really look the other way? I'd never been the type to allow others to walk all over me, so why was I okay with it now?

Damnit! I don't know!

The water in the bathroom shut off, interrupting my internal debate. My eyes darted around the room, catching on the door to my walk-in closet. It was the closest place I could get to as the bathroom door started to open. I dashed into the tiny room, regretting it instantly. *The closet, really, Maura?*

I left the door cracked, giving the windowless room a little light. Apparently I was a glutton for pain, because I couldn't stop myself from peeking out as Tom and most definitely Tina stepped out of the bathroom. *You don't want to see this,* I told myself, but I couldn't look away.

They were both naked, dripping wet from their shower. I watched my boyfriend carry my friend with her legs wrapped around his waist. Their lips were glued to each other while their tongues played tonsil hockey. One of his hands slid between them, making her squirm in his arms.

Unable to remove my gaze, I couldn't help but compare what

they were doing with what he did with me. The way he touched her, his fingers between her legs. I knew how those fingers felt, soft but firm as he stroked my sensitive flesh.

I think I'm going to be sick.

He threw her on the bed, amping up their foreplay to rough passion, then climbed over her and thrust little Tom between her legs. I covered my ears as she gave a gag-worthy performance by screaming out his name before they started going at it like rabbits.

The sounds made me feel like I was trapped in a bad porno. His grunting, her moans, and *my* bed shaking was worse than listening to someone scratch a chalkboard. I stepped away from the door in a futile attempt to put space between us.

Less than five minutes later—I assumed, because I knew from experience he couldn't hold out very long—the noises subsided. I peeked out again to find them cuddling under the bed's sheet.

"When will Maura be home?" she asked.

Tom leaned over to read the clock on my nightstand. "Not for another four hours. Her afternoon class is about to start."

Fuck! I forgot! This day was getting shittier and shittier.

"Good. I get to have you for a little while longer," she purred as she leaned in to kiss him affectionately. "Have you thought over what we last discussed?"

He sighed. "I need more time."

His response was apparently the wrong one. Tina jerked away from him, sitting up abruptly, causing the sheet hiding her breasts to fall. *Fake breasts!* At least mine were real; not as big, but they were nothing to sneeze at.

"I don't see how hard it is to just leave her, Tom! You can't stand her. The thought of having sex with her is a turn off because she's been milking the victim card. Which, I honestly think she's lying to get attention. If she was really raped, shouldn't she be over it by now? It's been seven years. Like, get the fuck over it already."

My breath hitched, my lungs constricting. *He told her?*

"Listen, Tom. Maura isn't what you signed up for. She's a frigid bitch with some serious mental issues, and if she *is* even telling the truth, that pussy is damaged goods. You need to end it."

My spine went ramrod straight. For years, I'd been working to close the wounds that horrible night had left behind. It hadn't been easy. Most of the time it had felt like a never ending uphill battle. I was still healing. I still had cracks where the gaping wounds used to be. Hearing her cruel words... it was like her boney fingers slipped through my cracks, ripping me open to expose all my pain and insecurities.

I trusted them! I knew there were bad people in this world. God, did I know. But there weren't supposed to be any in this new life I'd made for myself. Everything was supposed to be *normal*!

Was the universe trying to tell me that I was doomed to only know bad people? My assumptions and expectations about this life were just blown to smithereens by two people I thought cared about me. *Yeah, I think the universe just made my fate perfectly fucking clear.*

He sighed again. "I know. You're right."

My whole body started shaking. *How did I let this happen?*

Everything in me hurt. My chest burned with anger, but above all, my entire being—my soul—felt exposed.

The battle going on inside of me was making the walls of the small closet close in and the air nonexistent. I was having a panic attack. I'd had a few in the past, so I recognized all the signs. The best way to stop it was to regain control. I tried to grab ahold of said control, through the black hole of my overwhelming emotions, only to have it slip through my fingers like sand. I couldn't get a firm grip, not with the constant reminder in the other room.

Then get rid of the reminder, my darkness whispered from deep, very deep within me.

No! I shook my head violently. *I can't go back.*

The pain intensified in my chest. Sweat beaded on my skin, plastering my hair to my neck and face. Temptation slithered inside me as my panic attack worsened. My darkness rose and rose as my will faltered. I shouldn't have given in, but I was helpless to stop it. Enveloping me like warm water in a bath, the darkness consumed me, breaking to the surface.

I didn't know how much time had passed. A minute? Two minutes? I wasn't sure, but the change in me was fast.

A strange calmness took over, banishing the attack that had wreaked havoc on my body. It felt like a different *being* controlled me with its own thoughts and feelings. Except it wasn't a different being. It was me—a part of me—the darkness I'd suppressed for so long in my attempt to be normal. Now, the seal was broken.

As I reached for my gun safe on the shelf, I found myself numb. There was no internal debate or unsettled feelings with what I was about to do. Just purpose. The gun had been a gift from my father before I'd left for college, as a means to protect myself. I entered in the safe's code and pulled out a sleek silver pistol and matching silencer. The silencer had been a gift from my father's enforcer, Jameson. My family was... complicated.

I screwed on the silencer as I listened in on what was going on in the other room. Tom was talking about going downstairs to get something, then teased Tina about *round two.* I scrunched my nose.

I peeked out to see Tom leaving the room in only his boxers. Tina was laying on her stomach, playing on her phone. Her back was to me, which was giving me a direct view of her skanky ass.

I pushed open the closet door soundlessly and stepped toward the bed. The floor creaked beneath my foot. The sound wasn't loud but still pierced the silence like a bowling ball tossed through a china shop.

I froze.

"Back for round two, baby?" she teased, turning around. Her eyes widened when they met mine. I was too quick for her to react in any other way. Raising my gun, I struck her as hard as I could across the temple. Her body flew back on the bed, unconscious, blood trickling down the side of her face. I took a seat next to her legs on the bed and waited.

Tom had a smile on his face and a bounce in his step when he returned.

Until he saw me.

His smile fell as he stood frozen in shock. He noticed my gun before his focus shifted to Tina behind me. Fear took root in his light brown eyes. He lifted his hands, palms out. I knew he was going to try to *explain,* spewing nothing but excuses. It was what any cheating, lying bastard would do. What he didn't know was that he was already dead to me. He opened his mouth to speak; I took aim just like my father had taught me and shot him in the knee.

He yelled out in pain, falling to the floor. Time ceased as I stood to make my way over to him. I didn't rush, even though I probably should have with how loud he was being, but I couldn't bring myself to move any faster. I wanted him to suffer.

If I hadn't been so pissed off, it would have been comical the way he was rolling on the floor, cradling his knee, writhing in pain. I used the toe of my boot to push him onto his back and held him there. I aimed my pistol again, then started emptying the clip into his groin, pulling the trigger over and over again. His body jerked beneath my foot, his screams filling the room. I kept pulling the trigger, counting each release until I was down to the last bullet. I put that into his head.

The screaming came to an abrupt stop, but it still rang in my ears. I glanced over at Tina. Still lying there unconscious, her chest rose and fell with even breaths.

With empty pistol in hand, I walked back to the bed, only slowing to scoop up the silk tie Tom had been wearing that day off the floor. I set my gun on the nightstand next to the bed before I rolled Tina onto her stomach.

I climbed onto the bed to straddle her back, pinning her arms beneath my legs. Wrapping Tom's tie around her neck twice, I got a good grip and pulled it tight with all my strength.

She came to when her airway was cut off. She thrashed beneath me. I pulled the tie even tighter, until my muscles burned and my arms started to shake. She struggled longer than I'd thought she would.

Long after her body stilled, I released my hold on the tie. With labored breaths, I climbed off of her, grabbed my gun, and calmly made my way downstairs.

CHAPTER TWO

Whenever the discussion of my family came up with Tom or even Tina, I either was tight-lipped or lied. As far as they knew, I was an orphan. Yeah, that was a load of crap. I had a huge family. Some of them I missed and some I could go the rest of my life without seeing ever again, but keeping who they were a secret was imperative. So it was best to pretend they didn't exist at all.

Pulling my cell from my purse, I sat on the couch, sinking into myself. I closed my eyes to help calm my racing heart. What I'd done was unforgivable. I understood that. But I wasn't looking for forgiveness. There was zero guilt on the emotional rollercoaster currently doing loops and steep drops in the pit of my stomach. I was stressing about what was going to happen next, or rather, what I needed to do next.

Upstairs, the bodies... I was completely out of my depth when it came to cleaning that mess up. I didn't even know where to begin, nor was I going to try. If I did, I might as well take my own ass to prison. I wasn't accustomed to feeling helpless. I hated it.

What I hated even more was who I needed to go to for help. I stubbornly didn't want to call him. Not to sound dramatic, but my normal life would be over. He'd make me return home.

Who am I kidding? It was over the moment I reached for my gun.

"Damnit," I seethed, opening my eyes to look down at my phone.

Almost six years ago my father had asked me if I wanted out —of the family, that is, and I'd said yes. My plan had been to go to college, then create a new life somewhere along the West Coast, preferably California. Walking along a warm beach while sipping a margarita had been my dream. With a sizable trust fund, I'd left New Haven behind and been working toward that dream here in Hartford ever since.

No one in my family was allowed out, especially the women. Our lives were at the mercy and complete control of men. It was archaic, fucked up, and had never sat well with me. I wasn't wired to be at anyone's mercy but my own. Which was why I'd rebelled, *a lot*. If Stefan hadn't been my father, I probably wouldn't have lived to see my teens, or at least been beaten into submission a long time ago. I should have been grateful that wasn't my fate. A huge part of me was, but a tiny glimmer wondered *what if*, maybe even wished my life would have stopped before I'd reached my teens, because my life growing up hadn't been sunshine and rainbows either.

My father was Stefan Quinn, the boss of the New England Irish mob. He wasn't a good man. In fact, he was a monster, and now I was about to call that very monster for help.

Okay, now I'm feeling a little regret. Purely selfish regret though.

Was I even sure he'd help me?

Yeah. He cared about me, I guessed, even if he had a shitty way of showing it. Before I'd left home, I'd been in a really bad place. It had been just after *that night* and... well, let's just say I'd rebelled on a whole other level in hopes I'd push him enough to kill me. It had been dark times at Quinn Manor, and it had ended with him asking me if I wanted out. I'd left six years ago without looking back. Apart from an occasional email here and there I hadn't spoken to Stefan or anyone else in my past life in over a year.

I gripped my phone in my hand until it hurt.

I can't do it!

You have no choice.

I dialed the number to his cell. He wasn't saved as a contact in my phone. None of their numbers were. My heart was pounding in my chest, making my body buzz all over as I put the phone to my ear. It went straight to voicemail. Annoyed, because it had been hard enough the first time, I dialed the house phone. There was only one reason his cell would be off. *Family meeting.* The phone rang twice before a feminine voice picked up.

"Quinn residence. May I ask who's calling?" I didn't recognize the voice.

"It's Maura. Put Stefan on the phone, please." I tried to be polite. The apparent irritation and my curt tone, though, made me sound condescending. *Way to go, Maura.*

There was a pregnant pause. Despite not knowing who I was speaking to, there was no way she didn't know of me. It'd be hard not to. There were pictures of me growing up all over the house. *Unless Stefan removed them all.* As soon as that thought entered my mind, I instantly knew it was false. He would never have done that. Brody wouldn't have let him.

"He's in a meeting right now. I can tell him you called." Her tone told me she knew who I was, but her response wasn't what I wanted to hear, especially in my current mood. *Stay calm.*

"I know he's in a meeting, but this is urgent."

"I'm sorry, ma'am. I can't interrupt—"

Ma'am?! It never mattered if Stefan was in a meeting or naked in the shower. If I, his daughter, needed him, one was to put him on the phone. If Brody had answered, I'd already be speaking with my father.

"I didn't ask what you can or can't do." *So much for staying calm, Maura.* Then again, I'd never claimed I was perfect. This was really hard for me. I just needed to get Stefan on the phone before I lost my nerve.

"Excuse me?" she drawled.

This was going nowhere fast. I needed to backtrack, instead of acting like an asshole. "Listen," I sighed. "I wouldn't be calling if it wasn't important, believe me. It's an emergency."

"That's unfortunate. I'll let him know you called, or you're welcome to call back at another time. Have a wonderful day, ma'am!" She ended the call in a chipper tone that screamed sarcasm.

I dropped the phone from my ear to look at it in disbelief. Sure enough, the screen showed the call had ended. "What the fuck!" That was becoming my new favorite phrase today.

I was fuming, frantically bouncing my knee like a tweaker jonesing for their next fix. I debated on waiting to see if Stefan would call me back. Something about that lady didn't sit right with me. She wasn't going to tell him I'd called.

There was one more person I could call. Jamie.

He always had his phone on him. Even during meetings. He had to because of his position. I dialed his number and as I pressed the phone to my ear, memories of when I'd been seventeen, beaten, bloody, and hiding in a bathroom at a party flashed behind my eyes. *Wow, lock that shit down. Now is not the time.*

Taking in a shaky deep breath, I listened to the rings, counting them. On the fifth ring, I wasn't feeling optimistic and started preparing myself to leave him a message on his voicemail. Before the sixth ring, the mumbling sound of multiple voices talking in the distance filled the silence through the phone. "Maura?" Jamie's deep, silky voice poured into my ear, his tone filled with disbelief.

"Jamie..." *Shit, what do I say?*

"Maura's on the phone?" I heard Stefan ask Jamie and the mumbling voices in the background went quiet.

"Maura?" Jamie said again.

"I..." *Deep breath.* "I need Stefan." *Great, I sounded pathetic.*

Jamie was quiet for a moment. We'd had a call similar to this one before. Same tone, different circumstances, and it was probably bringing up the same shitty memories for him as it was for me. "Are you hurt?" That confirmed it. He was definitely walking down memory lane with me.

"No."

"You don't sound okay."

A dry laugh escaped me. "That's because I'm not. Can you please put Stefan on the phone? I've been trying to get ahold of him with no luck."

"Why didn't you just call the house?"

I went from zero to sixty with that question. "I did! The new lady refused to get Stefan for me even after I told her it was an emergency!" I snapped. Jamie was quiet again. *Damnit.* I was frustrated, but I didn't need to take it out on him. "I'm sorry. Please, put Stefan on the phone."

"Maura?" The deep confident sound of Stefan's voice was the essence of my relief but also my overwhelming regret. This was why I hadn't wanted to call him, because deep down, I knew the truth. I was a person torn. I just didn't want to accept it. Six years away from home, determined that I needed change, a normal life and poof, like magic or a slap to the face, I was second guessing everything. Did I really want a normal life or was I only running away from the pain of my old one?

Fuck, I don't need this right now.

"Maura?" he said again, more firmly this time, making me realize I hadn't responded to him.

I took a second to choose my words carefully. With a mob

boss as a father you learn never to say anything incriminating over the phone. You didn't know who might be listening.

"I'm coming home. I..." *Reel it in, Maura. You can't show him weakness.* "But I need help. Jamie might be the right person to send," I said, sounding monotone.

Silence stretched between us. Asking for help wasn't something I did. I'd always been independent and self-sufficient. Telling him I was coming home was probably the last thing he'd expected me to say as well, seeing how I'd given everyone the one finger salute as I'd walked out the door six years ago. I was stubborn. It was my gift as well as my curse and he knew this better than anyone. So I was sure it wouldn't take him long to figure out I was up shit creek without a paddle if I was willing to swallow my pride and come crawling back home.

"He's on his way."

I nodded, then realized he couldn't see me. "Okay." I leaned back into the couch, suddenly feeling very tired. I'd been so tense, sitting stiffly. Now my muscles were starting to ache. My arms more so. It was the adrenaline. It was wearing off and the urge to cry was strong. I never cried. At least, not for a long time I hadn't, and definitely not in front of others.

"Stefan, I—" My voice cracked, making me cringe. *Shit!*

"Don't chase the rabbit." He'd been saying that phrase my whole life. It meant, don't succumb to the temptation of being consumed by your emotions. "Are you hurt?" he asked like Jamie had.

At his concern, my heart warmed. Then, just as quickly, it turned to stone. This was what he did. He rarely showed he cared. When he did, it was just enough to keep me hooked or complacent to go through another long span of heartache and bullshit he'd inevitably put me through. "Nothing a whole bottle of whiskey can't cure." I tried to joke.

"I'll have one waiting here for you."

I didn't respond to that because I didn't know what to say. I hadn't spoken to him in over a year and for the past six I'd been trying to erase everything about him out of my life.

"I'll see you tonight," he stated before he hung up.

Three and a half hours passed before there was a knock on my front door.

Finally!

I only lived an hour away from New Haven. After waiting two hours, I'd started to pace anxiously. After two and a half hours, I'd raided Tom's liquor stash. For the remainder of the time waiting, I'd practically chugged four glasses of cheap bourbon without even tasting it.

I peeked cautiously through the peephole with my empty pistol in hand. If needed, I could at least threaten someone with it. Not that I was expecting a threat. I just hadn't put it down since I'd come downstairs.

Through the tiny hole, I saw Jamie standing on my doorstep. He wasn't alone. All I had to see was a head of golden hair to know it was Louie. I shouldn't have been surprised. Where one was, the other wasn't far. They'd been like that since high school.

Feeling nervous, I stepped back from the door. It'd been six years since I'd seen either of them. They'd been my best friends, once upon a time. A lot had changed since then—I wasn't the same person anymore. Being in the mob had undoubtedly had some effects on them, too. Before I'd left, they had already been working for my father for years, quickly moving up the ranks. I hadn't been blind to the toll it had on them, no matter how hard they tried to hide it.

Would I be opening the door to strangers?

Only one way to find out.

I opened the door slowly. My eyes instantly met Jamie's beautiful hazel depths, mostly green with dark brown flecks, before shifting to meet Louie's ocean blues.

I went to move my gun behind my back. The small movement caught their attention and their eyes dropped to my side. The tiniest flicker of surprise told me I hadn't been quick or discreet enough.

The three of us stood there, not saying a word as we took each other in. *Time was good to them,* I mused as I did a slow perusal of each of them from head to toe. They'd always had pretty boy looks with the bad boy appeal, which they'd used to their advantage from high school on. Girl after girl would throw themselves at them back then. Now they were men, with about twenty pounds of added muscle.

Feeling their eyes roam over me as well left me feeling a little self-conscious. I was a mess, still wearing the clothes I'd killed people in. I hadn't checked my jeans or fitted green T-shirt for blood splatter. Both garments were dark in color, so I wasn't too worried. As for my long red hair, I'd been either tugging on it or running my fingers through it for hours. *Oh well.* It was best not to dwell on something I couldn't change. Besides, both of them had seen me worse than this before.

My fingers began to itch to snap my bands as my mind drifted back to that night. They'd both seen the aftermath. Instead of pulling at my bands, I had to settle for squeezing my hand tightly around the grip of my gun.

"I see the bromance is still going strong," I teased, leaning against the door frame, trying to appear nonchalant, even though the thought of having two bodies upstairs poked at the back of my brain like a pickaxe.

Louie cracked a smile while Jamie just stood there as his normal unreadable, stoic self. He'd always been a brooding ass. Louie, however, rarely took anything seriously.

"We like to role play. It keeps the relationship interesting," Louie played along, making my mouth quirk a little.

"That just put a dirty visual in my head of you playing a naughty nurse who has to *blow* life back into Jamie. Talk about a whole new meaning to resuscitation." Could I be crude and crass with a potty mouth that would make a sailor blush? Yes, I grew up surrounded by men who were criminals.

I'd had to constantly watch what I said around Tom. The few times I'd slipped up, he'd looked at me with such disgust. With Jamie and Louie, though, I could spew as many vulgar things as I wanted with zero judgment.

Louie's smile fell, but I caught the corner of Jamie's lips twitching.

"Why am I the nurse?" Louie asked, sounding offended, but the gleam in his eyes gave him away.

"I don't think Jamie could pull off a naughty nurse outfit as well as you, Louie. At least not the one I'm picturing you wearing."

Louie threw his head back, laughing. "I'm glad to see that beautiful mouth of yours hasn't changed. When I heard you were dating a brief, I was worried you'd be all prim and proper now."

At the mention of Tom, I cringed. It didn't go unnoticed. Jamie narrowed his eyes in an assessing way.

"How'd you know he was a lawyer?"

I was answered with silence.

Louie looked to Jamie, telling me he'd heard it from him. How did Jamie know? I hadn't even told Stefan he was a lawyer. Looking to Jamie to push for my answer, I paused before the words could leave my mouth. It was the way he was staring at me, eyes fixated, appearing contemplative, like I was a puzzle he was trying to figure out.

"Was?" he questioned with a slight tilt of his head.

I shouldn't have been surprised Jamie had caught that. He'd always been perceptive, just like Stefan.

Jamie and I had grown up together under the same roof. His father Liam had been Stefan's best friend and used to be the family's head enforcer until he'd been killed when Jamie had been three years old. After the tragic loss, Stefan had stepped in as a father figure, helped raise him, and groomed him to one day take his father's place.

"Was," I repeated, pushing from the door frame. Jamie's eyebrows rose. Why else would I have asked for him and not Stefan to come get me? Why not just drive home instead of asking for help, which was something I didn't do? These were the questions I knew were running through his mind.

With the barrel of my gun I pushed my front door open wider, an unspoken gesture for them to come in. I took a step backward before turning on my heels, shoving my gun into the back of my jeans in the process.

"Maura?" Jamie's voice was just as I remembered—deep and smooth as silk. Hearing it again after so long made me feel a mixture of emotions. Relief, regret, nostalgia.

Ninety-nine percent of my memories growing up included Jamie. He had been a constant in my life. He had been my family, even though we weren't related by blood. As children in the care of Stefan, all we'd had was each other. No one understood what it was like to be born into a family like ours.

I walked across my living room to the foot of the stairs before turning back to face them. They stepped inside with Louie shutting the front door behind them. Their eyes roamed, taking in everything. The room wasn't big, but there was enough space for a couch, end tables, a coffee table and a flat screen TV before it flowed into the dining room, then into an open kitchen. The furniture was nice and newish. I didn't have anything hanging on the walls, but had pictures of Tom and I on the end tables next to the couch.

I tilted my head toward the stairs. "Upstairs, master bedroom... you'll see it when you reach the top." They both glanced at the stairs behind me before looking at each other.

I stepped away, giving them access to the stairs, to sit on the couch. They passed by me silently. I didn't follow. I just poured myself another bourbon.

CHAPTER THREE

L ouie's whistle traveled downstairs. Only he would make
light of two dead bodies. I scrunched my nose, envisioning them walking into my bedroom. I was sure it was
a sight—a scene right out of a horror movie with a dead naked
woman sprawled out on the bed and a bloody corpse on the floor.

I could hear them talking to each other but couldn't make out
what they were saying. Not that I cared what they thought, nor
was I worried about their ability to make it all go away. This
wasn't their first clean up job. It wasn't the first time I'd killed
either.

I knew they were coming back downstairs when their steps
caused my walls to shake like a small earthquake.

Louie was the first to enter the living room. He looked at me
with laughter in his eyes, then shook his head as he walked by,
heading for the front door. "Remind me never to piss you off," he
snickered before closing the door behind him.

I caught sight of Jamie in the corner of my eye. Turning, I
found him standing next to me, glaring. Someone wasn't happy.

"Are you judging me, mob man?" I asked, bringing my glass

back to my lips. I didn't look away as I tilted the glass back, sipping at the warm amber liquid.

"Did you kill them because he was cheating?"

I couldn't help but laugh. The sound was dry, lacking actual humor. He didn't care that I'd killed them. I was positive he didn't care about the motive either. He was fishing. Instead of just asking me outright what he really wanted to know, he was going about this in a shitty way. The jerk was playing me.

Jamie was very perceptive. However, sometimes it took more than just a keen eye to get what you wanted. Sometimes you had to play the *game.*

I knew this game. I'd grown up learning it from the master, Stefan. The goal of the game was to gain information or control. The weapons of choice were manipulation and deception. You always had to be one step ahead of your opponent if you wanted to win.

The game was why I'd chosen to study behavioral psychology. I liked to read people, know how they'd act or react, understand how they thought. I'd been able to hold my own at playing the game before I'd left home, but with what I knew now, I wondered how I'd fare.

I narrowed my eyes at him. "It definitely looks that way, doesn't it?"

His features turned cold. "Is that a yes?"

The thing about Jamie and I was that we'd promised we'd never play the game with each other. If either of us wanted to know something, just be straightforward and ask the other. We'd gotten enough of the shitty game from Stefan and the rest of our messed-up family. Why was he playing with me now? My best guess: this was the damage of six years of distance. There was uncertainty between us.

"Let's just get to the point, shall we? Am I a liability to the family?" I tilted my head and tapped my chin with my finger, pretending to really think about it. "I wonder." I clucked my tongue. "Daughter of Irish mob boss kills cheating boyfriend and mistress." I gasped, mocking shock. "That is by far the most scandalous thing someone in our family of killers, drug traffickers, and arms dealers has ever done. How will we get past such a blemish to the family name?"

His eyes were still narrowed as he stared down at me, but his features seemed to have softened. "The dramatics really don't help your case, but I see some things haven't changed. You're still as theatrical as ever."

Help my case? Interesting choice of words. *Hmm.* He thought I'd snapped. *Maybe I have.*

Since I'd been going to Trinity, I'd been playing the role of a demure, normal woman because I'd thought it was what I wanted. Not anymore. Pandora's box had been opened. I could no longer suppress my darkness. Even now, I could feel it bubbling inside me, ready to surface when I needed it.

"I wouldn't hold your breath, Jamie. If I've gone off the deep end... well, I guess only time will tell, but I certainly won't." In other words, I didn't answer to him. Even though he towered above me in what would be an intimidating stance to anyone else, I just cocked a challenging eyebrow. My father was Stefan Quinn. He'd taught me that you could be just as intimidating on your knees. As long as you had the confidence of a king, oozed the essence and mystery of a killer, people would think twice before fucking with you.

Jamie didn't say a word as we had our stare-off. I could see the wheels turning behind his eyes as he seemed to be searching mine. He'd always been intuitive, perceptive, and calculating. He'd been like that since we were kids, thanks to Stefan's tutelage. I didn't feel a flicker of intimidation inside me as I stared back at him despite knowing who he was and what he did for my father.

He was a killer.

Stefan had made Jamie kill for the first time when he was sixteen. I remembered watching as Stefan had led him into the basement of our home. A place I'd never been allowed to go. Stefan had sometimes taken people down there—people who'd wronged the family. I'd sat outside that basement for what had felt like forever with a twisted feeling in the pit of my stomach. Then a shot had rung out from behind the door. In that moment, I'd been convinced I'd never see Jamie again because every time Stefan had taken someone down there, they'd never come back out.

My heartbreak over losing my best friend had been short lived. Jamie had eventually walked out of that basement with Stefan not far behind. Both had noticed me sitting there. Stefan hadn't looked happy, but Jamie hadn't given him any time to chastise me. He'd pulled me to my feet and taken me outside. We'd walked along the stone walls that surrounded the five acres of our property in silence. I'd known not to push. Even at twelve years old, I'd known how hard Stefan's lessons were, and even if I hadn't, I was able to see how hard that one had been in Jamie's eyes. They'd been vacant, like the last piece of his soul had been chipped away. Now that I was older, I'd say it had been the last of his innocence that had been taken.

As he'd gotten older, even I'd known that killing had become as easy as breathing for him. I'd thought he'd even enjoyed it, turning it into a craft he'd worked hard to perfect. Some would have said he was the best. His death count in the crime world was the proof of that. His ability to make someone disappear was infamous. To some, he was the embodiment of the grim reaper, and that should have had me shaking with fear, but I wasn't. I didn't fear death anymore. My father was to be thanked for that.

While Jamie had been off killing people in the basement, I'd been going through a mental bootcamp of my own that involved mind games and desensitizing. When I'd been thirteen, Stefan had made me believe I was going to die for a whole summer. He'd been so convincing with the anger he'd exuded and his emotional detachment. For three torturous months, I'd thought I'd betrayed the family by spilling family secrets to a friend at school. Which had been impossible because I hadn't had any friends other than Jamie, but he'd broken me down, stripped away all that made sense until I'd believed what he'd been saying was true. Each day, I'd woken up wondering if today was the day he'd kill me.

His attempts had started off small. One time he'd ripped me out of bed in the middle of the night, sat me down at the dining room table, and placed a plate of food in front of me. He'd implied it was poisoned, then told me to eat up. I'd fought. Like anyone would die willingly. He, of course, had been stronger and ended up force feeding me. I'd trembled with fear as he'd shoved each bite into my mouth, but I hadn't begged, and I most certainly hadn't cried. In Stefan's eyes, crying was for the weak. After I'd swallowed the last bite, he'd stuck his finger down my throat and made me throw it all up, then told me poison wasn't the death I deserved.

It had only gotten worse after that, slowly progressing with each passing week. I think the time he'd finally broken me of my fear of death was when he'd had one of his men try to drown me in our pool. I remembered strong arms holding me under the cool water while Stefan had stood next to the pool watching, looking bored with his hands stuffed into his pockets. I remembered the very moment I'd stopped fighting. I'd stared up at my father through the rippling water, thinking, *Who the fuck cares anymore?* It hadn't been that I'd wanted to die, I'd just accepted that death was something I couldn't fight. The fear of it had no longer existed in me or weighed me down. It had been quite freeing, actually. Then I'd inhaled. My whole body had jerked as if trying to reject the water filling my lungs. The man holding me under must have noticed because he'd yanked me out of the water and tossed me out of the pool at Stefan's feet. I'd gotten a little bit of satisfaction from coughing up all the water I'd inhaled all over his expensive leather Oxfords.

The final time Stefan had attempted to kill me, he'd held a gun to my head. He'd asked if I had any last words. I'd told him to stop wasting my time and just pull the trigger. It must have been the look in my eyes or the boredom in my voice that had convinced him this lesson was over. He'd holstered his gun, given me a proud smile, warmth returning to his eyes. "Very good, Maura," he'd praised, like I'd aced a school spelling test, before he'd pulled me into his arms for a hug.

I was surprised Jamie and I hadn't ended up in a mental hospital with half of the fucked-up shit Stefan had put us through. Our childhood would have traumatized most and his excuse had been that we were stronger because of it.

When it looked like Jamie found what he was looking for in my eyes, his whole body relaxed. "There she is. I was wondering when the *Banphrionsa* would surface."

I suppressed an eye roll. "I'm not a princess." Banphrionsa was Gaelic and a nickname the family had given me. "But I'm still a Quinn."

"I don't know. You've been out of the life for a long time. I haven't seen you in, what... six years? The first time I hear from you and see you, you acted like a regular female. I had you read in less than two seconds with how much emotion you were show-ing. You never used to be this easy to read."

He was right. You couldn't survive in our world by showing vulnerability. No one could be trusted. However, I'd never had to worry about trusting Jamie and my gut had told me I could trust Louie as well. That was why they'd been my friends. *Had been.*

"Regular people show emotions, Jamie. It's how they interact. Believe me, it was a culture shock in the beginning, but I assimilated. I can adjust to my surroundings if needed. I just figured, since it was you at my door and not one of Stefan's goons, I didn't have to turn off years of conditioning like a flip of a switch. I've never had to hide anything from you before. When I needed you, you were always there, and in the back of my mind I figured that'd always be the case. It was wrong to assume that. I left everyone without looking back. Six years is a long time and people change." I failed to hide the disappointment in my voice. Maybe it was a little harder than flipping a switch.

Jamie's shoulders slumped. "No one blames you for leaving. It wasn't easy to let you go, especially for Stefan. But anyone close to you knew if we didn't, we would have lost you a different way without the option of you ever coming back."

I didn't argue that he was wrong. I was surprised they'd been able to see it. It had been a very dark time in my life. I'd been spiraling, consumed by internal turmoil that I'd believed I was the only one privy to. I'd challenged Stefan at every turn. Sometimes, I'd wanted him to punish me so my anger could focus on something else. Other times, I'd wanted him to kill me.

"And I'll always be there for you, Maura. Why do you think I'm here now? So if you want to be all emotional like a regular female, I guess I'll have to adjust. I just hope you haven't turned into a complete whack job who might murder us all in our sleep after we get you home."

And just like that, I felt like we were two young kids again, together, up against the cruel world. I smiled at him. "You should have just asked. We made a promise not to play each other, remember?"

He nodded. "At least you seem sane."

I snorted, shaking my head.

He gave me a small smile and looked like he was about to say something else when Louie walked back inside carrying two large black duffels. He dropped the bags on the floor with a loud *thunk*. Rubbing his hands together, he grinned evilly. "Are we ready to get this party started?"

CHAPTER FOUR

It took a lot longer than expected to clean up a murder. Not that I had any experience to go off of. I was restless and ready for this day to be over. Jamie and Louie did most of the work while I was told to pack a single bag of things I couldn't live without. When I questioned as to why only one bag, Jamie explained it had to appear like I had intentions of coming back even if I wasn't. I didn't understand what that meant, nor did I push him to explain further. It was an easy task. I had very little I couldn't live without. My one bag held my laptop, a few albums with old photos in them, a file folder full of important documents, and my jewelry box.

With my task complete, all I had left to do was watch the guys work. That didn't last long. Once Jamie pulled out a bone saw from one of the black duffels, I took my leave. Louie laughed at my back as I practically ran from the room.

Sitting back on the couch, I scrolled through my phone for hours trying to tune out the sounds of the saw and the occasional *thump* coming from upstairs. My phone's battery was in the red when Jamie came looking for me, asking for Tom's car keys. Then

I had to watch him and Louie cart heavy-looking black trash bags to the back of Tom's Jeep.

They left after the last bag was loaded, with Louie driving Tom's Jeep and Jamie following in his car. By the time they returned, I had finished off Tom's bottle of cheap bourbon and was sporting a really good buzz. They walked right in without knocking, startling me. I was about to blow up on them, but the smell of greasy food filling my nose pulled my focus, making my mouth water. Noticing Louie had a brown fast food bag in hand, my body moved before my brain could catch up.

Watching me approach him like a hunger-crazed zombie, Louie quickly lifted the bag of food out of my reach as I went to snatch it. I stumbled a bit, falling against his chest. His free arm circled around my back, steadying me. "Aw, Maura, I always knew you wanted me."

I chuckled. *Man, I missed him.* "What's a girl got to do for a cheeseburger?" I asked suggestively, yet showed him I was completely joking by wiggling my eyebrows.

The corners of his eyes crinkled before a dirty little smirk pulled at his lips. I knew him well enough to know, he'd tell me exactly what I could do in vivid detail. Which was why I pulled away before he could say anything gross.

I zeroed in on Jamie, who'd taken a seat on the couch to eat his own burger. Before he could protest, I planted myself in his lap by perching my butt on one of his muscular thighs and grabbed ahold of his wrist. While staring at Louie, I took a big bite of Jamie's burger.

Louie playfully frowned. "Tease."

A low moan escaped me at the explosion of flavor that hit my tongue. Closing my eyes, I savored the taste. It was a south-western burger with barbecue sauce, bacon, and onion rings on it. I hadn't eaten since six that morning before I'd left for class. It wasn't until that first bite I realized how hungry I was. Ravenous was more like it and I seriously considered stealing the rest of Jamie's burger.

"How much have you had to drink?" Jamie asked. I opened my eyes to find both of them staring at me.

"Enough to still understand what's going on but not care."

Jamie looked to the coffee table, eyeing the empty bourbon bottle.

"You just dismembered two bodies," I stated.

"You unloaded a clip into a guy's dick. I don't think cutting up two dead bodies is what's really bothering you."

Oh, the ever perceptive Jamie. He was right. Their methods were gross but not why I was stressed. As much as I wanted this day to be over, I was also dreading the end of it. It meant this chapter of my life would end. I'd be right back where I started—under Stefan's rule. All day I'd felt like I'd been waiting for my impending doom, ripping off the Band-Aid slowly, as it were. I didn't like that. I was a *rip that sucker off fast so I can get the pain over with and move on* kind of girl.

"I don't want to sound like an impatient child, but are you done yet?" I asked, deflecting.

Jamie relented with a nod. He tried to hand me his burger, but I shook my head. I'd lost my appetite.

"When was the last time you ate?"

My silence was his answer.

"It's a long drive home. I don't need you throwing up in my car."

I rolled my eyes, taking the damn burger, and went to get out of his lap. He stopped me by wrapping his arm around my waist. I questioned his hold on me with an arched brow. He ignored me by turning his attention to Louie. "Throw me another one, man."

"What, no offer of sexual favors in exchange for food? I'm feeling a little slighted." Louie pouted, reaching into the fast food bag to get him another burger. Jamie didn't feed into Louie's antics. Instead, he looked bored.

As I watched them, I tried to hide my smile. Jamie and Louie had been inseparable since they became friends freshman year of high school. They'd always reminded me a little of yin and yang. Both were polar opposites; Jamie's dark brown hair and hazel eyes clashed with Louie's blond hair and blue eyes, and their personalities were just as different. Jamie was stoic and reserved whereas Louie always seemed carefree and charismatic. Where one was weak, the other thrived. Together, they were like two puzzle pieces that fit perfectly.

When we'd been kids, before I'd really known Louie, I'd been a little jealous of him. I hadn't wanted to share Jamie. I'd never really been good at sharing, period, but that was beside the point. I'd been a major bitch toward Louie, but that hadn't seemed to faze him one bit. In fact, the asshole had encouraged my shitty behavior. It had thrown me for a loop, which had resulted in me liking the goof in the end.

"What's got you smiling, gorgeous?"

Busted. Sheepishly, I faced Louie. He was sitting next to us on the couch, eating. "I was just thinking back to when we were kids."

"Hmm," he hummed while he chewed. "Good times."

Some of it.

We ate the rest of our food in silence until Jamie asked if I had a candle. I retrieved one for him, along with some matches. He then asked me for my car keys. I handed them over without question. He tossed both his keys and mine to Louie. "Help her out to my car. I'll need you to follow us in hers. She can't drive," Jamie said before heading upstairs with the candle and matches.

"Come along, princess. Let's get you home."

The word *home* made my stomach drop. *Here we go.*

Louie scooped up my bag before heading for the door. I

followed, clutching my purse strap. I refused to look back as I put one foot in front of the other.

It wasn't until we were on the highway heading south that I thought to wonder why Jamie had needed a candle. I realized that setting my bedroom on fire to make it look like an accident was the easiest way to get rid of all the evidence. *Whatever works, I guess.* I leaned my chair back and drifted off to sleep.

I woke from a gentle caress along my cheek.

"Maura."

I opened my eyes, finding Jamie staring at me. We were still in his car.

"We're home."

I sat up in my seat and read the time on Jamie's dash. It was two in the morning. My eyes traveled outside, and sure enough, we were parked in front of my childhood home.

Stefan's home was monstrous compared to my little two-bedroom townhouse. It was a three-story Gothic Victorian on five acres of walled-off land. The house was, in my opinion, excessive for just one man, with its fourteen bedrooms, nineteen bathrooms, ten-car garage, and a three-bedroom pool house in the back, but it'd been in the family for generations since our ancestors migrated here from Ireland.

House maybe wasn't the correct term used to describe this place. *Castle* was more like it. The majority of the exterior was dark stone, accented with a lighter pale stone around the windows and chimneys. The driveway was paved with gray cobblestone and the property was sprinkled with big oak trees and lush green grass. Quinn Manor was just as I remembered. Beautiful yet ominous.

With a heavy sigh, I climbed out of the car.

Walking up the stone steps to the giant espresso wooden front doors, I noticed the security cameras. I hadn't missed those after I'd left, or all the guards who were walking the property. Stefan had better security than the president. He had men on guard outside as well as inside the house. Then there were the cameras *everywhere*. The only places without were the bedrooms and bathrooms. There was very little privacy. I was already missing the freedom of being able to walk around my house naked without a bunch of goons seeing me. Not that I'd done that all the time, but I had sexually christened every room of my little house with Tom.

Well, that thought just made me feel gross.

I walked ahead of Jamie as we entered through the giant doors. Once inside, I became overwhelmed with nostalgia. The smells, the sounds, they hadn't changed. Even the furniture in the foyer, apart from the flowers on the entryway table, were the same.

The house had that old gothic feel to it with a little bit of modern and Irish charm woven in. In some areas, the house still had its original mahogany-paneled walls, as well as a matching banister that ran along the grand staircase that greeted you as you walked through the front door. All the sleek wood was accented with breathtaking hand-carved Celtic lattice knotwork. The craftsmanship dated back to the eighteen-hundreds when the house had been first built.

"Maura, welcome home." I was greeted by Brody, my father's personal assistant slash estate manager, as he entered from the formal lounge to the right of the foyer. He, like every other man who worked closely with Stefan, was wearing a crisp tailored suit. He reminded me of a steward who'd been Americanized, modernized, and *Stefan-ized*.

Brody had been a figure in this house ever since Stefan had taken over as the boss. He managed everything from my father's day-to-day life to the staff in the house. If it was domestic, Brody took care of it. He'd even taken on the role of being a second parent to me. He'd been who I'd gone to when I couldn't have gone to Stefan and who'd watched over me when he'd been gone. When I'd started my period, I'd run to Brody. When I'd needed to start wearing bras, Brody had taken me shopping. He'd even given me the sex talk before I'd started high school. He'd been kind of like the mother I'd never had because mine had passed away in a car crash when I'd been a baby.

I greeted him back with a warm hug. "What are you doing up? It's way past your bedtime, old man," I teased.

"Old man? I'm younger than your father, who by the way isn't that old either," he stated as he stared down at me, smiling. Stefan was forty-six and Brody was only forty-one. I guessed you could say they were middle aged. I definitely wouldn't have wanted to be considered old in my forties. Apart from Brody's salt-and-pepper hair and the few wrinkles around his chocolate eyes, the rest of his face was youthful. The way he carried himself was that of someone who still had a lot of air in their tires, but that wasn't the point behind all my teasing.

"You didn't have to stay up. I know taking care of Stefan is exhausting."

"That is true. Especially after a day like today. He drove my staff crazy trying to make sure everything was perfect for when you arrived."

That's doubtful. I scoffed. "Are we talking about the same Stefan?"

Both him and Jamie seemed to go a little rigid. They had both witnessed the majority of the shit Stefan had put me through, but because of their loyalties, they'd never talked about it.

Brody's smile turned stiff. "He's waiting for you in his study. I'll take your things up to your room." He held out his hands to

41

take my purse and bag from Jamie. "Good evening, Jameson," Brody greeted Jamie.

"Brody," Jamie greeted back before following me as I made my way toward Stefan's study.

"Where's Louie?" I asked over my shoulder. He hadn't followed us into the house and I hadn't seen him or my car anywhere outside. He must have parked it in the garage.

"He went home."

"What about you?"

"Are you trying to get rid of me?" he asked, tone teasing and his eyes gleaming.

I stopped walking. "No. What's so funny?" He was acting weird.

He shrugged and walked ahead of me. "I live here."

What?! "When did that happen?" I was a little shocked. "And why? You loved your bachelor pad."

"I moved back in five years ago. Louie bought my condo and lives there now. As for why, I had my reasons."

I sighed dramatically. "Fine, don't tell me. I swear, getting information from you is like pulling teeth sometimes. You're lucky I love you, because you're extremely high maintenance."

Jamie's head fell back, his laughter echoing through the hall, startling me. "You're one to talk."

S tefan was sitting behind his big oak desk when we entered his study. Due to zero windows, the only light that filled the room came from the iron fixtures on the mahogany wood walls. The far back wall was a floor to ceiling built-in bookcase filled with hardbacks. His desk was slightly off center, facing the entrance, taking up some of the right side of the room, leaving just enough space for a large antique liquor trolley stocked to the nines with crystal tumblers and decanters filled with gold and amber spirits. The entire left side of the room was a fully equipped lounge with a leather couch against the wall and two matching leather armchairs facing each other.

I followed Jamie as he strolled right in. Stefan noticed him first before his intense gaze traveled to me.

I froze, planting my feet on the dark carpet. My expression relaxed, revealing nothing. Locking down everything I was feeling, I flipped that imaginary switch inside me. Six years of conditioning myself to act normal was wiped away in an instant. I was now in the presence of the most dangerous man alive. It didn't might find myself going through another one of his torturous lessons later.

Stefan got to his feet, buttoning the front of his black Armani suit jacket before smoothing away the nonexistent wrinkles, and walked around his desk to greet me. As he approached, his gaze wandered over me, reading my lack of reception. For a moment, I thought he was going to hug me by the way his arms started to rise, but he stopped his approach a few feet before me and shoved his hands into his pockets. Disappointment stabbed me in the chest. I refused to let it show.

We stared at each other in silence, awkwardness filling up the space between us. I took in his changes since we'd last seen each other, as I was sure he was doing with me. His light brown hair was brushed with a little gray at the sides of his temples, but his face was still as youthful as ever, maybe more so than I remembered. Even his forest green eyes were wrinkle-free. I had my father's eyes and some of his facial features, like his nose, but my dark red hair definitely came from my mother. Stefan was a quarter Italian and three quarters Irish due to an alliance marriage a few generations back. My mother had been full-blooded Irish with pale skin and freckles, which she'd cursed to me. I had a splash of them across my nose and cheeks. If I avoided the sun like a vampire, I'd save the rest of my body from gaining more.

"You can drop the facade, Maura. I think you've proven yourself. Believe it or not, I'm very happy you're home."

My eyes snapped to his before narrowing, searching for truth. I hated this. There was nothing right about what he said or how it gave me a whirlwind of bipolar emotions. I was thrilled he was happy to see me but pissed that he had to give me permission to trust him enough to show it—that I was *allowed* to relax around him.

His brow rose, waiting. My body slightly relaxed while my

mask held. Disappointment hardened his eyes. "I suppose that will have to do. May I hug my daughter now?"

Taking a step forward, I softened a little bit more. He pulled his hands from his pockets and closed the distance between us. His arms enveloped me with warmth. My arms hesitated for only a moment before squeezing tightly around his waist. Knowing he couldn't see my face, I let myself completely relax, allowing my emotions to surface.

It's been a long time since he hugged me like this. Instead of dwelling on that sad thought, I tried to focus on the moment and absorb his affection as much as I could.

As I felt him begin to pull away, I stepped back with my mask back in place. I searched around for Jamie. He had taken a seat in one of the chairs in front of Stefan's desk, giving us his back.

"So..." Stefan started, drawing my attention back to him. He gave me an amused look. "Am I going to find out why we had to dispose of two bodies?"

I glared at the back of Jamie's head. *The traitor couldn't let me tell him?* Sensing me, he turned, his expression schooled. *Jackass.*

Leaving me standing there, Stefan returned to his desk. Once he was comfortably situated in his chair, oozing the superiority of a CEO, he gestured to the open chair next to Jamie for me to sit. It was like we were about to have a business meeting and discussing killing people was normal. I guessed in their line of work it was— came with the territory, as it were.

I took a deep breath, strengthening my resolve before sitting. My eyes shifted from Jamie to Stefan, taking in his unbelievably youthful features again. Both waited patiently, watching me. I must have been staring for too long, looking contemplative, because he gave me a questioning look.

"Sorry. I'm debating whether it's really good genes or you've started dabbling in Botox. You're forty-six years old and your face is suspiciously youthful."

Being more experienced than anyone with the unfiltered shit that spewed out of my mouth, he smirked. "And which conclusion are you leaning toward?" he asked as if this were a serious topic.

"I need to see Samuel before I make a firm decision." My uncle Samuel was my father's identical twin.

"I'll await your final decision, but let's get back on topic."

My fingers brushed over the rubber bands on my wrist. They were a stress experiment I'd done for one of my classes last year. My conclusion had been that it was a successful technique to temporarily alleviate stress or anxiety. *Temporary* being the operative word. Ever since I'd started the experiment, they'd sort of become an addictive crutch, which was why I hadn't taken them off. The temptation to snap them right now was strong. To prevent my fingers from developing a mind of their own, I stuffed them under my thighs. That's when I caught Jamie staring in my peripheral vision. His eyes were fixated on the bands.

"I forgot my presentation at home," I started, pulling his eyes away from my wrist, "that I needed for my afternoon class." I continued on to tell them how I'd found Tom in the shower with Tina and everything that had transpired after. I skipped over their pillow talk.

They were quiet, absorbing the information. Stefan stared at me, wearing a frown while tapping on his desk with his fingers. "You killed them because your boyfriend cheated even though you were debating whether or not you should pretend you didn't see anything? That doesn't scream 'crime of passion' to me."

"Cheating's not a good enough reason?" *Was the boss of the Irish mob seriously nitpicking my motive?* I was blown away by the irony.

"From what you just told me, apparently not." He leaned back in his chair, appearing relaxed. I knew better. It was a facade—a technique to get your opponent to mimic and let down their guard. "You're withholding something."

"What happened in the closet that you're not telling us? You were very detailed about everything else but when it came to your time in the closet you rushed through it," Jamie asked.

The two most perceptive men in the world were sitting before me. *Damnit! I should have been more careful.* I fought the urge to shift in my chair. "I don't know what you want me to tell you. I was stuck in the closet with no choice but to listen to them fuck."

Stefan's features slowly morphed, turning cold. His eyes darkened into a monstrous shade. He began to exude anger and that detachment I knew all too well. I'd wondered when his true colors would show. The boss was a trembling sight. Too bad for him I wasn't thirteen anymore. With so many lessons I'd endured at his hand, there was very little he could do that would scare me.

"Don't play dumb, Maura," he said, voice eerily calm. It was like a predator giving false reassurance right before it struck.

"Am I?" I asked just as calmly, my darkness slithering to the surface, taking the reins. Everything in my body released from the tension of the moment to relax into a confident posture. Where he exuded hostility and sharpness like a knife's edge, my body screamed twisted excitement and eagerness to play. I was in the presence of a formidable opponent, after all. Imagining going head to head with him made an evil smile slowly pull at my mouth.

Easy, girl, he's not your enemy.

My eyes never left Stefan's, but I was still hyper aware of both men in the room. It was how I noticed their bodies stiffening at different times, one right after the other, realizing the change in me. Stefan's anger lessened, his head tilting slightly as he regarded me.

With the slight narrowing of his eyes, I read his next move before his mouth even opened to speak. "Careful." My voice sounded strange. It was still my voice, yet different. The tone was light, carefree—chipper-sounding, but laced with so much promise. I wasn't going to be messed with or blood would spill. Mine, theirs, it didn't matter. Just the thought of seeing blood excited my darkness. "We were doing so well. Let's not ruin this reunion with threats."

Having six years away from this family and this way of life had opened my eyes, giving me an outside perspective. My life, my decisions were no longer in the hands of others, especially Stefan. Yes, he had come to my rescue today—cleaned up my mess. I wasn't ungrateful. In fact, I was indebted, but that didn't mean I owed him everything. I'd come home by my own volition. I'd given up that beautiful dream of living by the beach. I'd explained what happened, omitting a few things, but they were vulnerabilities and mine to share only if I wanted.

"Is this how you want to do this?" he asked, ice seeping into his voice. He was feeling challenged. His body screamed it by the way his shoulders tightened and his fist resting on the desk clenched before he forced it to relax. He'd used to be the master of being unreadable. Had I gotten better at reading people or had he gotten lax over the years?

I felt equally challenged. That was why the darkest part of my soul rose, ready to take on anything, fight off anything. The rest of me didn't want to fight, not with Stefan. "No, but you leave me no choice. You want to know something I don't wish to share, yet you don't care and demand I tell you anyway."

"Do you honestly expect me to turn a blind eye to the fact you killed two people and not want to understand why?" He had me there.

"I don't trust you," I replied honestly, knowing it would hurt him. By the heavy silence that took over, I was right. I refused to let myself feel guilty. "How do I know you won't use what I tell you against me later?" At his blatant surprise showing all over his face, I got annoyed and lifted my hand, stopping him from arguing. I didn't want to be lied to or be placated. I wanted trust. I wanted a healthy relationship with my father. "Let's make a deal."

Stefan's brows shot up, surprised, before he quickly recovered. "A deal for the truth?" He was intrigued.

I nodded. "In order to tell you the truth, I'd be giving up a lot. I want something of equal value and a guarantee it couldn't be used against me, *ever*."

"And that is?"

"No more lessons, tests, or games." Stefan went statue still. I couldn't even tell if he was breathing. I wasn't sure what to make of that. "When it comes to me, I want you to be a father first and the boss second."

In the back of my mind, I knew forcing him to change didn't make it real, but I needed things to be different between us. I was done with short lived affection and the too few moments he decided to show he actually cared about me. Call me greedy or desperate, I didn't care. I wanted a father-daughter relationship with him.

Stefan's eyes were locked with mine, intensely so. For a good minute as he stared at me unblinkingly, I don't think he even saw me. He seemed far away, lost in his thoughts.

"No more lessons, tests, or games," he finally agreed.

I narrowed my eyes. "And the rest?"

"I don't understand why you'd even feel the need to ask for that," he grumbled, sounding beyond irked and frowning with disappointment.

I couldn't let that deter me, even if it made my chest tight. "I still need you to agree to it," I said, unrelenting.

He clenched his teeth, making the muscle in his jaw twitch. "If that's what you need to hear, daughter, fine. I'll agree to all of it. Now, let's get this over with."

My darkness faded, tapering down just below the surface. I leaned back in my chair, feeling more defeated than elated, but now I could at least let it show. Everything was catching up to me. Even though I was getting what I wanted, this moment didn't feel like a victory. I still had to fulfill my end of the deal. My eyes dropped from Stefan's. I couldn't look at either man. Instead, I focused on a dark spot that was a ripple within the wood of his desk.

Tom was the only man I'd willingly been intimate with. The only other time...

My whole body was tense. I didn't realize my hands were squeezing into tight fists until my nails started biting into my palms. The pain anchored me as I prepared to lay it all out for them, because if they were going to make me do this, then they were going to get it all.

I could use a drink. With that thought, I got up and made my way over to Stefan's liquor trolley. I poured whatever was in the tall decanter into a glass and took a big burning swallow. *Whiskey.* It was the perfect drink for the moment.

"I told Tom I was raped," I blurted as my eyes bored into the wall in front of me. "I kind of had to because the first time we tried to have sex, I flipped out." Looking back, I remembered thinking I'd found someone really special when he hadn't bolted after I'd told him. *I was a fucking idiot.* My desperation for normalcy had blinded me into thinking he'd been understanding as he'd patiently worked with me to get past my *issues*, when in reality, it had been mostly me forcing myself to push back my insecurities to make sure he'd been happy.

I didn't look back at Jamie and Stefan. I couldn't. I dropped my eyes to stare at the pretty crystal glasses on the trolley. "Our relationship was what I thought to be normal. We moved in together. I was happy. I thought we were happy...the fucking illusion was shattered when I came home and found myself stuck in a damn closet listening to him fuck that stupid whore who was supposed to be my friend." I was seething, breathing heavily remembering it. "What's funny is, I felt relieved. Betrayed, but still relieved that our relationship was over. I didn't have to pretend anymore." I took another huge swallow. "Their pillow talk is what killed them. Him cheating on me hurt my pride, but he really fucked me over when he told her that I was raped. That I was damaged goods. And that I've been nothing more than a disgusting pity fuck he had to force himself to be with." My words ended on an angry growl. "So I killed them. I killed them in a way that would cause them pain. The same pain they made me feel. I made sure I saw fear in their eyes just before I did it because otherwise it wouldn't have been as satisfying. Just like how I had to watch Zack and Tyson's fear before I killed them. I kill people who hurt me because that's apparently who I am. I'm a Quinn. No matter how many years I spent pretending I'm not. I will always be a Quinn."

"Maura—"

I stopped Stefan from saying anything by slamming my hand on the trolley, causing a loud bang and the glasses to clank. "Are you both satisfied with my reason now?" I was angry at them. Rationally, I knew they'd done nothing to deserve my anger. I wasn't very rational at the moment. I felt someone come up behind me and the last thing I needed was to be touched. "Don't," I snapped to stop whoever it was. No one touched me, but I could still feel a presence behind me. "You promised me a bottle of whiskey."

"It's in your room," my father replied. With how close he sounded, I had a pretty good guess as to who was behind me. I turned to face him. He held a blank expression, regarding me cautiously. I didn't even bother glancing at Jamie because I knew he'd be just as unreadable.

When neither of them said anything, I left.

53

By the time I made it to my room on the other side of the house, my anger was at a simmer. Once I stepped inside my old bedroom, it completely faded. Apparently all the prep work that Brody had talked about had been focused on my room. The last time I'd been here, it had been a room of a teenage girl, with dark walls, posters of hot rock stars, and hot pink bedding. Now it was completely redecorated for a woman. All the furniture was new and the bedding was a light lavender color. He'd even had the walls painted light gray with a white trim.

True to his word, a bottle of whiskey was sitting on my new dresser. I grabbed it only to place it on my nightstand. Climbing onto my cloud-like bed, I fell back against my pillows, letting all my emotions come to the surface. I allowed myself to feel everything. Tears poured uncontrollably out of my eyes, one after another until I finally drifted off to sleep.

CHAPTER SIX

even years ago...

S I didn't know how long I'd lain on that floor. The bass from the loud music downstairs buzzed through the tile, tickling my fingers. My adrenaline had faded and all the pain was trying to take over. I felt it everywhere. As I lay there, I tried to take inventory of every injury.

My head was pounding from the hits I'd taken to the face. The taste of copper coated my tongue from my split lip. The skin around my wrists was already discolored with bruises from when Tyson had held me down. My knuckles stung. They were sticky with blood from where they'd been cut open. I was proud of the way my knuckles felt because it showed I hadn't just lain there and taken it. I'd fought back, gotten a few hits in before they'd taken me down.

One of my breasts throbbed from where Zack had bitten me. The ribs on my left side were sore from where he'd kicked me. I could still feel his hands on my hips and thighs. His grip had been so rough I felt bruised down to the bone. Between my legs... the pain there was the worst. I tried not to focus on what had happened there, but each pulse of pain that ripped through me gave me flashbacks.

Zack shoving my legs apart while Tyson held me down. The feel of Zack pushing himself inside of me, ripping me apart.

I shook my head to clear my thoughts because I would never be able to leave this bathroom if I didn't gain some sort of control of myself.

"Don't chase the rabbit," I whispered, voice coming out coarse and broken. "Don't chase the rabbit," I repeated with little more conviction.

Slowly, I pulled myself to my feet, stumbling a little until I got my footing. The first thing I did was look in the mirror. My shirt was ripped open, exposing my bra that had been shoved above my breasts. My skirt was pushed up around my waist. My eyes bounced to all the places I saw blood. My face. My hands. Between my thighs.

I did my best to smooth down my hair and put my clothes back in place. I had to tie my shirt closed with a hair tie I found in the bathroom because too many buttons were missing. As I got most of myself covered, I thought of what needed to happen next. I needed to get out of here, but I couldn't go home. I couldn't let Brody see me like this. He'd blame himself for letting me go to Becca's tonight, when really, we'd snuck off to a party. I didn't want Stefan to find out either. He was out of town until tomorrow and I didn't want him to rush home because of me. I needed time to figure this all out... to process.

What do I do?

I remembered Tyson had taken my phone and tossed it into the bathtub when they ambushed me in here. Pain ricocheted through my whole body as I bent over to reach into the tub to retrieve it. I took a seat on the lid of the toilet and sent a quick text to Brody.

I'm going to spend the night at Becca's. She caught her

boyfriend making out with another girl at school today and is a mess.

Becca and I had come to the party together, but she'd quickly ditched me when her boyfriend had arrived. I hadn't been surprised. We weren't really friends. We had an arrangement. Her parents didn't like her boyfriend and I wasn't allowed to leave the house without Stefan's goons following me around unless I was dropped off at a friend's house. She used me as an alibi, saying she was hanging out with me when really she was sneaking around with her boyfriend. And I'd have Stefan's goons drop me off at her house, wait for them to leave, then sneak off to a movie or do whatever the hell I wanted to do, *alone*.

I'd been so excited when Becca texted me about this party. She and I had snuck away to a few before and I'd always had a good time. Like the last few parties, I'd drunk only canned soda and had a blast dancing my butt off in the living room with other kids from school before the urge to pee pulled me from the dancing crowd. I'd gone upstairs to avoid waiting in line for the bathroom downstairs. I'd done my business after I'd found an empty bathroom and before I could fully open the door to go back downstairs, Zack and Tyson had shoved their way in.

My phone beeped, notifying me of a new text message. It was from Brody.

Okay. Call me if you need me. See you in the morning. Be safe.

I was covered for the night. *But what now?*

There was only one person I trusted to help me. Convincing him to keep quiet for a while would be a challenge. Not impossible, though. Shaking, I dialed his number and put the phone to my ear.

The line only rang twice. "Hello?"

"Jamie." My voice chose that moment to crack. *Get it together.*

"Maura?"

Tears started spilling from my eyes. There was nothing I could do to stop them but quickly wipe them away.

"I need you to come get me," I said, doing my best not to sound like I was crying.

"Okay. Where are you?"

To be honest, I'd expected a million and one questions from him. So I was a little surprised that he'd agreed to come get me so easily. "You can't tell Brody or Stefan you're coming to get me."

"Damn it, Maura. Just tell me where you are," he snapped.

"Promise me you won't tell them," I shot back.

"Jesus Christ. I promise."

I told him where I was, and he told me he was fifteen minutes away.

The party was still raging on downstairs. I did my best to keep my head down. It took a few minutes to calm down enough and find the nerve to leave the bathroom. I didn't look around for Zack or Tyson. I didn't look at anyone. I kept my eyes to the floor as I tried to slip out of the house unnoticed. I got a couple of double takes, but no one stopped me. With the front door in sight, my heart sped up. When I was through it and making my way down the driveway, I felt like I could breathe again.

By the time I made it to the curb, Jamie's slick black muscle car came into view. Before he had time to even stop, I yanked open the passenger's side door and climbed in. Jamie's eyes locked with mine and his foot slammed on the brake, causing the whole car to jerk before he shifted it into park.

"What the fuck, Maura!" he yelled, flipping on the interior lights. His eyes bounced all over my body. Taking in my ripped shirt and every visible injury. I knew I looked bad.

"Did you get jumped?" a voice asked.

I glanced behind me, finding Louie sitting in the backseat. "You brought Louie! I told you not to tell anyone!"

"You told me not to tell Stefan or Brody. I was out with Louie when you called." He sounded angry. "What the fuck was I supposed to do? Kick him out of my car in the middle of nowhere?"

"Well, yeah." I was aware that I wasn't being reasonable, but I couldn't muster enough fucks to give.

"I'm really feeling the love, guys," Louie grumbled.

We ignored him as Jamie and I had a stare-off—a battle of wills. The muscle in his jaw was twitching and his eyes were dark with rage.

"I need to call Stefan," he said.

"No. You promised."

"He's going to find out when I take you home," he argued.

"I'm not going home tonight. You're taking me back to your place."

"Am I? Why the hell would I do that?"

I understood why he was upset, I would have been too, but I didn't have it in me right now to be patient. He just needed to give in because I wasn't going to budge on this.

"Because I need you to! I need time to myself to process what just happened. I just need fucking time! This happened to me. Not anyone else. Can you please just give me the night before I have to lay it all out for everyone to fucking judge?"

They both went quiet, glancing at each other. I closed my eyes. "Can you both promise me you'll keep quiet about this until tomorrow and then let me tell Stefan?" I included Louie on the promise because Jamie wasn't the only one who worked for my father. They both did.

"I don't plan on making any phone calls tonight," Louie stated from the backseat. Jamie stayed quiet as his eyes traveled over my body again.

"Please, Jamie? I don't know how much longer I can hold myself together. I'd prefer no one else sees when I fall apart," I whispered, pleadingly.

He turned away from me, looking torn. I watched as he thought it over as he stared out the windshield into the dark street.

"I have conditions," he stated before looking back at me. "I want to know everything that happened. I want to know who did this. You're clutching your left side. That tells me you got hit in the ribs. I don't know how severe your injuries are. You're going to show me every single one. No matter how small, I want to see it. If I think they are bad enough, we're going to the hospital and I'm calling Stefan."

The thought of showing Jamie everything made me want to scream *fuck you*, then jump out of the car. There was no way I could show him everywhere they hurt me. But what else was I going to do? Where would I go? He'd call Stefan the moment I got out of the car and would follow me wherever I ran off to. Within the hour, the whole family would know that Stefan Quinn's daughter was raped. *Damnit!*

I just needed one night of peace. Just one night!

Staring at Jamie, I asked myself if his conditions were really the price I was willing to pay. Could I do it? Was one night of silence worth it?

I nodded but reluctantly. "But I get to tell Stefan. Do we have a deal?"

Jamie nodded and put the car into drive.

We took Louie home first before we got to Jamie's condo. The entire drive was awkwardly silent. I could tell Jamie was on edge. He appeared calm, but the air around him was tense and almost suffocating. Once inside his condo, he dropped his keys on the coffee table in front of the couch on his way into the kitchen. I stood awkwardly in the living room as he ripped open his fridge. He pulled out a beer, then a water bottle.

Not one word was spoken as he walked back to me. He put the bottle of water in my hand, not really giving me any other option but to take it. He twisted off the lid on his beer before taking a seat on his couch, then took a swig all while staring at me.

He's waiting.

The entire ride here I'd debated how I was going to do this. I felt dirty. The strength I'd thought I had was shattered. For Jamie to see that… he'd never look at me the same again.

But I needed time.

It would only be one more set of eyes. I'd repeated that in my head over and over again on the way here, trying to convince myself. It wasn't until we'd gotten here that I'd figured the faster I got this over with, the faster I could let myself fall apart and cry. Before I lost my nerve, I set the water bottle Jamie gave me on the coffee table and started untying the hair tie holding my shirt closed.

"What are you doing?" Jamie asked when I tossed the tie to the floor and removed my shirt.

"You wanted to see what they did. You wanted to inspect every injury. Well, in order to do that, I have to take off all my clothes. That was the deal." I dropped my shirt on the floor, then winced as I reached behind to unclasp my bra. As Jamie's eyes zeroed in on the bite mark on my breast, I saw the foreshadow of comprehension. I unbuttoned my skirt next and started to move it down my hips.

"Maura, stop," Jamie ordered, jumping to his feet.

He was too late. My skirt and underwear hit the floor. I stood naked before him, but he wouldn't move his eyes from mine. It pissed me off. This was what he'd asked for.

"Look at me!"

He jumped from my loud outburst. Relenting, his gaze traveled down. I could feel his eyes landing on each spot they'd hurt me. When his eyes reached between my legs, he turned away from me as if the sight offended him.

Tears blurred my vision, then fell before I even realized what was happening. My time to be strong had run out. I didn't have it in me anymore. I didn't ever cry, but I was going to let myself tonight. When a sob escaped me, Jamie's head whipped around. I covered myself the best I could with my arms.

"I tried to fight them, Jamie. I promise I did, but they were too strong," I cried and crumbled to the floor.

Not a heartbeat later, he was pulling me into his arms. I tensed up and he froze, noticing. Before he could pull away from me, I fisted his shirt in my hands and buried my face into his chest. I cried, letting myself completely fall apart in his arms. My sobs were loud, messy, and wet. His shirt became soaked as he rocked me back and forth, soothingly.

CHAPTER SEVEN

S*even years ago...*
    Jamie held me until my sobs subsided into hiccups. I was exhausted both mentally and physically. As the awkwardness of being naked set in, I asked to take a shower. I made him promise me again that he wouldn't tell Stefan before I shut the bathroom door. I set the water to scalding, hoping it would burn away the dirtiness Zack and Tyson had left in their wake.

Jamie had laid out sweatpants and a hoodie on his bed for me to wear before leaving me alone in his room to go sleep on the couch. I tossed and turned in his bed for what felt like hours. My brain kept replaying everything that had happened over and over again. When lying there became unbearable, I sat up against the headboard and I tried to focus on what was going to happen after Stefan found out. *Would he blame me? Probably.*

He was going to kill them. There was no doubt and that really pissed me off. Shouldn't I be the one who deserved to get revenge? Why did Stefan get the satisfaction of watching them die? He'd never let me watch. After this, he'd never look at me the same. No one in the family would. I'd be nothing more than a weak, damaged female in their eyes.

I jumped out of bed in a fit of rage and started pacing. There had to be a better way to handle all this. I paced and paced some more, until I came to a decision. I was going to get revenge *myself*. I wasn't going to roll over and allow men to take control. I wasn't a weak female.

I quietly started going through Jamie's drawers and closet looking for things I'd need. I found a loaded pistol in his nightstand, a pretty sick switchblade in his dresser, handcuffs and zip ties in a bag in his closet. I put everything in the bag before creeping out into the living room.

Jamie was in a deep sleep. I could tell by his even breathing and soft little snore. Moving as quietly as I could, I collected my shoes and scooped up his car keys from the coffee table. I spotted his phone and grabbed that, too. I didn't want him calling Stefan the moment he noticed I was gone.

I backed up slowly, never taking my eyes off him until I reached the front door. I turned the deadbolt to unlock it and twisted the knob all the way before I pulled open the door. The door made a little *whoosh* noise when it opened. I cringed but Jamie was still sound asleep, none the wiser. I slipped out into the breaking dawn and closed the door most of the way, but not all the way because I was too afraid I'd wake him.

I didn't take a deep breath until I put his car in reverse and I pulled onto the main road.

***

It was evening when I parked Jamie's car in front of my house. Everyone was there. I didn't know if it was because I'd been missing all day or because of Stefan's weekly family meeting. *Only one way to find out.*

I walked into the house and was immediately intercepted by Brody, looking ready to strangle me. "Where have you been, young lady?" he roared, until he noticed my beaten face. His eyes widened. "My God, Maura! What happened?" He went to touch me, but I flinched away, stepping backward. His hand jerked back at my reaction.

"Where's Stefan?" I asked.

"He's in his meeting."

That was all I needed to hear. Nothing more was said between us because I was already walking in the direction of the enclosed secret room known as *the chamber,* located in the center of the house.

I passed the guards in the hall with my head held high. I got a few double takes from them, but no one uttered a word to me as I entered the chamber without knocking. Everyone stopped talking abruptly as heads turned my way. My eyes landed immediately on Stefan sitting at the head of the table at the other end of the room. He was surprised to see me and even more so when he noticed my face.

"What the hell happened?" He jumped to his feet.

Before he could step away from his chair, I walked further into the room and pulled out the empty chair at the opposite end of the table, where my grandfather had sat when Stefan had first taken over. I silently took a seat, refusing to wince as everything sore smarted. My eyes shifted to Jamie, who was sitting to the left of Stefan, in his late father's chair. He was pissed, eyes filled with scathing rage as they bored into mine.

I pulled his pistol from the big front pocket of his hoodie I still wore and I placed the gun on the table in front of me. I purposely avoided looking at anyone else as I watched Stefan stare at the gun before looking back at me.

"Last night I went to a party with Becca. When I went upstairs to use the bathroom, two guys from my school shoved their way into the room, cornered me, and raped me."

The room echoed with gasps and heads turned to look to Stefan. Without removing his eyes from mine, he slowly sat back down in his chair.

"I fought but it wasn't enough. They outnumbered me. They were jocks, they were a lot stronger. After it was done, I told Brody I was going to spend the night at Becca's place, but I didn't. I spent most of the night pulling myself together until I decided to break into Jamie's condo. He wasn't there. Probably out with Louie again. I took some of his clothes to replace mine that were ripped and borrowed his gun, along with a few other things." I sounded monotone and factual. There was zero emotion behind my voice as I told everyone what happened. They all silently listened. All men. My uncles, cousins, and their men. The room was filled with nothing but men and all of their attention was on me. It didn't matter because at this point, I was completely numb. Too numb to feel ashamed. Too numb to care.

"I was able to get Tyson first. He about pissed himself when he saw I had a gun and begged me to let him go. I lured Zack out by sending him a text from Tyson's phone. I started with Zack because Tyson seems to have a thing for watching." I paused as the memories flashed behind my eyes. "It went on for hours. Their cries. Their begging."

A deafening muteness overtook the room as everything I said sank in. I stood from the table and walked over to Stefan. His eyes never wavered from mine as I approached him.

I reached into the front hoodie pocket again and pulled out Jamie's switchblade and a sandwich bag that contained Zack's penis. It was the first thing I'd done to him as Tyson watched. I tossed the switchblade in front of Jamie and placed Zack's penis in front of my father. Everyone stared down at the penis.

"Please send this to Zack's mother. She should have taught

her son how to treat women better," I mumbled before turning to leave. "What's left of their bodies is in the old warehouse off of Stone Street just before the highway. You know, the place you all like to take certain individuals to ask a few questions," I informed them over my shoulder just before closing the door behind me.

The house was silent for days. I didn't see or talk to anyone other than Brody, and even those interactions were one-worded. I barely ate or drank. I just wanted to sleep. Stefan hadn't come to see me after I'd crashed his meeting and I was beginning to feel ashamed. He was probably angry with me for letting this happen. *He blamed me.*

Five days had passed and Brody was getting on my last nerve. He wanted me to eat and I just couldn't bring myself to do it.

"What's the fucking point? Just leave me alone!" I yelled at him and he stalked off, exasperated.

Later that night, while I numbly stared at the ceiling, my door opened. I didn't care enough to see who it was.

"Brody says you're refusing to eat." It was Stefan. I turned my head, finding him standing next to my bed. Shock pulled me from my numbness as I took in his appearance.

My father was always put together, dressed nicely, and oozing self-assurance. Even when he came home covered in someone else's blood. The way he held himself, he made it seem like blood was meant to go with his Armani suit. The man who stood before me now was anything but. This man was unshaven, clothes wrinkled, hair disheveled like he'd run his hands through it too many times. There were dark bags under his eyes. He looked miserable.

"Do you blame me?" I didn't mean to ask him, but I was dying to know.

My question was answered when he looked completely defeated by it. "I blame myself."

"Why?"

Stefan kicked off his shoes, climbed onto the bed next to me, and wrapped his arms around me. I was so surprised, I couldn't move. *Is he comforting me?*

"Because it's my job to protect you and I failed."

He is! He cares. He's not mad at me!

"Are you mad I killed them?"

"No. Strangely, proud. The whole family is a little shocked. I think your cousins might be afraid of you now. We all went to the warehouse."

My mind drifted back to the warehouse and how I'd left their bodies there. I'd butchered them for hours. Each cut or fillet I'd made with Jamie's switchblade, I'd gotten a moment of relief from my own pain and felt the slight taste of satisfaction as I'd watched them suffer. Just like I'd suffered. But it had been all short lived and I'd known it had been time to end things when they'd started to beg for death. With Jamie's gun, I'd put a bullet in each of their heads, leaving them behind in that warehouse still tied up in chairs and their blood staining the concrete floor.

I burrowed myself closer to Stefan. Everything was going to be okay. It had to be.

CHAPTER EIGHT

P *resent day.*
    In the two days I'd been home, I hadn't left my room. If it hadn't been a necessity to pee, I would have never gotten out of bed. No one bothered me, apart from the few times someone tried to call my room via the corded landline on my nightstand. I didn't answer, they didn't push more than that, and I was grateful. I needed time to work through my shit.

With my head buried under my pillows, I tried to will myself back to sleep. I had no plans of rejoining civilization today, but as I was about to drift off to La-La Land, someone banged on my door.

"Fuck off!" It was rude, I know, but I was almost asleep.

The loud banging was my first clue who was at my door. Stefan had never knocked—the man was too entitled—and Brody did a little tapping noise on the door before poking his head inside. My second clue was the boisterous hyena laugh coming from the other side of the door. *Louie.*

"Rise and shine, beautiful! It's time to get up!" he cheerfully yelled as he barged in. I ignored him by burying my face further into the mattress. "You've been cooped up in here for days. It's time to stop sulking and get that sexy ass out of bed."

I mentally rolled my eyes.

"You can come get lunch with us."

Us?

My curtains were thrown open at the same time my covers were ripped off my body. I was in nothing but black boy shorts which had ridden all the way up my ass and a very loose white tank I'd found in my closet. The arm holes were so gaping, the sides of my breasts and ribs were visible, and the thin material did nothing to hide my nipples. I was lying on my stomach, so my boobs weren't on display, but Louie and I was assuming Jamie were both getting a nice view of the serious wedgie I was sporting.

"Damn, Maura. You have a fine ass," Louie drawled as if enjoying the view. "Is that a tramp stamp?"

Oh, shit! I forgot!

Reaching behind me, I quickly pulled the back of my shirt down. Hands just as quickly wrapped around my legs and I was pulled toward the end of the bed. Before I knew it, Louie was straddling the back of my thighs.

"Louie!"

My hand was shoved away and the back of my shirt was pushed up. "It's a fucking shamrock! Jameson, look at this shit!"

"I'm Irish. I was also nineteen and drunk!" I exclaimed. I swatted at him and missed. I tried bucking him off, but he barely moved. *Asshole.* Giving up, I folded my arms under my head and stared at Jamie. He was just standing there, watching us from the side of the bed. "Your boyfriend is being annoying," I grumbled at him.

He shrugged. "Push him off." The jerk was completely abandoning me.

"I can't."

"We both know you can." He was right. Instead of tea parties and ballet lessons, Stefan had made sure my time was spent learning self-defense and shooting.

"If I try to push him off my boobs are going to fall out of my top. I'm not dressed to spar, Louie!"

Jamie's eyes raked over my body, taking in my sparse clothing, as if just noticing. Strangely, I felt heated, hyper aware of the parts of me that were on display.

Um... no! Don't go there, Maura.

Jamie and I were family. A relationship close to what I assumed a brother and sister had. Jamie was four years older than me. When we were kids, he'd treated me like an annoying kid sister he had to play with. As we'd gotten older, it had become apparent that our family was very different, and our bond had grown stronger, but it had never been more than friendship.

The way he looked at me now, though...maybe I was still half asleep, or maybe—

A strong hand came down on my right butt cheek. *Slap!*

I yelped.

"I don't think your tits will offend anyone in this room," Louie stated.

Alright, I've had enough of him.

I pushed up from the bed with all my strength. Catching Louie off guard, I was able to buck him off enough to pull a knee forward, gaining purchase. My back slammed hard against his chest, jolting him backward. Instinctively, his arms snaked around my stomach to save himself from falling off the bed. I quickly reached above me, my eyes locking with Jamie's as I fisted my fingers around Louie's soft blond locks. Jamie's attention dropped to my chest, fixated on what was undoubtedly a nip slip. I didn't give in to embarrassment. Instead, I pulled the knuckle-head behind me down by his hair. I landed back on my stomach with Louie on top of me, smothering my body into the mattress.

"Ow! Fuck, Maura!" Louie barked, pulling his arms from underneath me. His big hands locked around my wrists, holding them still, stopping me from tugging on his hair.

"You don't like that, baby?" I teased in a sultry voice, then giggled because I couldn't even pretend to be serious.

Louie's hands tightened their grip, body going still. Lips pressed against my ear as warm breath tickled along my cheek, conjuring forth a full-body shiver. "I'd like it better if you were naked," he whispered, his body going lax, molding along the curves of my backside.

This time, it was me that went still. My mind malfunctioned, focusing solely on the feel of him. His warmth, the heaviness of his muscles, his smell. *Wow, does he smell good.* He wore an earthy cologne that warmed in my nose.

He fidgeted, bringing my attention to the hardness currently pressed against my butt through the thick fabric of his jeans. Instead of being flattered or appalled, I got a shockwave of sickness I was well acquainted with. It wasn't because of Louie. It just happened every time I came into contact with a certain appendage of a man. My mind automatically flashed back to that night. The feeling only lasted for a few seconds before I was able to shove it away, pulling myself back into the moment. I wouldn't let what *they'd* done affect me anymore. If I wanted to be turned on—not that Louie turned me on—I was going to enjoy it, embrace the sexual rush, and not let the sickness it sometimes conjured dampen the moment.

I was only unsettled for a handful of seconds before I was able to bring myself back, but it was long enough to draw attention. "Get off of her," Jamie ordered firmly. Louie didn't argue, rolling off as quickly as he could, falling on the bed next to me. I didn't even realize I had released his hair. My hands were still held behind my head, opened wide, shaking. *Shit.*

Strong arms rolled me onto my back, and I found myself

staring up at Louie. His brows were puckered, looking contrite. I didn't like seeing him that way. His face was made to smile, and I felt bad knowing I had taken it away.

"Maura, I'm—"

"If you ever stop being yourself around me again, I'll never forgive you." I wasn't going to let him feel like he'd done something wrong. I was the one who was damaged. He'd been playing around. It was my mind that had traveled into that dark place and triggered that response. "If I wanted you to stop, I would have made you stop. I know I went a little weird there for a second, but if you'd waited a moment longer you would have seen I was fine." I tilted my head toward Jamie. He was still standing next to the bed, watching us. I gave him a pointed look, hopefully showing my words were meant for him as well.

Louie drew my attention back to him by gently brushing some of my hair away from my face. "Okay, beautiful." His infectious smile returned, reassuring me. He ran his fingers through his hair, rubbing his scalp. "Do I have any bald spots?" he asked, tilting his head down for me to look.

I chuckled. "That's what you get for slapping my ass." Sitting up, I clambered out of bed. "Where are you taking me for lunch?" I asked Jamie because Louie was still occupied with massaging his scalp.

"Do you want tacos?"

Jamie knew tacos were my favorite food. Looking back and forth between him and Louie, I bit my lip to hide a knowing smile. These two clowns were trying to cheer me up. It was like the past six years apart hadn't happened. We were falling back into who we used to be to each other. Friends. A huge part of me was overjoyed while a small niggling made me feel like I didn't deserve them. They had been the embodiment of my happiness growing up, but I hadn't spared them a glance when I'd left home.

"Maura?" Jamie's voice pulled me from my internal pity party.

His fingers wrapped around my upper arm, eyes full of concern. I was so zoned out, I hadn't seen him approach. "What's wrong?"

I shook my head with a smile. "I need to shower and find some clothes. Give me twenty minutes?"

He nodded. I practically skipped to my bathroom but stopped just as I reached the door. Looking over my shoulder, I asked, "We get to go alone, right? Just the three of us, no goon squad?"

Before I'd been ambushed at that party, things had been a little more relaxed. I'd been allowed to go to school and friends' houses without constant supervision. That night had changed everything. After, I'd never been allowed to go anywhere outside the house without an escort. Life had become too suffocating here. I had become resentful... hateful... suicidal.

"It'll just be us," Jamie replied, taking a seat on the couch facing the TV. Just like Stefan's study, my room was big enough to have a lounge. One side of my room was all bedroom furniture, with two dressers, two nightstands, and my huge bed between them. On the other side was my own little living room with a charcoal sectional couch facing the flat screen hanging over the fireplace, along with a coffee table and a plush, light gray armchair off to the side.

I was in and out of the shower in under ten minutes. I towel-dried my hair and used another to wrap around my body. Jamie was still sitting on the couch texting while Louie was still on my bed casually looking through my phone. He had no sense of boundaries.

"Find my naked selfies?" I teased.

Louie sighed dramatically. "No."

I chuckled. As I made my way across the room, I caught both of them staring at me. *Was I flashing them?* Tucking my towel tighter around my body, I kept my eyes forward. That didn't seem to help. I could still feel them tracking me. Heat began to creep up the back of my neck and by the time I made it inside my closet, I was a little flushed.

I'd be lying if I said they weren't attractive, and I wasn't ashamed to admit I'd done a little admiring. It was harmless—like appreciating art. Being in the mob gave them a dangerous appeal that made the rest of the female population drop their panties. However, both were commitment-phobes. They were the *love 'em and leave 'em* type of players.

It had to be loneliness getting to me. My ex had betrayed me and my self-worth had taken a nosedive. I was desperate to feel desirable. What woman wasn't? Unfortunately, Jamie and Louie were the only men I'd come into contact with since then and that was why I was misreading them. It made sense. *That has to be it.* I should take a trip to a bar or club to find a rebound soon or things might get awkward.

I completely raided my closet. Everything in there belonged to eighteen-year-old me. Two things on my body had changed since then: my boobs and my ass. They were both bigger. I tried on five pairs of jeans until I finally found one that sort of fit. They were skin-tight and I was barely able to button them. All my old bras were a big *nope* and my boobs were too big to go without. I'd be bouncing all over the place. There was no other option: I was stuck wearing the one I came here in.

"Hey, guys?"

"Yeah?"

"What's up, sweet cheeks?"

I grinned. *Oh, Louie.* "I don't have the chest of an eighteen-year-old anymore!" I shouted.

"Thank God for that!" Louie laughed.

I rolled my eyes and poked my head out of the closet. "I need my bra from the bathroom. Can one of you grab it from the laundry basket for me?"

Louie was the one who hopped up and disappeared into the bathroom.

"Why didn't you pack any clothes?" Jamie asked.

"You told me to pack what I couldn't live without. I didn't know you were going to burn my house down. Also, I thought I had clothes here that fit but apparently my body has changed in the past six years. You should see how many pairs of jeans I just tried on."

"We'll stop somewhere on the way home and get you some new clothes."

"You're going to take me bra shopping?" I asked incredulously. Jamie hated shopping.

"Bra shopping? Will there be modeling involved?" Louie teased, giving me a dirty smirk while he dangled my nude colored bra by one finger. *Cue eye roll.*

He handed over my bra and I rushed to finish getting dressed. I found a black blouse that fit nicely and really cute nude peep-toe boots among my old shoe collection.

After I was dressed, I found a hair tie and mascara in my purse. I used them to put my hair up into a messy bun and add a little volume to my lashes.

"Okay, let's go!"

CHAPTER NINE

Paco's Tacos had the best tacos in the world. I hadn't been there in years. I was so excited; I was bouncing in my seat as I looked over the menu.

"Calm down. They're just tacos," Jamie said as he read his own menu next to me.

"They're not just tacos. They're orgasmic tacos. Anyone would be excited for an orgasm." I could tell he was fighting to hold back a smile and a triumphant smirk pulled at my lips when he failed.

Returning from the bathroom, Louie took a seat across from us. "What about orgasms?"

"Want to share an order of nachos?" I deflected. I hadn't realized until we'd gotten here that I hadn't eaten in two whole days. Going days without eating wasn't unusual for me. I tended to forget to eat when stressed, like during finals week or finding my ex banging someone else. The longest I'd ever gone without eating was five days and that had been seven years ago. With all the yummy smells surrounding me right now, *oh man*, I was practically drooling.

"I thought you wanted tacos?" Louie questioned.

"I'm getting those, too. Oh! Their burritos look good. I'm so hungry, I want everything." I dramatically sighed as if this was the hardest decision ever, and of course, the waitress chose that moment to show up.

"Welcome to Paco's. My name is Sara. What can I get for you?" Her attention was solely on Louie. She stared at him like he was a tall glass of ice water and she'd been lost in the hot desert for a week.

Louie realized it too, but he didn't encourage her. He looked to me. "Why don't you order first, Maura?"

Did he just blow her off?

Wide-eyed, I tilted my head at him. *Are there pigs flying outside?* This was not typical Louie behavior. He'd normally be all over this waitress. She was totally his type. One, she had a vagina, and two, she showed interest—the only two things he looked for in a woman. Her being cute was just a perk.

Is he ill?

Normal Louie would have monopolized her attention and been screwing her in the bathroom before we were done eating. How did I know this? Because he'd done it before. *Five times!*

I handed over my menu to the waitress. "I'll take three steak tacos, a supreme nachos, a margarita, and two shots of tequila."

Both of the guys stared at me for a moment before placing their orders.

"A margarita and two shots?" Louie chuckled.

I shrugged. "When I'm in a shitty mood, I drink whiskey. When I want to have a good time, I drink tequila. I couldn't decide how I wanted it prepared, so I got both."

Louie smiled at Jamie. "Little Maura's become a lush."

I grabbed a tortilla chip from the bowl the waitress had placed on the table between us and threw it at him. "I've been in college. The first few years, I lived like a fish. I could drink you under the table."

Louie's brows rose at the challenge. "Don't get cocky, princess, or I'll call you out on it later."

"Oh, Louie, Louie. I'm not cocky. I'm confident you'll tap out long before I do. Just let me know the time and place, pretty boy." I gave him a sly and confident smirk. Both him and Jamie chuckled, clearly not believing me.

Laugh it up, gentlemen. Just you wait.

Our drinks came out first. I immediately downed the first shot, then decided to pour the second one into my margarita. The guys watched me quietly as they sipped their beers. Did I care? Nope. The food came a few minutes later and that first bite—it was better than sex. I moaned, "Oh my God."

"You think that's how she really sounds?" Louie asked Jamie and I flipped him off.

"Don't ruin this for me. Let me enjoy my foodgasm." I looked around at all the food and started digging in. After I ate a whole taco and some nachos, I couldn't stop myself from eyeing Jamie's burrito. It was shredded chicken with pico de gallo, rice, and sour cream. *Yum.* Jamie caught me staring, rolled his eyes, then offered me his burrito.

I took a huge bite and sighed with bliss. Jamie reached across me, grabbing one of my tacos. He ate the whole taco in three bites. Silently laughing at him, I wiped a crumb away from his chin with my finger. *Big mouth.* I took one more bite of his burrito, then handed the rest back to him.

"I forgot you guys used to do that shit," Louie stated, flicking his finger between us. "It's like six years apart didn't happen. You still act like an old married couple. You two are so weird."

I shrugged. I didn't think it was weird. Jamie and I had always shared food. "Don't be jealous. You want to split my taco?" A slow smirk pulled at Louie's lips and I knew the sick bastard was going to totally misconstrue what I said. "Louie, if you refer to my vagina as a taco, I'll kick your ass."

He just smirked at me and quietly continued eating.

⸻

"I'm dying," I groaned, climbing into Jamie's car.

"No, you're not," Jamie said and pulled out his phone. It had started beeping as we'd walked out of the restaurant.

"I ate way too much," I complained as I leaned my chair back to unbutton my pants.

"What's she doing?" Louie asked from the backseat. Jamie stared at my open jeans, then his eyes traveled to mine, looking like he was moments away from laughing at me.

"Hey, these pants are one size too small and because I ate more than the both of you combined, they now feel like they're two sizes too small. They're cutting into my stomach."

"We'll have to take you shopping later. Stefan just texted saying he needs us back at the house," Jamie announced, tapping away on his phone.

"That's fine. I don't think I could walk around a store right now, anyway," I said, rubbing my stomach, hoping to soothe my food baby like an expectant mother.

"What's going on at the house?" Louie asked Jamie.

"There's two cops asking to speak to Maura."

⸻

"You're not a child, Maura. I'm not going to rub your stomach," Jamie grumbled as we walked through the house. When we'd pulled up, there had been a gold sedan parked out front that screamed *cop car*. Brody had been outside before we'd even made it up the front steps and was directing us straight to Stefan's study.

"But my tummy hurts," I whined. It didn't. Not anymore. I

was just having fun messing with Jamie and I was warming up for what was to come. *Let the games begin.*

We walked into the study and I purposely ignored the two cops sitting in front of Stefan's desk. "Daddy! Jamie's being mean to me!" I exaggeratedly complained. My father only looked at me with a questioning expression mixed with genuine surprise for a brief moment because I'd never whined to Stefan. Ever. It wasn't something a Quinn did. And I hadn't called him daddy since I was thirteen. Not since that fucked up summer of hell he'd put me through.

As soon as the moment passed, he played along. "What'd he do?" he asked, getting up from his desk chair to wrap an arm around my shoulders.

"I had a little too much to drink at lunch and now my tummy hurts, and he called me a child." I made sure I slurred a bit, but not too much. Before Stefan could respond, I shifted my attention to the cops, who were still sitting in their seats, watching. "What's going on?" I asked, pretending like I didn't already know.

"These are detectives. They were wishing to speak with you. What for, I don't know. They won't tell me. Since you've been drinking, I don't think today's a good day to talk."

"But I want to know why they're here." I walked over to stand behind Stefan's desk, purposely using it to separate myself from them.

"Miss Quinn, I'm Detective Brooks and this is Detective Cameron." The younger of the two detectives introduced them by holding out his hand. I gave Detective Brooks a flirty smile as I clumsily leaned over the desk and daintily shook his hand. Brooks dropped his eyes, the corner of his mouth curled into a smug smirk. Brooks had to be about Jamie's age and was attractive for a cop, with dishwater hair and blue eyes. By his eager demeanor, I could tell he was still wet behind the ears. A baby cop. The other detective was seasoned, with tired lines wrinkling his face and ash colored hair. By his scowl as he glanced from Stefan to Jamie to Louie, he knew who my family was.

"Miss Quinn, when was the last time you were home?" Detective Brooks questioned.

"Uh, three days ago, I think?"

"You think?" Detective Cameron chimed in, tone harsh and full of suspicion.

"I hadn't gotten out of bed until those two meanies dragged me out to go to lunch today," I answered, pointing a finger at Jamie and Louie. Both of whom were standing by the door, holding veiled expressions I was sure looked intimidating, like guards quietly watching and waiting for an order or a threat to appear.

"Why were you in bed?" Brooks inquired.

"I was crying. My boyfriend and I broke up."

"Why'd you break up?"

I purposely looked at Stefan and then to my feet, trying to appear apprehensive. "Do you really need to know that?" I mumbled.

"Yes, we do." Cameron said firmly.

I crumpled into Stefan's chair and willed some tears to fall from my eyes. I quickly wiped them away and sniffled. "I thought I was pregnant," I said quietly. "The test came back positive and Tom asked me to marry him, but I refused. Then I got my period, but things couldn't go back to normal after that. He asked if I ever wanted to get married and I said no. I'm not ready. I've…I've only *been* with Tom, if you know what I mean. I'm just not ready to settle down." I looked up at the detectives and made sure I rambled as fast as I could. "I've never even had a one night stand or a threesome! Not that I'm sure I want one of those, but that's not really the point! The man could barely get me to orgasm! Do you know how many vibrators I've gone through during our relationship? Four! I just can't spend the rest of my life getting myself off. I need good sex! Mind blowing sex!" I said loudly and mimed my head exploding with my hands. "So I left. I got into my car and I left him and school. Shit! What am I going to do about school?" I groaned, covering my face with my hands, and cried some more.

There was an awkward silence. I knew everyone was shocked on both sides, but that was what I'd been aiming for.

"Uh..." Stefan cleared his throat. "Is there a reason you're asking my daughter about her ex-boyfriend?"

Detective Cameron sighed. "Yes, I'm sorry to inform you, but apparently after you left, the home you and your, uh... ex rented together caught on fire."

I shot up from Stefan's chair. "What? Oh my God! How bad is it? All my stuff is still there. Wait, what about Tom? Is he okay? Oh my God!"

"We walked through the scene. I'm sorry, it didn't seem like anything was salvageable," Brooks said, eyes holding sympathy.

"We haven't been able to locate Tom. We've spoken to his employer and they say he hasn't been to work for the past three days," Cameron said as he eyed Stefan. It was clear what he was thinking. Even though he was right on the money, I refused to feed his suspicion.

"Daddy, what am I going to do? All my stuff. Pictures of Mom. It's all gone," I cried hysterically, full on snotty sobs, and threw myself into his arms. *And the Academy Award goes to...*

"Shh, it's going to be okay, sweetheart," Stefan shushed as he rubbed my back.

"We don't know if Tom Morris is responsible. We need to locate him first. I think we're done here for today. Here's my card. If you have anything you want to add or have any questions, please give me a call," Detective Cameron said as he placed his card on Stefan's desk.

Jamie volunteered to walk them to the door.

After the door closed behind them, I waited a minute before

pulling away from Stefan and wiped my cheeks clean. "Well, that was fun."

Both Stefan and Louie stared at me with blatant shock on their faces. The room was so quiet, you could hear a pin drop. That was, until Louie practically fell over laughing.

CHAPTER TEN

"That was the best thing I've ever seeeeen!" Louie wheezed. "I almost lost it when you asked them about vibrators." Louie was laughing uncontrollably while holding his stomach with one hand and bracing himself on the wall with the other.

Stefan scrunched his nose, walking away to go sit behind his desk. I was sure it had been uncomfortable to hear me talk about sex and vibrators. Saying all that in front of him hadn't been easy for me either. "It was incredibly risky to lie like that. How did you know I hadn't said something that wouldn't have corroborated with your story?"

"You told me you didn't, remember?"

Stefan nodded, seeming pleased I'd caught that lifeline of information he'd slipped me.

"I swear, the shit that comes out of your mouth is amazing," Louie said after he calmed down. Catching his breath, he plopped down on the couch.

"They're gone," Jamie announced when he returned and took a seat on the opposite end of the couch from Louie. "Are you going to tell us what all that was?"

"We didn't discuss what we were going to say to the cops if they ever showed up. So I felt it was best to take the lead and make sure this situation was as uncomfortable as it possibly could be. By unloading information that is normally too uncomfortable for a sober woman to say, especially with her father present, I created an acute-stress environment." The three of them each gave me varying confused expressions. "When presented with stress, a distress signal is sent from the amygdala to the hypothalamus." I realized I was getting too technical when Louie's eyebrows puckered. "Have you ever heard of fight or flight?" They all nodded. "It's kind of like that. The basic human response is to flee in uncomfortable situations. Did you notice how they were asking me question after question in the beginning, trying to take advantage because I'd been drinking and my inhibitions were hindered? Then the moment I started crying and rambling on hysterically about threesomes and wanting mind blowing orgasms, they couldn't get out of here fast enough?"

Stefan leaned back in his chair, his head resting against the headrest as he pondered. "But your inhibitions weren't hindered?" he asked.

"No, but I certainly made it appear that way," I replied.

A proud smile slowly formed at his mouth.

"They'll be back. When they realize they didn't get everything they needed from you," Jamie warned.

"Yes, but we'll be better prepared next time," I said, taking a seat between him and Louie. "Speaking of being prepared..." I directed my question at Stefan. "Why didn't we go over what we were going to say to the cops?" Stefan didn't make mistakes or have slip ups. He was too meticulous. Too controlled. Everything he did or didn't do served a purpose.

The Stefan I knew wouldn't have cared how upset I'd been these past couple of days. He would have torn me out of bed and made sure my alibi was so ingrained into my brain, I would've believed it was actually true. He hadn't, though. That told me one thing. He'd wanted to see how I would handle this on my own. He'd just tested me. *Motherfucker.* "We had a deal." I glared.

Stefan's smile fell, his face relaxing to reveal nothing, but his eyes said everything. He was debating how he should respond. "We still do. You were upset. As any caring father would do, I gave you space. I knew the police would come, and soon. That's why I tried calling your room. You didn't answer. I didn't push. So I left this moment up to fate."

What a clever, word-twisting, manipulating bastard!

"Wow." I sighed, utterly frustrated. Saved by a technicality. One part of our agreement conflicted with the other.

He had tested me or he was playing one of his fucked up games. I could feel it in my gut. The question was, why? What did he have planned? Whatever it was, I wasn't going to figure it out right now. If Stefan didn't want me to know, then only time would tell. I just hoped he understood that if he reneged on our deal, there would be repercussions. He'd lose me. When we'd made this deal, I purposely hadn't mentioned that, and I never would. He'd find out after I was long gone.

I turned to Jamie, who was sitting there quietly watching. "Are we still going shopping? Because if so, I'm changing into sweats. These pants are too tight. Someone might have to cut me out of them."

"I can get the scissors?" Louie volunteered.

I crossed my eyes at Jamie. Louie was too much sometimes.

"Jameson informed me of your clothing situation. I've sent Angela out to restock your closet with proper fitting outfits. She got your sizes from the clothes she found in the laundry. I just need to inform her of your, uh... bra size."

Really? He still gets awkward about this kind of stuff? This was why we had Brody. I could drone on about cramps and how heavy my periods were, and that man wouldn't even bat an eye. It didn't faze him one bit. He'd talked with me about it as if we'd been talking about the weather.

"I'm a 32C." Then the rest of what he'd said registered. "Who is Angela?"

"She's one of the house staff. I think you spoke to her on the phone the other day," Stefan said while he sent a text to, I assumed, Angela.

"Oh, you mean the woman who wouldn't put you on the phone when I needed you?" Apparently, I needed to introduce myself to her. Or introduce my fist to her face. The latter sounded more appealing. I could have been dying and that bitch still wouldn't have connected me to Stefan.

Speaking of which, he stared at me pointedly. "I've already had a discussion with her about that and I believe Brody did, as well." In other words, *Leave her alone, Maura.*

"She sounded young. How old is she?"

There was a rule in the house when it came to hiring staff. Never hire a woman who was young, beautiful, or both, because the majority of the people who came in and out of this house were male. It never ended well. Someone in our family always ended up screwing the woman and because most of the men in this family were whores, the girl always got hurt. There was nothing worse for a *family business* than a woman scorned. It caused drama, put us at risk, and then the girl would have to disappear.

It had happened three times in my lifetime. Which was why Brody and I had come up with the rule. They had to be male, old or middle aged, or extremely ugly.

"She's younger," he replied, nonchalant.

"How young?"

Looking bored, he said simply, "Twenty-seven."

"Oh hell, is she pretty?"

Clearly over my questioning, Stefan gave me the brush off by busying himself with his phone. I turned to Louie because he was the biggest Lothario of them all. He refused to look at me as he picked at a nonexistent piece of lint on his shirt.

"Well, Louie's already sampled from her buffet," I said and narrowed my eyes at Stefan. "Old or ugly, Stefan." That earned me an eye roll.

I glanced at Jamie, who had been silent. With one leg propped up on his knee and his arm stretched along the back of the couch, he looked relaxed. Like his best friend, Jamie enjoyed the ladies. The only redeeming quality to his whorish ways was his standards. If he was interested in Angela or had already bagged her, then she had to be gorgeous. He caught me staring and smirked, looking smug as hell. He knew I was trying to get a read on him. I knew it was none of my business, but I didn't let that squelch my curiosity or stop me from proving a point. We had another stare off as he sat there with laughter in his eyes because the jerk was giving nothing away.

Giving up, I sighed. "Shit's going to hit the fan. I just know it."

"She's a sweet girl, Maura. You need to give her a chance." Stefan made it sound like I was the problem.

"That just means someone's going to chew her up and spit her out," I grumbled. "And don't make it seem like I'm the one with the issue. It turns into a damn telenovela around here when you all see a pretty girl with a feather duster. Need I remind you, Stefan, that Monica was your fault. She believed she was lady of the house after she bagged you, making everyone's lives miserable. She drove Jamie to move out. Young and beautiful house staff bring nothing but drama because they can't resist the bad boy charm."

Stefan sighed, "Maura, you're making it sound like we're taking advantage."

"Nah, she's just being territorial."

My jaw figuratively dropped to the floor as I gawked at Jamie.

"Yeah, now that you mention it, she was like that when we

were kids, too. She didn't like sharing you with me, do you remember that?" Louie laughed. "Oh man, she was a mean little shit. I think if it was socially acceptable, she would have pissed all over you, marking her territory to keep me away."

Jamie chuckled. "I remember you encouraging her to do just that. I've never seen her so pissed."

I frowned. "Laugh it up, gentlemen."

That had all of them laughing, including Stefan.

This was what it was like to grow up around men. They constantly teased you. It was never ending and either you learned to roll with it, give as good as you got, or you punched them where it hurts. Even if what they were teasing you about might be a tiny bit true. Yes, I'd been a huge bitch when Jamie had first brought Louie around and maybe continued to be for a few months after. I didn't like the term territorial. *Fiercely protective*, now that was a title I could roll with.

I looked at Louie and slowly shook my head at him. "Have you ever heard the saying 'don't shit where you eat?'"

They all laughed again.

"Don't worry, babe. I was just a fun time to her. She's moved on and set her sights on someone else," he informed me as his eyes pointedly shifted to stare behind me.

Great, now she was trying to jump into Jamie's bed. I didn't know how I felt about that, but I didn't get the time to dwell on it because there was a knock at the door.

"Come in!" Stefan said.

The door opened and in walked my uncle Samuel and his son, Dylan. Samuel was Stefan's identical twin, with the same green eyes and light brown hair but dusted with a lot more gray. Just like Stefan, he always wore a suit and was always clean shaven. They both looked more like rich entrepreneurs than criminals who'd been known to get their hands bloody.

I stood from the couch to greet them.

"Maura, welcome home," Samuel greeted politely.

"Cuz." Dylan smiled before pulling me in for a big bear hug. "You don't look like a little boy anymore, congrats."

Playfully, I punched him in the stomach.

He grunted, then released me to bend over, hugging his middle. I may have hit him a little harder than I'd intended, but he'd deserved it. *Asshole.*

Dylan was two years older than me and had always been a pain in the ass. He'd constantly made fun of me growing up, and not in the same way Jamie and Louie teased either. Maybe I was being biased because they were my best friends, but when Dylan had tried to make fun or tease, it had felt like he'd actually been trying to make me feel bad or put me down. Whenever Louie and Jamie poked fun, I'd always felt uplifted after. Despite them laughing and joking around, their tone and their smiles secretly told me they loved whatever they were teasing me about.

Dylan had light brown hair like his father's and brown eyes like his mother's. Unlike Samuel, he was rocking an edgy business look by wearing a button-down blue dress shirt with the sleeves rolled up, exposing multiple tattoos on his forearms. A lot of the men in the family had tattoos, especially Jamie. He was covered and I was slightly concerned he had an ink addiction. Before I'd left, he had just finished his sleeves with beautiful Celtic knots and been talking about getting more ink done on his back and chest.

Apart from a few new tattoos, Dylan looked pretty much the same since we'd last seen each other. I took in Samuel's wrinkle-free face next and I couldn't stop the corners of my lips from quirking up. "Stefan didn't tell me you were seeing the same doctor. Uncle, you look amazing! Stefan's been raving about the results and now I can see why. I'm starting to think this doc has a time machine with how good you both look."

Samuel's cheeks tinted. "Dr. Abell is known to be the best."

The sigh that came from across the room was comical. I turned, adorned with a triumphant smirk. Stefan was rubbing his forehead. "Really, Sam?"

"What?" Samuel asked looking between us, completely at a loss. I laughed at how easy that had been. Even Jamie was smiling from the couch while everyone else stared at us like we were crazy.

"I never told her about Dr. Abell," Stefan explained to Samuel.

"Am I the only one confused?" Dylan asked, frowning.

"Stefan and Samuel have been getting Botox. I wasn't sure at first, but your dad just confirmed it," I explained.

Dylan looked a little surprised as his eyes roamed over his father's face. "He has been looking more youthful lately. I assumed he was getting laid."

"Dylan!" Samuel chastised. It was no secret that Samuel wasn't faithful to my aunt.

I was a little shocked Dylan openly teased him about it. Then again, he hadn't specified that it wasn't my aunt Samuel was doing the deed with. If I were in Dylan's position, I'd be pissed if one of my parents cheated on the other. But that was me and they were the mob. *Morals* was just a word, not a requirement. And no one judged.

I wasn't saying every man in the family was an adulterer shit-head. My other uncle loved his wife and would never do anything to hurt her. Stefan had loved my mother, not that I could remember, but I could tell by how torn up he got whenever he talked about her. He hadn't moved on with anyone else, either. Just a couple flings here and there. I had a feeling as to why that was, but I didn't think it had to do with grief. Deep down, and I mean really deep down, I had a hunch Stefan might be gay. I didn't have any proof or ever would. As the leader of this family, Stefan had to uphold a certain image and sexual preference was woven into that. It was fucking stupid. Samuel could cheat on his wife and no one would bat an eye. If my father happened to like men, then there'd be an uproar and people would say he was not fit to lead. *Great, now I'm getting mad over something that may or may not even be true.*

"Maura?" The sound of Stefan's voice pulled me out of my thoughts.

"Yes?"

Stefan's head was slightly tilted, eyes studying me. He wasn't the only one. Looking around the room, I found I was the center of attention.

"You zoned out, babe," Louie said, taking pity on me.

Oh.

"Just thinking."

Stefan's gaze lingered until Samuel cleared his throat, drawing his attention.

"We've got the books you asked for," Samuel said, reaching into his breast pocket inside his suit and pulling out a flash drive.

"Good. Any progress this week?"

Samuel didn't answer as he handed over the flash drive. Stefan stared at him expectantly, which made Samuel look pointedly in my direction. "Maura, please excuse yourself. We have business to discuss."

Anger flaring, I bit my tongue. I had to love my uncle. I didn't have to like him. He was a sexist bastard like most of the men in the family. He'd always made it abundantly clear that women had no business knowing the *business* and that our place was either in the kitchen or in the bedroom, taking care of the men.

Stefan hadn't raised me, or even Jamie for that matter, to think that way. He'd demanded my strength and punished me if I'd ever showed him submission. When interacting with other members of the family who didn't agree with his *parenting style*, like Samuel, who expected my submission, Stefan had left me to stand on my own. He'd sat back, watched, never coming to my aid. As a little girl, I'd turned the other cheek. It had been what all the other females had done, or they'd been beaten. Sadly, abuse wasn't uncommon or stopped when done publicly in this family. Again, *morals* was just a word to the mob. It was why I hated holidays and family gatherings. What I hadn't understood until I'd been in my teens was that I couldn't be punished or put in my place by anyone other than Stefan. No one had outright told me that or explained what being Stefan Quinn's daughter entailed, which had left me terrified of being hurt. I had a feeling Stefan was to blame. He'd wanted me to be strong and earn respect on my own without the crutch of knowing he'd murder anyone who laid a finger on me. It had worked. Over time, something in me had snapped and I'd become fed up. Using all the stupid lessons my father had taught me, I'd held my head high and stood my ground against the men in this family. It had resulted in some angry mobsters looking to Stefan to deal with me. To their dismay, he hadn't come to their aid either.

"Let's go find some scissors, Louie. Anyone with a vagina apparently isn't welcome to know the goings-on of the big bad mob," I said caustically.

Samuel held a blank expression as he stared back at me, but the challenge was there. He was baiting me, and I so badly wanted to take it. *Bastard.*

"Are you saying I have a vagina?" Louie asked, trying to break the tension in the room like I'd known he would.

"You spend enough time with them. I'm surprised you haven't turned into one," I snickered. Without removing my eyes from Samuel's, I continued, "Besides, having a vagina is empowering. It can handle whatever a man can give, and it pushed all of you out into this world. Not to mention most men can't live without it. Some even pay for it, right, Uncle?"

Silence fell on the room with shock and tension speaking louder than words ever could. His infidelity wasn't a secret, nor were the high-end escorts he was unfaithful with. We just didn't talk about it.

Coming back to this life, I wasn't only going to change things between Stefan and me, but my position in the family, as well. I didn't want to be looked over as another female or Stefan's daughter. I was tired of seeing the line drawn in the sand. I wasn't going to just stand my ground anymore. I was going to rise. How was I going to do that? I wasn't quite sure. However, putting my sexist uncle in his place seemed like a good start.

Samuel's blank face faltered as his eyes narrowed. A cruel smile curled at my lips before I looked to Stefan, who had been quietly watching the two of us. I had caught the tiniest flicker of surprise in his eyes before he'd masked it.

"Enjoy your *no-girls-allowed* business meeting, gentlemen," I said, tone facetiously chipper, and spun on my heel.

"Will I see you at dinner?" Stefan asked before I could leave the room. Looking over my shoulder, I gave him a small smile and nodded.

"Why do you even need to ask her?" Samuel questioned disapprovingly. "If you taught the little bitch respect, she'd know what's expected—"

Stefan's passive demeanor faded, turning cold, eyes promising nightmares as he fixed them on his brother. Samuel had fucked up. Coming after me was one thing, but he'd pulled Stefan into it. *Tsk. Tsk.* Watching my uncle squirm under the intensity of Stefan's glare was a delight. I'd have liked to stick around for the ass ripping, but I was over all of the testosterone.

"You coming, Louie?"

CHAPTER ELEVEN

Louie and I spent the better part of an hour catching up. It was nice sitting with him, laughing and having light-hearted conversation. I told him about my time at Trinity—the people I'd met, the things I'd learned, the parties I'd experienced. He talked about his new position in the family that entailed him earning a seat at Stefan's table. The table symbolized Stefan's inner circle and it was where the leaders of the family sat during his weekly meetings to discuss business. Like Jamie, Louie was an enforcer, but he hadn't been born into our family. For an outsider to have a seat was a big deal. It hasn't happened since Jamie's dad.

"We need to go out to celebrate," I said.

"I got my seat a year ago."

"So what? I wasn't here. We'll drag Jamie along so he can sit in the corner sulking while we get hammered. We can make a game of it. Every time he frowns, we take a shot." *We'd be wasted within an hour.*

A knock on my bedroom door interrupted our laughter before Jamie let himself in. His eyes shifted between us, taking in our smiling faces. "We got orders," he told Louie, tilting his head toward the door. Louie sighed as he stood from the couch and the two of them left with a quick goodbye, leaving me to my own devices.

For the rest of the day, I forced myself to tie up loose ends. I contacted my insurance company to put a claim in for the fire. There was a lot of waiting on hold and questions I had to answer with lies. Seeing how I'd committed murder, you'd have thought insurance fraud wouldn't bother me, but for some reason, I still wound up feeling irritated. After I'd finished withdrawing from school, I was done adulting for the day. My foul mood had me absently reaching to snap the missing bands at my wrist for the hundredth time. I had taken them off yesterday and I ached for them like a chain smoker missed nicotine. Going cold turkey sucked ass.

Seven o'clock—Stefan's strict dinner time—rolled around faster than I wanted. With a frustrated sigh, I made my way downstairs.

Jamie and Stefan were already seated at the table by the time I entered the dining room. Stefan sat at the head of the long, maple wood table that was centered under a bright crystal chandelier. Jamie was seated to his left. I beelined for the large liquor hutch across the room to grab a crystal tumbler and one of the many decanters filled with amber liquid before heading to my spot on Stefan's right. I dropped my glass loudly onto the table, popped the crystal cork, and poured myself a generous amount.

I glanced at Stefan as I took a big gulp. His brow rose in question. I ignored it. "What's for dinner?" I asked, lifting my glass to take another sip.

Stefan reached out to grab ahold of my wrist, stopping the glass from reaching my lips. "What's making you drink all my good whiskey?" That was hilarious. All he had was good whiskey.

"I'm embracing my Irish heritage by drowning my feelings."

"I don't like repeating myself, Maura." *Oh, he pulled out his Boss voice.*

"I'm immune to intimidation, *Stefan*," I mocked, putting extra emphasis on his name. It wasn't wise to challenge the boss, but I was itching for a fight. His grip on my wrist tightened, not to the point of pain, just enough pressure to serve as a warning. I scoffed. "If you wanted me to be a timid female who toed the line, you probably shouldn't—"

"Enough!" he barked. Releasing a frustrated sigh, he leveled his calm eyes with mine. "Might as well spit it out because I'll find out one way or another."

A mean smile adorned my lips. "I'm almost tempted to see what you'll do."

His anger flared and his eyes narrowed. "I'm trying," he seethed. "No games. I'm asking you outright, but you're making this harder for both of us."

Taken aback, I looked away from him. If I wanted to talk about it, I would. But when he wanted to know something, he was relentless. We were both stubborn and our relationship was anything but easy. There were too many bad memories and too much lack of trust between us. He was trying, though. Could I say the same?

"I withdrew from school today," I relented.

"And that's why you're upset?" he asked with a puzzled brow.

"I feel... I don't..." I was floundering. Being forced to talk about it had left me unprepared to explain without sounding pathetic. "I feel like I wasted away six years of my life," I finally admitted. "I have no idea what I'm supposed to do now. I have my bachelor's, but there's not much I can do without my master's degree or doctorate. I refuse to take on the role of a typical female in this family. So don't get any ideas about marrying me off," I said, eyeing Stefan. "I have no purpose, no goal, no plan. I feel like I'm floating in limbo and I don't like it."

"Do you regret killing them?" he asked, dropping his hand from my wrist.

"No." I didn't hesitate in answering. "I just need to find something to do before you find a reason to wife me to someone."

"We both know you'll never have to worry about that," he assured.

About six months before I'd left for college, things had not been good between us and the De Luca family—the Italian Mafia who held territory west of the Housatonic River. I'd overheard a couple of goons gossiping about how the don, Giovanni De Luca, had been murdered. And because there'd always been beef between our two families, the De Lucas had accused us. Couldn't say I would have been surprised if we'd been responsible, but Jamie had assured me we hadn't.

There had been talk of war. Security around Quinn manor had doubled. There had been a few deaths on both sides before new rumors had started floating around that the *family*—all the leaders in Stefan's inner circle—had been trying to convince him to marry me off to the new don to broker peace. When those rumors made their way to me, I'd snapped. Being forced to marry a stranger and having to consummate that forced marriage? To me, that was rape. I would have rather died than face that again. I'd been barely holding on to my sanity as it was, and they had been going to feed me to the wolves to save their own asses? *Fuck the family.*

Blinded by betrayal, I'd pilfered a pistol and crept into Stefan's room in the middle of the night. Pointing the gun under my chin, I'd told him I was going to eat a bullet or he was going to give me his word as a *Quinn* that he wouldn't marry me off. There had been no doubt in either of us that I would have done it. Breaking me of my fear of death had bitten him in the ass. I'd been so emotionally fucked up, my finger had itched to pull the trigger. He'd given me his word he wouldn't, then hadn't spoken to me for weeks after. He'd been so mad, he'd refused to even look at me. I'd made the boss bend to my will. There was no greater sin.

Stefan's voice broke me out of my memory. "Take a couple of weeks to relax and really think before you make any decisions on what you want to do." It was an order, not a suggestion.

I nodded, because I was a little lost for words. Had he just made me talk about my feelings and instead of using them against me, he'd listened and kind of reassured me? He really was trying. *Wow. Now I feel bad for being an asshole.*

Hesitant at first, I did something I hadn't done in a long time. I reached out to place my hand on Stefan's arm. It was a small gesture of affection. For us, it felt huge. "Sorry for being a bitch," I mumbled. Stefan stiffened, eyes dropping to my hand. Feeling stupid, I was about to pull away when he stopped my retreat by patting the top of it. It was completely awkward.

I glanced at Jamie, who'd been quiet during the entire exchange. He appeared bored. This wasn't his first time witnessing our father-daughter drama and it probably wouldn't be the last. I noticed the whiskey decanter had been moved from where I'd placed it in front of me to his side of the table, out of reach. The klepto had lifted it without me realizing. "Why are we friends, again?" I asked, looking from the decanter to him.

A slow smirk lifted the corner of his mouth. "You're the one who was hogging it."

"You want a glass?" I asked Stefan as I stood and ventured back to the liquor hutch.

"I do."

I grabbed two crystal glasses and placed them in front of Jamie and Stefan.

The swinging door leading into the kitchen opened inward. Jeana, Stefan's personal chef who had been cooking in this house since I'd been two, walked in carrying our food. "Miss Maura, welcome home!" she beamed with a genuine smile as she served us each a plate of heavenly smelling food. Jeana was a very nice lady who liked to mother everyone.

"Thank you," I gave her a small smile back before looking down at my dish. Recognizing it, my excitement rose and my heart warmed. "Is this Grandma's cottage pie?"

"It sure is. Your daddy said you were coming to dinner tonight. I figured I'd make one of your favorites," Jeana said, giving my shoulder a gentle pat, then she returned to the kitchen.

I used my fork to cut through the crusty roof of mashed potatoes into the stew beneath. The vegetables were soft like butter and the meat was perfectly tender.

"Damn, that's good," I moaned around a mouthful of food.

Stefan chuckled as he dug into his own pie while Jamie gave me a strange look.

"What?"

"Did you not eat for the past six years? I swear every time you eat something, you do that."

"Is this you trying to be funny?" I teased him.

He shook his head, trying to hold back a smile. "You have a weird relationship with food."

"I'm sorry I'm not one of the anorexic skanks you like to pounce and bounce. I wouldn't want to get you all hot and bothered by pushing my food around my plate, pretending to eat."

He smirked. "You've been showing a lot of interest in my sex life today."

"Ha!" I laughed mockingly. *He's delusional.* "Someone needs to monitor your Louie exposure. The last thing we need is two egotistical boneheads running around."

"Deflecting?" The asshat was successfully ruffling my feathers, but I still grinned like a loon. If he wanted to play, then I'd play.

"Oh, Jamie. I don't think I'm your type. I don't have a gag reflex. How would I purge all this yummy food for you?"

"You learn that at your fancy college?" The muscle along his jaw looked strained, telling me he was fighting not to laugh. I was fighting it as well. I hadn't had this much fun in a long time. It was nice to have someone to spar with who wasn't easily offended.

"Children, play nice," Stefan said.

Like the boss man ordered, we stopped our bickering. Jamie and I both dug back into our food. I made it a point to enjoy my next bite loudly and obnoxiously.

CHAPTER TWELVE

After dinner, I went back to my room to find the couch, chair, coffee table, and every other flat surface covered with bags and boxes filled with clothes, shoes, and accessories. When I read the labels, I had a mini heart attack. All of it was designer. I opened a Louboutin box first and about cried when I saw the most beautiful shoes I'd ever seen. They were silky champagne satin pumps with tassels and the signature red soles. *Holy shit!*

Opening that first box was like a drug. A frenzy took over. I started ripping open bags and boxes one after another like an excited kid on Christmas morning. By the time I was done opening the last bag, my room was a mess. Tissue paper and packaging was thrown askew all over my floor as I sat on the couch surrounded by the best wardrobe money could buy. All the lingerie was French—each piece was sexy yet beautiful. The shoes were to die for. The clothes ranged from casual to evening gowns. There was even a few daring yet professional pant suits. *Where the hell am I going to wear those?*

Growing up, Stefan had given me an allowance that had allowed me to shop at the mall. Money had never been the issue.

He'd been trying to teach me the value of things and not raise me to be a spoiled brat. I respected that. All these clothes, though, they reminded me of what was in his closet. Stefan was an unashamed clothes snob. He didn't own anything that wasn't designed by Armani, Tom Ford, or Alexander McQueen.

"I see you discovered your new wardrobe."

I turned toward my bedroom door. Stefan was leaning against the frame with his arms crossed over his chest. His eyes roamed around the room, taking in the aftermath of my raid.

"Um..." I couldn't figure out what to say.

"If there's anything you don't like or if there's anything you still need, let Angela know. She's going out again tomorrow."

I loved everything. Angela had excellent taste. "Not to sound ungrateful, but isn't this a bit much? I would have been happy with clothes from a regular department store."

Stefan stepped into the room. Tossing a box off of the armchair, he took a seat. "Now that you're back, like everyone else in this family, you will have a role. What role that is, I'm not sure yet. I figured we could take the next couple of weeks to find where you're best suited."

"That doesn't explain the clothes."

"I wanted to give you a little more time to settle in before I approached you with this." He sighed. "I'd like it if you'd start shadowing me. Sit in on some meetings. See how I interact with those who work for and with the family. This will give you a crash course on how everything works. It's just for learning purposes. If you find you don't like something or if you are uncomfortable, we'll proceed from there. As for the clothes, you're my daughter and a woman now. You need to dress the part."

Befuddled, I slumped into the couch. That was not what I'd expected him to say.

"What are your thoughts on that?"

Half of me was intrigued while the other hated that aspect of the family. The business side. The crime. It was the source of everything that was wrong with us. Mine and Stefan's relationship, the death of Jamie's father, the difference between our family and everyone else's. "I don't know," I answered honestly.

"There's no rush. Why don't you take a couple of days to think it over?" he suggested and stood to leave.

I nodded. "Thank you for the clothes."

Stefan touched my shoulder, squeezing it lightly in another small gesture of affection before leaving.

There was a knock at my door as I was changing into something comfy to wear for bed. I'd found an old pair of black yoga pants and a baggy tee. I barely got my shirt on in time before the door swung open.

Both Louie and Jamie walked into the room only to stop in their tracks when they noticed the state of my bedroom. Louie whistled. "What happened here?"

"I opened all the new clothes Stefan got me. I, uh, went a little crazy. Designer shoes and dresses have that effect on some people. I didn't know I was one of them until it was too late." As expected, they both looked at me like I'd lost my mind. "Would it help if I told you there was some really sexy lingerie in the mix too?"

That brought a smile to Louie's face. "Now we're talking. Why don't you model them for us?"

"As tempting as that sounds, I was thinking about heading downstairs for a snack. What are you two up to?"

"We're going to watch a movie in the theater. We came to invite you," Jamie finally spoke. That sounded like fun. It'd been forever since I'd been able to laze around and watch a movie.

"Can we watch a comedy or a horror? I'll make some popcorn," I asked over my shoulder as we exited the room.

My room was on the second floor in the east wing, on the opposite side of the house from the kitchen. We debated over what to watch while I was putting the popcorn in the microwave. Louie wanted to watch the new IT movie and Jamie wanted to watch Deadpool. I didn't care either way because I hadn't seen either, but when they looked to me to decide I suggested we watch both and for them to *rock, paper, scissors* to decide whose movie we got to watch first.

I almost peed myself laughing at how serious they played. Two grown mob men facing each other, saying the words to the game at the same time while moving their fists up and down in the air. Louie won.

The theater was on the first floor on the west side of the house near the garage. The large room was dimly lit and filled with pillowy ash colored couches and recliners, all facing the wall with the projection screen. I chose the couch all the way in the back, intending to lie stretched out. That plan was ruined when Jamie took a seat next to me, just before scooping up the tablet that controlled the projector.

Louie snagged the bowl of popcorn out of my hands before plopping down on the other side of me. He shoved a huge handful into his mouth, making his cheeks puff out like a chipmunk. I bit my lip to hide my smile and reached into the bowl to grab a handful myself.

"You know there's enough seats in here for twenty asses to perch on. How am I supposed to lay down with you two sitting next to me?" I griped, eating the popcorn one piece at a time.

Louie handed the popcorn over to Jamie, grabbed one of the many decorative throw pillows in the room, and placed it on his lap. He patted the pillow. "Lay down. Jameson can have your legs. This couch is the best place to watch the movie. We're not moving." I stared at him, then looked to Jamie, who was munching on popcorn while fiddling with the tablet to get the movie started. He didn't protest. Instead, he placed the bowl of popcorn on the floor, showing me that he was already expecting me.

I put my legs in Jamie's lap first, then laid my head on the pillow in Louie's lap. Ominous music played from the speakers and I could already feel the nervous rush. I jumped and screamed throughout the movie and threw popcorn at the guys when they laughed at me. Every time an anxious moment came up, my body would tense up and I covered my eyes. To console me a little, Jamie rubbed my ankle with his thumb. Louie, on the other hand, kept pulling my hands away from my face to make me watch.

By the end of the movie my cheeks hurt from smiling.

The last thing I remembered was the beginning of Deadpool. I'd made the mistake of letting my eyes close. It only felt like a minute had passed before I was being shaken like a rag doll and yelled at to wake up. I startled, my eyes flying open, finding both Jamie and Louie hovering above me.

"Are you okay?" Louie asked.

I looked around, realizing I was still in the theater. My head was still in Louie's lap, but Jamie was kneeling on the floor next to me.

"What?" *Did something happen?*

Without answering me, Jamie gently brushed my cheek with his thumb. That was when I noticed my cheeks were wet. "You were crying in your sleep," he said, studying me with worried eyes.

Shit! I sat up, wiping at my face.

"Were you having a nightmare?" Louie sounded a little guilty, probably thinking it was due to the movie we'd just watched.

I shook my head. I couldn't look at them. The only person who'd known about this was Tom. He'd used to wake me up in the beginning of our relationship. When it had kept happening, he'd wait until morning to tell me. After about six months of being together, he'd stopped bringing it up. Which explained why I'd forgotten.

"What were you dreaming about?" Jamie asked.

"I'd prefer we didn't make this a big deal," I deflected before getting the nerve to look at them. Both of them were expressionless—keeping what they were thinking hidden, and I didn't know if that made me feel better or worse.

"Sorry to ruin the night guys," I said and got to my feet. "I'm going to bed. Goodnight."

They both mumbled goodnight as I left the theater.

CHAPTER THIRTEEN

I woke early the next day and zombied my way downstairs in search of coffee. While rubbing the fog from my eyes, I shuffled into the dining room.

"Good morning," I heard Stefan say. He was in his usual spot at the head of the table, dressed in an impeccable tailored suit, eating an omelet while scrolling through his iPad. As I took in the rest of the room, I noticed he wasn't alone. On his left were Jamie and Louie, who were both wearing suits with no ties and their shirt collars unbuttoned. Across from them, sitting to the right of Stefan, were my uncle Conor and my cousin Rourke, both of whom were dressed to impress. You'd have thought I'd walked in on a board meeting instead of breakfast with how sharp they all looked. I wished I could say the same for myself. I was in rumpled clothes I'd slept in and was undoubtedly sporting some major bed head.

Conor and Rourke stood from the table to greet me. Seeing my beloved cousin, I was suddenly energized with excitement. I dashed around the table, barely giving him time to brace himself before I full-body tackled him. We both hit the floor with matching *oomphs!*

"Ow, you heifer!" Not that I'd ever admit it out loud, but Rourke was my favorite cousin. He never acted superior. My aunt Kiara, Stefan's younger sister, would choke the life from him if he failed to show a woman respect. During my aunt's time as Banphrionsa, treatment of women had been at its worst. My grandfather had made my uncle Samuel look like a saint in comparison. He'd used his fists more times than not to ensure obedience, which had resulted in my beautiful grandmother killing herself.

"Who are you calling fat, you cherub-cheeked mama's boy!" I teased, squishing the sides of his cheeks until his face was smushed together, giving him squinty eyes and fish lips. Using a self-defense move we'd all learned as kids, he fluidly rolled me. The next thing I knew, I was pinned, and he was sticking a wet finger in my ear. I yelped. "Eww, you sick bastard!" Everyone laughed as we continued to wrestle on the floor.

"Let her up, son," my uncle Conor ordered.

Listening to his father, Rourke released me and got to his feet, then held out his hand to help me to mine. I gratefully accepted and he pulled me from the floor into his arms for a real hug. Rourke was tall like his dad. He towered over me by at least a foot. Despite his last name being Murphy, he had the looks of a Quinn, with light brown hair and green eyes. Thanks to his father, he'd been cursed with freckles. I felt his pain. With the same cluster across his nose, we looked like siblings even though our hair was drastically different.

"It's been boring without you around," he said, pulling away. He gave me a devious smile. "I heard you filleted another man's dic—ow! Damnit!"

I tried to stop him from talking by pinching the underside of his arm. Sadly, I was too late. Enough had been said and I inter-nally groaned at what was undoubtedly coming.

"Blew it to smithereens is more like it," Louie chimed in,

adding fuel to the fire. To be dramatic, he shivered as if trying to shake away the awful memory. Then he looked to Jamie. "Remind me never to piss off Maura."

Jamie rolled his eyes and returned to eating his breakfast.

"If you keep mutilating penises, people are going to start calling you *Dick Crusher* or something," Rourke snickered.

Louie's boisterous laugh followed before he snapped his fingers, pointing at me. "We should call her The *Castrator*."

The whole room erupted with laughter; even Stefan's shoulders were slightly bouncing.

My uncle shook his head, smiling as he opened his arms to hug me next. "They're almost thirty years old and they still act like teenagers," he said, his Irish accent standing out. He was the only one in our immediate family who had one. My aunt had bewitched him, so he said, while she'd been visiting some relatives in Ireland. At the beginning of their romance, his accent had used to be so thick, she could barely understand him. Pulled by love, he of course had followed her back to the States, which over time had helped to soften his words.

I stepped out of our hug. "How's Aunt Kiara?"

"She's doing grand. She's mad with joy that you're back home and was talking about visiting soon."

"That'd be wonderful. I'd love to see her."

"Are you hungry?" Stefan asked, already knowing the answer. I didn't like eating early in the morning unless I absolutely had to. I preferred to wake up and move around first.

I scrunched my nose. "Coffee?"

Stefan tilted his head toward the kitchen. I ventured off in that direction, through the swinging door. The gigantic gourmet kitchen was L-shaped, equipped with two restaurant grade gas stovetops, four ovens, a walk-in refrigerator, and a temperature-controlled pantry. The cabinets were navy blue with beautiful white quartz countertops. The room was filled with natural light coming in through the large window above the kitchen sink and the glass door leading out to the pool in the backyard. At the sink with her back toward me, Jeana was humming while washing the pots and pans she'd used to cook breakfast.

"Can I help you?" a feminine voice asked, tone far from friendly. My attention snapped to the large kitchen island where a pretty blonde was leaning over with a magazine open in front of her. *This must be Angela.*

Damnit. She was gorgeous. She had wavy golden hair that shone in the sunlight. Her lips were plump and heart shaped. Her makeup was flawless and made her tawny-brown eyes pop. Hell, if she and I were cellmates in prison, I'd totally want her to be my bitch. That didn't bode well for this family and, well... me. I could already tell that she and I weren't going to get along.

Her sleeping with Louie irked me. Thinking about her poaching anyone else in my family was making me feel extremely territorial—er, I mean fiercely protective. *I wonder what she'd look like if I ripped out all that pretty hair.* It was an appealing thought. I'd done it to my Barbies as a little girl and she closely resembled one of the plastic dolls before it had left its protective box. Maybe it was a sign? *Bitch better not hang up on me again or I'm going to make a generous donation to Locks of Love.*

I forced a smile. "No," I replied, making my way to the coffee pot on the counter behind her.

"Maura! Good morning, sweetie. I put some leftovers in the fridge. When you get hungry, let me know and I'll reheat them," Jeana informed me with a bright smile, then returned to the dishes.

I could feel Angela's eyes digging holes into my back as I fixed my coffee. I was stirring in vanilla creamer when I heard the door from the dining room swing open.

"Jameson! That's my job, silly. You didn't have to bring that in here," Maid Barbie said.

I pursed my lips at how overly friendly she was toward him. With a schooled expression, I turned and propped a hip against the counter. I watched Jamie stride through the room. He placed his plate and silverware next to the sink.

Jeana beamed at him with her motherly smile. "Thanks, sweetie!"

With his coffee mug still in his hand, I had a hunch where Jamie was headed next and I was blocking his way. His brows rose in question before his head tilted slightly. Refusing to move, I teased him with a mischievous smirk. "Want some coffee, big guy?" The corner of his mouth twitched. Placing my mug on the counter, I stepped closer, shrinking the space between us. "How bad do you want it?" I used a sultry voice as I cocked an eyebrow.

Thinking he was being clever, he sat his mug on the counter and picked up mine. The tiniest sip made him grimace.

"You put too much creamer in it," he complained, scrunching his nose.

"Not everyone likes their coffee black," I informed, grabbing his mug to fill it. I wiggled my fingers, gesturing for him to give me mine in exchange for his. He eagerly traded.

"What are you doing today?" I asked.

His gaze shifted to Angela, who was pretending to ignore us. I didn't like that. Thinking back, he probably didn't want to discuss work stuff in front of her. Unfortunately, at the time all I saw was red.

I invaded his space, plastering my body to the front of his as I hooked my arms around his neck. He was surprised for only a breath before he recovered.

"Do you get to be mine again today? Maybe this time Louie can watch while we wrestle around in my bed." I knew what I was implying was wrong, especially with Jamie, who thought of me like a sister.

His eyes narrowed. Thankfully, Angela took the hint or had

other things to attend to and left with Jeana trailing behind. I dropped my hands from around his neck to rest them on his chest. As if sensing I was getting ready to pull away, he put a hand on my hip.

"Did you enjoy that?" he asked, plopping his mug down with a loud clank, uncaring that his coffee sloshed over the rim.

Is he mad? I couldn't tell.

His voice was cold, but the way he was staring at me told me different. Stepping forward, he steered me by my hips until he had me pinned against the counter. His pelvis leaned into mine as his strong arms coiled around me, trapping my own between us. His hand traveled slowly along my spine until his fingers buried in my tangled hair. He tugged gently and my breath hitched as I was forced to look up at him. "Did you enjoy teasing me to get to her?"

Biting my tongue, I removed all emotion from my face.

"Maybe I should make you deliver. Louie does like to watch," he whispered in my ear.

Heat slowly crawled up my neck and I desperately fought to keep my heart rate steady. *Holy shit!*

In that moment, the veil that protected our friendship blew away, tumbling in the wind, and I was suddenly in unknown territory. My impassive mask was crumbling fast. I needed to turn this around because unlike my body, my mind knew he wasn't serious. "I've never been one to back down." I leveled my eyes with his. "And I'm pretty determined to keep her away."

"You'd let me fuck you?" His tone was harsh. However, the way the words *fuck* and *you* rolled off his tongue made my temperature rise. Could I? Would I?

"I..." His grip tightened around my hair, turning all my rational thoughts to mush. A gasp escaped me. My control slipped. The heat creeping up my neck flushed my cheeks.

Something shifted in his eyes as he took in my reaction.

Surprise, maybe? It only lasted for a second before they darkened. His gaze moved to my lips, lingering. I wet them with the tip of my tongue, and he inhaled sharply.

"Stop teasing me," I ordered in a confused mixture of angry and breathlessly wanton.

He bent forward, brushing his nose against mine. My fingers fisted around his shirt of their own volition, holding him in place. "I don't think you want me to stop," he whispered. He was so close, his breath tickled my lips.

Unable to take the intensity, I leaned forward, embracing the sting of his unforgiving grip pulling at my hair. I felt his body go so still the moment my lips lightly touched his that I wasn't sure if he was even breathing.

I didn't understand his reaction, but with the lack of recipro-cation, I pulled my head back. His arms tightened, making it diffi-cult to breathe.

"Maura, I—" he started, only to be cut off when the dining room door swung open. He quickly released me, stepping back, eyes dropping to the floor. To hide my flushed appearance, I gave my back to whoever walked into the room and tried to busy myself by topping off my coffee.

Rourke stepped beside me and took the coffee pot from my hand. "It's none of my business, but you look like a couple of guilty teenagers," he said, amusement lacing his tone.

I peeked at him out of the corner of my eye. He had this annoying smug look on his face, eyes sparkling with mirth as they traveled from Jamie to me. "You look a little flushed, cousin." He was laughing at us.

I grabbed my coffee and bolted. Like a coward, I didn't return to the dining room.

What the hell just happened? I kept repeating in my head as I retreated to my bedroom.

CHAPTER FOURTEEN

I spent all morning in my room overthinking and slightly freaking out. *Why did I kiss him?* I groaned. I'd crossed the line and now things were going to be awkward between us. *What if things don't go back to the way they were?*

I needed to get out of my room to clear my head. It was mid-September, still warm enough to go swimming. Unfortunately, there hadn't been anything swim related in the big clothing haul I'd received last night, but I was sure I still had an old suit still lying around. With my mind made up, I started digging through my closet. I found a robin's egg blue bikini in a drawer along with a white cover-up. As I was tying it on, I was reminded again that my assets were bigger. I ran into my bathroom to use the mirror to help me stuff my boobs behind two triangles of fabric. It didn't look bad. A lot more voluptuous versus the full coverage I was used to. My hips and ass looked amazing as they flared seductively from my small waist and bubbled tastefully in the tight bikini bottoms.

I pulled my hair up in a messy bun and put on my white cover-up. It was sheer with an open front and dolman sleeves that cut off just before they met my wrists.

I strolled through the house without seeing a single soul. Annoyingly, that didn't mean no one saw me. I passed camera after camera. I was sure one or two goons were currently monitoring them. That was, until I walked into the kitchen. Three of Stefan's goons were sitting at the island eating their lunch. Their conversation stopped abruptly as I entered the room. I didn't recognize or know any of them. *Fresh meat.*

I wasn't fond of Stefan's goon squad, be it grounds security or personal. Some were distant blood relatives, others were friends of and vetted by someone in the family. Regardless of how they'd joined or what type of security they did, all of them were obedient soldiers eager to move up the ranks. Grounds security for this property, or any property the family owned, was the bottom of the totem pole. It was where everyone started, apart from a few exceptions. The next step up was personal security. Who each goon was assigned to protect depended on how loyal and trustworthy they'd proven themselves to be. I was pretty sure Jamie had gotten to skip being a goon entirely and gone straight to shadowing Stefan. The same could not be said for Louie. Jamie had vetted him and he'd had to start at the bottom, walking Quinn Manor's property line at seventeen. He was the only goon I'd ever actually liked and that was because he'd been my friend for years prior.

Staring at these three new faces, an evil urge bubbled within me. Whenever new goons started working at the house, it was always a joyful pastime of mine to mess with them.

Walking to the other side of the island, directly across from them, I blatantly stared, taking in each of their appearances without saying a word. Each stared back at me with varying expressions. It was easy to tell who knew who I was and who didn't. The one sitting on the far right checked me out, while the one in the middle regarded me with respect. The last one on the left clearly had no idea who the hell I was because he glared. He was probably trying to intimidate me, which made me smile brightly. *This is going to be fun.*

"Ma'am," the one in the middle greeted. I ignored him. Without removing my eyes from the goon who was glaring, I leaned over the top of the island and rested on my forearms in front of him.

"You got a name, handsome?" And he was handsome. He had a sandy colored crew cut and milk chocolate eyes. From what I could tell, under the grounds security uniform consisting of a black long sleeve Henley, black cargo pants, and steel-toed boots, he was very fit. The sleeves of his shirt were stretched tight around his biceps. He was definitely eye candy despite what seemed to be a permanent scowl.

His glare shifted to disgust. "Don't you have a bed you should be warming?"

The guard in the middle winced. "Dean, that's—"

"Dean, is it?" I interrupted before he ruined my fun. "I'll make sure I remember that." I shifted my attention to the other two. "What are your names? I make it a point to know who's in my house."

"Your house?" Dean scoffed at the same time the others answered.

"Josh," the middle goon answered.

"Blake. You got a name, gorgeous?" the one on the left asked.

I gave him a fake smile. "I do, but I don't know if you've earned it yet. How long have you all worked for Stefan?"

"Seven months," Blake answered.

"Just over a year," Josh said, glancing nervously at Dean, who caught him doing it. His brow furrowed in confusion.

"Maura?" someone called out to me. The three goons shot up from their chairs as a formal greeting. Louie strolled into the kitchen. He glanced from the goons to me and shook his head.

"Babe, it's not nice to antagonize the guys even if you're giving them a great view of your rack."

I looked down. Leaning forward on my arms had made my boobs push up and out. There was a lot of cleavage on display and my small bikini top left very little to the imagination. It was hard to suppress the sly smile that was making the corner of my mouth twitch as I stood straight.

"She your girl, Louie?" Dean asked him.

The corner of Louie's mouth curled up. "Nah, man. I like my dick attached to my body," he joked and draped an arm over my shoulders. I lightly smacked his chest with the back of my hand. "She's the Banphrionsa."

Dean clearly didn't understand the Gaelic term and turned to Josh for clarification.

"She's the boss's daughter," Josh told him, sheepishly.

Both Dean and Blake stiffened.

Shrugging off Louie's arm, I held back the smirk threatening to pull at my lips. "Well, I'm going swimming. Enjoy the rest of your lunch, gentlemen."

"A heads up would have been nice," I heard Dean snap.

Josh sighed. "I tried."

Louie's boisterous laugher filled the room just before I stepped outside.

I did a lazy swim, letting myself get lost in the sensation of being weightless. It was peaceful and it helped dilute my worries.

Once my fingers started to prune, I got out and lay on one of the many plush lounge chairs around the pool. I soaked up the sun, most likely gaining more freckles rather than a tan. It was so comfortable and warm, I started to doze off.

"You'll burn if you fall asleep out here."

My heart tried to leap out of my chest at the sound of Jamie's voice. I hadn't even heard him approach. I cowardly kept my eyes closed, nervous at what I might see. I wasn't ready to face the ugly truth of what might have changed between us but knew putting it off would only prolong my suffering.

"It feels good out. Five more minutes," I said, finally opening my eyes.

He was sitting on the lounge chair next to me gazing out at the rest of the property. I followed his line of sight. Blake was walking the edge of the property with Dean, both of whom had guns and wireless radios holstered to their belts. Stefan typically had at least six grounds security on the property at all times. Two were posted at the gate in the guardhouse while another two walked the grounds and the last two monitored the cameras in the control room inside the house.

"What?" I asked.

"I think you're distracting the men from doing their job."

Yeah, right. "Have you come to tease me some more?" After the words left my mouth, I realized I was unintentionally picking a fight.

He studied me with a frown. He was trying to read me, and I put zero effort in trying to hide my irritation. I was confused, embarrassed, and beyond angry with myself... or should I say, my lack of self-control. I'd given in to a surge of hormones like a horny teenager. *Ah! Why did I kiss him?!* I didn't know what made me feel worse: me kissing him or him not kissing me back. I reached for my bare wrist out of habit, fingers searching for the bands. I missed the sting that helped reel in the shit I didn't want to feel.

Deep breath and just be mature about this.

He hadn't kissed me back because he didn't feel that way about me and that was fine. It wasn't like I understood my feelings either. Was I attracted to him? After this morning, I'd be lying if I said no. I had to take an ice cold shower once I got up to my room just to cool down. Jamie was fucking gorgeous. His muscled body was excitingly lethal. His tattooed skin, when he did show it, always made the temperature in the room go up. The fact that I trusted him more than anyone only added fuel to the fire. Maybe deep down, I'd always been attracted to him, and while growing up my need for his friendship had suppressed it. That was, until a little hair pulling had me go weak in the knees, making me hotter than I'd ever been.

"Do we need to talk about it?" Jamie asked, pulling me from my thoughts.

"No," I curtly replied. That was the last thing I wanted right now. "Can we pretend it didn't happen?"

He clenched his jaw, deepening his frown, which I found strange. I'd assumed he'd be relieved I was giving him an out.

His eyes locked with mine, as if searching for answers in the depths of my soul. Once he seemed to find what he was looking for, he gave me the slightest nod. Even though it was what I'd asked of him, his acceptance stung. I wasn't fast enough to hide the hurt in my eyes. So before he could say anything, I grabbed my cover-up and bolted. I felt like a coward for running away, but I couldn't be around him, not without making things worse.

Face downturned, I made my way through the kitchen into the foyer. I was so lost in my head, I collided with a wall of muscle. Hard. The impact sent me flying backward to the floor. "Ow," I hissed, landing on my ass.

"Watch where you're going," a venomous voice snarled. I peered up as I rubbed at my sore tailbone. A grisly goon glared down at me. *What the hell is his problem?* Running into him had been an accident, which I'd had every intention of apologizing for.

"Maybe you should have gotten out of the fucking way." It wasn't my finest moment. I was having a lot of those lately.

The goon's face hardened with anger as his eyes filled with murderous intent. He locked a hand bruisingly around my upper arm and yanked me to my feet. The pain caused me to yelp.

"Learn your place, you stupid cunt." His hand came out of nowhere. My head was forced backward by the roaring pain that slammed into the side of my face. My vision exploded and the taste of pennies filled my mouth. Flashbacks of that night seven years ago filled my head. All it took was one hit and pow! I was seventeen again. Zack had hit me in a similar way right before Tyson pinned my arms above my head. Then Zack ripped my legs apart...

Damnit! They're dead. Focus!

I blinked away the vision and slowly turned back to face my reality. The goon still held my left arm in his calloused, tight grip.

I made a show of forming a fist with my right hand and swung to punch him, knowing he'd block it. When he caught my wrist, I slammed my head forward, colliding my forehead with his nose. With that satisfying crunch, he shouted out in pain, blood gushing from his nostrils. I silenced him with a swift knee kick to the groin. He choked on a gulp of air, releasing my right wrist, but still held onto me tightly by my left arm. I tried yanking free to no avail. I was trapped. He refused to unclamp his strong coarse fingers and it put my head right back in that bathroom, pinned to that fucking floor. Tyson was squeezing my wrists while Zach's bruising fingers pressed into the tender area of my inner thighs, holding them open. *Fuuuuuck!*

I again crawled out of the trenches that were my memories and tried to figure a way out of his hold. My eyes bounced around quickly, until they landed on the gun holstered at his belt. I moved before my brain even thought to. I yanked his side arm from the holster, aimed the pistol at his head, and pulled the trigger. It happened so fast. I didn't think. I didn't hesitate. I just acted.

I watched the light leave his eyes as his body crumpled to the floor. The rush of it was intoxicating. Seductive. As quick as those feelings lit up, they were chased away by the ice water of guilt washing over me. I couldn't handle it. I shut down.

The shot had echoed throughout the house, followed by yelling. Numbly, I backed up from the body on the floor, taking step after step until I hit something solid. It didn't feel like a wall. Startled, I lifted my gun. A hand clasped around my wrist, stopping me before I was forcibly turned around to face whoever had ahold of me.

"Maura?" It was Jamie.

His eyes widened as his gaze traveled over the side of my injured face to the body on the floor behind me. From what I could tell, my lip was split and beginning to swell. Even the inside of my cheek was cut up from it smashing against my teeth. My cheek bone pulsated, sending a stabbing pain up behind my eye. I hurt and the pain was getting worse with each passing second.

One after another, goons showed up with their guns drawn. First Josh, next was Dean, and then another whose name I didn't know. Gun pointed in the air, Dean squatted next to the dead goon and checked for a pulse at his neck. Clearly not finding one, Dean looked to Josh, shaking his head slightly before all three goons looked over at me. Jamie quickly turned me away from them and pulled at my bikini top. I glanced down, finding my right breast had fallen out from behind the small fabric. Jamie did his best to yank the material back into place, covering my exposed flesh. Louie was the next to enter the foyer, gun at the ready. He saw the body first before his eyes traveled to me. He didn't even bother checking to see if he might be alive. Instead, he quickly shoved his gun in the back of his pants and started unbuttoning his dress shirt. He had it open by the time he reached us. I watched as he slid it off his shoulders and draped it around mine.

"What happened?" he asked Jamie.

"I don't know. She won't respond."

When did he ask me?

More bodies trickled into the room, goons, house staff. All were talking. It was loud, but I couldn't make out what anyone was saying. As more time passed, the more confused I started to feel. Every time I tried to focus on someone, thoughts of my finger pulling the trigger or the feel of the pushback after the gun fired would pull me away, flood me with thoughts of Zack, Tyson, that night and then that intoxicating feeling I'd gotten when I'd killed them. When I'd killed them all.

The memory from a few nights ago in Stefan's study played back like a movie behind my eyes. I'd told Stefan I'd had to see the fear in Tom and Tina's eyes before I'd killed them or else it wouldn't have been as satisfying.

Is this who I am? A monster? My conscience asked. *Who cares? You loved it. Embrace it,* my darkness argued. My soul felt split in two, putting me at war with itself.

Brody approached me, concern etched around his eyes. His mouth was moving but his words never reached my ears. When he looked to Jamie to talk to him, I was able to read one word his lips formed. *Stefan.*

"Should be here any minute." Jamie's voice reached me, a moment of clarity only lasting for the breadth of a second.

I tried to focus on Louie's shirt hanging off my shoulders, but I couldn't hold onto my thoughts of it—its color, the way the fabric felt against my skin. It wasn't enough.

Something was wrong with me. I was a psychology student for fuck's sake. *Why can't I focus?* I tried to still my mind long enough to understand, cataloging my feelings, my reactions, my surroundings, and then it hit me.

I was in shock.

"Maura?"

It was the only explanation.

"Maura?" Hands gently tilted my head back, forcing me to look up. My eyes met Jamie's. "You need to sit down. Brody brought you a chair." His hands traveled to my arms. As his fingers closed around my left arm, the pain caused me to cry out and I shoved him away. He jumped back with his hands in the air.

"My arm," was all I could muster.

Seeming to understand, he nodded, taking a hesitant step toward me again. This time he put a hand on my shoulder and his other at my hip. "The chair is right behind you. All you have to do is sit down."

I sat back, my butt meeting with a soft cushion. Jamie knelt in front of me, moving his hands to rest on my knees. His thumbs rubbed small circles against my skin, soothingly. The more I watched him, the more I was able to focus. Not on anything else. Just Jamie. He was anchoring me.

"Maura!" I heard Stefan yell. I listened to the slapping sound of his Oxfords hitting the marble floor as he rushed through the foyer. Jamie moved when Stefan approached. I reached out, frantically grabbing his hand, stopping him from going far. Stefan knelt in front of me, just like Jamie had. He looked me over, reaching up, hovering his hand over my hurt face.

His eyes traveled to Jamie. "What the hell happened?" He was angry. The fury in his tone was obvious, but the way his hands shook told me he was struggling with his control. I'd never seen him so close to losing it before. He was the boss. He couldn't afford to lose it in front of others.

"He wouldn't let me go, so I shot him. Here's his gun." My voice was drone-like and so matter of fact, even to my own ears. I held out the goon's gun and waited for him to take it.

Stefan tilted his head slightly, studying me as he took the gun. He glanced back to Jamie with a questioning expression.

"Josh has the camera footage ready for you to watch. She wasn't paying attention to where she was going and ran into

Greg. He hit her to teach her a lesson. She disarmed him and shot him in the head."

"Who found her?"

"I did."

"Has she been like this since then?"

"She's getting better. She was rambling before you got here, saying she's in shock and..." Jamie trailed off.

"What?" Stefan snapped, his patience dwindling.

"She said, 'Zack and Tyson.'"

Stefan bristled but quickly recovered and stood. "Alright. I'll take it from here. Help her get to her room."

Jamie took his place kneeling in front of me again. "Can you walk? If not, I can carry you."

If he carries you, you won't be able to look anyone in the eye tomorrow.

Jamie nodded and I realized I'd unintentionally said that out loud. He pulled lightly with the hand that still held mine. I got to my feet and let him lead me back to my room.

CHAPTER FIFTEEN

"I smell chlorine," I mumbled as we walked into my bedroom.

"You went swimming," Jamie reminded me. "Do you want to take a bath? Your muscles might be sore soon, if they aren't already."

I shook my head. He was still holding my hand and I was worried if he let go, my mind would spiral again. He tugged on my hand. "Come on, you'll feel better after." He tried to release my hand, but I tightened my grip and grabbed his wrist with my other hand to strengthen my hold.

"Please! Don't leave me." I hated the sound of panic in my voice. It was the sound of a helpless female. My need of him, however, outweighed my humiliation. If he stayed with me until I had a better grasp on myself, everything would be okay.

His free hand cupped the back of my neck. "I would never leave you," he said softly, pulling me closer. I rested the uninjured side of my face over his heart. The satin fabric of his black dress shirt felt soft against my cheek as I listened to the steady beat in his chest. "Let's get you into the bath. It will help, I promise." Trusting him, I let him lead me into the bathroom and stopped us as we came upon the porcelain clawfoot tub.

"I'm going to let go. I'm not going to leave. I won't go anywhere you can't see me," he said.

I took a deep breath and released his hand. My eyes never left him as he made quick work of unbuttoning the cuffs of his shirt before rolling up his sleeves to his elbows, exposing his tattooed skin. Bending over the tub, he turned the knobs, adjusting the temperature of the water pouring out of the faucet. Steam wafted above the water pooling at the bottom. He grabbed a bottle from the shelf on the wall and poured some of the liquid into the tub. Bubbles instantly began to form and the smell of lavender filled my nose.

Without saying a word of warning, Jamie slipped Louie's shirt off my shoulders, letting it drop to the floor. He pulled at the strings of my bikini, peeling the pieces that covered my skin away. I was as naked as the day I was born. My mind was too numb to care.

He grabbed my hand again and put his other at the small of my back, carefully helping me into the bath. The water was hot but not scalding. Just enough burn to feel good as I sank into it.

Jamie plucked a washcloth from a stack of many on the shelf and dropped it in the water. He knelt next to the tub after turning off the water. Sitting in the center of the tub, I bent my legs, bringing them to my chest. I felt Jamie reach into the water, scooping out the washcloth. Water dripped onto my back before the warm cloth slid down my spine. My eyes closed, relishing the sensation of it scrubbing gently against my skin.

"Do you need anything?" Louie's voice broke the silence in the room. I opened my eyes to find him standing in the doorway. Gone was his normal carefree smile. He seemed tense while holding a Jamie-like stoic expression.

"She's going to need an ice pack for her face and some clothes to sleep in. I'm putting her to bed after this," Jamie replied. Louie nodded and left.

"Something's wrong with Louie," I mumbled.

Jamie's head jerked back to me, seeming surprised. "He'll get over it," he replied.

I didn't understand, nor did I have it in me to ask him to explain.

Dropping the washcloth into the water, he sat back on his heels.

He brushed the back of his fingers over the bruises forming on my arm. They were dark, already taking the shape of fingers. He looked angry, staring at the marred skin, but his touch was gentle.

"Are you ready to get out?"

I nodded and took his offered hand. Water and bubbles sluiced down my body as I stood, splashing into the tub below. Turning toward him, I caught him watching a cluster of bubbles making its way down my stomach. He fixated on them just before they reached the top of my mound, then his eyes dropped to the floor. He took a step back, giving me room to get out.

Once my feet hit the plush rug, Louie entered the bathroom carrying some clothes. He stopped in his tracks, eyes wide as they traveled along my wet body. He recovered quickly, schooling his expression. "I got her a big shirt and underwear."

"Thanks, man. Can you toss me that towel hanging on the hook behind you?"

Louie grabbed the towel before tossing it to Jamie, who then wrapped it around my body.

"I can do it." My voice was low, but Jamie still heard me.

"Do you want me to stay?"

I nodded. "Out there."

Understanding, he left to wait in my room. Louie lingered behind, handing over my clothes. I took them and held them to my chest.

"I'm going to get you an ice pack and something for the pain. Can I get you anything else?"

I shook my head. Louie's eyes dropped to the towel around me, his expression turning pained before he turned on his heel to leave.

Slowly drying off, I slipped on the shirt and underwear Louie had brought me. The gray T-shirt had one of my favorite bands' logo on the front. It was baggy, soft, and the hem ended at mid-thigh, hiding the purple boy shorts I had on underneath.

I took a long look in the mirror. Bruises had already formed on my cheek bone and there was a little bit of swelling. The corner of my lip was split and also slightly puffy. Overall, it wasn't that bad. I'd looked worse.

"You alright?" Jamie's silky voice filled the room. He was standing in the doorway with his hands stuffed in his pockets, watching me.

"I'm seeing how bad it is," I said, sounding more like myself, and he seemed to notice, too.

"It'll fade in a week." He was trying to reassure me. "Louie brought you an ice pack and pain killers."

I turned around and walked over to him. Without stopping, I wrapped my arms around his waist and buried my nose into his chest. "I'm sorry." I didn't say what for because I meant it for everything. For the way I'd acted this morning and by the pool, and even for freaking out. Despite our fight and the unsureness between us, he'd still been there for me like always.

"Me too," he whispered, wrapping his arms around me and pressing his lips to my forehead. He gave me a tight squeeze before releasing me and stepping away. "You need to lay down, even if it's just for a little while."

I didn't argue. The covers on my bed were already pulled down and I climbed right in. Jamie handed me two pills and a glass of water. I swallowed them but refused the ice pack.

"Can you stay until I fall asleep?"

"I'll stay as long as you need me," he said. I patted the bed next to me with my hand, gesturing for him to lie down. He hesitated at first, then toed off his shoes and pulled his gun from the back of his pants. He slid it under his pillow before he lay down next to me.

Staring up at the ceiling, everything that happened that day started to replay in my mind.

"Don't think. Just close your eyes, Maura."

Letting out a heavy sigh, I did as he said, and I drifted off almost instantly.

"Maura, wake up."

I startled awake and almost jumped out of my skin when I saw a blurry figure hovering above me.

"Shh, it's okay. It's just me."

I blinked a few times and Jamie's face came into focus. His hand cupped my face and he wiped my cheek with his thumb. "You were crying."

I quickly wiped at my face. "I'm sorry."

"Don't be sorry. I just wanted to make sure you were okay. You were saying some weird shit."

I tensed. "Oh?" I didn't want to talk about my dreams, *ever*. Internally, I prayed he wouldn't ask.

"How are you feeling?"

Relieved, I relaxed. "Sore. Starving. I don't think I ate today. How long was I out?"

"About six hours. It's dinner time. Think you might be up to going downstairs or do you want to eat up here?"

"I'm not ready to face the world yet."

"By world, do you mean Stefan?" he asked, already knowing the answer.

"We could watch a movie while we eat. I'll let you pick," I said, deflecting.

He sighed and rolled over to pick up the phone on my nightstand. He only hit one button, which I assumed was the pre-programmed number for the kitchen. Someone picked up and he told whoever it was, likely Jeana, that we'd like dinner brought up to my room. The food arrived shortly after he hung up. It was Italian and smelled delicious. We ate on the couch as we watched TV.

"You're the only one Stefan allows to get away with shit. He'd never let anyone else avoid him because we weren't ready to talk. One time, he sent me to some dude's hospital room, demanding to know what happened. The guy had just gotten out of surgery after being shot in the chest."

"He'll interrogate me when he finds time to check on me," I argued, sounding bitter. The last time I got hurt like this, five days had passed before he'd come to check on me and that time I had been raped. This time I wasn't going to hold my breath.

"He came to check on you an hour after you fell asleep," he said. He must have seen my surprise because he gave me a tight smile. "He's trying."

I nodded, agreeing.

"He tried not to show it, but he was worried about you. You scared the shit out of us. You've never acted like that after..."

After killing someone.

I placed my fork down on my plate before setting the plate on the coffee table. "I'm surprised you aren't mad at me."

Jamie narrowed his eyes, perplexed. "Why would I be mad at you?"

"Because I killed him. I provoked him."

"He put his hands on you," he said as if that made it okay.

My stomach churned with guilt. "He didn't know who I was."

He shook his head. "You know that doesn't matter. Don't forget who you are—who we are," he said, eyes boring into mine. "Stefan would have made him suffer before he killed him to set an example."

I picked at the bottom of my shirt as I thought out how to say what I needed to say next. Jamie deserved to know, and I needed to talk about it. I took a deep breath and I just blurted it out. "I liked it. Killing him."

He stayed quiet, being patient, sensing I had more to say.

"It was so easy, pulling the trigger. Too easy. It was a rush, like that first high from a new drug or an orgasm. It was satisfying but left me wanting more." I kneaded the back of my neck with my fingers, trying to ease the tension and help stop the heat making its way up to my cheeks. *I just compared killing people to orgasming.* I dropped my eyes and went back to fiddling with the hem of my shirt again. "Feeling all that felt wrong, or it should. Zack, Tyson, Tom, Tina, they all hurt me, deeply. In my mind, I figured killing them was a kind of twisted form of self-defense and therefore justified. Today, though, all that guy did was hit me after I provoked him. He didn't hurt me deeply, even if that fucking backhand gave me some real fucked up flashbacks. One second I was standing there with him holding onto me and the next I was seventeen, being held down on that goddamned bathroom floor. It was the same exact hit to the face that gave Zack and Tyson the upper hand to take me down." I shook my head in disbelief. "I guess what I'm trying to say is that killing him—Greg, I couldn't justify it, but I didn't care. Realizing that, I felt guilty for not feeling guilty. I began battling with myself. I fought to hold onto the guilt because it's what you're supposed to feel when you murder someone. It was so difficult. The urge to enjoy the high was easy as breathing, but I knew if I gave into it, that'd mean I'm a monster. My mind just snapped."

Jamie set his plate on the coffee table next to mine before scooting closer. Fingers curled under my chin, gently forcing me to look up at him "You're not a monster," he said with so much conviction. "Do you think I'm a monster?"

"No." I didn't hesitate in answering. He would never be a monster to me no matter how bloody his hands ever got.

His hand moved up to cup my uninjured cheek. I couldn't stop myself from leaning into it, loving the feel of his strength and the comfort it provided. "We're not good people, Maura. We're the fucking mob. Those who don't learn to enjoy what we do don't survive in our world."

"What if I go crazy? What if I can't stop?"

He gave me an incredulous look. "You've always been crazy. I think you'll be fine."

I rolled my eyes, then sighed, deciding to let it go because I trusted him.

"Did Stefan tell you he wants me to start shadowing him?" I got my answer when his face became veiled and he dropped his hand. He knew, but didn't know what he could let on without breaking Stefan's confidence or the *code of honor*. I would never push him. I understood where his loyalties had to be. "I'm going to do it."

"Are you sure?"

"What else am I supposed to do? Get married and pop out a few kids? That's not who I am."

"You could finish school and get a normal job while still being part of this family. I don't think you understand what you're getting yourself into, Maura. Knowing everything this side entails... it's not easy. It's bloody and it's dangerous."

"I can't do normal. I tried for six years and I hated every fucking minute of it," I finally admitted out loud and it felt good. "I've already considered the repercussions and worked through my apprehensions. Even if there's a chance I might regret it later, I still want to do it because I know for a fact, I will regret it now if I don't."

Silence stretched between us as he mulled over my words. I waited for him patiently. When he found a reason within himself to accept my decision, he sighed and nodded.

CHAPTER SIXTEEN

I awoke to warm air tickling my neck and a heavy body
practically squishing me. For a second I thought it was Tom.
Then my brain roared to life, blowing away the drowsy fog.
Tom was dead. I was back home. Jamie had fallen asleep on my
bed when we'd lain down to watch a movie last night. I didn't
have the heart to wake him.

While we both slept, he must have gravitated to my side of
the bed. His face was buried in the crook of my neck. His torso
pinned my entire right side and one of his legs stretched across
both of mine. I wasn't sure if this constituted cuddling or if I'd
been rendered the human equivalent of a body pillow. Whatever
sleeping Jamie had intended, his hand had made its way up my
shirt and was currently groping my boob.

Oh boy.

Murmuring in his sleep, his whole body shifted, and his
fingers flexed around my breast. My breathing stalled. *Well, one
part of him is up.* I gaped at the hard rod now pushing into my hip
through his slacks. He was still wearing his clothes from yesterday. Having kept his promise, he'd never left my side even to go
change.

His hand slid to cup the side of my breast, thumb brushing over my nipple. I swallowed a gasp. When his thumb stroked over my puckered flesh once more, my heart rate took off at a galloping rate while I did my best to hold utterly still.

Mumbling incoherently again, he trailed his frisky hand down my stomach, making my skin break out in goosebumps. His pinky finger reached the band of my underwear first. Dipping underneath it, the rest of his fingers followed, sliding over my mound. My eyes nearly bugged out of their sockets.

I need to wake him.

That thought disappeared the moment his fingers grazed my clit. This time I couldn't contain my gasp. My eyes rolled into the back of my head as he began rubbing in small vigorous circles over my tiny bud of nerves. *If he keeps that up...oh my.* It was killing me not to move. His touch, even asleep, was determined and skilled. With the right amount of pressure and the right motion, my breathing increased. A sleeping man was about to get me off. *Fuck, am I taking advantage of him?*

With my one free hand, which had been fisted in the bed sheet, I grabbed his bicep, holding on for dear life as he pushed me toward the edge. "Jamie," I panted in a futile last second attempt to wake him. I got no response, and he kept working me.

Oh fuck. Oh fuck! "*Jaaamieeee!*" I cried out as my body exploded. His hand froze and his body tensed while my own shuddered from the euphoric waves of my orgasm.

He lifted his head from my shoulder, eyes meeting my hooded ones. I felt flushed, breaths labored. With his hand still touching my clit, it was obvious what just happened. A slow minute passed with us just staring at each other before his eyes widened. He lifted himself off of me, hand retreating from my underwear as he sat back. I sat up too, scooting myself back against the headboard. My cheeks scorched with shame.

"I...ah..." I stammered, not that he seemed to notice. He

appeared deep in thought as he stared down at his hand—the one that had just been in my underwear. My stomach twisted into a tight knot the longer the silence awkwardly stretched. "Please say something?"

His eyes lifted, traveling slowly up my legs, pausing at the apex of my thighs. He frowned with what seemed like disgust. "Did I...?"

"It's not a big deal." I instantly regretted my words.

"The fuck it isn't," he snapped harshly.

I winced, dropping my eyes. *You really fucked up this time, Maura.*

"I'm..." My throat felt like it was clogged. *What am I supposed to say? I'm sorry?* "I... I have to pee." Sliding off the bed, I bolted for the bathroom. I was running away like always. *Fucking coward.*

I hid, pacing the small room longer than I intended, which was just supposed to be until I got my bearings and conjured a genuine, heartfelt apology. My cowardice held me back. Jamie hadn't realized what he'd been doing. He had probably been having a hot dream about a past conquest or a future one. I'd been one hundred percent coherent while I'd just lain there letting him touch me, knowing it was wrong.

When I eventually returned to my bedroom, Jamie was gone. He probably had to get ready for the day; the sun was starting to rise. Or he was too disgusted with me to stick around. Either way, his absence left me feeling guilt-ridden.

I picked up my cell from the nightstand to look at the time. It was five in the morning and I was wide awake. I debated whether or not I should seek Jamie out. I decided not to. If he'd wanted to talk, he would have stuck around. *Right?* I'd wait until tonight to approach him after he got done doing mob stuff.

That reminded me that I still needed to speak with Stefan about yesterday's incident. I'd prefer to not go over it at the breakfast table. In fact, I planned on avoiding the dining room altogether. I wouldn't be able to mask my internal freak out with Jamie sitting across from me, which in turn would cue in Stefan that something had happened. I would rather swallow hot coals than tell my father I had taken advantage of Jamie. So that left me with no choice but to catch him before he went downstairs.

With a plan in mind, I threw on some yoga pants and made my way to the staircase that led up to Stefan's rooms, as in plural. His suite took up the entire third floor. It consisted of his gigantic bedroom that was double the size of mine, a walk-in closet that was the size of my room, his spa-like bathroom, and a private gym which had used to be my nursery when I'd been a baby.

Once I reached the top of the stairs, one of the solid oak double doors opened down the short hallway that led to Stefan's suite. At first, I expected it to be Stefan already heading down-stairs. To my jaw-dropping surprise, Brody stepped out with wet hair as if freshly showered and dressed in his usual suit. He didn't notice me at first as he quietly closed the door behind him. I took that as my opportunity to recover from my shock.

He took two steps in my direction before he finally saw me. His eyes widened, steps faltering. Brody had always been terrible at hiding what he felt, which was perfect for me, especially right now. All it took was the quick flash of panic in his eyes to confirm what I'd been suspecting for years. *Brody's doing the walk of shame.* Hmm, I didn't like that phrase. There was nothing shameful about two consenting adults bumping uglies. The only shame here was the reason for hiding it.

My lips curled into a *you-are-so-busted* smile.

He cleared his throat and straightened his shoulders. "Well?"

I had loads of questions. However, they were for Stefan, not his lover. When Stefan was ready to tell me himself about this, I'd ask everything I was dying to know. For now, I'd settle for just one question. "How long?"

He hesitated, contemplating how he should answer. "On and

off for twenty years." His honesty was as shocking as it was saddening. They'd been together for so long and I was just finding out about it now? I wouldn't have known at all if I hadn't caught Brody.

I had to be real with myself. Why would Stefan have told me? We weren't close. Nodding, I passed Brody as I continued to Stefan's room.

"You're not surprised?" he asked.

My hand hovered over the doorknob. I shook my head and glanced over my shoulder. "I always suspected he was into men. You, however, are a surprise. Looking back, though, I can't believe I didn't pick up on it. You've never dated, you agreed way too easily to no longer hiring hot maids, and you've devoted twenty plus years to taking care of a very difficult man." Stefan was very high maintenance. Brody's responsibilities went way beyond that of an estate manager. He literally worked twenty-four-seven attending to Stefan's every need. He made sure Stefan ate, bought his overpriced clothes, filled out his daily schedule, took care of me as a little girl, and tackled any other request Stefan threw at him while he also took care of this house and its employees. Just thinking about doing some of it exhausted me. Chuckling, I shook my head. "I used to think you needed to be sainted or you were a masochist. A lot of people would have quit a long time ago. Now, I see that you're his partner."

He smiled warmly, seeming happy I understood. Then his eyes drifted to my father's door behind me and his happiness dimmed. "If you're going to ask him about this—us—"

"Unlike Stefan, I want him to tell me something like this when he's ready."

Brody seemed relieved. He nodded his thanks and continued on downstairs.

I tapped lightly on the door before poking my head in. The

bed directly across the room was made, undoubtedly thanks to Brody, and the smell of a recent shower lingered in the air.

"Stefan," I called out, stepping into the room and walking toward the bed. His room was dim. The only light was coming from the open bathroom door and the muted news playing on the TV in the lounge area.

"Maura?" I turned, finding him standing in the doorway to his closet while buttoning a cufflink. He was wearing a light gray button-up shirt with black slacks. His satin tie hung loosely around his neck, waiting to be tied. "You okay?" he asked, clearly surprised to see me.

"I know you have questions about yesterday," I said and took a seat on the upholstered bench at the foot of his bed. I patted the empty space of bench, gesturing for him to sit down. With a small smile, he gracefully made his way across the room to sit next to me.

I didn't waste time and dove right into it. I recounted everything and I mean *everything* that happened yesterday. He asked why I hadn't been paying attention to where I'd been walking when I'd run into Greg and I answered honestly. I told him I'd kissed Jamie and had been confused. He looked a little surprised by that tidbit but made no comments about it. Then I explained why I'd freaked out, flashbacks, satisfaction, guilt, and all. I told him I felt like a monster.

"You're not a monster. You just take after me," he said and stunned the hell out of me by giving me a hug. He held me tightly, offering comfort. I didn't think I breathed the entire time. "Don't ever doubt yourself. You're strong and intelligent. Everyone in this family underestimates you. I'm guilty of it myself, sometimes. Trust your instincts and embrace what feels right and everything will work out. If not, I'll make sure it does."

Wow, who the hell is this guy and what did he do with Stefan? Did he really mean all that or was he playing the role of a caring father because of our deal? This would be the most fucked up thing he'd ever done to me if it was all an act.

I forced a smile as I pulled away. "By the way, I've decided to accept your offer."

Stefan held a fixed expression as he digested my words, then nodded. "I have a meeting with your uncles in my study at eight. That'll give you a few hours to get ready, unless you need a few days to recoup?" he asked as he brushed a finger over my bruised cheek.

"Nope, I'll be there. What's the meeting about?"

"Yesterday's incident," he answered. "News of what's happened has spread through the family and they want a clear understanding. Rumors have already twisted the story."

"I don't understand." I really didn't. Who was spreading rumors?

"I guess I should give you a quick rundown of how things work. Let's go down to the chamber. It'll be easier to understand if I can show you."

I followed him down to the first floor toward the center of the house. The chamber was windowless and had steel reinforced soundproof walls. When the house had first been built, the room had been a ballroom used for formal dances and lavish parties. Over time, as balls had become a thing of the past and our family's criminal empire had grown, the room had been converted to what it was today. Due to its length, there were heavy wooden doors on each end of the room leading out into the hallway. The east door was the one we used. He opened it, flipped on the lights, and gestured for me to go in.

Walking in, my eyes were immediately drawn to the massive espresso colored table in the center. The table looked like it had been cut from a giant tree, burned to give it its color, and varnished to give it a sleek feel. It had been in my family for generations. It amazed me that an old piece of furniture could hold such importance. Eight matching wooden chairs surrounded it, but the table was long enough to fit more. Three chairs sat on the right side of the table and three on the left, with one chair on each end.

The only lights in the room were hanging over the table. Stefan put his hands on the back of his chair at the head of the table before moving behind the chair to his right. He patted the top of the chair and said, "Samuel." Then moved to the next chair to the right. "Conor." He put his hand on the last chair on the right. "Your cousin Dylan." Stefan moved past the chair at the other head of the table and began touching the chairs on the left side, starting on the opposite end and working his way back to his chair. "Louie, Rourke, and Jameson." Jamie's chair sat to the left of his and directly across from Samuel's.

I walked over to the chair at the other end of the table, the other head, the one he'd skipped. "No one sits here?" I knew this chair. It was where my grandfather had sat before he'd passed away and it was where I'd sat when I'd told Stefan I'd been raped seven years ago—the only time I'd ever sat at his special table.

"That used to be my chair when I was your age."

"I thought this was Grandfather's chair?"

"After I took over, he sat there as an advisory role, but typically the *Prionsa* would sit there."

My brows shot up as I eyed the chair. *Prionsa* was Gaelic for prince.

"The *Ri* doesn't have an heir," I stated. *Ri* meant king.

Stefan nodded, nonchalant. He didn't seem bothered by the fact that he didn't have a son to follow in his footsteps. "Since I haven't picked a successor, whenever we have a guest attending the meeting, they sit there."

"Where do you expect me to be during these meetings? Do I stand behind you?"

"Where do you want to be?" The question was a loaded one. A

test maybe? Knowing that didn't immediately upset me because I couldn't see any risk in picking a chair.

I chewed on my lip. I knew where I wanted to sit, but I was worried I'd be overstepping, especially if I was just supposed to be shadowing him. Thinking back to what he'd said about who sat where, an idea formed in my head. "As of right now, you haven't decided what role I'll have in this family. Can I request that I temporarily take the title of *guest* until my role is decided?" I asked and pulled out the Prionsa's chair before sitting in it.

The corner of his mouth twitched. "Normally, our guests are someone of importance."

"I'm the Banphrionsa and the only child of Stefan Quinn, the boss of the New England Irish mob. Are you saying I'm not important?" I challenged with an arched brow.

He didn't argue. With a proud glint in his eye, he pulled out his chair and also took a seat. "The reason I brought you in here was to go over everyone's role at this table and why it's imperative they are always informed when something goes down." He pointed to Samuel's chair. "Samuel oversees drugs. Be it obtaining them, making them, or distributing them. Dylan works directly under Samuel. His main focus is getting the product out there and making sure it's being sold. They have men that help them man that pillar of the empire."

I quietly listened, digesting the information he was giving me. It was one thing to know your family was a bunch of criminals, but hearing it explained straight from the horse's mouth, as it were, was still a little eye opening. It hadn't felt real until now.

"It's sort of set up the same way with your Uncle Conor and Rourke, except they deal in guns. Conor works with our contacts in Ireland to get the guns. Rourke makes us a lot of money by selling them to other crime families and gangs across the States. They also have men who work under them who help move their product and man their pillar. Louie is our top enforcer. He helps

Jamie with a lot of tasks, but he's in charge of all our security. He oversees recruitment, placement, and passing along orders."

"What about Jamie?"

"Jameson is *my* enforcer. He's also my second pair of eyes and hands. He makes sure everything runs smoothly and if it doesn't, he fixes it. If we have a rat, he finds them and brings them to me. If I need information, he gets it. When I'm needed in more than one place, he steps in and we divide and conquer."

"How does the chain of command work?"

He seemed pleased by my question. "If I'm ever indisposed or otherwise occupied, Jameson runs things. If I die, Samuel."

"Samuel?!" I was going to be sick. No way could that man be in charge.

Stefan nodded. "Don't worry. I have a failsafe in place for you in case anything happens to me."

"What do you mean?"

"All I'll say is you'll be taken care of and out of Samuel's reach. He may be my brother, but I'd never trust him with you."

"Why haven't you named Jamie as your successor? You raised him."

Stefan sighed. The topic seemed to frustrate him. "He doesn't want it."

There was no way Samuel could be in charge. He'd undoubtedly destroy this family by ruling it like a tyrant. Not to mention, he'd either marry me off or beat me until I learned to be as submissive as he expected a woman to be, which would still probably end with me being married off.

"Back to the point of all this," Stefan said, pulling my attention back to him. "The reason your uncles need to be in the know is because the men who work under them have heard what's happened or what they think has happened. Regardless, all they know is one of our own is dead and that you killed him. I need to go over what happened with Samuel and Conor so they have the information they need to keep morale up among the men."

I supposed that made sense. Getting up from my temporary chair, I started for the door. "I'll see you at eight," I said before I left.

CHAPTER SEVENTEEN

L ike Stefan had said, my family underestimated me. I wanted to keep it that way until I had a better understanding of how things worked and how everyone interacted with each other on the business side. So instead of one of the suits Stefan had bought me, I chose an old white sundress I found in my closet. It was short sleeved and went to my knees. I didn't put on any makeup and made sure to pull my hair back into a tight bun. The white color washed me out, making my skin look paler than it actually was, which in turn made the bruises on my face and arm stick out. The look I was going for was battered and innocent.

Let the games begin.

I arrived outside Stefan's study at the same time as my Uncle Conor. He noticed my face and immediately hugged me.

"Are you alright, darling?" he asked, his accent coming out thick, especially the word *darling*. There was real concern in his voice, which warmed my heart. He was a good man—or rather, good to his family. He did smuggle guns in from Ireland and sold them to other criminals across the country. No judgment though.

I was distracted from answering when his eyes traveled

behind me, just before someone stepped into my peripheral. Every nerve in my body screamed it was Jamie. I glanced to my left to confirm it was indeed him and caught him staring down at me. My heartbeat accelerated.

"We need to talk," he said, voice like stone. It gave away nothing as to what he was feeling, yet still ravaged me with anxiety. We did need to talk, and I was compelled to beg for his forgiveness, but I'd fallen into a false sense of security where I'd thought I had more time before I had to face him again. I should've known he'd be present at this meeting.

Looking away, I nodded curtly. Glancing between us, Conor must have read our need for privacy because he excused himself and entered Stefan's study.

Jamie stepped in front of me and I found it extremely difficult to meet his eyes. My neck and cheeks flushed, betraying my overwhelming shame. "I'm so sorry. I don't... I should have woken you. I'll understand—"

"Why are you apologizing?" he interrupted.

My eyes shot up to his. They were darkened with a mixture of anger and confusion.

"Because I took advantage. You were asleep. I should have stop—"

He interrupted again by snorting with a rueful smile. It was my turn to be angry and confused. *Is he laughing at me?*

"I had you pinned underneath me. I woke up to you screaming and my hand..." He sighed. "I thought I hurt you—that I forced myself on you."

I shook my head quickly. "No. We could have avoided this whole mess if I'd woken you."

His eyes narrowed. "Why didn't you?"

My cheeks went from pink to crimson. "I...uh." I wasn't ready to answer that question with honesty. "I don't know." *Pathetic. What am I, a child?*

He stared at me intently, eyes searching mine. "You didn't make me touch you, Maura. You can't take all the blame."

"If that's how you feel, can we forgive each other and move on?" My voice bordered on pleading.

His expression softened before he cupped the back of my neck, pulling me closer and enclosing me in his arms. I buried my nose in his chest, relieved to be there and that we were okay.

Walking into the meeting together, I caught Stefan watching us, his expression blank. Conor was already seated in one of the chairs in front of Stefan's desk. Jamie and I each took one end of the couch. We were all waiting for Samuel to show up.

"Are you joining the meeting, Maura?" Conor asked, turning around in his chair. His seat was closest to the couch.

I just smiled. Conor looked to Stefan for confirmation. He nodded and Conor scratched the back of his head with a tight smile.

"This should be interesting," he mumbled before standing up and moving to sit in the other chair, furthest from the couch. It was obvious why he'd done it, and I couldn't blame him. He didn't want to be caught in the middle of the shit storm Samuel was going to cause.

"Pussy," Stefan teased. Everyone in the room chuckled and Samuel chose that moment to show up.

"Sorry for running late," he said, shutting the door behind him. He made his way to the empty chair in front of Stefan's desk. His gaze passed over me quickly as he glanced around the room. A second passed before he did a double take. "Maura, I didn't see you there." His eyes lingered on my face as he wrinkled his nose, then turned to Stefan. "She should be resting in her room. The poor thing has been through an ordeal and looks terrible."

"You should see the other guy," I grumbled.

Jamie rubbed above his nose with his fingers to hide his smile.

Conor did nothing to hide his and Stefan looked like he was fighting a losing battle as the corner of his mouth twitched.

"Maura's an adult. I'm sure if she wasn't up to being here, she wouldn't be," Stefan told him.

"And what is she doing here? I thought we were having a meeting." The man was completely dense.

"The meeting is about me. Why wouldn't I be present?" I fixed my tone with naive curiosity as if I truly didn't understand why I couldn't be here.

Samuel glanced at Stefan. "She shouldn't be—"

"*Stefan* asked me to be here in case you had any questions, but maybe he should have cleared it with you first. Shall I wait outside while the head of the family asks your permission?" Again, my voice was innocent, but my words held meaning. I was putting both him and Stefan on the spot. Stupid move on my part, and I was most likely going to catch hell for it later. I shouldn't have dragged Stefan into my fight, but I was over Samuel's small-minded, superior bullshit. For too long he'd overstepped his position and for too long Stefan had allowed him to do it.

The room filled with tension. Jamie and Conor seemed like they'd prefer to be anywhere else. Stefan's eyes kept traveling between Samuel and I with a blank expression.

At first, Samuel looked befuddled, mouth slightly ajar. He recovered quickly. His lips pursed and anger creased around his eyes. Within just a few days I was in another stare off with my uncle. It was a battle of wills I was clearly winning because the more carefree I looked, the more pissed off he got.

"Can we please get to the point of why we're all here?" Conor asked, sounding exasperated.

I cocked an eyebrow at Samuel, leaving the decision up to him. Samuel blinked before turning to Stefan. They stared at each other for a moment. I couldn't see Samuel's face, but Stefan's eyes shifted. The change was slight, barely noticeable, but it was enough to show his displeasure. The tension got even heavier, urging me to fidget at the awkwardness, but I held myself still.

"Shall we begin?" Stefan asked Samuel, but he wasn't seeking his permission. The question was laced with bait. Which way would Samuel go? Would his pride overshadow the good sense to stand down?

Samuel stayed quiet and that seemed to satisfy Stefan. Stefan's attention moved to me and the fierceness etching his face dulled. "Maura?"

Squaring my shoulders, I began going over yesterday's incident.

By Conor's annoyed sigh, I could tell the meeting was dragging on longer than it should have. Samuel, of course, was the one holding everyone up. After I'd gone into great detail and he'd watched the surveillance footage, he still had questions. We all knew what he was aiming to do, no matter how many times he reworded the same question. He wanted me to admit I was at fault.

"You should have apologized," Samuel huffed.

I ignored him because I was done defending myself to him. This wasn't a trial. I'd said my piece. He could do with it what he wanted.

"Are you saying you would have apologized?" Jamie, who'd been quiet the entire meeting, decided to chime in.

We all gaped at him. His focus was solely on Samuel as he held a challenging glare. Everyone glanced back to Samuel, waiting for him to answer.

"No, but—"

"Exactly," Jamie interrupted and dismissed Samuel by looking to Stefan. "Are we done here?"

I thought if my father's eyebrows could have reached his hairline, they would have. Even I was unable to hide my shock.

Stefan nodded.

Giving up, Samuel didn't argue, and everyone got to their feet to leave. Before I could take a step toward the door, Stefan stopped me. "Maura, a word."

I watched everyone else leave, then turned to face him with my head held high. I knew I was in trouble. There wasn't a doubtful bone in my body. I had put Samuel in his place, but in doing so, I'd forced Stefan's hand.

My father was unmoving as he stood behind his desk.

"I'm not going to apologize." Was I being stubborn? Yes, but I refused to feel guilty for something that had needed to be done.

"Then you're no different than your uncle." He didn't mean that, at least I hoped he didn't. Either way, my pride took a knife to the gut.

"There's a difference between undermining you and defending you," I argued.

"Which you managed to do at the same time," he snapped. His words were like a hammer, nailing his point before me, leaving little room to argue. "You can't do that."

"Yes, I did," I admitted with bitter tasting words. "But it was still different."

"How so?"

Did I really have to spell it out for him? What I'd done had been *for* him. Samuel, though, was a fucking snake waiting for the right moment to strike. I didn't trust him.

Stefan shook his head, clearly displeased. "You can't have it both ways. You can't demand the same respect as everyone else and expect to be treated special." He was right, but I didn't want to admit it. At the same time, I didn't think I could ever not defend him. Moving forward, I'd just have to go about it in a different way.

"Yes, I can. I'm a woman. I was born to be confusing to men. Learn to adapt." I gave him a little smile, showing him I was only joking. *Kind of.*

He let out a breath as he rubbed the side of his face. The tension in his body seemed to fade. "As punishment, you won't be attending tomorrow's family meeting."

I opened my mouth to argue, but Stefan arched a challenging brow—a trait I'd clearly inherited. Snapping my mouth closed, I pursed my lips. There was no point in fighting it. "Fine."

Seeming pleased that I'd relented, he stuffed his hands into his pockets, trying to appear relaxed. "I'm going to be out of the house for the rest of the day," he announced. "What do you have planned?"

I wanted to laugh at how quickly he'd switched from mob boss to father. "I was thinking about going out. There's still a few things I need."

Looking intrigued, he asked, "Like what?"

I shrugged. "Girl stuff."

"Girl stuff?" Tilting his head to the side, he eyed me with a curious expression.

For fuck's sake, did he think that's code for something diabolical?

We avoided talking about tampons and periods like it was taboo. As a teenager, I'd been embarrassed of my period, especially because I'd grown up surrounded by men. On the flip side, I could only imagine how awkward it would feel for a single father to talk about periods with his little girl. Thankfully, we'd had Brody to help us through those situations.

Right now, however, I was feeling a little spiteful. "Yes, girl stuff. Tampons, pads, panty liners. I'm going to start my period soon and the first day or two is always really heavy. Maybe that's why my periods only last four days? I hemorrhage everything in my uterus those first couple of days. Hmm, it's a good theory. Anyway, I'd hate to start and not have anything. It's a messy business being a woman." I smothered a smile as I held a stoic mask.

He tried his best to appear unfazed. With the clearing of his throat, I knew he was a little at a loss with what to say or do. His life was surrounded by death, drugs, and guns and the mention of tampons unsettled him? I coughed in order to hold back my laughter and took pity on him. "I was thinking about picking up some cute PJs and some athletic wear, as well. I need to exercise, or my hips will be the first to blow up from Jenna's cooking."

"Why don't you tell Angela and she can make sure you get everything you need?" he suggested.

"I've grown independent. I like doing things for myself. Plus, I need to get out of the house. I'll go stir crazy if I don't."

"You need to take someone with you."

I bristled. *Here we go with this shit again.* "I've been on my own for six years without your goon—uh, security following me around." Stefan didn't like me calling his men goons, but old habits and all.

He turned distant. The quick change in him caused unease to bubble in the pit of my stomach. Was there a threat to the family? Were we at war again? "What?"

He didn't answer. Instead, he looked down.

"Stefan?"

"You weren't entirely alone in Hartford."

My back straightened, preparing myself. I had a feeling I wasn't going to like what was coming. "What do you mean?"

He steeled himself, eyes determined when they met mine. "I hired a security team outside the family. Over the past six years, eight men were rotated in and out. Each stayed for a year or two at a time. All blended in as fellow students or neighbors to watch over you."

...What?!

Gritting my teeth, I bit out, "You mean they spied on me?"

"No. Watched over you. I couldn't risk someone going after you to get to me. Especially in the beginning, when things were still tense between us and the De Lucas."

This was a new low.

"You said I was out!" My outburst startled us both.

His shoulders squared and his expression hardened. "You're a Quinn and my daughter. You can never be out."

"So you lied to me?" I scoffed. "I don't know why I'm fucking surprised. It's what you do. It's what you always do."

"I was losing you!" he roared.

I reeled back, but still kept my feet cemented to the ground. He thought he could put this all on me?

"Yes, you were," I seethed honestly. "I couldn't trust *you* to let me fall apart—to feel the pain of what those assholes did to me in order to heal. I was worried you'd shame me for my weakness. So I held it all in. I stayed strong to make *you* proud. With each passing day, the burden of having to hold it all in became harder and harder until it was too much and I didn't see the point of living anymore."

His shoulders sagged slightly and the muscle in his jaw ticked. "I know," he said in a low defeated voice.

"You knew?" I repeated in disbelief. "And what, you just didn't care?"

"We both know that's not true. You may like to paint me as the villain, but at the end of the day I am still your father."

"Then why didn't you talk to me? I needed you, yet you kept your distance."

"Would you have believed my intentions were pure if I had?" he asked, eyes leveled with mine, waiting to read my reaction because we both knew I wouldn't answer. What would be the point? He knew I would have assumed the worst.

I folded my arms across my chest. It was a defensive gesture. I knew it and Stefan knew it, but in that moment I didn't care. I just needed something between us. "I'm assuming your spies reported everything they saw?" I asked, deflecting.

He hesitated before replying, "They gave me weekly reports on your activity."

I was starting to feel overwhelmingly exposed. *Wait...* If they'd been watching me, did that mean they'd seen what Tom had been doing? Had my sad excuse of a relationship been broadcasted like a fucking soap opera?

"Did you know Tom was cheating on me the entire time?"

I got my answer when he didn't respond. I stormed out of the room before I said something I'd regret later.

CHAPTER EIGHTEEN

I went to Jamie's room instead of mine. Stefan would undoubtedly come looking for me later and the last thing I wanted to do was make things easy for him. Jamie's room was in the west wing, the opposite side of the house from mine, on the second floor. I walked in without knocking. I had a feeling he wasn't there and the silence confirmed I was right. Right away, I was greeted with his masculine scent that was addictively fresh and woodsy. His furniture was set up with his bed up against one wall and with a dresser and large flat screen TV mounted on the opposite wall. The door leading into his private bathroom was in the far left corner and the door leading to his walk-in closet was on the far right. There were two cushioned window seats under large transom windows that overlooked the pool and property. His bedding was dark blue with white cloud-looking pillows. The room didn't have many personal items out in view except for two framed pictures on one of his nightstands.

Sitting on the edge of his bed, I looked over both pictures. One was of Jamie, Louie, and me at their high school graduation. The three of us were standing next to each other with me in the middle and them flanking me in their caps and gowns. We looked happy with genuine smiles adorning our faces.

The other picture was of his parents holding him as a baby. His father had been killed when Jamie had been a toddler. I didn't know what gang or crime family had been responsible. It didn't feel right to ask, but I did know it had been during a turf war. Right before Jamie had turned twelve, his mother had been diagnosed with cancer and Stefan had moved them both in with us. He'd gotten her the best medical care money could buy until she'd passed away, just after Jamie had turned thirteen. She had been a very kind woman and Jamie had been the center of her world.

I scooted toward the center of the bed. Lying flat on my back, I stared at the spots of sunlight shining on the ceiling. My vision drifted into a glossy daydream while my mind raked over the last six years. I tried to remember anyone who had stood out or seemed weird, but nothing came to mind. I thought back to the time Tom and I'd had sex in his car, then the time Tina and I had gotten drunk and she'd bet I wouldn't run down the hall of our coed dorm naked. Quite a few people had seen my naked ass that night. Both of those embarrassing moments were only a few that came to mind that were *public*. I was sure there were more. Had my every move or experience been spied on, written down in a report, and shared with Stefan?

What was the point of leaving at all?

To heal.

If I hadn't left, I would've killed myself. It was the sad truth.

There's zero room for weakness in this family. Having that ingrained in my brain had made me blame Stefan for the pain I couldn't make go away and it was what had laid the foundation for the past six years of my life.

Was my father really the crafty and insightful bastard he claimed to be? Had he really known I couldn't trust him, and thus formed a plan to give me an escape to have the freedom to accept what had happened, to feel it without fear of repercussions? Had I known I hadn't really been out, I wondered if I would have been as broken as the day I'd left. I probably wouldn't have been so determined not to come back, thinking a normal life was what I'd wanted or needed. Or maybe living a normal life was what I'd needed to show me this was where I truly belonged. Had that been part of Stefan's grand plan as well?

I didn't know how long I lay there as I watched the light from the sun move across the ceiling. It wasn't until I felt the bed dip and a feather-like touch across my cheek that I realized I'd fallen asleep. Opening my eyes, I found Jamie lying next to me with his head propped up on his hand.

"I'm mad at Stefan," I said, rolling on my side to face him.

He brushed a stray hair away from my face.

"Did you know?" I asked, already knowing the answer. There was no way he hadn't known Stefan had hired a private security team to watch me.

"I hired them."

Of course he did. I let out a frustrated sigh. "Do they still work for us?"

"Their contract ended when you came home."

"Can we get them back? If Stefan is going to insist I have a ball and chain, I'd prefer it wasn't someone already part of his goon squad. I want someone outside the family."

"Why?" he asked.

"They've already seen me at my worst, and they have zero to gain by using my vulnerabilities against me."

He frowned. "We train our men to be discreet and if anyone tried to hurt you—"

"I'm a woman." I gave him a tight smile. "Ninety percent of the men in this family see me as a bed warmer." Jamie opened his mouth to argue, but I continued on. "Yes, I'm the Banphrionsa and yet that title means shit if another leader—a male leader of this family—gives an order to contradict mine. I don't want someone whose loyalties will be torn. I'm not saying Stefan would order his men to hurt me, even though it was his goons who helped him *educate* me growing up, but I trust Samuel as far as I can throw him. If I want to survive in this family, I have to stay one step ahead of everyone else, imagine multiple outcomes. Did Stefan not drill that into you growing up or was that just me?"

"From the sound of it, not to the same extent," he muttered.

I wasn't going to explain the differences of being a female versus a male to him. Stefan had understood the hardships I'd face. *Fucking hell...* I was starting to understand why my father had been a complete and utter dick growing up. "Can you do this for me?"

"I'll need to talk to Stefan."

"He'll agree to it." I'd hire them myself if he didn't. Actually, that wasn't a bad idea.

"Okay," he said, sighing.

Wanting to ease the tension around his eyes, I brushed my fingers along the side of his face. His hand caught mine, holding it against his warm cheek as his eyes held mine. The intensity of his stare was becoming too much. It made me feel too much. It stirred feelings inside me that weren't reciprocated, which in turn added fuel to my anger. I didn't want to be angry at Jamie. Nor did I want to take my frustrations out on him.

To seek comfort, I scooted myself closer, burrowing my head under his chin. He let go of my hand to coil his arm around my back. The feel of his warmth and the strength beneath the hard planes of his body made my heart gallop. Memories from this morning flooded my mind, his fingers trailing over my skin, the way they'd worked me into a frenzy until I'd shattered.

I knew I was in trouble when the line between rational thought and the ache tingling within me blurred. Up this close, he was intoxicating. As if my body had a mind of its own, I arched, pressing more of myself against him. My nose rubbed along his neck and my hands fisted the front of his shirt, afraid he'd pull away.

His arm around me tightened. I couldn't tell if he was trying to hold me still or pull me closer. I tested the waters by pressing my lips to his neck. He let out a shaky breath. Removing his arm from my back, his hand cupped the back of my bare thigh before he hiked my leg over his hip. He leaned into me, pushing his leg between mine, thigh meeting my core. I shivered as his fingers glided up under the skirt of my dress. His touch was slow and tortuous. My body buzzing with need, I rocked myself against his muscular thigh. His hand jumped to the back of my neck, urging me to look at him.

Apprehensive, my gaze ascended slowly. When I finally met his gorgeous hazel eyes, I gasped. They were darkened and hooded with lust. He inched his face closer to mine until our noses brushed. I was dying to close the distance, but I still wasn't completely convinced he wanted this, wanted me.

His restraint seemed to break, and his lips slammed over mine. The kiss was bruising yet passionate, like he couldn't get enough. His tongue demanded entry by licking at the seam of my lips. I eagerly opened for him. His delicious tongue plunged and stroked along mine. The more our kiss deepened, the needier I felt. My core pulsated. It was consuming and I did nothing to fight it. I wanted to give in to this, to him.

My leg tightened around his hip, pulling him even closer until my pelvis kissed his growing desire. I was gifted a throaty groan. The sound was gruff, addictive, and urged me on. I snaked my fingers into his hair and tugged gently.

With little effort, he rolled me onto my back. He yanked my hand from his hair and pinned it to the bed. A muffled groan escaped him again as his lips traveled down my jaw, along my neck, nipping as he went. A full body shiver rippled through me as he reached that delicate spot below my ear. I moaned as his teeth grazed it.

He stilled, body going completely rigid above me. Then he ripped himself away, climbing off the bed so quick, the heat from his body still lingered on mine. I sat up slowly, slightly dizzy and also a little nervous. He stood a few feet away from the bed, head downcast.

Our labored breaths filled the silent bedroom. My lips felt swollen. I didn't dare touch them. My instincts were telling me not to make any sudden movements.

"Jamie?" I whispered, trying my best not to startle him. I slid to the edge of the bed. The slow movement drew his attention. His gaze lifted from the floor until it reached me. Tentatively, I reached out. He recoiled by stepping out of my reach.

"Don't touch me." His voice was harsh, and the words stung.

Refusing to let my hurt show, I masked my face and dropped my hand in my lap. *Why did I do this to myself again?* Yes, I'd practically thrown myself at him, but he'd kissed me! Was I delusional to think he wanted this as much as I did?

The sting of his rejection seeded deep before it sprouted a life of its own. Its roots and vines ripped their way through me before tearing me apart from the inside out. It was painful and suffocating and I couldn't stand to be in his presence any longer. I got to my feet and stiffly walked around him toward the door. He didn't try to stop me.

By the time I made it to my bedroom, I was feeling claustrophobic in this big house. I wanted to run away. I'd proven to be good at it, but I knew it wouldn't solve any of my problems. I needed to find a different way to deal.

Scooping up my cell from my nightstand, I hit the home button. The screen lit up, showing me that it was just after six on a Friday night. I was going out.

CHAPTER NINETEEN

It wasn't until I was out of the shower that I noticed the new cluster of bags sitting on my couch. I peeked in one and found an abundant number of tampons, pads, and panty liners. In the other bags, I found silky pajama sets, athletic wear, and everything a girl would need in her bathroom from makeup to hair accessories to irons.

Stefan had made sure I had everything I'd said I needed and then some. Was this his way of apologizing?

I grabbed some of the makeup and the iron before returning to the bathroom. Smearing on enough concealer to hide the bruises on my face, I went with dark colors around my green eyes, making them pop. I put wavy curls in my blood-red hair and pinned it all to one side.

The dress I chose to wear was burgundy and skin tight with long sleeves and cut off at mid-thigh. The back was jaw dropping. It was backless, exposing my entire spine and shamrock tattoo. The dress was sexy as hell. However, it had a flaw. I couldn't wear any underwear. Panty lines ruined the allure.

I put on a new pair of Louboutin black lace peep-toe pumps and stuffed my phone, ID, and credit cards into a wristlet. With car keys in hand, I made my way downstairs to the control room where I knew at least one goon would be stationed. Stefan's rule was I couldn't go anywhere without security. Fine. I was going to do exactly that.

The control room was near the garage. The door was slightly ajar and I could hear voices inside as I approached. Pushing the door open, I stepped into the small room. Josh was sitting in a swivel desk chair with his back to a wall of monitors surveilling different areas of the house and property. On the opposite side of the room was a huge gun cage. Leaning against it was the grumpy Dean. They both stopped talking when they noticed me.

Glancing from one to the other, I wondered, *Which one will be the most entertaining?* My gaze landed on Dean. "Come on, Grumpy. You're coming with me. Stefan's orders."

They exchanged a look with each other before Dean pushed off the wall and followed me out. Obediently, he walked behind me through the rest of the house to the garage. Passing the many sleek and expensive cars, I hit the unlock button on my key fob as we came upon my little Audi. I tilted my head toward the passenger side. "Get in."

Planting his feet on the ground, he eyed me with suspicion. "Where are we going?"

"I'm not allowed to leave the house without security and I'm craving gummy worms," I lied, opening my car door to get in.

He stayed rooted in place, clearly having an internal debate under his pissed off exterior.

Losing my patience, I poked my head out of the car and snapped, "We'll be right back. Just get in the car."

He released a heavy sigh, walked to the passenger side and got in. I backed out of the garage and we made our way down the driveway.

"You're a little dressed up to get candy," he stated as his eyes roamed over my dress. He was really good looking, despite his resting bitch face, with buzzed sandy colored hair and a good amount of scruff on his face. He looked like he was growing out his facial hair along his jaw, chin, and around his lips.

I smiled coyly. "Am I? I didn't know there was a dress code to get gummy worms." Approaching the gate, I hit the brakes, jolting us in the car. "Oh crap!" I gasped. "I left my phone in my room. Can I borrow yours? I want to see if Stefan wants anything."

His eyes never wavered from their narrowed state as he reached into his pocket and retrieved his phone. He handed it over. Rolling down my window, I tossed his phone and hit the gas.

"What the fuck?!" he yelled, turning in his seat to look out the rear window.

"Chill, it landed in the bushes. I'm sure it's fine."

"That's not the point. Where the hell are you taking me and don't tell me it's for damned gummy bears!"

"I said worms. Gummy worms," I corrected, pissing him off more. "I needed to get out of the house. You already know I'm not allowed to go anywhere alone. No one said I had to tell them where I'm going or who I had to take with me," I said in a sing song voice, a little too happily. I was following the rules while sticking it to the man at the same time. Was it going to piss some people off? Namely Stefan and Jamie? *I sure hope so.*

"Why did you have to toss my phone?"

"We both know you would have called Louie the first chance you got when you realized this wasn't a trip to the corner store. I need a break. If you can't be understanding of that, I will leave you in the middle of nowhere and you can explain to Stefan why you let his daughter run off on her own or worse, why her body was found in a ditch somewhere."

"I'm going to catch shit no matter what if I don't report in. I'm just grounds security," he argued.

"If you watch my back tonight while I blow off a little steam and get me home safely, you won't get more than a slap on the wrist."

"I could make you take us back."

I felt rather than saw his body go very still. By how deep his voice got, I knew he was really considering it.

I laughed, breaking the seriousness of the moment. "You could try. Let's play that scenario out, shall we? I won't go back willingly. You'll need to put hands on me. Remember *that*." I paused for a moment to let that sink in. "Something you should know about me is that I've been learning how to defend myself since I was a little girl. I won't fight fair and I'll do whatever it takes to win. If you try to take me back, two things could happen. One, I will kill you. Don't doubt that I can't. Look how well your colleague Greg turned out. Or two, you could try to subdue me, but it won't be easy. You'll have to hurt me, and how will Stefan feel about that? You will die either way."

He deflated, body relaxing into the seat. "Where are we going?"

I smiled triumphantly. "A club downtown."

He sighed. "Fucking fantastic."

Located in a renovated warehouse downtown, Anarchy was a popular club that had an industrial underground feel and played live music. Tonight's genre was rock.

We snaked our way through the dim crowded club toward the bar while loud music boomed around us. I perched on a vacant stool and patted the one next to me, gesturing for Dean to take a seat. He pulled out the tall chair but swiveled it around to face the rest of the room before sitting down. I waved a hand in the air to get the attention of one of the bartenders. One of them gave me a nod, signaling he'd be right with me.

Once he finished up making his current drink, he made his way over.

"What can I get for you?" he shouted over the music.

I ordered whiskey before handing over my credit card. The bartender and I both looked to Dean. "You want anything?" I asked him. He shook his head, never removing his eyes from the crowd. The bartender nodded, taking my card and quickly returned with my drink. I sipped from the glass, relishing the burn alcohol always brought. Instantly feeling warm, I remembered I hadn't eaten today. *I might regret this later. Oh well.*

"Why so glum all the time, Grumpy?" I asked, leaning closer to Dean. By the death glare he was giving me, I knew I wasn't going to get an answer. I smirked. I'd break through his surly exterior eventually. I was patient. Crossing my legs, I turned my stool to watch the crowd with him.

Three refills later, I was sporting a good buzz. A couple of cute guys tried to approach me, but with one mean look from Dean, they spun on their heels and moved on. My head fell back laughing the second time it happened.

"You are the definition of a cock block," I said, wiping a tear from my eye.

Dean eyed me soberly.

I shrugged. "Works for me. The last thing I want is to be bothered by men. Especially since the ones already in my life like to hurt me." I winced, realizing everything I'd just spewed. Thankfully, he made no comment.

The music was amazing. Dean refused to dance with me. He also refused to let me go out onto the dance floor. *Too many risks.* His words, not mine. Therefore, I decided to go easy on him and dance in front of him by the railing that protected people from falling onto the dance floor a few steps down from the bar. I had a great view of the stage and the band, who performed a mixture of covers and a few originals. The crowd ate it up by singing along and dancing to the beat. I closed my eyes, letting my body move to the music. All the tension from today seemed to fall away with each sway of my hips. I danced until the current band ended their performance and they began to set up for the next group.

"They were great, weren't they?" a man standing next to me asked.

Feeling like the question was directed to me, I glanced to my right and found a gorgeous man staring down at me. He towered over me by a foot or maybe even a foot and a half. I wasn't short either at five feet six inches. He had the most striking bluish-gray eyes I'd ever seen and dark brown hair that made them pop.

Even in my buzzed haze, I took in everything about him from what he was wearing to any possible branding. I'd been raised to be cautious after all. He was wearing a skintight black V-neck tee tucked into black slacks and dress shoes. I could tell right away his shoes were designer and with the expensive watch on his left wrist, I became suspicious. I caught what looked like an eight-pointed star peeking out from under his shirt collar. Last time I checked, Stefan had an alliance with the Russian mafia.

"Yes, they were amazing." Then I switched from speaking in English to Russian. "But that's not what you really wanted to ask me, is it?"

His eyes widened for only a second before he quickly hid his surprise.

Along with guns and self-defense, I had also been tutored in French, Italian, Spanish, and Russian. I switched back to English and sighed, "Listen, I've had a shit day and all I want to do is have a good time tonight and forget about my shit day. So if you're here to bring me more shit, then I'm going to tell you to eat shit. Also, I'm too buzzed to have any serious conversations at the moment. Tonight, I'm just Maura. I'm checked out."

My rambling made his eyebrows rise before a slow smile pulled at his lips. "Why was your day shit?" he asked.

I wagged my finger at him. "I'm here to forget, remember? Ask me something better. Like what my favorite color is."

His smile grew. "What's your favorite color?"

I smiled. "I don't know. You weren't really supposed to ask me that. You're terrible at this," I teased.

Amused, he chuckled.

"Do you know if the next band is any good?" I asked, taking charge of the conversation.

"I only book good bands," he stated with a cocky glint in his eye.

"Smooth. Owner or manager?"

"Owner," he said proudly.

"So tell me, Mr. Owner, how'd you know who I am?"

He leaned closer and whispered in my ear, "I didn't. I thought Stefan was here, but when I noticed they were all watching over you, I became curious."

It took a moment for the information to compute in my whiskey-soaked brain. "They?" I tilted my head, confused before the rest of what he said caught up. I spun around, looking back at the bar, finding not only Dean, but Jamie and Louie as well.

I let out a frustrated sigh and turned back to the owner. "Did I piss in someone's Cheerios by coming here?"

He stared down at me for a moment and then one side of his mouth lifted up in a smirk. "No," he finally replied. Then his eyes looked past me before a hand came down on my shoulder.

"Sasha," Jamie said from behind me.

"Jameson." The owner, who I guessed was named Sasha, greeted. "Tell Stefan his daughter is always welcome here." Then he looked back to me. "It was nice to meet you, Maura." He gave me a tight smile before walking away.

I shoved Jamie's hand off my shoulder and walked back to the bar. I wasn't ready to deal with him. I caught Louie glancing between us, reading our interaction with questioning eyes.

"How'd you find me?" I asked him as I climbed onto the stool next to him. I shot a glare at Dean over his head. *Did he call them?*

"We tracked your phone," Louie answered honestly.

Of course they did. I waved a finger at the bartender, telling him I was ready for another. In the back of my mind, I knew I shouldn't drink anymore. Having Jamie so close made me not care.

The bartender dropped my drink down in front of me and I tasted nothing as I swallowed half of the amber liquid in the glass.

"How much have you had to drink?" Jamie asked from behind me. I hated how my body reacted to the sound of his voice. We'd kissed, like, twice! Okay, maybe a little more than twice and there had been this morning. That wasn't really the point. *Why does he have this effect on me? I never reacted like this with Tom.*

"Not enough," I snapped loud and clear.

It went strangely quiet behind me. Peeking over my shoulder, I found both Louie and Jamie staring at Dean expectantly. The assholes were trying to get an answer from him. He genuinely surprised me by just standing there with a blank face and his arms folded over his chest.

"How much has she had to drink?" Jamie questioned Dean. Despite his calm tone, I could tell he was pissed he even had to ask. Other goons would have thrown me under the bus by now.

Dean shrugged. "I didn't know I was supposed to keep track."

Louie's brows shot up and he smirked a little. I couldn't tell if he was proud or impressed, both of which I'd never expected. I think my jaw would have dropped to the floor if I hadn't recovered as quickly as I did. *Isn't he Dean's boss?* Jamie, on the other hand, glared at him. If Dean was intimidated, he didn't let it show. Now I was impressed.

"Leave him alone," I ordered. The steel and authority behind my words could rival Stefan and seemed to surprise the men around me. Jamie's anger traveled to me. "He did his job by keeping me safe. If you punish him, you'll not only lose his respect but mine, as well."

Done saying my piece, I turned back toward the bar and waved at the bartender again for one more before I threw the rest of my current drink back. When he placed another glass in front of me, I asked to close my tab. Ignoring everyone, I threw back my last drink, then slammed the glass down on the bar. Louie swiveled around and bumped his shoulder playfully into mine.

"Why are you here?" I grumbled after the bartender handed me my bill.

"Why do you think I'm here?" he asked, sarcastically.

"Stefan send you?"

He shook his head. "I don't think Jameson's told him yet." That surprised me. "If you wanted to go out, babe, all you had to do was ask. You didn't have to kidnap one of my guys."

I laughed at how infuriating that was. Why the hell should I have to ask? I was a grown-ass woman. "I was in the mood to piss some people off."

"I think you succeeded," he said, tilting his head toward Jamie. *Good.*

Louie whistled and I realized I'd said that out loud. "I don't know what happened between you two, but you guys need to fix it because you're both shitty company tonight," he said in a low voice only I could hear, then held his hand out with his palm up. "Give me your keys. I'll drive you home." I fished them out of my wristlet and dropped them into his hand. He smirked mischievously and I immediately realized my mistake. He turned to Dean and I heard him say, "I'll drive you back to the house." Dean nodded and they both walked away, leaving me alone with Jamie.

CHAPTER TWENTY

Jamie sat on the stool Louie had vacated and rested his arms on the edge of the bar. An awkward uncertainty bubbled between us as the next band began to perform. The room filled with loud music. Not that I could hear it, though. I was too consumed with the man next to me.

How did we get here? With that thought, through the thick cloud of my frustration, I realized there was no going back for us. At least not for me. I had crossed the line that should have never been crossed. I rubbed my chest, hoping to ease the wrenching regret that had taken root there. It didn't help.

I wanted to place blame. He'd kissed me too, but...I had thrown myself at him.

Did he kiss me out of pity?

Shit, I'm going to cry.

With blurry sight, I hopped off the stool. As if I had sea legs, I took two steps before stumbling. I barely caught myself in time on the railing. A hand wrapped around my arm, holding me steady. Without thinking, I looked up. My eyes met Jamie's for only a moment before I remembered I was on the edge of tears and quickly turned away.

He was so close, I could smell him. His intoxicating scent should be an illegal substance with the way my body betrayed me. I was tempted to crumble, so he'd have no choice other than to hold me, giving me one more chance to be enveloped in all that was him, his smell, his strength, his soul. I wanted it all.

Then I remembered everything I felt for him was completely one sided. That knowledge was like being doused in gasoline and lit on fire, consuming me with white hot anger.

I jerked my arm away. I didn't need his help. He grabbed ahold of me again, tightly this time, and I couldn't shake him off. Pulling me forward, he helped me walk through the club, out the entrance, and into the parking lot. I tried to yank my arm free to no avail. Then my instincts took over. Turning toward him, with my free hand, I slapped him across his face.

He let go, leaving both of us standing there shocked.

"You kissed me," I blurted as a single tear escaped. "Did you do it because you were afraid to say *no* to poor little Maura? Do you think I want your fucking pity?" More tears fell. I couldn't stop them. I was blaming this show of weakness on whiskey.

His shock and anger seemed to fade. Frustratingly, he said nothing. After a long span of silence, I'd come to the conclusion that my needing to know didn't matter anymore. Either way he answered, our friendship was ruined. We'd never get back what we had.

"Forget it. You've made it perfectly clear you're not interested. It's my fault for pushing." I took in a deep breath, held it, then let the air out of my lungs with a heavy sigh. "Go home, Jamie. I'd rather take on the wrath of Stefan than stand here—"

"I don't fucking pity you, Maura," he snapped. He rubbed his hands down his face. "I don't know how to do this." His fingers flicked between us. "I don't know if I can, and you deserve better than that."

"Do you even want me?" The sound of defeat was blatant in

my tone. I expected him to say *no* and no matter how much it'd hurt, I still needed to hear it to move on.

He gave me an exasperated look. "It doesn't matter what I want."

"Yes, it does," I argued. "Since I've been home, things have been changing between us. The looks, the touching. I need to know it wasn't all in my head. I need to know I'm not the only one wanting more between us."

He seemed a little taken aback, eyes widening slightly, but he didn't answer me, which set me off. "Damnit, Jamie! Just put me out of my fucking misery and tell me!"

"Yes, I want you! Fuck, I've wanted you!" His body turned away, angrily running his hands through his hair. His jaw clenched as he stared off into the distance. He looked torn. *Why?*

Stunned, all I could do was stand there and watch as he seemed to battle with himself. My fingers ached to comfort him, but I kept my feet rooted to the ground. I wouldn't pressure him anymore. I couldn't do that to him, and I couldn't do that to myself. Instead, I replayed this moment in my head. Rewound everything he'd said, trying to understand why this was so hard for him.

"Why?" I asked. "Why do you think you don't deserve me?"

His eyes closed slowly, looking pained.

When his eyes opened, they shifted to mine. My breath hitched. They were filled with so much emotion. He was letting it all show. Anger. Defeat. Sadness.

"I've never given women respect for more than a night and I don't think I ever can give more than that," he explained, sounding bitter. "A relationship could pull me from my priorities and that's protecting this family and Stefan. If it ever comes down to it—and I know it will—where I'll be stuck in the middle between you two, I'll have to choose..."

"You'll choose Stefan," I finished for him, not at all surprised.

I'll admit, it wasn't easy hearing it out loud.

"It's our code. We all follow it. Even you, in your own way," he explained.

Stefan's code of honor was like the Mafia's omertà. All the men in the family took the code seriously, but as a woman, it wasn't really something Stefan had sat down and talked about with me. I'd only heard about it because teenaged boys liked to talk when they thought I wasn't listening. It wasn't like anyone had expected me to be introduced to the business side of things. Women in the family were kept naive because most of the men thought we were too weak to handle what they did, which in turn gave us deniability if anything were to happen. Now that I kind of had my foot in the door, I had a feeling I was going to be hearing about the code a lot more.

I sighed heavily and wiped away the wet tracks along my cheeks. "I don't know what scenarios you've drawn up in your head, but boo fucking hoo. Your loyalty to Stefan is the last thing that'd wreck me. Stefan and I have always butted heads and probably always will. I'm kind of pissed that you're comparing me to the normal, anorexic, air-headed bimbos you're used to screwing. Who the hell do you think you're talking to, Jamie?" I practically growled my words.

Everyone wanted to be the center of someone's world. It was human nature. You couldn't have those kinds of expectations in our world. I'd always understood that. I'd known there would come a day where I'd meet someone, and I'd prayed they'd be understanding that my loyalty to Stefan had to take priority. Code or not, he was the king of our family's empire. Everything our family relied on rode on his shoulders. And if anything were to happen to him, it would be chaos.

"In all the years we've known each other, I've never tried to get you to pick me over him. The fact that you think I would makes me want to punch you in your perfect face," I fumed.

"I just don't want to hurt you, Maura."

Well, shit. How can I be mad at that? My shoulders slumped as my anger simmered. Shifting from one foot to the other, I tried to find the courage to say what I needed to next. I wouldn't beg him to want me. The ball was in his court. "If I'm going to have a semblance of happiness in this life, I'll take you any way I can have you because a piece of you is still better than nothing. Even if it's only friendship. I don't want to lose you. I need you too much."

We stood there in the middle of Anarchy's parking lot just staring at each other. Jamie reeled in his emotions, locking everything down. The longer time passed without his answer, the less confident I felt about anything. My feet shuffled again before I gave up.

"Where's your car? We might as well head home. I'll give you space to—"

Jamie startled me by cupping the back of my head and pulling me to him. His lips came down onto mine. I quickly recovered from my shock, seized his shirt in my hands, and stood on my tiptoes to help deepen our kiss.

"I want this. I want you—in every way I can have you. But I'm going to fuck it up. I don't know how to do this," he said, sounding pained in between kisses.

I nodded and pulled away slightly. "We're both going to mess up. It's inevitable. As long as we don't set out to hurt each other, I think we'll be okay," I reassured him. "Let's just take this one day at a time."

My words seemed to get through to him and the tension in his body eased. He molded his lips back to mine and I felt his tongue sweep out, demanding entry. I opened, groaning when his tongue brushed mine. His hand roamed down my bare back until it reached the base of my spine. He hesitated before his hand continued its descent and smoothed over my butt. His fingers flexed and squeezed, causing the fabric of my dress to ride up. A cool breeze hit my bare bits, making me gasp. I pushed away from him to pull down my dress.

"I think I just flashed the world," I said, looking around us, a little embarrassed. I didn't see anyone close by. *Phew.* When I turned back to Jamie, he was staring down at me like I'd lost my mind. "My dress rode up and I'm not wearing any underwear."

He stepped back, eyes traveling down my body. On his way back up, he lingered on my breasts. My nipples were hard and pushed against the thin fabric of my dress.

"You're not wearing anything under that dress?" he asked.

I smirked. "No."

He groaned. "We should go home," he said, reaching out for me.

I took a step back out of his reach. "Hmm, I don't know if I'm ready to go home just yet," I teased, trying to appear serious. "I'm having a good time right now. Unless you can offer me a better time—"

"Maura, get your ass in the car before I throw you over my shoulder," he warned, voice coming out deep and gruff. He pulled out his keys from his pocket and hit the unlock button on the key fob. Five cars down, the headlights on his black sports car flashed, signaling that it was unlocked. I gave him a defiant look by lifting a brow, daring him.

He shook his head at me, smiling, then moved faster than my mind could register as he swooped down and—like he'd said he would—threw me over his shoulder. I screamed, startled. Jamie's hand came down on my ass with a good slap, causing me to yelp.

"Jameson!" I growled. He just chuckled as he started for his car.

The sexual tension in the air was getting thicker and thicker the closer we got to home. Now that things were cleared up between us, what now? The whiskey was set in my system and it was giving me all kinds of naughty fantasies and the liquid courage to act them out.

I kept sneaking peeks at Jamie when I thought he wouldn't notice. Of course, he caught me every time and teased me with a knowing grin before returning his eyes to the road. *Man, he's beautiful.* Strong jaw, beautiful greenish-brown eyes, lush mocha colored hair. Don't get me started on his body. I wanted to explore every inch. My current debate was whether I should use my fingers or my tongue. His arm that gripped the wheel flexed a little and his tattoo covered skin bulged. It made me itch to start my exploring right then and there.

He caught me checking him out again. "You need to stop looking at me like that," he said, voice sounding strained.

"What will happen if I don't?"

His knuckles turned white as his grip on the steering wheel tightened. "You've had a lot to drink tonight," he stated, like that was supposed to mean something to me. I knew he was just as sexually charged yet was holding back, trying to do the right thing. I needed to break him of that annoying habit.

Unbuckling my seatbelt, I leaned over the center console and kissed him just below his ear while I slid my hand down his inner thigh. "We're not good people, remember. Don't turn honorable on me now. Especially when I want to do really, really bad things with you," I whispered before nibbling on the lobe of his ear. His body stiffened.

My hand slid further between his legs until I was cupping him over his pants. "Fuck," he hissed after I gave him a light squeeze. I teased him by alternating between nipping and kissing along his neck. I tugged his leather belt loose around his black slacks.

"We're pulling up to the house," he announced. I didn't stop. I felt the car slow when we approached the gate and I undid the button on his pants. I got the zipper down and slowly inched my hand inside his briefs, wrapping my fingers around him. He inhaled sharply, making me smile. I loved that my touch could draw such a reaction from him.

He was already hard, skin velvety smooth. I stroked his length slowly, memorizing every ridge from his base to his tip. He blew air through his lips while bumping the back of his head against the headrest. Once the gate was opened, he slammed his foot on the accelerator and sped up the driveway.

As soon as he parked the car inside the garage, he pulled my hand from his pants and unbuckled his seatbelt. Then he lifted me under my arms over the center console to straddle him. "That was mean," he growled and captured my lips with his in a punishing and demanding manner. His hand tangled in my hair, holding me in place. His tongue caressed mine and I moaned, loving the taste of him.

My hands slid over his arms and down his chest, feeling his taut muscles through the thin fabric of his shirt. His free hand traveled down my bare back to my ass and squeezed while I ground myself on his hard bulge.

A groan rumbled in his chest. Lips moving over my jaw, to my neck, his teeth nipped at my sensitive skin before his tongue soothed the sting. I was a panting mess as the ache between my legs became unbearable. My fingers moved frantically to unbutton his shirt.

"We need to go upstairs." He tugged on my hair to make me look up at him. His eyes were heavy-lidded with desire, but he was trying to fight it. Determined to do the right thing.

"Don't you dare stop." I gave up on the buttons, deciding to rip his shirt open the rest of the way instead. I took a moment to admire his beautiful tattooed skin and rippling muscles beneath them before I pressed my lips to his collarbone.

"The garage—" he started to say, but I quickly covered his mouth with mine.

"Shh, stop thinking and just be here with me," I whispered pleadingly against his lips.

His resolve snapped and his hands grabbed ahold of my dress, pulling it from the back down my arms. It bunched around my waist, exposing my breasts. He pushed me back gently to look his fill. "You're so fucking beautiful."

He leaned forward, lips capturing one of my dusky-pink nipples and cupped the other breast with his hand, kneading it. He suckled and tugged lightly with his teeth, causing my head to loll back, moaning.

I snaked my fingers in his soft hair and pulled lightly. "I need you," I said breathlessly.

His lips released my nipple and trailed up my chest, along my neck until he reached my ear. "You have me," he mumbled against my skin. His hands fell to my hips and pushed the skirt of my dress up over my hips. He slid a hand over my bare ass cheek before smacking it and giving it a good squeeze. I chuckled at his playfulness while I reached into his pants to pull him free.

Wow.

He was bigger than I'd been expecting. I pumped my hand up and down his cock a few times, assessing its length and enjoying the heaviness. The noises I coaxed from him fed my ego and turned me on even more than I thought possible. He caught my proud little smile and kissed it away.

"Do you enjoying teasing me?" His husky voice made me shiver.

I leaned forward and angled him at my entrance. "I'll let you have your way with me later. Right now, you're mine," I said and leaned back.

We stared at each other as the head of his cock slowly slid inside me. I gasped at the feel of being stretched. With my hand still buried in his hair, I couldn't stop from tugging it as I took more of him in. Jamie's brows furrowed, almost as though in pain as his grip on my hip and ass tightened, fingers biting into my skin. We were both panting heavily, enduring the same amazing torture. He pressed his lips to mine in a passionate kiss before slamming me down his shaft the rest of the way. I cried out from the abrupt intrusion.

He gave me a moment to adjust around him before he began to rock my hips. I grabbed ahold of the top of his seat with one hand and placed my other on the roof for purchase, then took control. I lifted my hips up until he was almost out before slamming back down. We both groaned. I kept moving like that until I found an addictive rhythm. Up, down, grind, and repeat. It felt amazing.

Jamie seemed to think so too because he urged me to ride him harder with his bruising grip. There was nothing slow or sweet about what we were doing. It was pure, *I-can't-get-enough* fucking and it was perfect.

At the new pace, pressure started to build where Jamie and I met. My boobs bounced in his face. He cupped one of them and his fingers tweaked my nipple, sending a jolt of electricity down to my clit, causing me to clench around him as my body exploded.

I whimpered and his breath hitched as my core contracted, milking him. Chasing his own release, his hips pumped at a frantic pace until he let out a throaty moan and I felt him come inside me.

We were both breathless and slick with sweat. That didn't deter him from pulling me close, crashing his lips down on mine.

He tucked my hair behind my ear and caressed my cheek with his thumb, spoiling me with affection, while his other hand rubbed up and down my bare back, soothingly. The sensation of his fingers trailing along my skin gave me goosebumps. Relaxing against his chest, I let myself enjoy the feel of him around me.

CHAPTER TWENTY-ONE

We were still so entangled, kissing nonstop in the afterglow of mind-blowing sex, that we didn't notice someone approaching outside. Knuckles rapping on the window startled us and caused us to jerk apart. Standing next to the car smiling like a smug loon was Louie. I pushed the button on the door to roll down the window.

"Glad to see you two made up," he teased. Eyes bouncing between us, something seemed to change in him. His smug look quickly faded as his expression turned serious. "You know there's two cameras pointed at you, right?"

Jamie's body stiffened.

"Dean and I just walked in on three of my guys eating popcorn in the control room watching you two shake the shit out of this car on the CCTVs."

Oops.

I'd forgotten about the cameras. I gave Jamie a sheepish smile. It quickly faltered when I noticed the tension around his eyes. I could already feel him closing off, thinking he'd messed up in some way. He'd tried to get me to go upstairs, but I hadn't listened. As long as Stefan didn't see the footage, I'd get over being watched. It was a little embarrassing, but we'd done nothing to be ashamed of. Surprisingly, a tiny part of me found it exciting and hot.

"Are they not allowed to have popcorn in the control room?" I asked.

Louie's eyes narrowed, not taking the hint and making light of this situation. Instead, he got annoyed. *Hmm...*

"She's plastered and her tits are out. The camera over my shoulder got a great recording of her riding you for everyone to see. How do you think she'll feel about all this when she sobers up?"

I really wasn't that drunk. I'd burned all the alcohol out of my system with the workout Jamie had given me. Sex was the best exercise. I was a little peeved he was talking about me like I wasn't there. I turned back to Jamie and sighed. His afterglow was starting to fade the more Louie spoke.

I brushed his cheek reassuringly. "I think he's worried you took advantage, but if anyone is the victim here, it's definitely you," I said with a proud smile. "I'm grateful you're looking out for me, Louie, but drunk or not, I'm always in control. If you watch the video, you'll see I was the aggressor and rode him like a professional cowgirl. As for the guys in the control room, tell them I'd like a copy of the video."

I ran my fingers through Jamie's hair, unable to stop touching him. A small smile tugged at the corner of his lips and I knew I'd eased some of his worry. I gave him a quick peck on the lips and whispered, "Since you let me have my wicked way with you, I'll play the willing victim next time." That earned me a bigger smile and he kissed me deeply, jump starting my heart. Despite the earth-shattering orgasm I'd just had, I found myself growing wet again with him still inside me. I rocked my hips ever so slightly and he grew hard almost instantly.

He growled, nipped at my bottom lip, then pulled away to look at me. "Fuck, already?"

I smirked. He brushed his thumb across one of my pebbled nipples. I clenched around him, causing him to exhale shakily.

Louie cleared his throat. "Alright, alright, break it up and get out of the car. You guys need to take this shit upstairs behind closed doors." Louie's voice was deeper than usual. I couldn't tell if he was uncomfortable or turned on from watching.

Jamie didn't seem bothered that he was standing there. If Louie hadn't just told us to take it upstairs, I'm pretty sure we'd be going at it again while he watched. Louie had watched Jamie have sex with another woman in the past. Maybe that was why he seemed unfazed. As for me, I don't know if I was caught up in the moment or if I didn't care either.

"You might want to turn around. We're, uh... still attached," I explained.

Louie just blinked at me.

***

"I left my shoes in your car," I said to Jamie over my shoulder as we walked through the house. He and Louie were quietly trailing behind me. They both hadn't said a word to each other since Jamie and I got out of the car. Louie was unusually quiet. I was a little surprised he wasn't cracking jokes or teasing the hell out of us. Instead, he seemed pissed off and from how pensive Jamie looked, he could tell something was up with Louie, as well.

Jamie's eyes traveled to mine and softened. "I'll get them for you later."

We had to pass the control room to get to the stairs in the foyer and as we were passing it, two goons walked out. Their eyes widened when they saw me, but once they noticed Jamie, they quickly looked to the floor.

"Enjoy the show, gentlemen?" I snickered. They both flinched, making me chuckle.

Louie stayed behind to talk with them. It wasn't until Jamie and I reached the second floor that I asked, "What crawled up Louie's ass?"

He shook his head. "Don't worry about it."

"Do you think he's mad we had sex?"

"Maura," he snapped in a tone that warned me to let it go.

"Fine," I growled, stomping ahead of him while I mumbled, "Cryptic, brooding asshole."

A smack came down on my ass, hard, causing me to yelp. I stopped walking and turned to glare at him as I rubbed a hand over my smarting left butt cheek. His expression was blank, but there was a glint full of mirth in his eye.

"You're an ass man, aren't you?" I asked.

A slow smile pulled at his lips. Coiling an arm around my stomach, he pinned my back against his chest. His fingers brushed against the back of my bare thigh, just past the hem of my dress. I stiffened when they traveled up under the skirt until his palm covered my sore cheek. With a slow, gentle caress, he rubbed, soothing the sting he caused. "You do have a nice ass, but if I had to choose, my preference would be between your legs," he whispered in my ear.

If he hadn't been holding me, I think I would have melted to the floor.

"Now who's teasing who?" I asked, leaning my head back on his chest and tilting it to the side to peer up at him.

He moved his hand from my ass to place it around my neck just under my chin, holding me firmly but gently. "A deal is a deal, baby," he smirked, then brought his mouth down to mine in a sensual kiss.

Did that mean he was going to have his wicked way with me right now? *Oh, I hope so.*

I turned in his arms without breaking our kiss. Pushing up onto my tip toes, I wrapped my arms around his neck. His hands fell down my back, tickling my flesh, until they smoothed over my ass. He lifted me up and instinctually, my legs locked around his waist.

I felt him walk with me in his arms, holding me up like I weighed nothing, with one arm under my ass and the other at my back. He took me to his room, set me down, and turned on the bedside light. Standing with my back to the bed, I stared up at him waiting for his next move. As promised, I'd let him be in control. Downstairs in his car, he'd let me take what I'd needed from him. Now, it was his turn to take from me and my heart raced with anticipation.

"How do you want me?"

He gave me a heated look.

"Take off your dress." It wasn't a request and his tone wasn't one he'd used with me before. It was deeply calm, authoritative, and dangerous. I suddenly felt like prey. I didn't know if his intentions were to kill me or fuck me, but either way, it made me wet and pulsing for him.

I did as he'd said and slowly pulled my arms from the sleeves of my dress before pushing it down my stomach, over my hips, and letting the fabric go at my thighs to fall at my feet. I stepped out of the dress and returned my eyes to his. They began their descent, taking in every inch of my body. I stood there unabashed, letting him look his fill. I wanted him to see me just as much as I wanted to see him.

When his eyes reached between my legs, they jumped up, locking with mine. "Lay on the bed."

I backed up without hesitation until the back of my legs touched the bed. Scooting back, I lay down. With my knees bent and hands resting at my sides, I waited.

Jamie hadn't moved an inch from where he stood, still fully

dressed. "Spread your legs," he ordered. I did, slowly baring myself to him. "Wider." I opened my legs until it was almost uncomfortable.

I could almost feel his eyes roaming down my slit. He groaned. "Fuck, baby. Your pussy is perfect. Pretty and pink. It makes me want to devour it." His dirty talk was going to drive me insane. I loved it. "Touch yourself."

Feeling a little rebellious, I touched my knee. "Right here?"

His eyes narrowed and I couldn't hide my smile. "Lower," he grumbled, clearly not thinking I was funny. I slid my hand down just an inch.

"Maura," he growled in warning. I was tempted to see what would happen if I didn't heed it, but I was done poking the bear.

I slid my hand down the inside of my thigh until I reached my soaked pussy. My fingers glided between my folds and my breathing hitched as I grazed over my clit. I rubbed over it again and again. With my other hand, I tugged and tweaked one of my nipples. My eyes closed and a moan fell from my lips.

"Put your fingers in your pussy, baby." My eyes popped open at the sound of his gruff voice. His whole body looked rigid as he watched. He had taken off his shirt and was slowly loosening his belt.

I dipped my middle finger inside me, pumping it in and out a few times before adding a second finger. My eyes never left Jamie's while I fucked myself. After he stripped away his pants and briefs, he stood before me in all his naked glory. My mouth went dry. He had the body of a god. His muscles were well defined under his silky skin, from his bulging arms and chiseled abs to his strong thighs. I wanted to run my tongue along the sculpted lines on his abdomen and brush my fingers through the dark little trail of hair that led past the V shape of his hips to his delicious cock.

While I plunged my fingers in and out, the palm of my hand ground against my clit and my orgasm started to coil. My breaths turned into pants. *I'm so close.* My legs shook and inched closer together.

He groaned as he stroked himself slowly. "You better keep those legs open."

I strained to hold them open, crying out, "Jamie, I can't!" But apparently, I could, because my back arched off the bed, my eyes squeezing shut as my orgasm sprung and exploded around my fingers. My body shook and spasmed.

As I was riding the sexual high, hands grabbed me by the hips, and I was pulled to the edge of the bed. My hand between my thighs was shoved away and I felt something probe at my entrance. My eyes snapped open just as Jamie slammed himself inside me. I groaned at the unexpected force and intrusion. Not giving me a moment to recover, he began thrusting into me, hard and unrelenting.

The pressure was too much, and my nails dug into his hands that were holding me firmly by my hips. Before I could even wrap my head around what was happening, I was coming again. I screamed, body thrashing from the pleasure overload. I was falling apart around him, yet he still didn't stop pumping into me. He was insatiable.

One of his hands traveled up my body, brushing over one of my breasts along the way before his hand cupped the back of my neck. His other arm moved behind my back, then I was being lifted. I locked my legs around his hips and snaked my arms around his neck. With us still connected and me in his arms, he climbed onto the bed and laid me down in the center. Bracing himself over me, he brought his lips down to mine and gave me a tender kiss. His hips rocked again but this time it was slow. He ground into my sensitive sex with each deep plunge, making my breath hitch every time. My whole body was shaking from the sexual torture. I honestly doubted I could survive another orgasm, which was already building.

"Jamie," I panted in between kisses and raked my nails down his back. "I'm—" I couldn't finish telling him because I was coming, and it completely shattered me. Tears clouded my eyes. My core began contracting again and it felt so good yet so painful. His thrusts picked up until I felt him swell and explode, filling me with warmth.

His body collapsed on top of mine. He was careful not to crush me as he burrowed his face into my neck. His labored breaths puffed against my skin while tears fell from my eyes uncontrollably.

What we'd just done had been absolutely perfect. It had never been like this with Tom. Hell, he'd barely gotten me to orgasm each time we'd had sex, let alone three times, but that wasn't why I was so overwhelmed. It wasn't until right now that I noticed I didn't cringe or feel fear when Jamie touched me intimately. With him, I found myself, or at least the closest I'd ever be to the self I'd been before I'd been tainted that awful night. *I don't feel damaged with him.*

Fingers brushed away the wetness on my face and I opened my eyes to find Jamie staring down at me, worry and confusion etching his features. "Did I hurt you?"

I shook my head and smiled. "No," I said and kissed him, reassuringly. When I pulled away from him, he still looked confused. "I didn't know it could be like that," I tried to explain.

"Like what?" His eyes narrowed, not understanding.

I sighed, a little nervous about answering. I didn't want to scare him away and I definitely didn't want him to think I was comparing him to Tom.

"I don't know...amazing," I finally replied.

With a look of understanding, he brushed my hair behind my ear, then pressed his lips to my forehead. We held each other and it wasn't long before my eyes started to feel heavy.

CHAPTER TWENTY-TWO

The bright morning light woke me the next day. Tucked under soft dark blue blankets, I was naked with a larger, equally naked body spooning my back. My head was using one of Jamie's arms as a pillow. Hugging me close, he draped his other arm over my stomach. His pelvis was pressed against my ass with his hard shaft nestled between my cheeks. Remembering the events of last night, I was suddenly wide awake and extremely turned on. He was like a drug who should have come with a warning label. *After riding once, you may find yourself addicted.*

Feeling naughty, I rolled my hips. A muffled moan sounded behind me. His hand flattened on my stomach. I bit my lip and moved my hips again. This time, he met me with a thrust of his hips. His hand traveled up and closed around one of my breasts.

"If you keep grinding your ass on my dick, I'm going to take it as an invitation," he mumbled, sounding half asleep.

He rolled my nipple between his fingers before giving it a tug. I gasped as wetness pooled at my core.

"It's definitely an invitation, but you're not going anywhere near my asshole, Jameson Coleman. With the size of your cock, you'd tear me wide open."

The bed shook from his silent laughter. "Baby, if you want me in, I'll get in," he whispered in my ear before he thrust against my ass again. I rolled my eyes.

"You can have me any other way," I whispered, turning my head to see him. He was wearing a lazy smirk before his lips touched mine. I licked and nipped at him to open up for me. He took the hint and I caressed my tongue against his. We devoured each other as his hand released my breast, moving down my stomach to the apex of my legs.

His fingers slid between my folds and circled over my clit. "You're so fucking wet," he growled into my mouth and pushed a finger inside me. He stroked in and out a few times before adding a second. His fingers were magic and had me so wound up, I was dying for release.

"Jamie, please," I pleaded. His mouth released mine as he shifted down the bed. I rolled onto my back and he settled between my legs, pressing his lips to my skin just below my belly button. I got butterflies in my stomach when his eyes looked up at mine as he dipped lower.

"Jamie, I—" I didn't get to finish that statement because he planted an open mouth kiss over my clit and I lost the ability to form words. This was a first for me. Tom had never attempted to go down on me and because I'd still been learning how to have sex without flinching, I'd never asked him to.

Thinking back to my relationship with Tom, I'd never fully trusted him. Jamie, on the other hand... There were no doubts, no fears. We fit like two halves of a whole and words couldn't describe the sense of comfort my soul felt when it touched his.

I fisted the sheets, anchoring myself as his hot mouth enraptured me. He hooked my legs over his shoulders and his large arms circled around my thighs to hold me in place. His tongue stroked over my clit and my eyes rolled back into my head. *Oh wow!*

His tongue alternated between circling and lapping before sucking my clit between his lips. My hips bucked and my legs began to shake. He had figured out that the closer I was to coming, the louder my moans got. The bastard would pull back just as I was about to reach the peak. Then he would start the tortuous process again. When he did it to me for a third time, I was ready to kill someone for an orgasm.

I dug my fingers into his hair and pulled. "Damn it, Jamie! Don't fucking stop!" My voice was strangled, a mixture of pleading and demanding, but my delirious frustration was apparent. He chuckled against my sensitive nub, making me whimper, then he began working my clit with determination. This time as I reached the peak, instead of stopping he grazed my delicate bundle of nerves with his teeth and I fell off the edge screaming, back arching off the bed. It was the most intense orgasm I'd ever had.

My body turned languid. Jamie smirked proudly as he scooped me up and carried me into the bathroom. He held me in his arms while he turned on the shower.

Once I was sure I could stand, he set me down and we both stood under the hot water, enjoying the feel of it cascading down our naked bodies. He washed every inch of my body, getting me worked up again. *He's turning me into a nympho.*

When it was my turn to wash him, I started at his shoulders, kneading his thick muscles, slowly working down. The moment I started stroking his cock with soapy hands, he picked me up and fucked me against the shower wall.

Jamie practically kicked me out of his room to go change in mine. Apparently, I was giving him "fuck me" eyes while he was getting dressed and if I didn't leave, we'd never make it out of his room.

Getting ready for the day, I skipped doing my makeup and only ran a comb through my hair. I didn't have the energy to do much else. A night and morning of marathon sex took a lot out of me, it seemed. Even my clothes were picked lazily. A green tank and leggings.

I need coffee bad. I sighed, plopping my tired ass on the couch.

Jamie showed up not a minute later, looking sexy as hell. He was dressed in a button-down red shirt with the sleeves rolled up to his elbows, displaying his tattooed arms. His dark jeans looked starched and had been paired with black leather Oxfords.

My eyes slowly roamed over him and my mouth went dry. He watched me while I looked my fill, smirking knowingly.

"Do big bad mob men get sick days? We could play naked doctor or just be naked. All. Day."

He put his hands on his hips, shaking his head with the biggest smile. "I'd love to spend all day in bed with you, but I have today's family meeting."

Well, that wiped the smile off my face. I was uninvited to today's meeting. Remembering Stefan's punishment killed my naughty mood.

"We need to talk about something," he stated, pulling me from my thoughts. His features returned to their stoic facade.

"We do?" I asked, erasing my own emotions, preparing for the worst.

"We had sex."

I was unsure what he was getting at. "We did. Quite a bit, actually."

He nodded in agreement, then rubbed the back of his neck.

Why would he be uncomfortable?

Then it hit me. He had a history of pouncing and bouncing.

My heart rate spiked. It took everything in me not to sound hurt and keep my voice calm. "If you're here to end this—"

"No." The one word was said curtly, leaving zero room for argument.

I inwardly relaxed. He wasn't ending *this*. I didn't know what else to call what we were doing. We hadn't exactly discussed it. I wouldn't say it was just sex. Feelings were on the line. We'd been friends for so long, there was nothing to stop that from happening. This little scare, however, revealed my feelings were stronger than expected, unsettlingly so.

"We didn't use protection." My eyebrows shot up, surprised. "I always remember to wear a condom, but when I'm with you... nothing else exists. You mess with my head." He sighed. "I'm clean and I trust you are as well. I just want to know if I should be preparing for a baby?"

Understanding washed over me. "There will be no baby. I'm on the pill." Kids were the last thing I wanted. Ever. I wasn't the maternal type and I refused to subject a child to this life.

He visibly relaxed.

"It's nice to know I have the same effect on you that you have on me," I admitted.

"I told you I wanted this. Have I given you the impression I felt otherwise?" He didn't sound upset or accusatory. His tone was gentle while implying I shouldn't doubt *this*, us, or him.

I shook my head. He hadn't given me that impression at all. I felt bad at how quickly I'd assumed the worst.

"Get your beautiful ass up and let's go to breakfast. We're already late as it is, and I don't trust myself to be alone with you behind closed doors."

That put a smile back on my face. I stood. The entire world tilted, and my vision became spotty.

"Maura?"

I immediately sat back down and waited for my vision to clear along with a weird pulsating pressure in my face.

"Maura?" Jamie called out to me. Then I felt hands cupping my face. I blinked the last of the spots away and saw him kneeling in front of me, worry etched around his eyes. I quickly plastered a smile on my face.

"I think I stood up too fast. I got a little dizzy, but I'm fine now." I didn't know who I was trying to convince more, him or myself.

Slower this time, I got back on my feet. When nothing unusual happened, I believed what I'd said to be true. As we made our way down to breakfast, I added a bounce to my step, showing Jamie I was fine. It seemed to help ease the tightness around his eyes, but once we approached the stairs, he took ahold of my hand. His concern was sweet and made me grin like a loon.

It was crowded at the breakfast table. Louie, Rourke, my uncle Conor, my aunt Kiara, and, of course, Stefan were all seated and already eating. Stefan noticed us right away, eyes flicking from my aunt sitting across from him to Jamie and I, or more specifically, our joined hands. I released Jamie's hand and we went our separate ways with him heading for his seat and me making my way over to my aunt.

"Maura, how are you?" she asked, beaming with warm affection as she got up and hugged me. My aunt Kiara was awe-strikingly beautiful with long golden-brown hair and the Quinn green eyes. She was Stefan's baby sister and had an aura about her that radiated grace and sophistication.

"I'm great, Auntie. How are you?"

"I'm good, honey," she replied. She touched the bruises on my cheek, then turned to glare at Stefan. "She is the Banphrionsa," she seethed disapprovingly at him. "Papa would have never allowed one of his men to put their hands on me or their whole family would be dead. You need to educate your men, Stefan."

The whole room muted. I noticed Conor had his elbow resting on the table with his face planted in the palm of his hand. Rourke was wide-eyed but staring down while biting the inside of his cheek. Louie was clearly feeling awkward as he pushed the food around on his plate. Jamie looked bored and Stefan regarded his sister with a displeased frown.

I sighed, feeling the need to ease the tension. "He was new and didn't know who I was." I put a hand up to stop before she could argue. "I know it's no excuse and I made sure he got what he deserved. I appreciate your concern, Auntie, but times are different. I can fight my own battles. Stefan respects this and so should you."

Kiara pursed her lips, clearly not happy. I gave her a forced smile before walking around the table to sit to the right of Stefan. "Morning," I greeted him out of politeness.

"Good morning."

I could feel him staring at me. I chose to ignore him. I was still pissed. "What's for breakfast?" I asked, peering at Rourke's plate next to me. He had bacon, eggs, hash browns, and toast. I reached for his last slice of bacon. He intercepted me by scooping it up and shoving the whole thing into his mouth. *Pig!* He smiled triumphantly with his cheeks puffed out around his food.

"You're going to eat breakfast?" Stefan asked, sounding surprised.

I shrugged. "I woke up starving."

"I wonder why that is?" Louie muttered caustically from across the table. Both Jamie and I frowned at him while Stefan eyed the three of us. *What is Louie's problem?* I was about to ask him just that when Maid Barbie decided to walk in from the kitchen.

Angela glanced around the table. Her gaze landed on me. The faintest hint of annoyance narrowed her eyes until she noticed

Jamie. I watched as she zeroed in on him like a predator, licking her lips.

"Jameson, I was wondering if you were going to make it to breakfast. It's not like you to be late. Would you like your usual?" she asked him sweetly while touching his shoulder.

I bristled. I was going to sever that appendage. So help me, I'd use a damn butter knife if I had to. "You can blame me for that," I said just as sweetly. *Back off, bitch.* "I can be a little distracting in the shower."

Rourke choked on a bite of food before releasing a fit of coughs. Thankfully, Jamie didn't look at all upset that I had basically just announced we were sleeping together. In fact, he looked downright smug about it. Angela on the other hand was glaring at me. The meanest smile pulled at my lips. *Bring it on, Barbie.* In the back of my mind, I was already smashing her face against the table. Who didn't like entertainment with their meal? "If you're taking food orders, I'll have whatever Rourke had, but with extra bacon and hash browns."

Angela's lips pressed into a firm line before she retreated back into the kitchen.

"Well, that didn't stay a secret long," Louie commented around his food. I ignored him and everyone else at the table. My focus was solely on Jamie.

He was smirking at me. "You done marking your territory?"

I steeled my features, showing him this was anything but funny to me. The only other relationship I'd been in had ended because of infidelity. I wasn't saying Jamie would ever cheat on me. I trusted him more than anyone, but I still felt doubt. I fucking hated it. "If she touches you or you her, I will kill her. It won't be quick and she will suffer." My warning didn't shock him in the slightest. It amused him. I directed the rest of my warning to Stefan. "You will never find her body and if we ever hire another beautiful maid again, don't be surprised if pieces of Maid Barbie get mailed to her replacement."

His brows arched as a small smile pulled at the corner of his lips. I couldn't tell if he was proud or laughing at me. Either way, I was surprised he wasn't mad I'd threatened him.

"That's kind of morbid," Rourke said, pushing his plate away.

"She's too much like you, Stefan. You should have raised her to be more like a lady who deserves respect and a lot less like a mobster who kills to earn it," Kiara lectured.

"Kiara," Conor snapped, chastising her for berating Stefan again.

Stefan ignored them and leaned back in his chair, still holding my gaze. He reached into his pocket and retrieved a dark blue velvet box. "I got this for you," he said, handing me the box.

I schooled my face as I flipped open the lid. I guessed the tattoo on my lower back was no longer a secret, like everything else in my life. Inside, pinned by two satin snaps, lay a rose gold necklace with a shamrock pendant. Four heart-shaped diamonds made up the sprig's petals and a cluster of smaller diamonds encrusted the stem. It was beautiful.

"Are you trying to buy my forgiveness?" I asked him.

He didn't immediately respond, clearly choosing his words carefully. "I've agreed to hiring back someone from the team who watched over you in Hartford," he said, as if that righted the wrong, the violation I'd felt. "Which, I'll have you know, is almost double what I normally pay for security."

Manipulation. Guilt. Tools of the game. I wondered if it was on purpose or after playing it for so long, he didn't even realize he was doing it. Either way, he was skirting the line, threatening to break the terms of our deal. "Am I not worth it?" I asked, using his own tools against him while acknowledging his transgression, accidental or not.

Of course, he hid what he was thinking or feeling. The only

hint I got was his hand resting on the table. It was curled into a fist.

I didn't need jewelry. I needed two words. But I knew I'd never get them. Along with three other words I'd give my left arm just to hear once.

"I won't explain myself again."

"I don't need you to." I understood why he'd done it. He'd been trying to protect me. That still didn't erase how I felt. *Exposed. Lied to.*

Closing the lid on the beautiful pendant, I slid the box over to him, leaving it next to his clenched fist. "I need time."

"It's a gift, Maura. No expectations. I had it made for you," he said, pushing the box back to me.

I locked my eyes with his. "It's an insult."

He let out a frustrated sigh. "You're being stubborn."

I clenched my jaw, preventing myself from lashing out. I glared at the box. I couldn't accept it. Not like this. Relaxing my face, I put on an empty mask before meeting his eyes. "I want to meet the person you've chosen before we hire him. To see if it's a good fit," I said, hoping to change the subject.

Stefan studied me with narrowed eyes for a few heartbeats before relenting with a slight nod. Angela returned with mine and Jamie's breakfast. She placed our plates in front of us without a word or a lewd glance at Jamie before disappearing back into the kitchen.

Looking around the table, I sighed. We really needed to invest in a coffee carafe. Standing, I drew Jamie's attention right before he was about to take a bite of eggs. "Want some coffee?"

He nodded. I took one step away from the table. Just like in my bedroom, the world tilted, but a lot faster this time. Pressure built behind my face and my vision spotted to black.

"Maura?" I heard Stefan say as a hand touched mine.

I was falling before everything went black.

CHAPTER TWENTY-THREE

"Maura?" Jamie called to me through the darkness. When a hand brushed against my cheek, I knew it was him.

"Maura, damn it! Wake up!" Stefan yelled. I felt myself being shaken awake.

I groaned and blinked my eyes open a few times, getting glimpses of blurry bright light before I squeezed them closed. *Why is it so bright? Am I hungover?* My head was killing me.

"She's waking up," a woman said. *Aunt Kiara?*

"The doc is on his way," I heard Louie say.

I tried to open my eyes again, this time squinting to help shield them from the light. My vision was less blurry, and I found myself staring up at a bunch of faces peering down at me. *Am I on the floor?*

Stefan and Jamie were sitting on the floor with me, hovering. Louie, my aunt, my uncle, Rourke, Brody, and a few goons were all standing around me.

"What's going on?" I asked, rubbing my forehead.

"You passed out, babe," Louie answered.

"You went down like a sack of potatoes," Rourke stated.

The more they talked, the more my memories came back to me. I'd been heading to get coffee from the kitchen. I'd been in the dining room about to eat breakfast. *Shit, I didn't eat. When was the last time I ate? Damnit!* This was freshman year at Trinity during finals week all over again. I'd gone days without eating because I'd been stressed about passing my classes, and I'd almost fainted. I guess this time I actually did. *Great. Just great.*

I tried to sit up only to get pushed down by Stefan.

"I know this looks bad but I'm fine. I just need to eat—"

"No. Stay down until the doctor gets here," Stefan ordered, his tone brooking no argument.

"Maybe you should move her somewhere a little more private until then," my aunt suggested. *Bless her.* I was not enjoying the audience.

"Let's take her to my study," Stefan agreed, exchanging a look with Jamie.

Jamie nodded and scooped me up into his arms. I let out a frustrated sigh. I was fine. Well, if you didn't count the mind split-ting headache and feeling shaky. If I ate a PB&J, I would be back to normal, not that I could convince them of that. I had no choice but to ride this out and see this doctor they called. Pouting, I mourned my breakfast left behind in the dining room. "I really wanted my bacon and hash browns. It's why I ordered extra," I told Jamie as he carried me to Stefan's study. "Maybe we can ask someone to bring—"

"Let's see what the doctor has to say first," Stefan snapped.

Jamie laid me down on the couch. I got into a seated position. Thankfully, they didn't protest. Jamie took a seat next to me on the couch and with Stefan leaning against the front of his desk, we waited.

Embarrassingly, my stomach growled loudly multiple times as the three of us sat there. Jamie's phone beeped a few agonizing minutes later. I about cried with joy when he told us the doctor was at the gate.

"I know me passing out was scary and I'm very sorry to cause you both to worry, but I promise I'm going to be fine. If I just eat something—"

"You're seeing the doctor, Maura," Stefan said.

"I'm fine with seeing the doctor. That's not what I'm trying to say. I'm hungry. You ever reach the point of hunger where you'd stab someone for a cheeseburger? Well, gentlemen, I'm starting to feel stabby."

They both ignored me until the doctor walked in with Louie leading the way. The doctor was unexpectedly young. For some reason, I was imagining an old man looking like Santa Claus who did house calls with a black leather medical bag. This guy, however, was in his mid-to-late thirties, was covered in tattoos, had long golden hair tied at his neck, and was carrying a duffel bag. *Hello, Doctor.* He was *fine.* His skin was tan with a golden hue and he had caramel colored eyes. Don't get me started on the muscles. He was bulkier than Jamie and had the perkiest ass. I was awestruck.

"Ben, thank you for coming so quickly," Stefan greeted the doctor, shaking his hand.

"You're drooling, baby," Jamie whispered in my ear. I turned to find him smirking. *Oops.*

"Jealous, *baby?*" I teased him.

With a mischievous glint in his eye, he walked away to go greet Dr. Ben. Louie took Jamie's spot next to me and threw an arm over my shoulders to offer comfort.

"Louie said someone fainted?" Dr. Ben inquired, looking between Stefan and Jamie.

"My daughter," Stefan confirmed, gesturing to me. Dr. Ben gave me a dazzling smile. *Oh, jeez.* If I hadn't been completely consumed by everything that was Jamie, I might have blushed.

"Do you get fainting spells a lot?" he asked, kneeling in front of me. He sat down his duffel bag on the floor next to him and pulled out a blood pressure cuff along with a stethoscope.

"No," I answered, lifting my arm for him to strap the cuff on.

He tapped his cheek. "When did this happen?" It took me a second to realize he was asking about the bruises on my face.

"Most doctors would ask how it happened."

Dr. Ben's eyes dropped from mine.

Anger bubbled in the pit of my stomach. "Have you worked for the family long?"

"Five years."

"Seen many battered wives?"

"Maura," Stefan said, tone full of warning. Dr. Ben's golden face paled and he swallowed audibly.

"I got hit in the face two days ago. You'll be happy to know this happened during a...I guess we'll call it a sparring match and the other person lost," I somewhat lied. "As for wanting to know if other women are being beaten in my family, I'll let that go. For now."

"And what do you plan on doing with that information, daughter?" Stefan questioned, not at all pleased. I just smiled at him.

Dr. Ben cleared his throat, regaining my attention. "Any medical history I should know about? Diabetes or high blood pressure?" he asked and began pumping air into the cuff. He was smart, beautiful, and cared for others. He almost seemed too perfect. There had to be a catch.

"No. I didn't pass out because of an underlying condition. It's because I haven't eaten, but no one will listen to me. I'm about to take a bite out of Louie here if I don't eat something soon."

"When was the last time you ate?"

"Day before yesterday," I mumbled sheepishly. The men in the room stilled and Dr. Ben released the air in the cuff.

Louie dropped his arm from around my shoulders. "What the fuck, babe? Are you anorexic or something?"

"Does my ass look like it's anorexic?" I snapped.

"Do you normally go long periods without eating?" Dr. Ben asked as he took the cuff off my arm.

"No. Only when my emotions run high. At those times, the last thing I think about doing is eating. I think the only exception is when I'm on my period. I swear the amount of ice cream I consume should put me in a sugar induced coma."

"Why were your emotions running high?" Dr. Ben inquired.

I glanced at Stefan, then Jamie. "Let's skip the therapy session. I'm sure you have better things to do than listen to me drone on about my daddy issues or my love life. Just feed me a damn cheeseburger and I'll be square."

Jamie stormed out of the study. He was clearly pissed. I sighed and returned my attention back to Dr. Ben, ready for this to be over. "So, Doc, am I good here?"

He gave me a dazzling smile again. "I don't think we have anything to worry about. I recommend you eat something right away and take it easy for the rest of the day." He got to his feet and turned to Stefan. "She's going to be fine. Sounds like her blood sugar dropped. It's explains why she fainted," he reassured him. They shook hands again and the beautiful doctor took his leave.

"I'm just going to say this out loud because I know we're all thinking it. That man was so beautiful. I swear Fabio and Aphrodite bumped uglies and the result was him."

"I'm sure his boyfriend thinks so, too," Louie laughed. *Ah, there it is, ladies. The catch.*

"I need to speak to my daughter alone," Stefan said to Louie. Obediently, Louie stood from the couch, squeezing my knee before leaving. Even he knew I was going to get my ass chewed.

"If you're going to lecture me, just know I already feel like shit."

Stefan didn't say anything. Instead, he quietly stared at me, looking deadly still with his arms crossed over his chest. He did nothing to hide his anger.

"I've been like this for years and don't tell me you're not the same way. If Brody wasn't here, I highly doubt you'd remember to breathe."

"You're right. I recognized my faults and I found an alternative way to fix them. You, however, have failed to do that."

"Are you saying I should hire someone to remind me to eat?"

"I don't care what you have to do, but what just happened will not happen again. You won't like what I'll do if it does, am I clear?"

I was a weird mixture of contrite and happy. I'd scared him. "Okay."

His frown took some time to fade. He eventually sighed and walked behind his desk to take a seat. Jamie barged in with a plate in hand the instant Stefan's ass met the cushion of his leather chair. He beelined for me, still looking pissed, and placed the plate in my hands without really giving me much choice but to take it. I beamed once I saw what was on it. It was a cheeseburger with a side of bacon and hash browns. My mouth watered at the delicious sight.

"I think I might actually cry. This is the best thing anyone has ever given me."

Jamie rolled his eyes. "Just eat it," he ordered, taking a seat next to me.

I bit into the cheeseburger and moaned. "I think I'll hire Jamie as my own Brody," I said in between bites. He'd be perfect for the job. He'd bring me all the foods I loved, and I wouldn't have to worry about getting fat because he'd help me burn off all the calories with multiple orgasms. It'd be heaven on earth.

"He already has a job. Find someone else."

Well, that just shattered that fantasy. I frowned at Stefan. How come Brody could do both his job and take care of him, but Jamie couldn't? It frustrated me that I couldn't call him out on that. At least not until he was ready to talk to me about their relationship.

"Speaking of hiring someone, when should I expect my own personal goo—I mean, security?"

Stefan gave me a look that said he wasn't fooled.

"It's like smoking. It's a bad habit to kick. Especially since the nickname fits so well."

"Your new security should be here next week when he's done with another assignment."

I nodded. "Until then, I want Dean assigned to me and possibly for the future along with my new security."

"He's not ready for that. He's barely been with us a year," Jamie argued.

"Then make him ready." I wasn't going to budge on this. If I had to have security with me, then I was going to choose who I was going to be stuck with. "I will not be cooped up in this house for a week." Plus, I liked that he was new and that he was an asshole. He wasn't a kiss ass like the rest of them. He was perceptive and thought for himself. He'd sure as hell questioned my every move yesterday until he'd found out I'd been lying. He was also loyal and didn't feel the need to throw me under the bus to prove it.

Jamie didn't appear happy as he turned to Stefan for back up. They exchanged a look before Stefan sighed tiredly. For once, he was in the middle. "I'm good with it."

Jamie frowned.

"But you need to tell Jameson or myself where you'll be going when you leave the house." That seemed to placate Jamie a little and it was a compromise I was willing to make.

"I'm fine with that...for now." I wasn't a child anymore. I should be able to come and go without having to tell someone. Stefan didn't seem pleased but didn't argue. I took a bite of hash browns. "Yum," I moaned around my food. I noticed the side of Jamie's mouth twitch. I think he secretly liked that I loudly enjoyed my food.

As I chewed, I caught Stefan looking from me to Jamie. "Something you want to know?" I asked.

"No," he replied with a strange look in his eye that I couldn't decipher.

I didn't dwell on it because, well, bacon was calling my name.

CHAPTER TWENTY-FOUR

Chocolate chip cookie dough ice cream. It was a magical concoction I wholeheartedly believed was the cure for bitchiness and homicidal tendencies when Aunt Flow came to visit. That was why Ben and Jerry's was always stocked in the freezer.

I fondly remembered when Stefan had discovered ice cream was the key. I'd been fifteen, Aunt Flow had been rearing her ugly head, and Stefan had received a call from my principal to come get me. I'd been sent home and possibly expelled for making a fellow student cry. In my defense, the pimple-faced jerk had groped my ass and I'd given him the beat down he'd deserved. Had I taken it a little too far by breaking his nose? Maybe. Had I lost sleep over it? Not a wink.

I'd still been itching for another fight when Stefan had strolled into the school's office, looking superior in his tailored suit, while giving off an intimidating aura. At one look from Stefan, my principle had paled and nervously fidgeted while he'd explained their zero tolerance for violence policy.

I hadn't gotten expelled. I'd had no doubt I ever would, but I had gotten sent home for the rest of the day.

Stuck in the car with a raging hormonal teenage girl, Stefan had taken all my lashing and bashing like a pro. He hadn't engaged. To my complete and utter surprise, he'd silently driven to an ice cream parlor. I'd immediately cooled down and sweetened after two bites of my favorite cookie dough ice cream. Stefan had then explained that I was just like my mother.

It was one of my favorite memories because it had been eight months, fourteen days, and eleven hours since the last time he'd been kind to me, let alone spent one-on-one time with me. And yes, I had been counting. I'd been beginning to think he hated me because I'd made the mistake of allowing Dylan to get the upper hand while we'd been sparring, showing off what moves we had learned in self-defense training. Stefan had walked in when Dylan had me in a choke hold. What he hadn't seen before that was Dylan getting pissy because he hadn't been able to take me down the previous three times we'd sparred. Dylan had a fragile ego. To be nice, I'd been letting him win so we could call it a day. Well, suffice it to say, Stefan had not been happy. He'd switched out my private self-defense teacher, in other words, fired him. And he'd made my new one push me. I'd hurt after every session. The smallest injury I'd received had been a sprained wrist. My worst had been a cracked rib. I'd stopped showing up for my training after that. Which, in turn, had set Stefan off even more. He had become cruel. He wouldn't really acknowledge me. If I'd ever needed something from him, like signing a permission slip for school or permission to go the movies with Jamie and Louie, he'd forced me to use the game to try to get what I wanted from him, which had always ended with me losing. We'd kind of stopped talking after that.

Frowning at how quickly my venture down memory lane had turned unhappy, I took one of the many pints of ice cream from the freezer and grabbed a spoon from the silverware drawer. My period had come after this morning's fainting drama and with each passing hour I'd been getting more and more irritable.

My period meant no more sexy time with Jamie. Being a girl fucking sucked.

Digging into the creamy goodness, I made my way back to my room. Stepping into the foyer from the kitchen, I was startled by Jamie and a goon crashing through the front door, dragging a bleeding, barely conscious man behind them. I gaped at them with the spoon hanging from my mouth as they dragged the bleeding man down the hall toward the basement door, leaving behind a crimson trail across the tile floor.

My feet moved without thought and I followed them down to the basement.

They threw the bleeding man into a lonesome chair centered under the only hanging light in the dark room. The basement was pretty barren, apart from a table up against the far wall and a few folding chairs. The floor and walls were concrete and there was a single drain in the center under the bleeding man's chair.

This room was used for one thing. Interrogation. Which always ended in death. In the past, I'd seen Stefan and his goon squad drag people down here, but never followed. Stefan had never allowed me. I understood. He hadn't been ready for me to see everything the family did. Now that I was older, nothing could happen down here that would shock me.

I took a seat at the bottom of the stairs. The goon zip tied the bleeding man's hands to the back of the chair. My eyes flicked to Jamie, finding him staring at me. He gave me a questioning look that said, *What the hell are you doing here?* I rose an eyebrow, daring him to try and make me leave. Giving up, he returned his attention to the man in the chair.

The goon took a step back from the man tied to the chair as Jamie approached. The man glared up at Jamie in a defiant show of strength. He'd taken some hard hits to the face. His right cheek was gashed open along the bone and his lip was split. One of his eyes was completely swollen shut. His breathing was labored and even though the man was obviously in a world of pain, he still had the balls to give the death stare to Jamie.

This was going to be entertaining.

"We know you lied about getting jumped. You sold the guns and pocketed the cash. You're going to tell me where you stashed the cash and who you sold the guns to, because we know De Luca doesn't have them."

I got goosebumps watching Jamie. His voice...it was ruthless yet excited. He was looking forward to this.

I looked back at the bleeding man and tried to imagine what he must be thinking while Jamie towered over him. Fear. Pain. Death. He had to know what was to come, especially if Jamie was the one sent after him.

The man's glare fell away and an unexpected calmness came over him before his eyes went vacant. With a tilt of my head and a mouth full of ice cream, I studied him. My best guess for his unusual response was that this man had accepted his fate. He was ready for whatever came. Unfortunately for Jamie, this guy was going to be a tough nut to crack.

Jamie retrieved a switch-blade from his pocket and jammed it into the man's thigh. The man screamed out in pain, but quickly recovered and willed his body to relax. Jamie alternated between cutting, punching, and breaking bones to no avail. Even the goon took a turn, inflicting torturous pain. Still the man said nothing.

"What are you doing down here?" I heard over my shoulder. I turned, finding Stefan standing a few steps up, staring down at me. His eyes moved to roam over the beat down going on in the room.

I shrugged. "There was nothing good on TV," I fibbed and took another bite of ice cream. Stefan opened his mouth to say something. I anticipated him asking me to leave. His eyes dropped to the pint of Ben and Jerry's in my hands. He closed his mouth and stayed quiet.

Jamie's breathing was labored after delivering another pointless punch. He backed away from his prisoner, finally realizing he wasn't getting anywhere. The man looked ten times worse than when they'd brought him down here. Blood dribbled from his mouth as his head awkwardly rested on his shoulder. He was going to die before they got anything from him.

Feeling compelled to help, I stood and padded my bare feet on the cold concrete floor over to the stack of chairs against the wall. Grabbing one, I dragged it over to the guys. "Take a break, fists of fury," I said, passing Jamie and unfolded my chair in front of the prisoner. Jamie looked to Stefan, whose attention was on me. I took a seat and I shooed away the goon who was standing too close with my hand. I guess Stefan gave the *okay* because the goon backed away without question.

I caught the prisoner staring at me. He was clearly confused as his one good eye took me in, from my long open black silk robe, silky green shorts, and matching tank pajama set to my bare feet. I had just painted my toes a hot pink color this afternoon and was second guessing the color, especially in this terrible lighting.

We sat there in silence while I dug through my pint for any remaining cookie dough buried in the ice cream. When I couldn't find anymore, I set the pint on the floor. I rubbed my lower belly. "I have the worst cramps. I swear I have a sadistic uterus," I complained dramatically.

The prisoner gaped at me like I'd lost my damned mind.

"What's your name?" I asked.

He was quiet for a moment, debating whether or not he should answer. "Ian," he mumbled. More bloody drool spilled from the corner of his mouth.

I was surprised he'd answered, but I didn't let it show. "Do you have a girlfriend or wife, Ian?"

"A wife."

"Do her cramps try to kill her like mine do?" I shifted in the uncomfortable chair to help relieve the pain in my lower back.

"No."

"Lucky woman," I mumbled, finding the perfect position, which was somewhat slouching in the chair with my legs crossed. "Do you have any kids?"

His single unswollen eye softened as he stared down. "A daughter." He refused to look at me when he answered. *Hmm...*

"You're a brave man. I don't think I could handle having a daughter. Girls are scary," I rambled. "How old is she?"

"Seven."

My attention was drawn to Jamie's switchblade, still embedded in his thigh. I leaned forward and nodded to the blade. "Do you mind if I take that out?" He didn't answer me. I had a feeling pride was standing in his way. I wrapped my hand around the grip of the blade and pulled it from his leg. His body went rigid and he hissed.

Holding the bloody knife, I stood and made my way over to Jamie. He and Stefan were both leaning against the wall by the stairs. Jamie watched me with his arms crossed over his chest. I invaded his space. Smiling up at him, I wrapped an arm around his waist. My hand brushed over the gun I knew was tucked into the back of his pants. He let me take it without question. "I'm borrowing this," I said, waving the gun a little. He didn't protest. Both he and Stefan just continued to watch me, waiting patiently to see what I'd do.

With the switchblade and gun, I walked behind Ian and cut the zip ties, freeing his wrists from the back of the chair.

"Maura!" Jamie pushed away from the wall. I stopped him in his tracks by cocking the gun. I gave him a pointed look that said, *I got this.*

"Ian's not going to do anything stupid, now are you, Ian?" I asked sweetly as I held out the switchblade to Ian. He stared at the blade, then at me and made no move to take it. "Take it," I ordered.

He lifted his hand to take it but hesitated halfway. I grew tired of waiting and placed the grip of the blade in Ian's hand, then returned to my chair with Jamie's gun.

Stefan pushed away from the wall as well, taking a couple of steps forward. I could see worry etched around his eyes as they bounced back and forth between Ian and me.

Ian stared at the blade in his hand, beyond confused. It wasn't the norm when it came to interrogating someone, I was sure, but Ian was a special case. The guy was prepared to take his secrets to the grave and that wasn't going to work for me. We needed to go about this a different way.

I pointed the gun at him. "I'm going to give you a choice." Ian eyed the gun. "Two, actually. I'm going to let you pick how you're going to die. You knew how this was going to end. You've already accepted it. That's why I'm going to let you pick how you go out." I studied him as the wheels turned behind his one good eye. "Option number one...you can kill yourself, right now, with the knife. I recommend the wrists. It's less painful, but it takes a while. You'll bleed out slowly. Panic uncontrollably sets in about the same time the cold does. Soon after that, you won't be able to move because there's no more blood pumping through your body. I hear your sight goes first, and while you sit there in complete darkness, your brain will go haywire. Some say as you're dying, you see your entire life flash by. Others say you see and feel everything you regret. I think you just remember random shit, like what you had for breakfast, because how can the brain bring forth all your memories if it doesn't have what it needs to function?" I said, tapping my finger to my chin, as if pondering, before I shrugged. "That's dying for you. It's still the unknown." The room was so quiet, you could hear a pin drop. "Option two is probably painless." I wiggled the gun in my hand. "I'll make it quick. All the pain and fear you're feeling will be over in an instant," I told him, snapping my fingers. "It'd be the more dignified way to go out. I'd take it, but option two has a price." I paused, leveling my eyes with Ian's. "I need to know who you sold the guns to."

Ian's eye narrowed in disbelief. I knew what he was thinking. His skepticism confirmed what I suspected. The right question wasn't *where* the money was but *why* he would be willing to die to keep it hidden. "I already know where the money is." For only a brief moment, his eye widened. "You see, you've already told me. Human behavior is a fascinating thing. When pushed or presented with the right questions, it's amazing how someone will react. Like how I asked about your family. When speaking about your daughter, your reaction was stronger compared to when we talked about your wife. Love is a strong emotion but when paired with sadness, it's hard to hide. When grouped with fear, any human would do something drastic. I'm assuming she's sick or was sick and that's why you needed the money? Why else would you break the code and betray the family unless it was for someone you loved?" I watched as panic took root. I could see it in the way his breathing picked up and how his eye was unblinking. "You know what? Let's sweeten option number two. If you tell me who you sold the guns to, we won't go after your family for the money." I refused to look at Stefan. I was probably going to catch hell for making that kind of promise because it wasn't my place to make, but I'd deal with that later.

I sat back, waiting for Ian's decision. He stared down at the ground and his grip around the knife tightened. "The Aryans," he finally answered. I knew of them. White supremacist gang. I quickly turned to Jamie to see if he was satisfied. When nothing was said by either him or Stefan, as promised, I pointed the gun at Ian and pulled the trigger. The force behind the bullet caused Ian's head to fly backward and his body to fall to the floor. I stared at his lifeless body for a moment, feeling the finality of his death. He'd wronged the family; even if I understood the reason behind his betrayal, his death was necessary.

I padded my way back over to Jamie and Stefan. They both held different expressions. Jamie was unreadable, whereas Stefan looked like he was calculating or scheming. I wasn't quite sure. I held out the gun for Jamie to take. "Will you be done with this soon? I figured we could watch a movie?"

He took his gun from my hand and he tucked it into the waistband of his pants behind his back. He then surprised me by taking the sleeve of his shirt and wiping at my cheek. "You have blood on your face."

Eww. A shower was in my near future. "You didn't answer my question."

Jamie's eyes softened as they looked torn.

"He'll be done in an hour," Stefan answered for him while texting on his phone. "I'll have someone take over."

"I can finish the job," Jamie argued. *Uh oh.*

Stefan peered up from his phone, seeming slightly surprised but still authoritative and chilling. "I'm not doubting you, Jameson. I'm giving you the opportunity to enjoy the rest of your night. We have other people who can do this," he explained and dismissed us by walking up the stairs while tapping away on his phone. Jamie watched as Stefan left with a puckered brow.

"You're upset."

Jamie's head jerked around to face me. He shook his head. "No. Just surprised."

"Are you sure? I did kind of take over..."

The corner of his mouth twitched. "I didn't mind. It's hot watching you play with people."

Well, alrighty then.

"I'm not the only one who's sexy when they're getting bloody." I invaded his space and ran my hands down his chest.

"You use your bedroom voice when you're on the edge of killing someone."

His arms wrapped around me before his head dipped down to kiss me. I eagerly met him halfway and molded my lips to his. Almost instantly, fiery need sparked inside me and I had to pull away before he stroked it into a blaze. *Stupid period.*

CHAPTER TWENTY-FIVE

T he next day was spent in ratty sweats surrounded by everything I could find containing chocolate while vegging out in the movie theater on one of the fluffy couches. Jamie had been gone when I'd woken this morning. Both he and Stefan were working away from home today and I'd been left alone to entertain myself. There wasn't anything wrong with that. I was independent, but with how hormonal I was, my moods were giving me whiplash. One minute, I was going stir crazy, dying to get out of the house and the next minute, all I wanted to do was lie down. I was a hot mess.

I ended up in the movie theater with an armful of what I called *happy food*. It was all junk that would probably go straight to my ass. Each bite of ice cream, cookies, and chocolate candy bars was bittersweet.

Brody found me that afternoon in a sugar-induced haze, covered in cookie crumbs and candy wrappers while watching a sexy romantic drama. It was just getting to the good part where the sexy rich man was showing the young innocent girl his *play-room*. Oh yeah, things were about to get *hot*! I wasn't getting any right now, so I had to live vicariously through the two fictional characters on the screen.

Brody walked into the room with his cell at his ear. He took in the train wreck that was me and the mess surrounding my prone body. I'd eaten a whole pint of cookie dough ice cream and a whole box of chocolate chip cookies, not to mention ten fun-sized chocolate bars.

The corner of his lips twitched. "I found her. She's in the theater." Brody looked to me. "Your father wishes to speak with you," he said, holding out the phone.

I took it and brought it to my ear. "What?" It came out harsher than I intended, but my hot moment was being interrupted. And Brody was standing in the way!

I barely heard an audible sigh coming through the phone as I tried to look around Brody to see the screen. He had busied himself by scooping up the mess on the floor. Chuckling while shaking his head, he pulled a candy wrapper from my hair.

"Maura?" Stefan said calmly, drawing my attention back to the phone.

"Yes?"

"You didn't hear a single thing I just said, did you?"

Uh...he said something?

With my silence, Stefan got his answer. "There will be a car waiting for you outside in two hours. Get ready. You'll be joining me for dinner."

"Have you become a masochist since I've been gone?" I asked seriously. "I'll be shitty company and I won't feel bad about it. In fact, I might enjoy it. I just need to stay home and not come into contact with the human population. It's safer for everyone that way."

"I certainly didn't miss your flair for the dramatic once a month, that's for sure," he mumbled but was still clear enough for me to understand.

"Are you trying to pick a fight?"

He sighed again. A clear sign I was trying his patience. "Put on a dress. We're going somewhere nice." It wasn't a request. "There's a bakery next door that has the best chocolate cake. We can get some after."

I chewed on my lip as temptation chiseled away at my cranky mood. He didn't play fair.

"The cake better be worth it," I murmured and hung up the phone.

Despite feeling bloated, I picked out a skin-tight black cocktail dress with sheer lace cut outs around my ribs and above my breasts. I paired the dress with ruby-red pumps.

Two of Stefan's goons who I didn't know but recognized from them following Stefan around were waiting for me outside next to a black Escalade. It was a silent car ride with the two goons up front and me by myself in the back. From what I could tell through the heavily tinted windows, we were headed downtown. After a twenty-minute drive, we pulled up to a fancy steak house in the center of downtown.

The valet in front of the restaurant quickly jumped up to open my door, but Stefan's goon riding in the passenger's seat hopped out and stopped him from touching my door.

They take their job way too seriously. I mentally rolled my eyes while I waited patiently for the goon to open the door. He held out his hand and I took it. Once my feet were planted on the ground, I walked ahead toward the entrance of the restaurant. People waiting by the valet stared, probably wondering who I was and why I needed a bodyguard.

The restaurant was elegant inside, decorated with black wood, gold accents, and burgundy painted walls. It was busy.

Every table was occupied with dressed-up people and more waiting in the lobby.

When I didn't see Stefan seated anywhere, I approached the hostess. Before I could utter a word, she grumbled, "Do you have a reservation?"

Hackles rising, I wanted to be a grump back at her. Then I glanced around. It was busy and she'd probably been dealing with impatient assholes all night. So I tapered my anger down. "I'm meeting my father here. Stefan Quinn?"

The hostess's back snapped straight and she gave me a forced smile. "Yes. Would you please follow me?"

With my goon in tow, we followed her through the dimly lit restaurant. I scanned the room and still didn't see Stefan anywhere. I looked ahead and saw she was leading us toward the back of the restaurant. We came upon a set of black painted doors with floor to ceiling mirrors on either side of them. The wall of mirrors had rust looking spots blemishing them, making the glass look aged or antiqued.

The hostess opened one of the doors, holding it for us to enter. My goon went in first before I followed him. Inside was a private dining room with a ten-seater table in the center and a rustic golden chandelier dangling from the ceiling in the center. The whole room was walled with windows, giving a view of the street where cars passed by and inside the restaurant where everyone was eating. Those antique mirror walls outside were two-way mirrors. We could see everyone dining in the restaurant, but no one could see us. *That's cool.*

Seated at the head of the table was Stefan and seated to his left was Jamie. Both looked dashing, dressed to the nines in their tailored suits. Standing guard along the far back wall and near the entrance were two more goons. Seated to Stefan's right was an older gentleman in his late fifties. I didn't know who he was, but as I took in his white chef's jacket, I had a good guess.

Stefan and Jamie both stood when I entered, and the older man followed suit.

"Maura, you look beautiful," Stefan greeted and stepped away from the table to meet me halfway. He embraced me with a quick hug before planting a kiss on my forehead. I tensed slightly with the sudden show of affection but quickly recovered and forced myself to relax. It was going to take time for me to get used to him doing that.

Circling his arm around my back, he ushered me over to the older gentleman. "Adrian, this is my daughter I was just telling you about. Maura, this is Adrian, the executive chef of this restaurant."

Adrian gave me a smile and held out his hand. I placed my hand in his and he covered it with his other hand before shaking it gently. "Your Papa is right. You're stunning," he said with a thick Russian accent. I thanked him in his native tongue and his smile grew.

"Vy govorite po-russki?" he asked. *Do you speak Russian?*

I smiled back at him. "Da." *Yes.*

That seemed to please Adrian. He started firing off in Russian at Stefan about how I was not only beautiful but smart and that he should be proud. Stefan smiled genuinely down at me before he replied in English, "Yes, I'm very proud."

"I must get back to my kitchen. Please, enjoy my food and yourselves," Adrian said before leaving. I took the seat Adrian had vacated at Stefan's right. We were all looking over our menus when our waiter came in with some appetizers. He asked me for my drink order. I noticed the men were drinking whiskey and ordered the same.

"So what's the occasion?" I asked. They both looked at me then at each other. Jamie stayed silent, sipping at his whiskey.

"Does there have to be an occasion to go out to eat?" Stefan answered with a question.

I found that suspicious. "That doesn't answer my question." Both stayed quiet. I glanced at Jamie, who was refusing to look at me. He took a big gulp of his drink and kept his eyes down. I turned my attention back to Stefan. He was purposely acting obtuse. "We don't go out for dinner. You don't like to unless it's a special occasion or business. You always said it was too risky," I explained.

"I didn't like to take the risk when you were younger. You're not a little girl anymore and less vulnerable if anything were to happen."

I could sense he was telling the truth and as much as it warmed me to hear that, in a small way, his explanation left me feeling patronized.

Deciding to let it go, I looked back down at my menu and stated, "I believe I was promised chocolate cake."

Jamie chuckled at that.

"You can't just eat chocolate cake, Maura. After dinner, we'll get some," Stefan admonished.

"I wasn't planning to. I'm getting a big juicy steak and garlic fries. I was just reminding you about the cake."

The waiter returned with my drink and took our food orders. While we were waiting on our food to come, we drank, nibbled on the appetizers, and interacted with small talk. It was nice, actually, and I was kind of glad Stefan dragged me out.

Our food arrived shortly after that. It looked so delicious and succulent, I might have drooled a little. With my steak knife and fork in hand, I was getting ready to cut into my steak when the door to our private dining room opened suddenly. In walked a big, dangerous-looking man, dressed all in black and obviously armed, followed by a similarly dressed, dangerous man, and then another.

An uneasiness spun into a ball in the pit of my stomach. I didn't know these men, and with one look at Stefan and Jamie, I could tell they didn't either. Our three goons standing around us all widened their stances. As each unexpected visitor walked into the room, my instincts screamed at me that something wasn't right. Without even thinking, I swiveled my steak knife inward, hiding it under my arm before placing it in my lap as I continued to watch as more men entered the room.

Four more mean-looking men filed in, followed by a less bulking man in a gray suit with Russian tattoos on his hands and neck. The last man to enter the room was Sasha, the Russian owner of Anarchy, looking as tall and gorgeous as I remembered from the other night.

I felt a little relieved it was him, but as I looked around the room at all his men, I couldn't pull myself off the edge of my seat. Something still didn't feel right.

With my back painfully straight, I watched Sasha walk toward us. Stefan got to his feet and they clasped hands.

"I heard you were here and wanted to pop in to say *hi,* but I see my timing was poor. Your food just arrived. Please, sit down."

Stefan gave him a tight smile, not liking the order, but he took a seat anyway.

Sasha looked to me, his remarkable gray-blue eyes filled with recognition. Before he could say something to me, Stefan intercepted, "What can I do for you, Sasha?" His tone was polite. Only someone paying attention could tell it was forced.

"Like I said, I was just popping in to say hi." He glanced at Jamie. "I heard someone tried to hit one of your trucks yesterday."

Across the table, I noticed Jamie had tensed up.

After an uncomfortable amount of silence, Stefan schooled his face into a polite facade. "How'd you hear about that?" His eyes traveled the room, studying all of Sasha's men and how they were surrounding us. His gaze flicked to Jamie and they exchanged a look.

The man in the gray suit pulled out the chair next to mine. As he took a seat, his jacket opened just enough to flash the gun holstered under his arm. "It happened in our backyard. How could we not hear about it?" he stated, slouching back in the chair before looking at me. His eyes traveled slowly down my body, blatantly checking me out. I tightened my hold on my steak knife, squishing it between my arm and thigh, making sure he couldn't see it. I ignored his wandering eyes by staring forward at Jamie, who was glaring at the man sitting next to me.

"We heard you caught someone from the raid," Sasha said, pulling my attention from Jamie.

"No," Stefan replied, and his eyes locked with mine, warning me. It was only for a breath. I almost missed it. My heart rate spiked as adrenaline surged through my veins.

"Are you sure? I had multiple witnesses say otherwise. Unless you killed him?" Sasha was fishing and he wasn't fooling anyone. I was beginning to think that our truck being hit in Sasha's *back-yard* was a little too big of a coincidence.

"I think I'd know if we captured someone," Stefan replied.

Sasha turned toward me. "Maura, it's good to see you again."

"You two have met before?" Stefan questioned me.

I opened my mouth to speak but Sasha beat me to it. "Yes. We met in my club the other night." He reached toward me and grabbed a piece of my hair, twisting the ends around his fingers. "You have a beautiful daughter, Stefan. How have you kept her secret for so long?"

"I'm a lesbian," I blurted, putting on a stoic mask. "I'm what you call the black sheep of our very Catholic and old-fashioned family." I gave Stefan a pointed look and the corner of his mouth twitched.

"A lesbian?" Sasha repeated.

"Yup. I'm all about the pussy."

Sasha shifted his attention to Jamie, who looked ready to lunge across the table. His eyes were glued to where Sasha held my hair. When he looked up at Sasha, his murderous glare spoke louder than words. Pain was in Sasha's future.

Sasha returned Jamie's glare with a knowing smirk and reached inside his jacket. My lungs seized as Sasha's gun came into view and was aimed at Stefan. The rest of Sasha's men mimicked their leader, pulling out their own pistols and turning them on our men. Jamie shot to his feet, reaching into his jacket, but froze when the barrel of a gun was placed to the back of his head. He was shoved back down into his chair by one of Sasha's guards.

The sound of something plonking onto the table pulled my focus and I glanced at the man sitting next to me. He had taken out his pistol and set it on the table with his hand lazily resting on top of it. In the corner of my eye, I caught his other hand coming at me. I held very still. I was proud of myself for not jumping when he put his hand on my shoulder and squeezed. He didn't hurt me. It was a warning: *Don't do anything stupid.*

Sasha's men made quick work of disarming our security, including Jamie and Stefan. Our guards were pushed down to their knees and made to face the window walls with guns held to their heads.

"I'm going to ask again and let's answer truthfully this time, Stefan. Your men took a man hostage yesterday, yes?" Sasha questioned.

"If you already know the answer, why are you wasting your breath?" Stefan shot back. He sounded so calm, bored even, all while staring down the barrel of Sasha's sleek black pistol.

If Stefan's challenging tone rubbed Sasha the wrong way, it didn't show. "Where is he?"

Stefan's mouth stayed shut. He wasn't going to tell him. If he did, we were dead. As I looked from him to Jamie, I came to the gut-wrenching conclusion that there was a big chance we weren't going to get out of this alive. We were outnumbered.

Knowing all of that, a rush of determination surged through me.

"Maybe one of your children knows where he is?" Sasha moved his gun away from Stefan's head and placed the barrel against my temple. "Would be such a waste," he murmured. Next to me, the man's hand dropped from my shoulder. Sasha's free hand came up under my chin. His fingers forcefully turned my head to look up at him as his gun shifted to my forehead.

His eyes softened before he asked, "Do you know where he is?" Like my father, my mouth stayed closed. "Your father took someone very important to me. He's my blood and I just want to get him back."

He was trying to gain sympathy from me because he assumed I was a weak female. My unwavering silence made him see his error, which in turn angered him. The fingers cupping my chin tightened and the gun pressed harder into my forehead, causing my head to tilt backward.

"She doesn't know anything," Jamie snapped.

"I don't know about that. I barely know her, but I can tell she's clever and an excellent liar. If I hadn't seen you two practically fucking outside my club, I'd believe she was really a lesbian. The women in our lives are not as naive as they appear. They hear things. She could have overheard where he is," Sasha explained. "Your father has warehouses, homes, businesses. Where do you think he's hiding my guy?"

The meanest smile I could muster slowly curled my lips. I could think of a bunch of places Stefan could have the man hidden and I'd die happily knowing Sasha would never find him.

Sasha moved the gun from my head and pointed it across the table. "I'm going to count to ten and then I'm going to shoot your lover..." He shifted the gun toward Stefan. "Or your father unless you give me what I want."

"How am I supposed to answer something I don't know?" I

argued, finally breaking my silence. My heart was beating painfully fast, making my chest hurt. Helplessness and hopelessness were taking root in my soul, making me want to cry or scream out. *Why is this happening?* I looked to Stefan and then Jamie, the two strongest and most dangerous men in my life, to see if they could fix this, but with just one look, I knew they couldn't. It wasn't until that very moment I realized I was scared.

My darkness hummed within me, trying to coax me to let it out, but I felt frozen as I was being reacquainted with a feeling I'd long forgotten.

"One...two...three," Sasha began counting as he swung his gun back and forth between Stefan and Jamie.

The man in the seat next to me chuckled like this was five-star entertainment. He reached in front of me, intending to take a fry from my plate. I eyed his tattooed hand grabbing the fry and then glanced at his other holding his gun loosely. My paralysis broke and my fingers twitched around the steak knife that was cutting into my inner arm from how tightly I was holding it. Sasha continued to count, up to six now. I only had an instant to strike. My darkness rushed to the surface and I swiveled the knife outward, fisting my fingers around its grip. As the man was pulling the fry back toward him, hovering over the table, I lifted the knife. I slammed it down, stabbing him through the hand and embedding the knife into the wooden table below.

He screamed out next to my ear and he frantically let go of his gun to grab at the knife. I scooped up his gun as I sprung to my feet. My chair fell backward and before it hit the floor, I had the gun pointed at the back of Sasha's head. He froze with his own gun pointed at Stefan.

I sensed someone step behind me before something hard pressed into the back of my head. I shifted slightly, seeing one of Sasha's guards behind me, who I assumed had a gun at my head.

With a gun pointed at me, my gun pointed at Sasha, and

Sasha's gun pointed at Stefan, we were in our own unique Mexican standoff. The room was quiet. Well, except for the man I'd stabbed. He had removed the steak knife and was groaning while clutching his bloody hand.

"She fucking stabbed me!"

"Maura?" I heard Stefan say. I didn't remove my eyes from Sasha.

"You underestimated me," I said ever so quietly. My voice sounded so cold and disconnected that even I didn't recognize it. "If you shoot him, I will kill you."

"If you kill me, my men will kill everyone in this room, yourself included," Sasha said over his shoulder.

"You still underestimate me," I droned, void of any emotion. The longer I stood there, the more numb I felt. I'd already accepted death long before this night. However, if I had to watch Stefan or Jamie die, I'd welcome it with open fucking arms. "I'm not afraid to die. Are you?" I pushed the barrel harder into the back of his head. "Because I'm thinking about taking you with me. It'd be quick. We might not even feel it. The next thing we'd know is our two souls being dragged down to hell to pay for our sins."

"I told you this was a bad idea," I heard Jamie say. I was too far gone to pay him any mind. I was going to die. There was no other way out, but I could still try to save him and Stefan.

"Maura?" Stefan said gently. I couldn't look at him. He'd hinder my resolve because this was goodbye.

"I'm going to count to ten," I said, copying Sasha. "If you don't drop your gun, I'll pull the trigger."

"Maura!" Stefan barked but I tuned him out.

"One...two."

"Stefan?" Sasha looked pointedly at Stefan.

"Maura?" Jamie called to me.

Nothing else mattered. Not until Sasha dropped the gun. "Three...four."

"Dammit! Let me go!" Jamie roared.

"Five...six."

"Put down the gun. She'll do it if you don't," Stefan said.

"She just stabbed Eitan," Sasha argued.

"Just do it!" Stefan yelled.

"Seven...eight."

Sasha lowered his gun and set it on the table.

"Nine..." I still counted, finding it hard to stop. Sasha lifted his hands into the air as an act of surrender. I released a slow breath.

"Maura, drop the gun. Sasha did as you asked," Stefan ordered.

If I did that, how would he and Jamie get out of here? Without taking my eyes from the back of Sasha's head, I directed my words toward Stefan. "You need to leave."

"Maura," I heard Jamie. He sounded right next to me. "Baby, look at me." His soft voice pulled at me with irresistible strength. My eyes shifted to my left and found him standing there. "Everything is alright. It wasn't real," he said in a soothing voice. "It was just a test. You need to put the gun down before someone else gets hurt."

"A test?" my voice croaked as emotion filled me and my darkness relinquished control.

"Yes. It was a test to see if you'd crack and give up information," Jamie explained.

My eyes narrowed as I processed his words. My body was slowly un-numbing and my adrenaline was starting to fade.

A test, I repeated in my head. I looked to Stefan for confirmation. His expressionless fucking face said it all. *This was a fucking test!*

My fear and desperation were quickly being replaced by

blinding rage. I moved the gun from Sasha's head to point it at Stefan. He stayed still as stone while his eyes bored into mine.

"You promised," I seethed.

"Maura?" Jamie said calmly, but uncertainty underscored my name.

I shifted the gun slightly and pulled the trigger. The shot rang out, zipping past Stefan's head and through the two-way mirror, shattering it. Screams and chaos erupted in the restaurant.

"Have fun cleaning this up," I sneered at him before I tossed the gun on the table and scooped up my wristlet. I walked out of the private dining room into the chaotic restaurant, leaving nothing but stunned and speechless criminals in my wake.

CHAPTER TWENTY-SIX

I walked around aimlessly. My feet were killing me. My beautiful heels were scuffed to ruin. I decided a break was needed when I came upon a playground in a park. I kicked off my tortuous pumps at the edge of the sand pit surrounding the swings, and that first bare step I took into the cool sand was agonizingly good. Each step after that, my feet sunk deep while being massaged by a million grains of exfoliating dirt. I groaned with relief.

I was rocking gently back and forth on one of the swings while my toes drew in the sand when I heard a car approach. I listened as multiple car doors opened, followed by the sound of gravel crunching underfoot. I didn't look up to see who it was because I already knew.

There had been no doubt he'd eventually find me. I contemplated what I was going to do. When I'd originally made the deal with Stefan, things had been different. I'd had every intention of disappearing if he fucked up by sliding back into his old ways. I had enough cash in a safety deposit box and a contact I'd met at Trinity who could get me new identification for the right price. That was my plan a week ago, but now the thought of leaving...

Like I'd said, things were different. I was different.

Stefan had broken his word and my trust. What was worse, he'd made me feel real fear, something I hadn't felt in a long time. His stupid test had scared the shit out of me because I'd truly believed he and Jamie had been about to die—the two people I loved most in this world. The fucked up thing was that I valued their lives over my own, despite not knowing if they loved me in return. I couldn't really fault Jamie, though. We'd just started whatever it was we were doing, but we still had the love of friendship. Stefan, however, he'd never told me he loved me. Ever. We'd made some progress this past week, but was it enough for me to forgive and forget tonight's betrayal? What kind of message would that send if I did?

In my peripheral, Oxfords planted themselves at the edge of the sand pit next to my discarded pumps.

"It's getting cold out," Stefan said, breaking the silence.

Now that he mentioned it, I guessed it was a little chilly out. Having it brought to my attention, I shivered.

I held my emotions at bay as I looked up to face him. He was standing there with his hands in his pockets, fog puffing into small clouds around his face each time he released a breath. With the way he regarded me from a distance, it was as if I were a coiled snake at the ready and he was hesitant to approach or make any sudden movements, fearing I might strike. It was an unusual look for him to seem so unsure, especially around me. I'd also never threatened him with a gun before. Tonight was becoming full of firsts for us.

"You never allowed me to play at one of these when I was little," I said, gesturing at the playground. His eyes left mine to slowly roam over the jungle gym with a steep slide and monkey bars. "I remember driving past these all the time, seeing kids around my age looking carefree and happy as they played. They had an innocence about them I've never known. I was envious." I was aiming to sound nonchalant, but I couldn't hide the bitterness and resentment I felt.

He listened silently, standing there like a statue until his eyes flicked back to mine.

"You don't make it easy, you know that?" I laughed dryly while shaking my head.

His eyes narrowed with puzzlement.

"You've put me through one fucked up test after another and have made me play too many mind games to count. Do you ever stop to think, maybe you've gone too far? Or are you trying to make me hate you?"

He didn't respond for the longest time, but I could see the wheels turning, or should I say, grinding angrily. I'd successfully pissed him off. You'd think I'd slapped him with how hard his features became. *Good. He should know how it feels.* He'd toyed with me tonight, completely disregarding my feelings and our deal. He'd taken what I'd say was my worst fear and played it out in front of me, torturing me. And for what? To see if I'd break? *Screw him!*

"Everything I've done, or you think I've taken from you, I did for your own good. You don't know what it's like to be a parent. You don't know what sacrifices or hardships I've had to endure to make sure you were safe. So don't you sit there and give me that oh-woe-is-me bullshit, Maura," he snapped, pulling his hands from his pockets to rest at his sides. They opened before they squeezed shut into white knuckled fists, then he relaxed them again. "The innocence you're so envious of is a prison and you should be grateful I freed you from it. To be innocent is to live in a constant state of ignorance and a false sense of happiness. I'd be damned if I left you that weak and vulnerable. We live in a cruel and harsh world. If you haven't figured that out by now, then I have failed," he said, pointing at me, chest heaving. He was struggling to keep his voice calm.

I stopped swinging to listen to him, to watch him because I'd never seen him so emotional. I'd wanted to piss him off a moment ago, in a childish attempt to seek revenge for what he'd put me through, but now I kind of felt bad. Only a teeny tiny bit, though.

"You were just six weeks old when I lost your mother. I was alone with a new baby and had more enemies than I could count barking at our doorstep. If you were going to survive, you needed to be smart and strong." The conviction and pain in his voice made my chest hurt. Even to this day, it still pained him to talk about her. I didn't want to imagine how hard it must have been for him at that time in his life, but he painted a vivid picture.

To calm himself, Stefan took a deep breath. A large cloud of fog formed around him when he released it.

"You are," he whispered, pulling my attention back to him. "You are so smart. The way you read people and situations...you see things that other people don't and you're quick about it. Tonight, you knew right away something wasn't right. I was watching you, Maura. You looked Sasha and his men over and came to a decision in less than five seconds. I watched as you swiveled that steak knife inward to hide it, knowing, preparing." He smiled as he stood there remembering. "Your strength is even more remarkable. You stared down the barrel of Sasha's gun with the cruelest smile I've ever seen, and I've never been so proud of you."

"I don't understand why I was given a test to begin with. What was worth going back on your word?" I asked, allowing my hurt to be heard.

"It's tradition. A test of loyalty. A lot of people break when pressed with fear. I needed to know you wouldn't. Since you're not afraid of dying yourself, I had to find something that would make you equally afraid, if not more. You gave me the idea last night when you were talking with Ian. He betrayed us because of his love for his daughter. You were right, by the way. His daughter is sick. He and his wife couldn't afford her treatment. I decided to let his wife keep the money." He gave me a pointed look, reminding me of the promise I'd made when it hadn't been my place. I'd considered writing Stefan a check to replace the money, but now I felt like he deserved to eat the loss.

"Back to the point." He cleared his throat. "I used your love for Jameson and myself against you and it worked. You were frightened when you wholeheartedly thought we were going to die. It took strength to work through that fear instead of rolling over and giving them what they wanted to try and save us."

"Some fucking tradition," I grumbled, still not seeing the point.

"I test everyone when I've decided they're ready to join the fold," he said. *The fold?* "I even tested Jameson." My brows shot up, curiosity piqued. "It was a similar test. He didn't break, but he wasn't as quick thinking as you were. Nor did anyone get hurt. That was a first and I'm so happy I got it recorded. I'll be showing off the video in next week's family meeting." He chuckled.

My father was certifiable. He was acting how a normal father would act when their child came home with macaroni art and he wanted to proudly show it off by hanging it on the fridge. I hadn't made him macaroni art, though. I'd stabbed someone and he was going to boast about it just the same.

"What do you mean, the fold?" I asked. "I'm supposed to be shadowing."

Stefan pondered for a moment. "I only suggested that you shadow because I wanted to slowly introduce you to this world versus scaring you off before you were ready. I was worried if I offered you a job right off the bat, you'd turn me down. I've always planned to bring you into the business, like I did with Jameson. I've just been waiting for you to be ready, to find the strength I knew you had."

I was stunned, speechless.

"No more tests. Tonight was the last one. I've seen and learned all I needed to know you can handle this. I give you my word as a Quinn."

Should I believe him? I guess I understood why Stefan had tested me. That didn't mean I had to like it. Understanding was the best I could offer. At least he was honest as to why he'd done it, which was a first. My shoulders sagged because deep down, I had already forgiven him. I wanted to give him another chance, like always. I just hoped I didn't regret it later.

Stefan stuffed his hands back into his pockets while shuffling his feet in an attempt to warm up. He noticed my pumps on the ground next to him before he looked back at me, eyeing my bare feet and short dress. "It's time to go home. You'll get sick if you're out here much longer, bare footed no less," he said, holding his hand out to me. It was awkward for him to do that from so far away. Then I remembered where he was standing, just outside the sand pit.

Smiling deviously, I rocked in the swing a little. "I'm tempted to see if you'd ruin your shiny shoes to come and get me," I teased.

He frowned, clearly not finding me funny, and looked down at the sand with distaste. Nope, he wasn't going to do it.

He tilted his head toward his black Escalade parked in the street, which had two of his goons standing next to it. "I have that chocolate cake waiting for you in the car."

I stopped rocking in the swing and my evil little smile dropped. *Well played, Stefan. Well played.*

The chocolate cake was sinfully good. Stefan had bought me a whole eight-inch round and I ate almost half of it on the drive home. Well, Stefan had a few bites. In my defense, I hadn't gotten to eat dinner. When we got home, I cut one more slice off and placed it on a plate before putting the rest in the fridge.

With plate in hand, I walked up to my room to find Jamie waiting for me. As soon as I stepped through the door, he jumped to his feet from the couch and cautiously approached.

"I know you're upset, but please let me explain," he pleaded.

Huh? Why would I...oh.

I had never been upset with him. Looking back, I could see how he'd gotten that impression with how I'd stormed out of the restaurant, not even giving him a second glance. All my anger had been directed at Stefan. I understood what Jamie's loyalty entailed and I'd never held it against him. Clearly he hadn't believed me when I'd explained that to him in the parking lot of Club Anarchy or else he wouldn't be tiptoeing around me right now, looking guilty as hell.

It was good to know he understood what he'd done was wrong, despite having no choice, and I wasn't going to complain about the groveling. The thought of this big, bad mobster begging me to forgive him tickled me in a twisted way. So I thought I might just see how far this would go.

"I understand how fucked up tonight was. Believe me, I really do," he said, probably thinking back to his own test. I wondered if Stefan had recorded his, as well?

He stopped walking to stand a few feet before me. Damn, he was sexy as hell in his suit. Downright drool worthy. It took some serious restraint to keep my eyes up when all I wanted to do was objectify every delicious inch of him.

"You have to know, it gutted me seeing that fear in your eyes and knowing I had to take part in putting it there." He took another step closer, invading my space, and his hand came up to cup my cheek. His eyes were filled with such remorse as they locked with mine, pleadingly. He truly felt bad and I wanted to cave, but I could be stubbornly wicked sometimes.

"What can I do, baby?" he whispered, thinking I wasn't going to relent. "What do I have to do to make it right?"

Ah, shit. I couldn't take it anymore.

Splat!

We both stood in stunned silence as pieces of chocolate cake fell from Jamie's shocked face. His hand dropped from my cheek and I curled my lips inward and bit down to stop myself from laughing. I hadn't exactly been thinking. I'd just reacted, wanting him to stop giving me those damn puppy dog eyes.

His surprise quickly washed away once he saw I was struggling not to laugh. His tongue slipped out to get a taste of the cake coating his lips before his hand wiped most of it off his face. "Do you feel better?" he grumbled. I could tell he wasn't mad at me. The laughter in his eyes gave him away.

"Seeing how I was never mad at you to begin with? Yeah, I feel great."

He nodded before the hand that had swiped away most of the cake from his face came up to mine and rubbed all over my mouth, cheek, and neck. I squealed as he smeared the remnants of the cake on my skin and I fought to hold back his hand from doing any more damage. He outsmarted me by wrapping his other arm around my back, pinning me closer to him before he started rubbing his face against mine. He chuckled evilly as I struggled to get away.

"Jamie!" I laughed, letting go of his cake-covered hand to push against his chest. Stupid move on my part because he just snaked those sticky fingers into my hair to get a better hold. I tried to dip backward, putting all my weight in his arms. He, of course, held me effortlessly.

"You started this," he snickered before his lips slid over mine.

Smelling the chocolate on him, my tongue slipped out and licked at his lips. *Jamie and chocolate? Yes, please!* "Hmm..." I moaned.

He smiled against my lips. "Do I taste good?" he teased, his voice sounding husky. *Oh, yeah.*

My arms went up around his neck and I ran my fingers in his hair, pushing him more firmly against my lips. I deepened our kiss by plunging my chocolate-coated tongue into his mouth and brushed it along his.

We kissed, sucked, and licked at each other until it became too much and we had to break apart. Our breathing was labored. I felt hot and achy. I knew he felt the same from the hard bulge pressing into my stomach. Unable to control myself, I rocked myself against it.

"Maura," he growled in warning.

I bit my lip to keep from smiling. I grabbed ahold of the lapels on his jacket. He let me push him backward until the back of his thighs hit the back of the couch.

I reached for his belt. "There's another place I'd like to lick chocolate from," I said as I undid his belt and pants. His eyes darkened with understanding. I pushed down his pants and briefs and let them fall at his ankles. I grabbed his cake-covered hand and brought it to his cock. "Stroke yourself," I ordered, releasing his hand and taking a step back to watch.

His hand wrapped around the base of his thick member. With hooded eyes, he stroked upward to the tip before pulling back, smearing chocolate cake crumbles and frosting along the shaft. I licked my lips, imagining what he was going to taste like.

My eyes flicked back to his. "Rest against the couch and hold on." He did as he was told. I knelt before him. My fingers slowly brushed against his thighs. Staring up at him, I dipped forward. My tongue lapped at his length, tasting the chocolate cake before I glided him into my mouth, wrapping my lips around the mushroom tip. I swirled my tongue and sucked more of him into my mouth until he touched the back of my throat. Then I pulled back, sucking and grazing my teeth along his sensitive flesh as I went.

He hissed and removed his hand from the couch. I caught his wrist firmly before he could reach me and released him from my mouth. I gave him an evil smile and warned, "If you touch me, I'll stop." I wanted to be in control while I touched him, knowing it was all me making him come undone.

He didn't argue, letting me guide his hand back to the couch. I grabbed him at the base of his cock and licked along his length while staring in his lust-filled eyes, then took him back into my mouth. I sucked, hollowing out my cheeks, and bobbed, taking him in as far as I could while stroking what didn't fit.

His grip on the couch tightened, turning his knuckles white. His chest heaved with labored breaths and when his hips thrusted forward uncontrollably, I smiled around him.

"Fuck, baby," he groaned, and his head fell backward with rapture.

Once his legs began to shake, I knew he was close. I took him in even deeper, to the point that my eyes watered while my hand cupped his balls, massaging them.

His head fell forward to watch me as he swelled and began pulsing on my tongue. Jets of cum hit the back of my throat and I continued to suck on him until his pulsing subsided. Then, my lips released him with a pop.

In a lust-induced haze, Jamie lifted me to my feet and slammed his lips down onto mine. He kissed me so passionately, my toes curled and I melted in his arms.

He broke away and rested his forehead on mine. "I don't think I'll ever get enough of you," he said breathlessly while running his hand up and down my back.

"Ditto," I replied and his body shook with silent laughter.

CHAPTER TWENTY-SEVEN

I woke the next day to the sound of my bedroom phone ringing. I ran my hand down the other side of the bed in search of Jamie, finding it empty. It was morning, but I had no idea of the time. Turning, I reached over to my nightstand and picked up the black corded landline.

"Hello," I mumbled into the phone.

"It's eleven in the morning, Maura," Stefan said on the other end.

Is it? Oh, well. I always slept more while on my period. It was honestly safer for everyone the longer I spent in bed. I rubbed my eyes and stretched. "What's up, Stefan?"

"I'll be home in an hour. Meet me in my study. There's something I need to discuss with you."

Discuss with me? I didn't know if it was just me, but when a parent said they needed to talk to you, I immediately thought, *Oh, shit, what did I do?*

"Okay. I'll be there," I told him, and I returned the phone to its cradle.

As I sat in one of the chairs in front of his desk, my stomach was a knotted mess and my back was stiff. I couldn't believe what I was hearing, and it certainly was not what I would have guessed when I'd met Stefan in his study.

"Do you understand what I'm telling you?" His tone was low and serious.

I released a heavy sigh before slouching back in my chair, deflated by the news. "How sure are you?"

"I'm sure. I just don't know how or why and I'm not quite sure who exactly, but it's either Samuel or Dylan or both."

Please don't let it be Dylan.

"I want you to be the one to look into this. You're still on the outside of the business. You'll have fresh eyes and if you start poking around into things, you'll have shadowing as an excuse and you're most likely to be underestimated if caught. I'm going to provide you with all the books and the flash drive. Those will give you a crash course on how we run our drugs. I'm also going to put my tech specialist at your disposal. He typically doesn't leave his home but is making an exception and will be staying here until we find what we need. He's not really a people person. No one in the family has met him in person apart from Jameson and myself. He should be here any minute."

I was speechless. All I could do was sit there while I processed. Something weird was happening on the drug front of the family business. The money the family brought in had dropped drastically in the past couple of years. Samuel was in charge of the drugs and his excuse was the economy: there weren't enough people who could afford to pay the asking price.

Over the years, revenue had slowly dropped to the point where we were only slightly making a profit. The economy excuse was bullshit because we had no problem selling guns. When Stefan had brought that argument to the table, Samuel had then blamed the government. He'd said cops were cracking down on our clientele and with so many free programs to help people get clean there weren't enough people with a habit to sell to. Dylan was, sadly, backing up all the shitty excuses his father was spewing.

Just listening to Stefan, I could tell things weren't adding up. He'd looked into their bank accounts to see if they were lining their own pockets and lying about making the bare minimum, but there was nothing out of the ordinary. Just the income Stefan paid them. He suspected they had offshore accounts under different names. Without the names, more investigating would be needed, and that required finesse.

Samuel had his own pillar of power within the family, which included a good number of men and spies who were loyal to him. If anyone loyal to Stefan got caught sniffing around Samuel or Dylan, an internal war could ensue, which was why I was shouldered with this task. I guessed this was my initiation.

If Samuel or Dylan were guilty of stealing from the family…

Deep down, I'd never trusted my uncle. Those doubts stemmed from being treated unfairly and how he interacted with Stefan. I'd never thought he would do something that would hurt the family.

Unless he assumed what he was doing wasn't hurting the family. We still made money from the drugs. Just not as much anymore. Maybe this was a ploy to undermine Stefan or dethrone him.

Dylan had to be naive to all this. I was sure of it. Even though Dylan was older than me, he could be weak and wasn't the brightest. He was emotionally driven and easily riled, which could be deadly for a mobster. There was no way he could pull off something like this on his own.

My best theory was that if someone was guilty, it was Samuel. He was the one behind it all and Dylan—if he knew about what was going on at all—was being manipulated by his father. Not that it mattered. He was a dead man walking. They both were.

"This task is going to be more than just reading books and internet hacking or else you would already have the answers you need. I might have to get my hands dirty and with that comes risks. Are you going to allow me to do that to get this job done?" I asked. He refused to let me leave the house without a goon glued to my hip.

With raised eyebrows, he sat back in his chair. "To a certain extent. Last night's test was more than just about proving your loyalty." Just mentioning the stupid test irritated me. I wasn't completely over it just yet. "What we acted out in front of you could really happen. It's a bloody business we're in. We have a lot of enemies and I needed you to show me that you could handle it."

"And did I?" I asked, already knowing the answer, but I'd like to hear him say it anyway. *I kicked ass.*

"Just be smart and stay safe," he drawled, disappointing me. He pushed his chair back and walked over to his liquor trolley. He reached for the painting on the wall above the trolley. Sliding his fingers behind it, he pulled, swinging it to the side on hidden hinges.

In the wall was a sleek black safe with a keypad lock. Stefan entered in a code, unlocking the safe door, and took out two tan leather books with a flash drive resting on top of them.

"The leather books are from when your grandfather ran things. I modernized us by switching to the flash drive when I took over," he explained. As he handed over the books and flash drive, there was a knock on the door. "Come in!"

The door opened and in walked a few of Stefan's personal goons with a young man apprehensively trailing behind. The first few things I noticed about the young man were his shoes and his hair. His sneakers were neon red, which was the only color of clothing he wore apart from black. His hair was bright pastel blue and had a spiky messy style to it. Compared to his pale skin and dark clothes, the two colors popped in contrast.

His age really threw me. He was just a kid. Eighteen or nineteen, maybe.

"Vincent, thank you for coming," Stefan greeted, and I stood from my chair.

"You really didn't give me much of a choice. I still don't see why I can't do this from home," the kid grumbled. I smiled. He had spunk.

"As we discussed, my daughter will be the one working with you, and for her safety, it's best you stay and work together here rather than at your home." He made the word *home* sound like there was something wrong with it. *What is so wrong with where this guy lives?*

At the mention of me, Vincent's eyes traveled to mine. I gave him a schooled expression as I continued to study him. Stefan hadn't shaken his hand, therefore, I didn't either. The poor kid seemed ready to bolt. Not that I could blame him. *How the hell did he get mixed up with Stefan?*

I looked to the goons towering over him and stepped ahead of Stefan. "I got it from here, gentlemen, but on your way out, can you tell Dean I'd like a sandwich and some chocolate chip cookies? Oh! And some French fries and a chocolate shake. Would you like something?" I directed my question to Vincent. He appeared a little surprised by my offer. "You can order anything you're craving. It's lunch time. Unless you already ate..."

Vincent's eyes shifted down. "A sandwich with some fries sounds good," he said in a low voice.

I looked back to one of the goons. "Please pass on our orders specifically to Dean and tell him we'll receive it in my room." I smiled sweetly. One of the goons nodded before pulling out his phone on their way out the door.

"Oh, I didn't want anything. Thanks for asking though," Stefan said sarcastically.

I turned my smile to him and saw that he wasn't at all hurt. "I'm sure Brody already has lunch on its way for you."

"And why didn't you give your food requests to Brody or the kitchen staff?" he asked.

"Angela might be in the kitchen. I don't want skank with my food."

Stefan sighed, slightly annoyed. "What about Brody?"

"Dean is my Brody in training." Plus, I got a twisted pleasure from ruffling his feathers. He was too easy to rile, and it was highly entertaining. Was I being a bitch? Yup, but it was all in good fun. Mine, specifically.

"Maura, he already has a job and that is to protect you."

"He can do both." I brushed off Stefan's protests with a wave of my hand. "Has anyone told him he's been assigned to me yet?"

Stefan paused. "No. I haven't passed on that news to Louie yet and I don't think Jameson has either."

"Good. I want to do it." I turned back to Vincent, who had been quietly watching our exchange. "I guess we better get started."

CHAPTER TWENTY-EIGHT

D ean was not happy, especially after I told him about his new job responsibilities, which he doubted right away and called Louie. Stefan, I assumed, had informed Louie of Dean's new position in between the time we'd left his office and when Dean showed up with my and Vincent's lunch. Dean physically paled as Louie confirmed what I had already told him.

"I wouldn't look at guarding me as a bad thing, Grumpy. It's a promotion," I tried to reassure him while fighting back the bubbling laughter in my chest.

Louie showed up soon after that to take Dean away to go over what his new position entailed. The following day, I found Dean standing outside my room looking like one of Stefan's personal goons dressed in an all-black suit. Gone were his cargo pants and steel-toed boots. He reluctantly got into the routine of watching over me and making sure I didn't starve only after I told him that keeping me alive included feeding me.

Poor Jamie got neglected over the next couple of days. The first night he came to my room, it was late at night. The way he had reacted after seeing I was still up working and not alone had me biting my cheek to hold back from laughing. He didn't even question what we were doing or why Vincent was there. Obviously, Stefan had told him. Instead, he looked from Vincent to me and grumbled, "It's time for bed." Then he pulled out his gun from the waistband of his pants, making sure Vincent got a good look at it, before placing it under his pillow in my bed.

Vincent took that as his cue to leave, scooped up his laptop, and scurried to his temporary room I had assigned him across the hall.

"Why'd you do that?" I asked. Jamie hadn't needed to intimidate the poor kid to get him to leave.

"It's late," he said curtly. *Someone's in a mood.* He wasn't even looking at me. He was focused on unbuttoning his shirt.

I was about to ask him what was wrong, but he took his shirt off. My attention was pulled to his naked chest and my mind seemed to short circuit because I'd forgotten what we were talking about.

My gaze roamed slowly as I took him in, inch by chiseled, tattooed inch. *Man, he's beautiful.* Even with the two nasty scars that marred his velvety skin. I had noticed them in the shower yesterday while I'd washed him. As my soapy fingers had run over the jagged skin, I'd asked him, "Are they dead?" It was obvious they'd been inflicted by someone else, with the intent to kill. It had angered me—I'd felt downright murderous. I'd wanted to hunt down whoever had hurt him and make them suffer. I would take my time with them, drag it out, until their voices became so hoarse from begging for death and then, and only then, would I kill them.

The bigger of the two started on his side just below the ribs and curled around down to the top of the V shape at his hips. It was long, like someone had tried to slice him open. His other scar was smaller, maybe three inches long, and located just under his right collar bone.

As water had spilled down our bodies, he'd run his hands down my back, soothing my rage, and replied, "Yes." *Good.*

He must have gotten the scars within the last six years. I'd seen him shirtless many times before I'd left to attend Trinity in Hartford, be it while swimming, working out, or playing sports, and I wasn't ashamed to say I'd looked. It would've been impossible not to. He'd always been good looking. He'd been a lot leaner back then. Someone had definitely hit the gym while I'd been away. Maybe his scars were the reason for his drool worthy transformation.

Catching me staring, his irritation faded away and he gave me a cocky little smirk. I rolled my eyes at him because if his ego got any bigger, I'd be pushed out of the room.

I turned away and returned to my research. I felt him move through the room and come up behind me. It was crazy how in tune my body was with his. I'd never felt this with Tom. Maybe it was Jamie's magical tongue? He'd reprogrammed me to be in sync with him while he'd been down in Lady Town. I wasn't complaining, but it would explain why he'd driven me to madness with how many times he'd teased me, only to give me the most intense and earth-shattering orgasm I've ever had.

Great, now I'm turned on just remembering it.

I cleared my throat and adjusted how I was sitting, trying anything to bring down my lady boner. I was sitting on the floor with my arms resting on the coffee table with my laptop open in front of me.

He took a seat in the armchair behind me, positioning his legs at my sides, cocooning me from behind while trapping me between him and the table. His fingers brushed my hair away from my neck before his lips pressed where my neck met my shoulder, causing a shiver to rock through my body. "You look flushed," he teased and began kissing up along my neck.

"You make me that way," I mumbled and gasped when he bit

down hard on my sensitive spot. "Are you trying to brand me?" I groaned from the mixture of pain and pleasure.

The next thing I knew, hands slid under my arms and I was being lifted. He shifted me to sit sideways across his lap, with his arm around my back for support and my legs dangling over the arm of the chair. His free hand went to my neck and his thumb rubbed over the spot he'd just marred. "I'm just marking what's mine." I sucked in a breath. His eyes traveled to mine, showing me he meant it.

"Are you mine?" I asked, barely breathing.

His hand moved up to cup my cheek and his thumb brushed over my lips, pulling them apart slightly. "What do you think?"

He kissed the hell out of me by nipping and sucking at my lips. He'd successfully turned me into a wanton mess. Running my fingers through his hair, I gave it a light tug in order to break away from him.

"You're being mean. Lady Town is out of order for a few more days."

He chuckled. "Then get your ass in bed. You need sleep and I need sleep. This shit will still be here tomorrow."

I gave in. "Fine." I squealed when he got up with me in his arms and carried me to bed.

That became our routine for the next three nights. Vincent and I would research all day and Jamie would come in late at night to make us stop.

It took some time to get Vincent to open up. It was literally like pulling teeth, but by day two things got a little easier. He was incredibly smart, especially for someone at the young age of nineteen. His parents had died in a car crash when he'd been a kid and we kind of bonded over it because my mother had passed the same way. He'd lived with his grandma until cancer took her life when he'd been sixteen. Refusing to go into foster care, he'd run away, making money by hacking for anyone who would hire him.

Or if he was in a pinch, he'd illegally wire money into his account. Which was how he'd come to work for Stefan a little over a year ago. Vincent had wired money from one of Stefan's accounts and it hadn't gone unnoticed. Stefan had found Vincent and instead of killing him, he'd offered him a job.

The poor kid had been through some major losses in his lifetime. No wonder he didn't like to leave his home, which I most definitely asked about. Turned out, he lived past the border in De Luca territory. There wasn't anything wrong with his home, just its location.

After three long days, my brain was ready to explode from everything I'd learned. The upside, we got a lead.

We'd begun our research by tearing through the books and electronic records on the flash drive. The books were the financial records of what we put out and brought in from selling cocaine and the ledgers were all dated back during my grandfather's time as boss. The flash drive was the same thing, but dated from when Stefan had taken over.

We received the cocaine from a supplier in Colombia. We paid fifteen thousand per kilo to the Colombians, then turned around and sold it for forty thousand per kilo here in the States. After paying our courier slash smugglers to get the drugs from Colombia to here, the family profited twenty grand per kilo.

That had been the case until about two years ago.

Over the course of two years, our profits had slowly been decreasing down to a profit of ten grand per kilo. The drop of revenue had happened gradually in the first year, starting with us losing a thousand, then two, three, until we'd reached an even ten thousand lost per kilo. The ten thousand had been a consistent loss for the past eight months.

Stefan was right. And it was slightly insulting that Samuel thought he wouldn't be caught. When we'd reached this point in our research, I'd had Vincent dig up all he could on Samuel,

Dylan, and every man that worked under them. I'd wanted pictures, backgrounds, bank accounts, anything that was tied to their name and fingerprints.

Everything we could find on Samuel and Dylan had come up as Stefan had stated. There had been no extra money in their accounts, which just meant they had it hidden under different aliases. Vincent had worked his ass off to find out what they were. I'd learned a lot that I hadn't wanted to know about my uncle and cousin. Samuel constantly cheated on my aunt with high end prostitutes, which I'd already known, but what I hadn't known was he liked them young—eighteen, to be exact. Dylan watched too much anal porn. I could have gone my whole life without knowing that.

Hours of research and I'd known pretty much everything about Samuel's men. It had been information overload, but it had been worth it when Mark Ferguson's file had been the next one for me to go through. He was our lead. Mark was Dylan's head enforcer.

Two years ago, Mark's brother had opened a new bank account. Mark's brother who had been deceased for five years. How did a dead guy open a bank account with routine deposits of large sums of money for the last two years? I had no idea, but I was going to find out.

The amount of money being deposited into this dead man's account wasn't enough to cover all our losses, not even close, but it was enough to be suspicious. Mark was the key.

CHAPTER TWENTY-NINE

Showing off the platinum wig, I twirled around in the costume shop. "What do you think?"

Dressed casually in a T-shirt, denim jeans, and the ball cap I'd bought him at the sporting goods store we'd just left, Dean looked positively bored out of his mind as he watched me.

Last night, I'd realized I wasn't equipped to spy on someone. That someone being Mark Ferguson. The first thing on my list of spy supplies had been binoculars because...come on? *Who spies on people without binoculars?* I'd gotten a pair at the sporting goods store along with Dean's hat. Next on my list was a disguise. "The black wig or the blonde?" Putting my hands on my hips, I stared at my fellow sleuth expectantly.

Dean eyed the platinum blonde wig I was wearing. This morning, before we'd left, I'd gone over the plan with Vincent and Dean. Vincent's job was to track Mark's phone and give me updates on his whereabouts. As of right now, he was at McLoughlin's, a bar owned by the family and one of the many fronts Samuel and Dylan used to conduct business, I'd recently learned. Dean and I were headed there next.

"The blonde," he answered. Without taking the wig off, I ripped off the price tag and paid for it at the register.

Sitting in my parked car at an unnoticeable distance down the street, I peered through my new binoculars at McLoughlin's.

"I don't know what you think you're going to gain from doing this," Dean grumbled from the passenger's seat while scrolling through his phone.

"I already told you. We're going to follow him until something happens."

He sighed. "Whatever you say, Nancy Drew."

"None of Stefan's personal security are mouthy," I murmured under my breath.

Out of my peripheral, I caught Dean's head lift from his phone. "Then you should have picked one of them to babysit you."

Well, there went my good mood.

"Do you think I like having a ball and chain all the time? At the end of the day you get to go home, enjoy your independence of running errands, have the privacy of going on a date, feel the freedom of just walking out your front door without having to *ask* someone to accompany you." I squeezed the curved sides of the binoculars. Envy was a bitter bitch. "I'm sorry you don't like being stuck with me. Just remember your agony is only nine-to-five. You get to clock out. As for me, I'll be shackled to someone else."

He didn't respond to my spew fest. For the longest time, the only noise was the cool air being pushed through the car's vents until he quietly asked, "Why did you choose me?"

I lowered my binoculars to meet his eyes. He was staring at me intently, waiting. "I have many reasons," I said with a smirk. "Mainly, I don't like ass kissers. But most of all, you surprised me.

Underneath that surly personality of yours, you have a moral sensibility I find refreshing."

He scoffed. "Just because I didn't tell Jameson how much you had to drink at Anarchy doesn't—"

"Then explain why you did it?"

He looked away to stare out his window. "Do you want something from this coffee shop? A drink or a cookie?"

Is he deflecting? I wondered as I eyed him. Regardless, he'd surprised me yet again by the kind offer. "A cookie."

He nodded and climbed out of the car. "*Do not* go anywhere," he ordered just before shutting the car door.

Hours passed by at an agonizingly slow rate. Temptation to give up was poking at me like a woodpecker, but I imagined shooting that annoying bird. Dean, on the other hand, was completely relaxed, not bothered in the slightest by being cramped in my small car. Fidgeting in my seat for the thousandth time, I caught the corner of his mouth lifting. The jerk was laughing at my discomfort and probably assumed I was getting ready to cave soon. Unbeknownst to him, I was too stubborn to quit.

Both Stefan and Jamie had texted, checking on me. I hadn't been entirely forthcoming as to what I was doing today. Stefan had said he trusted me to handle this. I wasn't convinced. My gut had told me he would still meddle. So I'd lied by omission and said I was out doing a little shopping.

"Isn't that your guy?" Dean asked, nodding in McLoughlin's direction as I paused in the middle of rubbing my stiff neck. Forgetting about the binoculars in my hand, I squinted in that direction. Sure enough, there was Mark Ferguson crossing the damn street toward his gold '67 El Camino.

I made quick work of starting my car, shifted it out of park, and pulled out into traffic the same time Mark did. We followed him through the city.

"He's getting on the interstate," Dean said, eyes glued to the El Camino three cars ahead of us.

Mark took the ramp heading south on I-95. We passed exit after exit and as we got closer to the Housatonic River, a knot started to form in the pit of my stomach.

"He's heading into De Luca territory," Dean voiced what I had already concluded.

Quinn territory took up most of the New England area. We had family and businesses spread out across the states from New Haven to the top of Maine. Within our territory, there were gangs like the Aryans and other smaller crime families like the Bratva who coexisted alongside us but still paid homage to Stefan. The Italians ruled over New York, New Jersey, and a small corner of Connecticut. The Housatonic River was the line drawn in the earth that separated our two territories and we were about to cross it.

Mark's destination was a strip club called Show 'n Tail in Bridgeport, southwest of the river. *What the hell is he doing here?* I pulled into a spot on the opposite end of the lot from where Mark had parked. Both Dean and I watched as he went through the front entrance.

"It's kind of early for a lap dance, isn't it?" I mumbled.

Dean snorted. "What time of day do you think is acceptable for a lap dance?" His caustic tone made it clear he was making fun of me, but *seriously*? It was one in the afternoon. Wasn't that a little creepy or was I just being a judgmental prude? *Whatever*. My point was, I didn't think he'd drive into another city just for a lap dance.

I chewed on my lip, debating what to do. Movement toward the back of the club caught my attention. Standing by the back door was a couple of girls in robes. They were standing with a bouncer, talking while they smoked. An idea popped into my head and before I lost my nerve, I unbuckled my seatbelt.

"What are you doing?"

I glanced at Dean as I reached for the door handle. "If I'm not back in twenty minutes, call Jamie or Louie." I had the door open and a leg out when he grabbed ahold of my wrist.

"You're not going in there," he said firmly.

"I have to find out why he's here. If—and that's a big *if*—anything happens, it's better if you stay out here and call for help." I shoved his hand off. He let out a frustrated sigh. "It's going to be fine," I said before closing the door.

I approached the girls and the bouncer with a small smile on my face. "Hi." The three of them stopped talking and eyed me curiously. "Today's my first day..." The bouncer didn't even hesitate in opening the door and held it open for me to enter. It must have been the wig.

Stepping inside, I was immediately greeted by loud music and a dressing room with a huge mirror taking up the left wall and lockers taking up the right. I had romanticized what a stripper's dressing room looked like in my head. I'd imagined vanities full of makeup, with lightbulb framed mirrors and racks full of skimpy costumes. This room was barren, and I found myself a little disappointed. I got over it quickly when I spotted a door at the other end of the room. I beelined for it and pushed it open slightly. "The Beautiful People" by Marilyn Manson filled my ears as I peeked out into the dark club. The showroom had dark mood lighting, multiple platforms with poles, a bar surrounded by stools, and lounge chairs and tables strategically placed to view each one of the stages the dancers performed on. I'd only been inside of a strip club once, and that had been years ago with Tina. It had been her birthday. Her friends and I had paid for her to get a lap dance. It had been fun.

Scanning the room for Mark, I spotted him sitting at the bar.

How do I get close without being noticed? Eyeing one of the cocktail waitresses walking the room with a tray in hand, I took in what she was wearing. Black bra, matching boy short underwear, and heels. I was wearing something similar to that. Shutting the door and opening up an unoccupied locker, I quickly stripped down to my underwear and heels. I shoved my shirt and pants into the locker before heading into the showroom of the club.

On my way to the bar, I scooped up a discarded tray sitting on an empty table. Passing Mark, I strutted like I actually worked there to the drink drop off station at the far end of the bar. There, I had an unobstructed view of him. He was alone. The drink in front of him was clearly just for show as it sat there untouched.

"You must be new," the woman behind the bar asked, placing a couple of bottled beers in front of me.

"Yes," I replied.

"Can you take these to table four?"

I glanced down at the beers then back up at her. "Table four?"

She pointed at a table in the center of the room where a group of guys were laughing while watching a dancer swing around topless on a pole in front of them. I hurriedly placed the bottles on my tray and went to drop them off. As I passed out the drinks to the guys, one of them put a dollar in the side of my underwear and asked when I performed. I forced myself to smile at his drunk ass and walked away.

I made the mistake of only staring at Mark on my way back to the bar. My shoulder bumped into someone, knocking the tray from my hands. "I'm so sorry," I said as I started to bend to retrieve my tray from the floor. The gentleman was faster, moving fluidly as he bent over, scooping it up, then returned it to my hands. I gave him a brief once over, not wanting to take my eyes off of Mark for long. His pretty gold eyes and his tailored charcoal suit stood out. Besides that, I didn't pay him much attention.

"Thank you." I smiled genuinely and returned to the drink drop off station.

Setting my tray on the counter, I tried not to blatantly stare at Mark and glanced at him every once in a while. A man dressed very similar to Stefan's personal security—black tight T-shirt with a black suit jacket and black slacks—approached Mark at the same time a bouncer of the club and a dancer approached me.

"You've been requested for a private dance," the bouncer said. *Huh? I thought the cocktail waitresses didn't have to give lap dances!* "Come with me." He turned, expecting me to follow, and left with the dancer trailing behind him.

Fuuuuck! I hesitantly followed. Searching for Mark, I noticed the bouncer was leading me in the same direction he was being led, toward a somewhat private room off to the side of the showroom. *Maybe I'm dancing for him? But why the other dancer?*

Mark disappeared into the private room. The bouncer I was following stopped just outside the open archway and gestured for us to enter. The dancer strutted in there like this was just another day at the office. I supposed it was. Me, on the other hand, I was wondering what the hell I'd gotten myself into as I followed her in.

The private room was small with mirrored walls, an armless upholstered bench bordering the entire U-shaped room, and a pole in the center. Stepping further into the room, we passed the guy who'd approached Mark at the bar. The way he stood guard at the entrance cemented my assumption he was security. Mark was sitting on the right side of the room, body tense despite the at-ease facade he was failing to pull off by a relaxed pose, one leg resting on top of his knee. I could only assume his nervousness was due to the man sitting across from him. Achieving the relaxed look with one arm draped across the back of the bench was the gentleman I had bumped into in the showroom. I recognized his gold eyes right away. How could I not? They were locked on me, assessing me from head to toe.

The first thing I noticed as I actually took the time to take all of him in was that I recognized him. From where, I didn't know. All I was certain of was I had seen him before.

He was Italian. His thick hair and designer stubble were dark as coffee. He had a strong, lean build and a sharp jawline. He was devilishly handsome. There was something about him that put me on edge, though. It was the way he held himself—confident, superior, dangerous. He reminded me of Stefan.

"What do we have here?" Mark asked the man seated across from him. "Are we finally going to get some entertainment during these meetings?"

The man removed his eyes from me to stare at Mark. "I figured I'd humor you this one time." A small yet excited grin pulled at the corner of Mark's mouth. "Mind if I have the blonde?" the man asked.

I glanced at the other dancer's raven hair, confused. Then I remembered I had a wig on. Mark shrugged as if he didn't care either way. My fellow dancer made her way over to him, unclasping her glittery neon green bra before straddling his lap in only her matching neon green thong.

Fucking hell. Am I really doing this?

Mustering the determination I needed, despite the over-whelming urge to run out of here like a bat free from hell, I reached behind my back and unclasped my black bra. *You can do this, Maura. They're just boobs. Just channel your inner stripper and gyrate that ass.*

I straddled the man's thighs, but instead of facing him like the other dancer did to Mark, I went about it reverse cowgirl style. I took in a calming deep breath and exhaled, willing my stiff body to relax. Thinking back to the dancer who'd given Tina a lap dance all those years ago, I reenacted some of the same moves she'd done the best I could, grinding my ass against him as I moved along to the music. After that first awkward minute passed, I started to actually relax. My body embraced the beat and I gave my first lap dance, ever.

CHAPTER THIRTY

Dancing sensually in a strange man's lap, I multitasked by listening in as he and Mark began to talk.

"My delivery is late," the man said.

Mark tilted his head to the side so he could see past the raven-haired stripper currently gyrating her practically naked ass in his lap.

"That's why I'm here. It'll be here tonight. Our boat transporting the shipment ran into a weather issue," Mark explained. He was talking about the cocaine we had coming in from Colombia. According to the flash drive, we were expecting one hundred kilos to be smuggled in. It had cost us one point five million dollars, paid via wire transfer to the Colombians. After we'd paid the couriers, the goal profit was two million. Lately, we'd only been making half of that.

"A weather issue?"

Mark nodded. "A storm. Our boat took damage. Delayed the shipment. Dylan sends his apologies."

"And why isn't Dylan here himself?" the man questioned, sounding put off and the tiniest bit distracted. I didn't think Mark noticed as he was pretty distracted himself with the stripper rubbing her boobs in his face. *Shit, do I have to do that?* I still hadn't turned around.

Fingers lightly touched the tattoo on my lower back, pulling me from my internal debate. I stood abruptly and spun around on my heels. Stepping between his legs, I moved my hands seductively up his chest, around his neck, and into his hair. Straddling his lap, our eyes locked. His golden eyes were captivating and scrutinizing. It was distracting. Breaking away from his intense gaze, I stared through the mirror behind his head at Mark as I rocked my hips over his hardening bulge.

"He meant no disrespect, Nicoli. He's ensuring there are no more delays." Mark's voice held a hint of nervousness.

The name Nicoli made my fluid dancing stagger for only a breath. Flicking my eyes back to the man beneath me, I finally realized why I recognized him. He was Nicoli De Luca, the don, a.k.a. the boss, of the Italian Mafia.

A few days ago, Stefan had handed me a file with profiles of the other crime lords and their top affiliates. I'd briefly looked over each profile. I'd had enough shit to research as it had been, but I'd made a note to go back and intently study them all later. If I could kick myself right now, I totally would. *What have I gotten myself into?*

"What about Samuel? He's the one in charge, is he not?" Nicoli pushed, clearly unhappy. His alluring honey eyes met mine again. I wouldn't have said they were intimidating. Hypnotizing, definitely. They sucked you in, making it difficult to break the compulsion of getting lost in them. I forced a sultry smile and stood again to get back into reverse cowgirl position. As the other dancer and I faced each other, I did my best to mimic her moves.

"Samuel handed the reins over to Dylan. He stepped back into an advisory role." That was a big fucking lie. There was no way in hell Samuel would step down and allow Dylan to run things unless forced. He was too power hungry.

"What time tonight?" Nicoli asked, seeming placated.

Mark outwardly relaxed. *Why the hell would Dylan send him to negotiate with Nicoli?* He reeked of unease. It was clear as day he was intimidated by Nicoli and the don knew it, too. "Ten tonight. Same spot."

"Same amount?"

Mark's hands fisted. "That's another reason why I'm here. Our shipment is double this time. We were wondering if you'd like to take another fifty kilos off our hands? For the same price, of course."

"That's another two million," Nicoli said.

I quickly did the math in my head. *Damnit.* They were selling it to the De Lucas at forty thousand a kilo. Which meant they'd been selling it at our standard price all along. Stefan had been right. If they'd been pocketing half of the profit all this time, where the hell were they hiding all that money?

Nicoli was quiet as he mulled it over. Music from the show-room filled the silence as us girls continued to dance. "I'm going to need time to get the cash. Two days."

Mark smiled, triumphantly. "We'll deliver your regular order tonight. In two days, we'll bring you the rest." That seemed to conclude their meeting. "Thanks for the dance." Mark slapped his dancer's ass. She yelped, jumping from his lap. Without having to be told to leave, she scooped up her bra and scurried from the private room. Mark followed her out.

Taking that as my cue to get the hell out of here as well, I stopped dancing and went to stand. The don's arm quickly snaked around the front of my waist like a seat belt, holding me firmly in his lap. I glanced in the direction of his guard, who had been standing by the entrance during the entire meeting, and saw another had joined him. Both of whom were blocking the way out.

I was caught. I could feel it in my bones. What was worse, I was practically naked. Hell, I *was* naked! There was a saying, never get caught with your pants down. Yeah, I was learning that lesson the hard way.

"You must be new?" He phrased it as a question, as if wanting to draw up an innocent conversation. I knew better.

"First night. Was it obvious?" I asked, keeping my voice calm.

"Only to someone paying attention." His voice was an alluring mixture of low, smoky, and pure sin. Just listening to it, my ears warmed and an exciting rush pulsed through my veins. He'd make a killing as a sex phone operator.

"I don't know if that's good or bad, but you know there's a no touching the dancers policy, right?" I did my best to make my tone seem light and humorous.

"The rules don't really apply to me." He shifted beneath me, his free hand reaching for something. "Besides, you don't work here." Cold metal pushed through my fake hair, kissing my skin just below my left ear. I didn't have to see to know it was a gun. *How did I not feel that when I was rubbing all over him?*

Steeling myself, I drew forth my darkness. I'd never needed it as much as I did right now. As the strongest part of my soul took over, my empathy and my moral sensibility slept, allowing my ruthless side to do what needed to be done without anything holding it back.

A cocksure smirk pulled at my lips as my eyes peered into the mirror-covered wall directly across from us. "I'd love to know what gave me away." I took in our reflection of me sitting on his lap, in nothing but a black scrap of lacy underwear and heels. My eyes met his hovering behind my left shoulder.

He only showed a flicker of surprise at my lack of fear. "Your shoes. The girls here can't afford Louboutin."

Hmm...not buying it. "That's quite a stretch. Maybe I have an unhealthy obsession with shoes, and I need to strip to support my habit?" I arched an eyebrow at him.

"I own this club. I know everyone who works here."

"You could have started with that, instead of picking on my fabulous shoes. Did you at least enjoy the dance? I might add erotic dancing to my resume."

The cool metal of his gun pushed bruisingly against me, forcing my neck to extend to the side. "Judging from your pale skin and the shamrock tattoo on your lower back, I'd say you're Irish. Want to tell me why the fuck you're in my club?"

"Yes, I'm Irish. The last name's Quinn." I relished the surprise he let slip. His eyes bounced all around my face as if finally seeing me for the first time before he reached up and pulled the synthetic blonde wig off my head. My blood red hair fell to my shoulders. "I didn't come in here with ill intent. I needed to know why one of my guys was visiting a strip club that belonged to Nicoli De Luca."

"Your guy?"

I lifted my chin, gesturing to the area of couch across from us. "Mark."

"Yes, I knew who you were talking about. What I want to know is, how is he your guy."

"Now, now, Nicky, I've played nice." I tsked. "If you want answers, you'll point your gun somewhere else. It's distracting and not to mention rude."

"I don't think you understand the position you're in. You won't be leaving here. Whether or not I'm going to kill you or pass you around my men is still up for debate."

I laughed at that. Head thrown back and all. This situation was far from funny, but his intimidation act was hysterical. "I haven't ridden an Italian before, but I do enjoy the food." He released my waist to yank my head back by my hair. I gasped, then chuckled. "I should tell you that's kind of turning me on."

"You don't know when to shut up, do you?" he snapped.

"Save yourself the headache, pull the trigger."

"I wouldn't do that." The voice startled both of us and we both looked toward the entrance. There stood Jamie, Louie, and Dean with their guns drawn at Nicoli's two men. "Drop it," Jamie ordered.

Both guards had their guns pulled from their holsters but pointed at the ground. The sound of two heavy thuds vibrated through the room as their matching black pistols hit the carpet.

Jamie shoved the barrel of his gun into the back of his guard's head, pushing him forward further into the room. "Walk." His voice was impassive. His eyes said otherwise. Louie wasn't thrilled either. In fact, I'd never seen him look so cold, glaring down the barrel of his Glock at Nicoli's other guard.

Nicoli's eyes followed their movements until they were standing before us. His demeanor was sedate while the wheels behind his golden depths calculated.

"Jameson Coleman," Nicoli said with recognition. "Want to tell me why Quinn sent a spy into my club?"

"She's not a spy. She's his daughter," Jamie corrected, eyes traveling to me, taking in my naked state. *He's going to kill me later.* "I don't need to tell you the repercussions if you hurt her."

Nicoli's eyes narrowed at the threat. "I'm surprised. Here I thought you were looking for any reason to start a war."

I looked between them as the hostility in the room grew. There seemed to be a history here I wasn't aware of. The pure hatred in Jamie's eyes was a clear indication of that.

"Why would Quinn send his daughter here?" Nicoli asked.

Before Jamie could answer, I took back control of the conversation. "Jamie." My voice was low but summoned his full attention, nonetheless. Locking my eyes with his, I shook my head slightly, silently telling him I had this. When he stayed quiet, I knew he'd gotten the message. I returned my attention to Nicoli through the mirror. "That's enough talking on our end. If you want answers, you know what you have to do."

Nicoli looked from Jamie to me, noticing the power dynamic. Jamie had complied without question, which had been a relief as much as it had been a surprise. According to Stefan's hierarchy, Jamie technically outranked me since my place in the family was still being determined, but in my mind—the mind of the boss's daughter—no one outranked me except for the boss himself. The power here was mine and I wasn't giving it up.

"The ball is in your court, Nicky."

His eyes held mine, still seeming unsure.

"If it makes you feel better, I planned on approaching you after Mark left. You just saved me from giving you a cheesy pickup line. You have questions. I have questions. Shall we have a civil conversation?"

The corner of Nicoli's lips pulled up slightly. He removed his gun from my head. With his hand still tangled in my hair, I knew he was waiting for me to make the next move.

"Put your guns down," I ordered. Dean immediately lowered his. Louie looked to Jamie for reassurance while Jamie just stared at me, the muscle in his jaw flexed. He was not happy with me. I understood why, but the part of me that cared was smothered at the moment. Reluctantly, he removed his gun from the guard's head and stepped back, with Louie following suit.

Nicoli released my hair. I stretched to my feet slowly and took a step toward my guys. Squaring my shoulders with confidence, I placed a hand on my hip, not giving a fuck what I had on display. I looked between the three of them. Dean's and Louie's eyes wandered, taking in my goods. Jamie's, however, stayed leveled with mine. "Wait for me out there," I said, tilting my head toward the showroom. "I want to speak with the don alone."

"Maura—"

My expression must have stopped Jamie from saying more.

His disobedience made me itch to spill blood. Now was not the fucking time for him to question me. He briefly glanced at my state of undress, which only further angered him. As his eyes met mine again, I saw a small flicker of hesitance within the fiery blaze of his rage. He took a small step forward and in a low voice, he said, "I'm not going anywhere until you put some fucking clothes on."

"Alec, go fetch a shirt from the office," Nicoli ordered as he watched us. The guard next to Louie nodded and rushed out of the room. While we all waited silently for him to return, Jamie and I glared at each other in our usual battle of wills.

When Alec returned, a black T-shirt with the club's logo on it in hand, he went to give it to me. Jamie intercepted him and snagged it from his hand. Without a word, he shook out the cotton shirt and pulled it over my head. I shoved my arms through their designated holes, and he pulled the hem down until it ended at mid-thigh.

"I'll give you ten minutes," Jamie said loud enough for everyone to hear. He glared at Nicoli before he stalked from the room.

I took a seat across the room to face the don and crossed my legs. I masked my face, leveling my stare with his.

His brow narrowed, eyes studying me. "I believe we had a deal. I removed my gun. Why are you here?"

My lips curled slowly into a mischievous smile. "Didn't I answer that already? I believe it's your turn to answer one of my questions."

His features hardened.

"Were you aware Stefan had no knowledge you were a customer of ours?"

He didn't even hesitate in answering. "I had the feeling he didn't. Never really cared enough to find out for sure. They delivered the drugs. I paid Dylan's lackeys. Transaction complete." My lack of reaction seemed to intrigue him. He was trying to get a read on me. *Good luck, buddy.* "Why were you following Mark?"

I also didn't hesitate in answering. "Because our profits have decreased by a suspicious amount. I'm looking into it. Who approached you with the offer to be your pipeline?"

"Dylan." He leaned forward, resting his elbows on his knees, and placed his chin on laced fingers. He stared at me intently, making me arch a brow in question. "You don't intimidate easily, do you?"

"Would you prefer I quiver with fear? I could try, if your ego is in dire need of it. I've been known to be quite theatrical."

The side of his mouth curled up. "Were you really going to approach me later?"

The honest answer was yes...after I'd spoken to Stefan. I didn't know how or if he'd want to proceed with the current dealings with the Italians. As of right now, things were civil between our families. To my knowledge, there hadn't been any *incidents* in years, which was probably due to the arrangement Dylan and possibly Samuel had with Nicoli.

Getting caught put me in a *damned-if-you-do-and-damned-if-you-don't* situation. I was a complication to Nicoli's pipeline to our drugs. As a *family* man himself, he knew Stefan would be cleaning house if I revealed my discovery. This meeting was going to end in one of three ways. One, he could kill us, preventing me from telling Stefan; two, he could inform Dylan we were on to them and Dylan would either go on the run or civil war would ensue within the family. I couldn't let either of those scenarios happen. Which left me no choice but to push for scenario number three. The only downfall...I would be facing the wrath of Stefan. Yet again, I was going to be overstepping.

"Yes. We both know the deal you have with Dylan is over. However, I don't want to lose your business. What if I made you a better offer? Say, thirty-eight thousand a kilo?"

Nicoli leaned back, draping an arm across the back of the couch. "Is this a deal with Stefan or just you? I'd hate to be back in this predicament again. That's excluding the lap dance, of course." He smirked. I would've been lying if I'd said his dark and dangerous appeal wasn't attractive. I apparently had a type because I was already enthralled by a sexy dangerous man in the next room.

"Any deal I make will be backed by Stefan. In fact, I'd love for you two to meet. That way we could solidify our agreement and erase any doubts. A dinner, maybe?"

"Such trust Stefan has in his princess," he said with a slight tilt of his head. "I'll agree to thirty-eight a kilo. Moving forward, though, I want every liaison to be with you. Don't ever send me someone like Mark." His eyes raked over my body unabashedly, lingering on my bare legs. "Also, I want one night with you in my bed."

It was painful not to show my annoyance. "I'm as flattered as I am offended. Like you said, I'm a princess, not a whore. A night between my legs isn't for sale."

"Everyone has a price. Even princesses."

He was right, I supposed, not that I'd sit here playing the *what-would-it-take-for-me-to-sleep-with-him* game. "Thirty-seven a kilo and all future transactions will be handled by me as per your request."

His brows lifted before a knowing little smirk pulled at his lips. "Alright, Princess, I'm a patient man. Let me take you out to dinner and you'll have a deal."

I weighed my options. One dinner wasn't so bad, I supposed. I could keep it professional. That was, if Jamie didn't kill me.

"Fine," I relented, my voice sounding tight.

Nicoli's smirk morphed into a triumphant grin. He reached into his suit jacket and retrieved his cell phone. "Your contact information," he said, holding the phone out. "I'm assuming my new discount will go toward the fifty kilos I'm expecting in two days?"

I stood to take it. To be a little bit of a sass, I entered my personal cell's number under the name Lesbian Princess. "Of course," I assured, handing him back his phone.

CHAPTER THIRTY-ONE

T o say the drive home was an easy one would be a fucking lie.

"Are you going to tell me why I found you naked in Nicoli De Luca's lap?" Jamie's voice sounded strained and his fist was white knuckling the steering wheel.

"Dylan's been selling all our drugs to De Luca. I followed his enforcer to Show 'n Tail," I explained briefly.

The muscle along his jaw tightened. "You found that out by rubbing your tits in the don's face?"

I bit my tongue. The urge to lash back was, well, bad enough to make my tongue bleed. *Don't chase the rabbit.* Yes, what I'd done looked bad. It wasn't like I'd set out to give another man a lap dance. I'd been doing my job. His accusing tone was implying otherwise.

Enraged silence made the air in the small space between us thick enough to choke on. I should have fought to drive myself home instead of allowing Jamie to practically drag me to his car, then shove me into the passenger's seat. I just had to be understanding, didn't I? Pick my battles, as it were. I could sense Jamie needed some semblance of control back. Not to mention, I felt like I owed him, finding me the way he did.

Once we were pulling into the garage, I was out of Jamie's car before he even shifted it into park. A woman on a mission, I walked briskly through the house. Blake and Josh stepped out of the control room as I rushed by. They did a double-take and I groaned internally. I bet I was a sight. I was still only wearing the Show 'n Tail T-shirt, my underwear, and Louboutins. Brody and I entered the foyer from opposite ends at the same time. Pausing in his steps, he gaped at my appearance.

"Stefan?" I asked him, confirming I was headed in the right direction.

"In his study," he replied, eyes following me.

I nodded my thanks and continued on.

Approaching Stefan's study, the hairs on the back of my neck rose. I knew without a doubt Jamie was closing in on my heels. Forgoing knocking despite the door being closed, I barged in not giving a damn what I might be interrupting.

Per usual, Stefan was sitting at his desk. He appeared to be having a private meeting with a stranger sitting across from him. Both of them turned their heads in my direction, startled by the abrupt intrusion. With one glance at my shirt, Stefan's demeanor hardened instantly. Jumping to his feet, he directed his livid attention behind me. "What the fuck is she wearing?" *Whoa, Daddy-O is mad.*

I stepped into Stefan's line of sight. "I am perfectly capable of answering that for myself. *Alone.*"

At the sound of rustling footsteps on the carpet, I risked peeking over my shoulder. Behind Jamie, who was currently glaring a hole into the back of my head, stood Dean and Louie. "Dean, please go get Vincent and grab Mark's file," I ordered. Dean nodded before turning to leave.

Jamie hadn't moved. Like a petulant child, he folded his arms over his chest, blatantly ignoring my request to speak with Stefan alone. "I said alone, Jamie," I bit out, voice noticeably strained.

Louie looked between us. Frustrated, he shook his head. He was wise enough not to argue and left the room.

I had to turn away from Jamie. If I got sucked into his rage filled eyes, I was going to lose my shit. I didn't have time for that. I looked to Stefan and for the first time in probably my whole life, I tried to convey my need for backup with my eyes.

With what sounded like an annoyed sigh, he sat back down in his chair. "Jameson, wait outside."

There was no argument, just the wall-shaking slam of the door as Jamie stormed out.

The stranger stood from his chair, eyes traveling from me to Stefan. "I think I'll give you two a moment." Up until this moment, I had ignored his presence entirely. There was more stressful shit steering my focus. Looking at him now... *Damn*. He was a beast. The muscles on him were huge, bulging, and very apparent as they stretched the fabric of his button-up blue dress shirt and black slacks. He reminded me of a hunky lumberjack or one of those really ripped Navy SEALs you saw on the cover of romance novels. He had the most stunning aquamarine eyes and tan skin that made them pop. His brown hair had a slight red tint and was cut short. The length of stubble along his jaw, chin, and lips was bordering on a beard. He had to be at least six and a half feet tall. By how bulky he was, I swore he could crush someone with a hug.

"Who's Hercules?" I asked Stefan. The corner of the stranger's mouth twitched, and his eyes squinted slightly.

"Your new security," Stefan answered.

"Right." I stepped closer and held out my hand. "Maura Quinn."

My new goon stared down at my offered appendage before his big hand engulfed mine, making it look somewhat childlike in comparison. *Jeez, he's part giant.* "I know," he said, shaking my hand. "Asher King."

I tilted my head slightly, mulling over his words. "I'm so glad Daddy Dearest was able to get someone who was part of the team he hired to spy on me for the past six years."

Stefan sighed again, drawing both mine and Asher's attention. "Is there an issue, daughter?"

"Not at all. Just making conversation. I'm sure he got to see *a lot.*" Understanding my meaning, Asher smirked. *Yup, he's definitely seen me naked.* "When does he start?"

"As soon as we sign the contract. You said you wanted to meet him first. I was just about to call you, but you saved me the trouble by barging in here," Stefan said in an admonishing tone.

Yeah, yeah, I won't do it again. "May I see the contract?"

Stefan's brow furrowed at my request. Scooping up a small pile of papers lying in front of him on his desk, he held them out to me. I took the contract and began reading it over. It entailed exactly what I'd assumed. It went over confidentiality, liability, and expectations. Asher was to take all directives from Stefan that had to do with protecting me. The last page went over contract term, which was a year, and it listed his pay.

Reading back over the confidentiality section, doubt had me chewing on my lip. "Are we sure we can trust him or this security firm?" I asked Stefan. When I first had requested outside security, I hadn't been aware of how far Stefan was going to pull me into his world. "It's one thing to watch over a college girl. It's another to bear witness to everything—"

"Aiden, Jameson's uncle, is the founder of the security firm," Stefan said, interrupting me.

Oh.

That explained a lot. Aiden was Jamie's only other living blood relative. He was ex-military and had stayed at our house a few times to visit with Jamie. He was a recluse, yet a kind man. He and Jamie shared some familial features, like their eyes and stature. After Jamie's mom had passed, he'd had a choice to stay here or go live with Aiden in New York. He, of course, had chosen to stay with us. Due to Aiden's long stints overseas in the military, Jamie barely knew his uncle. Aiden hadn't held Jamie's decision against him. In fact, I'd thought he'd been relieved.

"Do you know why I wanted to hire you?" I asked Asher.

He stuffed his hands in his pockets, appearing lax. "I wondered. You have plenty of security already on the payroll."

I nodded. "As you are aware, my family is...unconventional. I trust few among them. The security we already have are ambitious and eager to move up the ranks. As a woman and the only child of Stefan, I refuse to be used as a stepping stone to get in someone's good graces, my father included. Which is why I'm willing to increase your pay by fifty percent if you sign a contract with me and not Stefan."

"Maura!" Stefan roared, jumping to his feet again.

"You will suffocate me," I snapped. He could get as mad as he wanted. I wouldn't budge on this. "I can't live my life if my security is constantly reporting my every move or my every word to you. I need some sort of privacy and people I can trust, who are on my side. Samuel, Conor, Rourke, Dylan, Jamie—everything they do doesn't get reported to you, so why do you expect that of me?"

"I could freeze your trust fund," he threatened.

Go ahead, old man. "I moved that money years ago," I scoffed.

Stefan set his hand on the back of his chair, grasping onto it tightly as he stared down at his desk. "I'm not trying to suffocate you. I'm trying to keep you safe."

"I know." I understood his intentions. It didn't change anything, though. He was still going about it the wrong way. "You still have Dean."

Stefan frowned. "For now. How long will that last, I wonder?"

It took a lot of effort not to roll my eyes. He was unhappy I'd pulled one over on him. If we were to tally up the number of times he'd done something like this to me, he'd have no ground to stand on. "Do we have a deal, Mr. King?" I looked back at Asher, who had been quiet this whole time.

He pulled his phone from his pocket. "Fifty percent increase?" he asked. I nodded and he began tapping away on his phone. "My guy back at the home office is going to fix the contract and resend it. Anything else you want to change?"

Stefan was still pissed but didn't protest. I sighed, shaking my head. The new contract was sent back to Asher's phone within minutes, and we both signed it electronically.

"Perfect. Take a seat, Thor. This will be the best time to get you up to date on the clusterfuck we're currently facing," I said, taking a seat in the vacant chair next to him and crossing my bare legs.

As Asher sat, Dean walked in with Vincent. I gestured to the couch. "Take a seat, Vin. You might as well stick around too, Dean." Dean nodded as he handed over Mark's file. I passed it to Stefan, who stared at me expectantly as he opened it.

I went over everything from the money we'd found in Mark's deceased brother's bank account to Jamie and Louie showing up at Show 'n Tail, finding me with a gun held to my head and wearing nothing but my panties in Nicoli De Luca's lap. By the tightness in Stefan's jaw, I could tell he wasn't particularly thrilled about my hour as an exotic dancer, but he made no comment about it. With a deep breath, I steeled myself for what I had to tell him next. The deal I'd made with Nicoli.

My body was stiff. I was expecting my impending doom by the time I was done telling him. The room had fallen mute as everyone processed. Stefan leaned back in his chair. With his thumb brushing his bottom lip, he stared absently at the painting over his hidden safe. Shockingly, he didn't look mad. Which was freaking me out.

"Stefan?" I said, apprehensively. His eyes flicked back to me. "If you're debating how you're going to kill me, can you at least not be so calm about it? It's unsettling."

He rolled his eyes at me. "I'm surprised at Jameson. I wonder if he realizes what he did."

... *Huh?*

"What are you talking about?"

"My enforcer just took orders from you, a novice to our world, in a...*pressing* situation and without question. I don't know if I should be proud of you or disappointed in him."

Seriously? I sighed, slumping back in my chair. I was tired. Today had been a whirlwind. Imagining having to face Jamie after this exhausted me further. "When's the next family meeting?" If Stefan wasn't going to wring my neck, it'd be best to move on.

"Day after tomorrow," Stefan answered.

"I still don't have the proof we need against Samuel. Everything we've found all points to Dylan. You and I both know there's no way Dylan could have pulled this off on his own. Vincent is still searching for offshore accounts. All that money they've been pocketing has gone somewhere. I highly doubt they have it stuffed under their mattress—" I palm smacked my forehead. *Why didn't I think of it before?* "Vincent, search for any storage facilities leased just prior to or within the past two years. Don't just look for it to be leased by Samuel or Dylan but by my aunt or another close relation, as well." Vincent nodded, getting to his feet to leave. "If he can't find what we need by the time of the meeting, I have something else I want to try."

Intrigued, Stefan's brow arched. "And that is?"

"I'm Stefan Quinn's daughter. When people hear that, they imagine a little girl." An evil grin grew slowly across my face. "I think it's time to change that.

CHAPTER THIRTY-TWO

Due to his deep seated hatred for the Italian Mafia, Stefan wasn't thrilled about the deal I'd made with Nicoli. Still, he said he would honor it. I came to find out that if it meant keeping myself alive, I was allowed to make whatever deals I wanted. "Just don't make a habit of it, Maura," he ordered.

Putting myself in danger seemed to upset him more than anything. That was the father side of him coming through. His *boss* side didn't hold my actions against me. I did the job he'd tasked me with. It was what he'd expect of Jamie or any other loyal member of this family.

Leaving Stefan's study with Dean and Asher in tow, I wasn't surprised to find Jamie waiting outside. He was pacing the hall, seeming more pissed off than before. Louie was leaning against the wall, arms folded over his chest with a calm yet closed off expression while he watched his best friend. That alone should have warned me of how bad things were going to be.

Noticing me, Jamie stopped his pacing abruptly. Meeting his burning eyes, my heart picked up speed. If we were going to argue, which I had no doubt we were, we should at least do it in private. Dropping my eyes from his, I walked in the direction of the stairs, intending to take our conversation up to my room.

I barely made it into the foyer before a hand locked around my arm. "Stop walking away from me, Maura," Jamie growled, yanking me harshly around to face him. *Damnit, here we go.* "Do you have any idea how fucking stupid that was? Christ!" he yelled while shaking me roughly by the arm. He wasn't hurting me, but his uncontrolled rage still shocked the hell out of me, and I wasn't the only one. Dean, Asher, and even Louie stepped closer to us with unease written all over their faces as they continued to watch. "What if I hadn't gotten there in time, huh?"

Narrowing my eyes, I yanked my arm free from his grip. "I'm sorry I worried you, but I'm not a child. Stop berating me as one," I snapped, stepping backward, needing to put space between us.

"Then stop acting like one!" he snapped back.

Well, shit. That lit my metaphorical fuse. "I had it under control. In case you've forgotten, it was me who got us out of there, not you! So get off your fucking high horse!" And thus, our screaming match began.

"You had nothing under control! You were naked with a gun pointed at your head when I showed up! What were you going to do, hmm? Fuck your way to freedom?" He was so lucky I didn't have anything to hit him over the head with.

A wide-eyed Brody stepped into the foyer from the kitchen. I guessed our heated argument was being heard throughout the house.

I took a deep breath to calm myself. "I'm sorry you had to see that—"

"You're sorry I saw that?" He scoffed with disdain, like he couldn't believe what he was hearing. "Are you fucking kidding me? How about you show a little remorse that you got naked for another man and rubbed yourself all over him!"

"I did what I had to! I won't apologize for that!" *So much for staying calm.* I didn't just chase the rabbit, I outran the bastard straight to hell. Staring at Jamie, all I saw was red. Hell fire red. "What did you think was going to happen when Stefan tasked me with all of this?"

"I didn't expect you to act like a whore!"

I reeled back from him. *Did he really think that?* Why couldn't he see it hadn't meant anything? Did he not trust me or was it his pride that was smarting? Maybe a woman taking charge wasn't something he could handle. "Fuck you! If I were a man, we wouldn't even be fighting about this! It's because we're fucking!"

"You're damn right it's because we're fucking!"

I shook my head, disappointed. He was just like the rest of the men in this family. "So tell me, is it your jealousy or a fractured male ego that's the issue here? Or is it both?"

Jamie went eerily still before taking a step toward me. I stood my ground. What the hell did he wish to gain from his stupid posturing? Intimidation? He knew it'd be a waste of time, just like I knew he'd never hurt me. Dean, on the other hand, didn't seem to feel as confident. He stepped between us, forcing me to take a step back.

Jamie's fevered rage shifted to Dean. The look in his eyes as they locked on my unneeded protector caused an uneasy feeling in the pit of my stomach. "Move." It was one word, but the threat behind it made my heart race.

Dean didn't even blink. If anything, his demeanor changed slightly. He looked ready to take on whatever was to come. Even though it wasn't necessary, his willingness to go up against Jamie again to protect me proved that I'd read him right. I'd picked a good goon.

"You need to back up," he told Jamie as he put a hand to my stomach, gently pushing me back even further.

Jamie's eyes dropped to Dean's hand. It was that moment when things went from bad to worse. I knew what Jamie was reaching for when he moved his hand behind his back. It wasn't just the movement that gave it away. It was the murderous intent that flared in his eyes. As his gun came into view, I pushed Dean's hand out of my way and stepped between them, putting the barrel of Jamie's gun level with my head.

I could feel the nervous shock blanket the room. Asher took a stealthy step behind Jamie. Dean, as if in tune with Asher's thought process, grabbed the back of my shirt. The longer Jamie continued to point his gun at me, the more anxious everyone else seemed to get. As for me, my rage and hurt grew. My eyes held his while I lifted my arms straight out at my sides in a daring gesture.

"Jameson," Louie said, cautiously stepping toward us.

It was the perfect distraction. Jamie's eyes slid slightly left to look at Louie and I took advantage. I smacked his inner wrist with one hand and yanked the gun out of his grasp with my other, disarming him. Before he even had a chance to stop me, I had his own gun pointed at him.

I shoved the barrel into his chest, wanting him to take a step back, but was met with a huge wall of unbudging muscle. "Don't you ever pull a gun on one of my men again."

A twisted smirk lifted the corner of his mouth, like he was laughing at me. "Your men, huh? I think you're forgetting how things work—"

"I think you're forgetting who the fuck you're talking to." I paused for a breath, unblinking as I held Jamie's eyes. "I don't give a shit where you sit at Stefan's table. I am the Banphrionsa. No one outranks me. Not even you."

Silence fell on the room once again despite the large audience we had drawn. Not only had Brody trickled in from the kitchen, but also Jeana and Skank Barbie. I was sure she was enjoying the show. A few goons had come from the direction of the control room. What was worse was Stefan's presence. He was standing behind Jamie with his arms folded across his chest, frowning at the two of us.

Louie took another step closer, putting his hand on Jamie's shoulder. "Let's go for a walk."

Jamie shrugged Louie's hand off his shoulder. Closing his eyes, he took in a calming breath. When he opened them to meet mine again, some of his anger had faded. I thought I saw the tiniest hint of hurt shadowing his rage, but he turned away from me and stormed off.

Louie looked from his best friend's retreating back to me. His shoulders sagged. "He loves you," he said as if that statement alone was supposed to make everything that had just happened go away or make it alright. *If that's true, he has a shitty way of showing it,* I thought, clenching my jaw. Louie must have realized his stupid excuse wasn't reaching me because he let out a frustrated sigh and took off after Jamie.

I glanced around at everyone remaining and grit my teeth. "Why don't you all grab some fucking popcorn and pull up a chair if I'm that entertaining!" I bellowed, startling them, and almost everyone scurried away apart from Stefan, Dean, and Asher. I stared at Stefan as I released the magazine from Jamie's gun and tossed both the clip and gun on the foyer table.

"Do you want to talk about it?" he asked, eyes bouncing all over my face, reading me.

Is he expecting me to cry? I wanted to.

Looking away, I shook my head. It was taking everything I had to hold myself together. *What if I screwed everything up with Jamie?* I couldn't think about that right now. I needed to make it to the privacy of my bedroom first.

Biting the inside of my cheek to help hold my emotions at bay, I pivoted toward the stairs. With each step I took, the burning behind my eyes intensified, causing me to stumble on the last couple of steps before reaching the top. Arms steadied me, preventing me from falling. By the hands alone, I knew it was Dean. Asher's hands were a lot bigger.

Stupid heels! Blaming my clumsiness on them was better than admitting the truth. In an uncontrolled fit, I kicked them off and tossed them as hard as I could. One hit the wall in the hall with a thud while the other bounced on a slim table standing along the wall, knocking over a vase. I watched it roll its way off the table and shatter on the floor. The shattering of the vase shattered my remaining strength. My eyes flooded and hot tears escaped, sliding down my cheeks. Not giving a damn about the mess, I continued on toward my room.

CHAPTER THIRTY-THREE

J amie spent the night at Louie's. I became privy to this information via Stefan. He assumed by telling me that I'd be willing to get out of bed and join him for dinner. It didn't work. Closing my puffy red eyes, I rolled over and tried to bribe the Sandman. I'd sent Dean and Asher home hours ago. I wasn't planning on going anywhere and there was no need for them to hang around outside my bedroom, hopefully not listening to me cry. I wanted to be alone.

I heard Stefan sigh. "Men act stupidly when they're jealous."

I turned over slowly and glared at him. "Are you making excuses for him?"

Stefan shoved his hands into his pockets. "No. I think you're both being stupid."

"He's not just jealous. He expects me to be a demure and submissive woman, like all the rest of the assholes in this godforsaken family. If Louie or Rourke had done what I did, or hell, even slept with someone for information, they'd get a high five or congratulated for a job well done. Me, oh no, I get shamed and called a whore." *It's bullshit!*

"I'm not going to coddle you, Maura—"

"I never expected you would." I was snappy and acting bitter. He didn't deserve it, but he was starting to get on my nerves.

With pursed lips, he gave me a displeased look. "You're allowing your desperate need for acceptance to cloud your judgment."

"Thanks for the pep talk, Stefan. I feel so much better," I drawled caustically and flopped onto my back to glare up at the ceiling.

Stefan turned to leave, muttering something about me being impossible and stubborn under his breath.

I stared at the stupid ceiling all night. The Sandman was giving me the middle finger. I itched to run my hand down Jamie's side of the bed. I was so mad at him but missed him more than my heart could handle. I had gone over our fight a hundred times in my head and taken apart everything that had been said word by word until my brain couldn't take it anymore. Could we get past this? Did I want to? If he wanted a submissive woman then we wouldn't work. I couldn't suppress who I was to save his ego. No matter what I felt for him, I just couldn't.

There was a knock on my door come morning, or at least I assumed it was morning. I hadn't been able to fall asleep until the sun had started to peek through my curtains. So it could have been afternoon for all I knew. By how tired I felt, though, it sure as hell still felt like it was morning.

"Go away!" I growled and smushed my face deeper into the mattress. The door to my bedroom opened and I groaned. "Leave me alone, Dean."

"Guess again, doll."

I rolled my head to the side and found Asher standing next to my bed, smirking down at me with a mug in his hand. I scowled at him before turning my head back the other way, willing myself back to sleep.

"You better get up. Dean is bringing your breakfast."

"I don't eat breakfast. Dean knows this."

"Your father said you didn't eat dinner last night and according to Dean, all you ate yesterday was a cookie. By everyone's lack of surprise, I'm guessing starving yourself is a known issue with you?"

"Fucking hell, you're chatty in the morning," I snapped, pulling a pillow over my head.

"You not eating isn't going to work for me. Starting today, you will be eating at least three meals a day."

I snorted. *Good luck with that, buddy.*

"Knock, knock," a voice said with a little tap on my door.

What now? I pushed my tired body up to a sitting position. From what I could see hanging down my chest, my hair was a tangled mess. I was only wearing a baggy shirt, boy shorts, and fuzzy tube socks. My feet had gotten cold last night. My eyes were burning and felt like sandpaper was scraping across them every time I blinked. They were undoubtedly still puffy and bloodshot. I glared at the second person to disturb my sleep.

Vincent stood in the doorway with his laptop open in his arm. He took in my grumpy and disheveled appearance with wide eyes. "Sorry, your door was open. I thought you were awake. I can come back," he said sheepishly and took a step backwards.

"You might as well join the party, Vin. I have a feeling I'm up for the day," I grumbled. Vincent nodded and made his way for the couch while I eyed the coffee mug in Asher's hand. "Is that for me?"

Asher held out the mug. *Thank fuck.* I took the mug from him and took a sip. It was just how I liked it. I assumed Dean had prepared it. I'd been training him for the past couple of days on how to make me the perfect cup of coffee. If I was going to make it through the day without falling over, I was going to need about ten refills.

Both Vincent and Asher watched as I took five more sips, then sighed. "What's going on, Vin? Did you find anything?"

He shook his head. "No storage units, containers, or lockers registered to Samuel, Dylan, or any close relation. But I decided to broaden the search on our storage theory. Like a home safe. A really high-tech home safe." He grinned like a cat who'd caught the canary.

"You found something?" I asked and clambered out of bed, careful not to spill my coffee. I made my way over to sit next to him. Asher followed and took a seat in the chair. I caught Vincent staring at my bare thighs. My shirt only went to mid-thigh. He cleared his throat and looked down at his computer with rosy cheeks.

"Yeah. Just over two years ago, Samuel hired a personal security contractor to set up and update security systems in pretty much every property owned by the family. Businesses, warehouses, homes, your house included." I nodded to show him I was following. "The contractor your uncle hired is famous for his state-of-the-art panic rooms and home safes." My brows rose, finally seeing where this was going. "I was able to track down an invoice emailed to your uncle. It didn't specify what was done exactly, but it did list parts ordered, labor, and a broken-down cost list associated with each property."

"Did anything stand out?"

"Two properties. Your uncle's house and a warehouse off of Stone Street. The cost and work done was astronomical compared to everywhere else."

My stomach sank. "The warehouse off of Stone Street just before the highway?"

Vincent's brows shot up. "Yeah. Have you been there recently? Seen anything out of the ordinary?"

I shook my head. I hadn't been to that warehouse in seven years. I released a shuddering breath and set my now empty mug on the coffee table. "Can you send me that invoice to look over?" I asked. He nodded. "Good work, Vin." I stood tiredly. "I'm going to get ready for the day and pass everything you've found to Stefan."

"Speaking of Stefan," Vincent started. "He signed all the checks to that contractor."

I sighed. "I'm sure he's going to be thrilled to find out he footed the bill so my uncle and cousin could steal from him." Today was going to suck. I could already tell.

Stefan was out of the house until almost dinner time. Alone in his study, we went over what Vincent found. I supplied him the invoice with my uncle's address and the warehouse address highlighted. After reviewing it, he frustratedly tossed the invoice on his desk and slumped back into his chair. He did nothing to hide the mixture of pissed off and possibly hurt he was feeling as he stared off into space.

Crap, now I felt like an insensitive ass. I'd been so determined to prove my uncle was guilty, I didn't stop for a minute to think of how his betrayal might be affecting Stefan. Even though Samuel was a dick, he was still Stefan's brother.

I stood from my chair. His eyes caught my movement and followed me as I made my way around his desk. He swiveled his chair to the side, reading my intentions. I took a seat in his lap and hugged him. "I'm sorry, Daddy," I whispered. His body was tense at first. He slowly relaxed, then tightened his arms around me.

Stefan and I left his study together around dinner time. We ran into Asher in the foyer. He was waiting on Dean and Vincent as they made their way down the staircase.

I held back with them while Stefan continued on towards the dining room. "I don't plan on going anywhere for the rest of the night if you guys want to take off?" I said. Dean and Asher took me at my word and both left, leaving Vincent and I alone. He fiddled nervously with the hem on one of his sleeves. He was invited to dine with us tonight before one of Stefan's goons drove him back home after. Up until tonight, we'd been taking all our meals in the sanctuary of my room. Sadly, our partnership was coming to an end and it was time to rejoin civilization. At least for me it was. I slung an arm over his shoulders, hoping to provide comfort. "You can sit by me."

Entering the dining room, we were greeted with a feminine giggle. My steps faltered. Stefan was seated at the table, wearing a frown as he stared across the room at the couple standing by the liquor hutch. Except it wasn't a couple, or they shouldn't be, because Jamie was mine, not Angela's. By the body language alone, they could have fooled me.

There was very little space between them as his hand was rested intimately on her hip. They were smiling as they talked in hushed tones. The way they looked at each other made it seem like the rest of the world didn't exist. Jamie reached out to grab a lock of her golden hair, twisting it around his finger as he leaned in to kiss her cheek. When she blushed, something in me fractured, sending all the pain straight to my heart.

I went dark. I not only let my darkness surface, I relinquished everything to it. My will. My sanity.

I stormed towards Skank Barbie, fisted my hand around her beautiful golden hair, and yanked her backwards to the floor. She let out an ear piercing shriek. Still holding her hair, I straddled her stomach on the floor and just started swinging. I delivered closed fisted punch after punch. I barely registered my knuckles splitting, but I definitely felt her nose crunch. It gave me a fucking high. It made me wonder what else I could crush. I released her hair to wrap both hands around her neck and squeezed until the muscles in my arms shook.

"Maura, that's enough," I heard Stefan say. I ignored him. "Alright, Jameson. You may intervene."

Arms wrapped around my waist and ripped me off of her. *No!* I kicked and struggled. I dug my nails into the arms around me, drawing a hiss from my captor.

Stefan stepped into my line of sight, blocking my view of Skank Barbie, who I thought looked a lot better with a bloody face. "Take a deep breath," he ordered.

I didn't want to listen to him. I wanted to kill her. Bleed her dry as I watched her pain and fear. So I fought by kicking and hitting. My captor grunted when I landed a kick to his shin and my hand smacked flesh behind me.

"Maura!" Stefan roared, startling me. "Regain control."

I didn't want my control back. Be it a split psyche or a split soul, regardless, my other half was doing what it was created for. To protect me from what I couldn't handle. I didn't want to face the reality that another man had betrayed me. Except this wasn't just another man. This was Jamie. The last person I'd ever assumed would hurt me. I trusted him more than anyone. I love —no. I wouldn't say it and I'd never admit it. There was only one thing in common between my relationship with Tom and what I'd had with Jamie. Me. I was the reason they'd left me. If Jamie could do this to me, it proved it.

Stefan stood before me, refusing to back down until I did. *Damn him.*

With no other choice, I relented. While holding my father's eyes, tears pooled in mine. My pain surfaced first, slowly followed by everything else. Rage. Sadness. The longer my sight was cut off from Angela the more in control I felt. I looked over Stefan's shoulder and saw Vincent standing by the dining room entrance. He was wide-eyed and his face was a little pale. With

Stefan and Vincent in sight, that told me Jamie was the one holding me.

I grit my teeth. "Put me down." Stefan looked over my shoulder and nodded at Jamie, who slowly released me. I stepped away from him, still giving him my back. "I warned you," I said over my shoulder, refusing to look at him. He didn't deserve to see me like this. "If you touched her, I'd kill her. You're lucky Stefan let you stop me, or she would be dead." I took in another calming breath, but it was futile. "Whatever we had, it's over. I don't want to fucking see or speak to you again." I glanced at Stefan. The shift of my eyes caused the tears to fall. He was hiding what he was feeling as he watched them roll down my face and drip off my chin. "Get your whore out of my house." It was the last thing I bit out before I stormed out of the room.

I had to leave the house. I couldn't be there with him and I didn't want Stefan hunting me down to talk about it either. So I left. I got in my car and drove around for a while until I found myself at Louie's. Jamie's old condo. I didn't know why I'd ended up there. Maybe I just needed a friend. I sent a quick text to Stefan telling him where I was, then decided to send a text to Dean and Asher as well. That way I'd hear zero bitching later for running off on my own.

I numbly knocked on Louie's door, ignoring the sting of my split and swollen knuckles. I'd been crying nonstop and had no doubt I looked like it. At the moment I couldn't find it in me to care.

Louie opened the door, surprised to see me. He took one look at me and pulled me into his arms. After crying for so long, thinking I had no more tears left, another dam broke within me and I sobbed into his chest.

He scooped me up, carried me inside, and held me until I calmed down. Once I was able to speak without hiccuping, he quietly listened as I told him what had happened. We were sitting on his couch in his living room. I was curled up, hugging a decorative pillow, while he sat hunched over, feet planted on the ground with his elbows perched on his knees. He occupied himself by picking at the label of a beer bottle he had been drinking before I'd showed up.

"Are you going to offer me one of those?" I asked.

He smiled down at the bottle. "I think you need something stronger than this."

"I think you're right."

He jumped to his feet and made his way into the kitchen. I heard cabinets opening and closing before he returned with a bottle of whiskey and two glasses.

"Didn't you challenge me to a drinking duel?" He winked, handing me a glass. That was right. When we'd gone to lunch at Paco's Tacos, he had called me a lush and I'd told him I could drink him under the table. In true Louie fashion, he'd taken that as a challenge.

"It wasn't a challenge. I was stating a fact."

His eyes filled with mirth as he filled our glasses. "Shall we find out?

CHAPTER THIRTY-FOUR

Sitting on the floor with our backs leaning against the couch, we laughed at each other. We'd attacked Louie's unopened whiskey like a couple of true Irishmen. The bottle was down to its last inch of amber liquid and I was beyond buzzed. I'd passed that happy-giggling stage so quick, I hadn't even gotten a chance to enjoy it before I'd been in the I-can't-feel-my-face drunk stage. I refused to let it show. I had a competition to win, after all. Sure, the world kept tilting, but as long as I kept reminding myself to stay sharp, I was able to reel a little bit of myself back to lucidity.

"Craziest place you've had sex?" he asked, slurring a little bit. This was the game we'd been playing. Well, it had started off as *would you rather.* The more we'd drunk, the harder it had become to think clearly and thus our game had turned into risqué questions.

My loopy smile fell. I had gone almost an hour without thinking about Jamie. Now here I was, my head consumed with thoughts of him. He'd hurt me but I still loved him. *Crap!* I vowed to never admit it. *Stupid whiskey.* "My father's garage in Jamie's car while being watched by a bunch of goons eating popcorn," I answered, drone-like.

He grimaced, obviously recalling the time he'd caught us.

"Your best sexual experience?" I asked, taking a big gulp, finishing off the amber liquid in my glass.

He scrunched his nose as he refilled my glass, then topped off his. "I don't think you want to know that," he said. "It involves Jameson."

I didn't think I blinked for a whole minute. My poor drunk brain was overloaded with dirty visuals and questions. *Did they sleep together?* "Now I'm dying to know."

Louie studied me for a moment. His cheeks were flushed, and he had hooded eyes—the kind you got when you were past-the-point-of-no-return drunk. "Are you sure?"

Oh, you bet your perfectly tight ass I am. Bring on the hot mobster on hot mobster action. I played it cool by smiling. He took a sip of his whiskey before releasing a breath through parted lips, amping himself for what he was about to say, then turned back to me. "It was about a year ago. Jameson was going through a shitty time. I knew the best thing for him was to blow off steam and hit the bar. We drank a lot and by a lot, I mean we didn't even know we were taking home the same girl until the three of us were climbing into the same cab. Not wanting to ruin the night for each other, we brought the girl back here and shared her."

I was too intoxicated to contain my burning curiosity. "How did you share her?"

He tried to give me a cocky smirk but failed. Instead, I got a drunk goofy smile. "You want details, huh?"

I nodded.

"It started on this couch," he began, patting the center cushion. "Jameson was sitting right here, and the girl got on her knees to suck him off while I watched."

It slightly irritated me to hear about another woman blowing

344

Jamie, so I envisioned it was me instead. The tiny voice of reason in the back of my head was telling me that it was a bad idea. I took another sip of whiskey to drown it out.

"Once she was done on her knees, she pulled Jameson's pants down to his ankles, stripped off her dress and straddled him. Refusing to leave me out, she looked over her shoulder at me and like the dirty girl she was, she gave me the come hither crook of her finger. I slid into her from behind and she rode us both."

"Rode you both," I repeated in a daze. I felt the need to fan myself. Picturing the three of them together—the three of *us* together...*holy hell.* I knew what it felt like to have Jamie inside me as I rocked my hips. Imagining Louie as his bare chest molded along my back had my eyes glazing over, desperate not to lose the scene playing out in my head. Louie's hard cock would slide between my ass cheeks, probing at my back entrance, threatening to take me where I'd never been taken before while I moved back and forth, grinding myself on top of Jamie. I squeezed my thighs together to help ease the throb between them.

Louie stared at me with a slight tilt of his head. "Have you ever done anal?" he asked, eyes dropping to my lips, then back up to my eyes.

In the past, the thought of anal had turned me off, but envisioning Louie taking me from behind felt like a forbidden fantasy. I shook my head.

"Does it make you hot hearing about me and Jameson sharing someone?"

I gave him a slight nod. If I hadn't drunk enough liquid courage, I doubt Sober Me would have ever answered that.

His sapphire eyes darkened at my response and he scooted closer, erasing the space between us. "Would it turn you on if I told you we took turns with her for the rest of the night, barely getting a minute of sleep, while the other watched?" Lips parting slightly, my breathing began to pick up. His hooded eyes dropped to them. "The second time we shared her, I bent her over, slammed myself into her pussy while Jameson shoved his cock between her lips to fuck her mouth." His hand came up to cup my cheek, thumb brushing across my bottom lip. "You have to stop looking at me like that, babe."

"Why?" My voice shook.

"You've been drinking. I've been drinking. We're not think-ing...just feeling," he said, inching his face closer to mine.

"I like what I'm feeling," I whispered, licking my lips, sliding the tip of my tongue across his thumb in the process.

That seemed to snap the tethers holding him back and his lips molded against mine. He nipped at my bottom lip, coaxing from me a breathy moan. Taking advantage of my parted lips, his tongue glided into my mouth. He tasted good. Like warm whiskey.

His hand made a slow descent from my cheek, fingers gently exploring as they went. They tickled my skin as they trailed down my neck, caressed over my breast, and curved around my hip. He pulled me closer. Without breaking our kiss, I straddled his lap. He grasped my hips with both of his strong hands and rocked me over his hard shaft. I whimpered. The movement caused a delicious friction against my core, leaving me wanting more.

Things were quickly becoming heated. Our kissing turned frantic and rough. Until something changed. His lips ripped away from mine. "I can't." He squeezed his eyes closed before dropping his head back to rest on the couch cushion with a frustrated sigh. I froze on top of him. Being drunk could help numb a lot of things, but not the sting of rejection. As if sensing the change in me, his head popped back up to look at me. "No." Both of his hands cupped my cheeks. "I want you. Believe me, I really do," he assured. "But fuck, I can't hurt him. Jameson loves you. He's always loved you and as much as I want you for myself...he's my best friend," he said, ending on a pleading note, willing me to understand.

I did. We were both drunk and had allowed our hormones to take control. I was hurt and angry with Jamie, but no matter how bad I felt, I'd never want to come between them.

"That's good to know," a voice said from behind me, startling us both. Louie's eyes widened when they saw whoever was standing behind me. I peeked over my shoulder apprehensively. Standing by the front door, which was currently wide open, was Jamie. He held an unreadable mask as he stared down at us.

"How long have you been standing there?" I asked, anger seeping into my voice. The longer I looked at him, the more the memory from this afternoon replayed in my head.

"Does it matter?" His voice was calm, giving away nothing as to how he felt.

"You're right. It doesn't matter," I bit out and stood from Louie's lap. The world tilted, causing me to tilt with it. I caught myself on the couch. Once I was sure footed, I scooped up my phone and purse.

"What are you doing?" Louie asked, watching me from the floor.

"Going home." I scrolled through the notifications on my phone. Dean had texted me saying he was outside if I needed him. *Perfect!* That saved me from calling a car service. I stepped towards the front door to leave, but Jamie hadn't moved and was blocking my exit. "Please, move," I said to his chest, refusing to look at him. He was dressed casually in jeans and a black long-sleeved shirt. He looked sexy as hell, like always. I hated it.

"You can't drive. We drank an entire bottle of whiskey," Louie argued, then groaned as he rubbed down his face with his hands. "I'm fucked up. Which means you're definitely fucked up."

"I'm not driving. Dean's outside," I said, placing my hand on the wall to prevent myself from falling over.

"Give us a minute?" Jamie asked, staring at Louie.

They seemed to do that silent communication thing until Louie eventually nodded. He got to his feet, stumbling on his way up. "Take all the time you need, man," he said, shuffling into his bedroom, and shut the door. Jamie kicked the front door closed with his heel and leaned against it with his arms folded across his chest.

Fuck my life! I angrily tossed my purse on the couch before plopping down on it. Hunched over with my elbows resting on my knees, I rubbed at my temples. I was too drunk to deal with this shit right now. "What part of me not wanting to see or speak to you again did you not understand?" He stayed silent as he continued to stare at me. "Why the hell are you even here, Jamie?"

"Stefan said you were here."

I scoffed, shaking my head. "Wow, talk about answering without actually fucking answering."

"I don't want to fight with you anymore, Maura."

"Then why are you here! What do you want?"

"Is it so hard to believe that I'm here for you?"

"Is that so?" Skeptical, I narrowed my eyes. "Where's your new whore?"

An angry fire lit in his eyes. It was the first glimpse of emotion he'd let slip since he arrived. "There's nothing going on between me and Angela. There never has and never will," he declared with such conviction, it was almost convincing. Almost.

I leaned back against the couch, exhausted. Closing my eyes for only a moment, I got the spins. *Bad idea. Abort! Abort!* Vomit threatening to erupt from my stomach like a volcano made me sit back up. I took a breath in through my nose and out through my mouth. *Please don't throw up.*

"Did you know the De Lucas are who killed my dad?" Jamie asked. I'd known his father was killed during a turf war, but I hadn't known who'd been responsible. "Things have been hostile between us and the Italians for generations. Nicoli's uncle Giovanni, the don before him, was who put the hit out on my dad. One of Giovanni's enforcers hid in the backseat of my dad's car and shot him in the back of his head."

"I'm sorry." I truly was. I understood what it was like to lose a parent and grow up not really knowing who they were. "Did the family or Stefan...I know he wasn't the head of the family at the time, but did we get back at them?"

"Stefan took out the enforcer and mailed him back to Giovanni piece by piece." Jamie smiled a little. "If you ever wondered where you get your sick sense of justice, look no further."

Remembering how I had threatened Stefan to do the same to Angela had me fighting back my own small smile. That explained why he'd looked proud instead of mad. "I'm surprised he didn't go after Giovanni."

Jamie's tiny smile fell. "At the time Giovanni was too protected. Then you were born, Stefan lost his wife, and he took over the family. It was one thing after another that prevented him from going after Giovanni and over time, things settled down. With you still being a child, despite his best efforts to keep you hidden and protected, Stefan didn't want to risk another war between the two families. It was when I came to live with you he passed the revenge torch to me. As long as it didn't lead back to the family, Stefan would train me and teach me everything I needed to know to go after Giovanni."

"And did you—wait..." Giovanni had been killed just before I'd left for Trinity. "I asked you if Stefan had anything to do with Giovanni's death and you told me no."

"Stefan didn't kill Giovanni. I did," he said. "I left zero evidence that would lead back to the family."

I shook my head. "They still suspected us. We lost men. There was even talk of marrying me off to the De Lucas to broker peace.

Jesus, Jamie, I'm happy you got your revenge but shit!" I would have killed myself if Stefan hadn't given me his word he wouldn't go through with it.

"Stefan shot that idea down the moment it was brought to the table. Hell, he threatened to shoot the next person to ever suggest it again."

I went back to rubbing my temples. That time of my life had been a huge cluster fuck and it hurt my head just thinking about it. "Is there a point? Why are you telling me all of this?"

"When Dean called me yesterday and said you were in De Luca's club, I was so fucking scared I wasn't going to get to you in time. Then I get there and find that not only are you naked, but you just got done giving the enemy a lap dance." Nostrils flaring, he took in a deep calming breath.

"I didn't have a choice. I was posing as a waitress. De Luca took one look at me and knew I wasn't supposed to be there. Then I was requested for a dance. At first, I thought it was Mark who requested me because we were headed towards the same room. It wasn't until I got there that I realized it was De Luca who requested me and by that point I didn't have the option of leaving. He had a guard at the door. I was outnumbered and unarmed. I hated every minute of it, and it killed me knowing it was going to hurt you."

With a furrowed brow, he nodded curtly. "I know. If it had been someone else, I still would have been pissed, but...the way he looked at you. He wanted you. He had touched you and I couldn't handle it."

"You were jealous, and it set you off even more because it was De Luca?" I asked, clarifying.

He gave me another curt nod.

"You called me a whore," I seethed, making him wince.

I dropped my eyes to the floor. What was I supposed to do with this information? Forgive and forget? Just because he hated

De Luca didn't excuse how fucking badly he'd made me feel. How was he going to react when he found out I had a date with the don? Was he going to lose his shit again and we'd be right back where we started? Not to mention what had happened today with Angela. Should I believe there was nothing going on between them? Then why had he touched her? Kissed her? This whole situation was fucked.

My eyes bored into the carpet, feeling hopeless. Feet stepped into my line of sight and Jamie knelt before me. His hands cupped my face, gently lifting my head to face him. "I'm so sorry, baby. I didn't mean any of it. I didn't know how to handle what I was feeling, and I lashed out."

I looked back and forth between his hazel eyes, reading the sincerity in them. "What about Angela?"

His jaw clenched and his hands dropped from my face. "What about her?"

"Explain what the fuck that was—what I saw?"

This time his eyes dropped to the floor. "Nothing happened. I was still pissed. She was there. I knew you were coming. All I did was whisper in her ear. That's it. I wanted you to understand what I was feeling."

My spine went ramrod straight as I sat there barely breathing. I would've sworn I was dying if my fucking heart hadn't hurt so much. A part of me wanted to shut down, block out the world and let myself break or cry, anything to ease the pain. The other part of me wanted to lash out, set the world on fire, stoop to his fucking level. Seeing how I wasn't in the best place to fall apart...

I pulled my phone from my purse and sent a text to Dean, telling him I was coming out before I stood, slinging my purse over my shoulder. Jamie stood with me, eyeing my purse, then he stepped in front of me. "I know I fucked up, but you have to know—"

"Do you know the difference between me giving De Luca a lap

dance and you pretending to be interested in Angela? I didn't purposely set out to hurt you. I forgive you for yesterday. Couples fight. There's no escaping that, but today...you knew that would fucking gut me. Tom cheating on me messed with my self worth. You, though, fucking destroyed it, along with my trust." Tears filled my eyes again. This time I was determined to keep them from falling. I'd be damned if I shed a single one in front of him.

"Please—"

I sidestepped him before he could spew any more excuses. I made it to the door and got the handle turned before his hand slammed down on the door, preventing me from pulling it open. His chest molded along my back, caging me between him and the door.

"Nicoli De Luca asked me to dinner and I accepted," I said over my shoulder. Hurting him was the only way he was going to let me go. When I felt his body stiffen behind me, I knew I'd succeeded. His hand dropped from the door and he stepped away. I didn't let myself glance back. I kept my eyes forward, pulled open the door, and walked out.

Dean was standing by his car waiting for me. My tears fell freely the moment I saw him. The determination and strength holding them back dwindled to nothing. My emotions were overwhelming, and I was drunk. Which was why I didn't make it to Dean. Instead, I veered to the right behind a tall bush and threw up.

CHAPTER THIRTY-FIVE

Pain. That was what I woke up to. To be more specific, I woke to a mind-splitting, eye-blurring, oh-God-this-is-how-my-life-is-going-to-end hangover. I knew I'd drunk a lot at Louie's but not enough to feel like this. I turned over onto my side and groaned. My mouth tasted like acidic roadkill that made my stomach roll.

I squinted my eyes open, blinking away the blurriness. The light was dim, thanks to my curtains blocking out most of the sun. I was home and in my room. For the life of me I had no idea how I'd gotten there. The last thing I remembered from last night was throwing up in the bushes while Dean held my hair back. After that, nothing.

Very slowly, I sat up. The room spun and I had to focus solely on breathing to keep whatever was left in my stomach down. I needed to pee, and I desperately wanted to brush my teeth. A shower was definitely in my near future. I just needed to make it to the bathroom first.

Shoving the covers off, I climbed out of bed. I was still wearing my shirt and panties from last night, but my pants and bra were gone. Dragging my feet and grabbing onto each piece of furniture to help keep me standing upright, I started for the bathroom. Once I made it to the couch, the halfway point to the bathroom, I nearly jumped out of my skin when I realized I wasn't alone. Dean was sprawled out on my couch in a deep sleep. *Why is he sleeping on my couch?*

I tapped on his sock covered foot. He startled awake, blinked a few times before his eyes met mine. He was lying on his back with a throw covering his hips down to his ankles. He was fully dressed, apart from his shoes kicked off in front of the couch. He rubbed down his face, wiping away the fog of sleep before he yawned and sat up.

"How are you feeling?" His voice was gruff, and his scowl was already in place.

I put a hand to my queasy stomach. The moment my fingers touched the thin fabric of my shirt, I remembered my state of undress. No bra and my light blue panties were on full display. Then I remembered Dean had seen me practically naked at Show 'n Tail and that helped taper my embarrassment.

"I feel like shit. I can't remember how I got home."

Dean shook his head. "I doubt I'd be able to remember anything with how much you drank last night and that was after we got back here. I have no idea how much you drank at Louie's, but you were already puking before we left."

I nodded. "The last thing I remember is throwing up in the bushes. After that it's a black hole."

"It took a while to get you into the car. You threw up everything but your stomach, and it wasn't for a lack of trying."

I scrunched my nose. That explained why my stomach muscles were sore.

"Once I was able to get you in the car, you, uh...cried. You said some stuff about Jameson. It's probably best you don't remember that. You asked if we could go kill someone. Skank Barbie, I think you called her? You went into vivid detail on how you wanted to kill her. Which was fucking terrifying. I don't know what your obsession is with neck ties, but I will never wear one around you. Ever."

Neck ties?

"After we got back to the house, you stole whiskey from the boss's study and started chugging it like it was water. It was a task to get you up to your room. You took off your shoes and pants on the way up the stairs. Because you valued the whiskey bottle you were carrying more than yourself, you would have broken your damn neck if I wasn't there to catch you." Dean shook his head again as if in disbelief. "It was a fucking battle to get you to give it up. The only way you'd hand it over is if I promised not to leave you."

Heat scorched my cheeks. I couldn't remember any of it. "Thank you," I mumbled, sheepishly.

His brows furrowed. "It's not like I had much of a choice."

Well, that didn't last long. "You couldn't just accept the gratitude, could you, Grumpy?"

Dean's cell vibrated on my coffee table. "Not when I have that name to live up to." I thought I saw a tiny smirk lift the corner of his mouth, but as quickly as it came, it went. He scooped up his phone, light illuminating his face as he read what I assumed was a text. "Asher's here. I'm going to head home and change."

"Family meeting today. I need you both there," I said. Dean nodded and left.

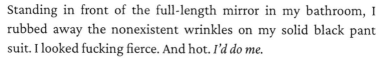

Standing in front of the full-length mirror in my bathroom, I rubbed away the nonexistent wrinkles on my solid black pant suit. I looked fucking fierce. And hot. *I'd do me.*

The suit jacket was sexy, molding to me perfectly like a second skin. The neckline plunged open until just below my sternum, showing off the sexy black lace bustier corset I had on underneath that gave my breasts a drool worthy push up. The suit jacket stayed closed with two shiny black buttons. The pants hugged my hips and were skintight all the way down to my ankles. I finished the outfit with dark purple Louboutin platform pumps.

My makeup was dark, especially the shadow around my eyes, making my green eyes pop. My cheeks were shimmery and my lips were blood red to match my hair, which was curled into tight waves.

"We're going to be late," Dean said, stepping into the bathroom dressed in an all-black suit sans tie. I turned and caught him checking me out with a slight lift of his brow. If the way I looked could lightly crack his resting bitch face, that meant the outfit I'd chosen was perfect.

"I'm ready. Do you have it?"

Dean nodded and pulled a silver .357 Magnum revolver from inside his suit jacket. I took it and opened the cylinder, finding it fully loaded. Pleased, I stuffed the gun into the back waistband of my slacks and pulled my suit jacket over the top half, hiding it.

"The other leaders will have their enforcers there. Seeing as I don't have an enforcer of my own, you will stand in."

Dean only let his surprise show for a second. I had already filled Asher in on the plan. He was going to stand in the hall with Stefan's security to hold Samuel's and Dylan's security out. Stefan's personal security, along with the rest of the security in the house, were already on alert for what was going to go down. Dylan and hopefully Samuel, if I played my cards right, would be forcibly removed from their positions in this family.

I had tiny butterflies fluttering in my stomach as I approached the chamber. I knew I was going to be the last to arrive. I'd planned on it. Passing the goon squad and Asher standing along the walls of the hallway, I steeled my nerves and waited for Dean to open the door for me to enter. *Let the games begin.*

The rumbling of men talking trickled into the hallway once the door was opened. With squared shoulders and my darkness taking the reins, I stepped into the room.

Like it had seven years ago, silence blanketed the room and heads turned as my presence was noticed. I had entered through the east door behind Stefan's chair at the head of the table. To his right sat Samuel, then Conor, then Dylan. To his left sat Jamie, then Rourke, then Louie, leaving the Prionsa's chair, the other head of the table, empty. Six enforcers stood along the walls. Three on the left and three on the right side of the room. I didn't recognize most of them. I assumed who they belonged to was who they stood behind. How I came to that conclusion was Mark, who was standing behind Dylan.

Without stopping and Dean following in tow, I walked behind my uncles and Dylan to the other end of the room.

"Gentlemen," I greeted as I strutted like I was walking a fucking runway. At the other end of the table, I pulled out the Prionsa's chair and took a seat. "I hope I'm not late," I asked Stefan.

Stefan's face was void of what he was feeling as he regarded me. "Right on time."

I leaned back in my chair and glanced around the table. Jamie was predictably expressionless, but I'd caught his eyes traveling up and down my body, taking in my attire, when I'd first entered the room. Rourke looked surprised to see me, as did Louie, but the moment my eyes met his, he looked away. We needed to talk about last night. Apparently, I wasn't the only one affected.

To my left sat Dylan. He had *what the fuck is she doing here* written all over his face. My poor uncle Conor looked from me to Samuel and sighed. Last but not least was my uncle Samuel, who pursed his lips, openly frowning. "What are you doing here?" he questioned.

I smiled. "I'm here to attend the family meeting, silly." I flicked my eyes to Stefan. "Does the Ri have an issue with the Banphrionsa attending today's meeting?"

The corner of Stefan's mouth twitched before he steeled himself. "I don't," he said.

Knowing Samuel was going to argue, I beat him to the punch. "Perfect! Shall we begin? Uncle Conor, why don't you start? I'd love to hear how much our family has made recently selling guns." Conor's brows rose, surprised. "Or should I ask Rourke, as he's really the salesman?" Rourke smiled and looked across the table to his father.

"Conor?" Stefan said, urging Conor to begin.

Pretty much everything Conor and then Rourke said didn't reach my ears. It took lot of will power not to look at Mark. I wondered if he recognized me. I risked a quick peek. He appeared beyond bored as he leaned against the wall. Who was I kidding? I'd been wearing a wig and my tits had been out the entire time. He'd probably never even seen my face.

When Conor and Rourke were done talking, Stefan moved the topic of discussion to drugs. Samuel stated things were still rough and there had been *another* decrease in profits. Stefan asked to see the numbers. Samuel then looked to Dylan, who made a show of holding his hand out to Mark. It wasn't until now I noticed Mark was holding a thin file folder. Mark stepped next to Dylan and handed over the folder. I took that as my chance. I reached out and placed my hand on Mark's forearm.

"Well, hello there. I haven't seen you before." Unsure what to make of me, he glanced at the rest of the table. Ignoring the audience of the entire room, I gave him my full attention as I stood from my chair. "You got a name, handsome?" I asked, drawing his eyes back to me as I tugged on his dark blue tie.

He smirked. "Mark."

I looked down, trying to appear demure. I took a tiny step towards him while pulling on his tie, making him close the space between us until the fronts of our bodies molded.

"Well, Mark...I just got out of a relationship and I'm on the hunt for a rebound. You know, the kind with a marathon of nonstop dirty sweaty sex?"

Rourke gagged behind me. "I didn't need to hear that."

Mark's brows shot up before a heated look of intrigue followed. His eyes traveled down to my pushed up voluptuous cleavage.

"I have to warn you. I'm kind of in the mood to try some new things. I've been having nothing but generic missionary sex for over a year. I really want to get my hair pulled, if you know what I mean?"

"Yuck, cuz," Dylan said, scrunching his nose.

It took everything in me to make the rest of the room disappear. "What do you say, Mark? Think you can handle me?" I playfully challenged him.

Thankfully, Mark seemed too oblivious to the rest of the room as he held his cocksure smirk. "Maybe."

I arched an eyebrow. "Maybe? I guess I need to think of a better way to entice you. Hmm, what to do?" I put my back to the table before I used one hand to help me sit on it. I pulled Mark with me until he was standing between my legs. "What if I told you my dirtiest fantasy?" I wrapped my dangling legs around his hips and pulled him by his tie until his face was inches from my own. His strong cologne filled my nose and I had to fight the urge to scrunch it. "You see this table? It's been in my family for generations," I said, rubbing my free hand along its smooth black wooden surface. "I fantasize about being fucked on this table until I scream." I arched, falling backwards slowly until my shoulders met with the table and I was laid before him. "Just like this."

A whistle pierced through the silence in the room. "This is not what I expected from today's meeting," Louie said.

"How long are you going to let this go on for, Stefan?" I heard Samuel ask. I was sure everyone was looking to my father to stop me. What they didn't know was he wasn't going to.

I sat up and unlocked my legs from around Mark's hips. I flattened my hand on his chest and pushed him back until the backs of his legs hit my chair. With a not so gentle shove, he sat down. I quickly hopped off the table and straddled him. "I think after I get mine, I'll straddle you in this very chair and ride you until you scream," I said and rocked my hips, grinding myself on him.

He chuckled and put his hands on my thighs. "Sorry to tell you this, gorgeous, but I'm not a screamer."

"That's a shame. How will I properly return the favor?" I tapped my chin with my finger as if really thinking about what I'd do. "I could give you a lap dance instead?" I asked, reaching behind my back for my gun. "I've been told I'm very good. Would you like to know by whom? He's a very powerful man." I rocked my hips again, making sure he was plenty distracted as I lifted the back of my jacket and pulled the gun from my waistband.

"Who?" he mumbled, fingers digging into my thighs.

I brought my lips to his ear. "Nicoli De Luca." His body tensed beneath me at the same time I brought my gun up under his chin. The don's name and the cold barrel sobered the lust from his eyes. I climbed off of him slowly, gun pointed at his head, and hopped back on the table.

"Can someone tell me what the fuck is going on?" Samuel demanded.

I glanced over my shoulder at Stefan. He was sitting back in his seat like a stoic king, ignoring my uncle. He'd promised to trust me by not interfering. He was going to let me do my thing— to let me prove myself, and I wasn't going to let him down.

I turned back to Mark. His smile was gone and in its place was a narrowed glare as he stared up at me.

"Get your gun out of my fucking face," Mark demanded.

"You don't recognize me, do you?" His glare lessened as confusion took over. "Day before yesterday. Nasty ass strip club called Show 'n Tail. Do you remember a platinum blonde stripper gyrating her ass in Nicoli De Luca's lap?" I watched the color drain from his face. "Yeah, that was me. Not that you would have noticed. I don't think you looked past my tits. I can't blame you, though. I do have a nice rack."

"I've seen better," he scoffed.

I chuckled at his attempt to take a jab at me. "I've never given a lap dance before, but I guess I did alright. You were none the wiser with how you just started yammering on, not even caring about what the women dancing in the room would overhear. That's a big *no no*, by the way. What if I had been a cop?" I tsked. "Oh, the things I learned. For two years we've been selling our drugs to the De Lucas and what shocked me the most is we've been selling it at forty thousand a kilo all this time. My, my, you've been a bunch of naughty boys, haven't you?"

Mark grit his teeth. "If you know everything, then why the fuck am I still alive?"

An evil smile pulled at my lips. "I wanted to see how they would react knowing that you were the one, the weak link in their master plan that got them caught. I wonder what they would do to you if I handed you over to them right now."

The eye shift was so quick I would have missed it if I hadn't been watching him intently. In one fluid eye movement, Mark looked to Samuel, then to Dylan, and back to me. That was all the confirmation I needed from him. I pulled the trigger and Mark's head jerked backwards, then his body leaned to the side and crumpled to the floor.

The room was silent like the dead. I slid off the table, careful not to trip on one of Mark's legs, and turned to face the rest of the room. Most of them were shocked.

"Stefan," Samuel said, voice low and calm. Stefan still refused to acknowledge him. The only other person who didn't look shocked was Dylan. He was staring down at the table, refusing to meet anyone's eyes.

CHAPTER THIRTY-SIX

"Uncle Conor, can you please go stand by Rourke?" I asked. Conor stood, pushing his chair back in the process, and quietly made his way to the other side of the table, his enforcer following him. I glanced at Samuel's enforcer standing behind him. He was staring at Mark's body on the floor behind me, worry etched around his eyes. I glanced back at Dean. We exchanged a look and he moved across the room to be closer to me, but his eyes were fixed on the worried enforcer.

Using Conor's chair as a step, I hopped back onto the table, sitting myself between Dylan and Samuel. Dylan had yet to look up as he stared at the table like a scared puppy. I sighed. "Oh, Dylan." His cowardice further cemented my belief that he wasn't the mastermind behind this betrayal. I felt bad for him. Sure, growing up he'd pissed me off by teasing the hell out of me, but he was my blood. My uncle was the one who had led him astray. As much as I wished I could put all the blame on Samuel, Dylan had sealed his fate by choosing to follow him.

This is our way of life.

"Let's play a game," I said, opening the cylinder on my

revolver, and dumped the remaining bullets in the palm of my hand. I started tossing one bullet after another down onto the table where Dylan was staring. The first bullet loudly hitting the table startled him, the third finally drew his eyes up to mine. I continued tossing bullets, each obnoxiously loud as they bounced on the table until I was down to one, which I pointedly showed to Dylan as I reloaded it into my gun, spun the cylinder, then clicked it back into place.

I pointed the gun at Dylan before turning my head to face my uncle. Samuel's eyes were narrowed and filled with murderous rage as he looked from the gun pointed at his son to me. "This is how we play," I said cheerfully with a smile full of mirth. "I'm going to ask you a question and you're going to answer. If I feel like you're lying, I pull the trigger. If you don't answer in a timely manner, I pull the trigger. I'm not looking. I don't know if the gun is going to click or if your son is going to eat a bullet. It's your gamble."

Samuel turned back to Stefan, whose eyes finally met his brother's, completely void of all emotion as he regarded him. "Are you seriously going to just sit there and let this shit show continue? She is threatening to execute my son and is accusing two leaders of this family without providing a scrap of proof. This is not how things are done, Stefan. Your daughter is about to start a war."

Revealing nothing as to what he was thinking, my father's eyes shifted to me. "Maybe you should tell the room why you're accusing your uncle and cousin before you continue your game?"

"Of course. How silly of me to forget that not everyone is privy to Samuel and Dylan's betrayal," I said as I continued to point my gun at Dylan. Samuel stared with disbelief like a fool. "Twelve million dollars. That's what's missing from the last eight hundred kilos you moved over the past two years."

"That's the drug business. Not everyone can afford asking price."

"Well, according to Nicoli De Luca, the don of the Italian Mafia, we've been his pipeline for the past two years and he's been paying asking price at forty thousand a kilo. I followed Mark, Dylan's head enforcer, to Show 'n Tail down in Bridgeport, where he had a meeting with the don. I was in the same room while Mark ran his fucking mouth, telling me everything you and Dylan have been up to."

Samuel went quiet, his mind clearly scheming. Trying to think of any excuse or lie he could use to save him.

"So, Uncle, here's my first question...was it your idea to sell to the De Lucas?" I asked, cocking the gun.

Samuel glanced at his son. He was trying to hide what he was feeling by steeling his expression. The void facade made him look just like Stefan, but his eyes always gave him away. They were permanently full of anger, resentment, and jealousy. He'd always hated having to follow Stefan's rule. He wanted the keys to the kingdom, but like his son, his emotions controlled him.

"No," he answered.

I pulled the trigger and the gun clicked.

"Fuck!" Dylan roared, voice shaken with fear. He closed his eyes as he released a trembling breath. "Maura, please. You need to listen to me. I—"

I whooped and laughed. "Talk about a rush!" I peered over my shoulder. "Anyone want to place some bets? I have a feeling it'll fire next time." They just blinked at me. *They seriously need to lighten up.* I looked back at Samuel. "Let's try this again. Uncle... same question?"

Samuel's void facade faltered back to murderous rage. His eyes filled with the promise of everything he'd do to me if he got his hands on me. The pain he would inflict played out like a fire dance in his depthless pupils.

"You think this is funny?" he seethed. "You think just because you hold the gun you hold the power? You're just a sniveling little girl desperate for Daddy's love."

My finger pulled the trigger and the gun clicked again. In my peripheral, Dylan jerked in his seat, but neither Samuel nor I looked away from each other.

"If Stefan had married you off to De Luca like I suggested years ago, I wouldn't have had to send Dylan to make a deal with him. His hate for the Italians and his love for you clouds his judgment. We needed peace between our two families. We've been fighting for too long and have lost too many of our own."

"If you did this for the good of the family, why are you lining your own pockets?"

Samuel's hand slammed down on the table in a fit. "Who do you think your father is going to name as his successor, hmm?" he asked caustically, then looked to Stefan. "You think I've been fucking blind all these years? You've been grooming her," he sneered, and his eyes traveled around the room until they circled back to me. "He's going to put a bitch in charge. A woman cannot rule over this family. You will ruin our entire empire and I'll be damned if I sit back and let that happen."

Without removing my eyes from Samuel's, I pulled the trigger over and over and over. The click after click of the gun sliced through the silence in the room to the same effect as a loud drum. *Boom. Boom. Boom.* Panic and fear took root in Samuel's eyes with each click of the gun until it was clear the gun was never going to fire. I pulled the bullet I'd pretended to load into the gun from my sleeve. "Sleight of hand," I said, wiggling my fingers at my uncle. "I swear you can learn anything on the Internet these days." I placed the bullet upright on the table in front of Dylan. Both him and Samuel held mirror shocked expressions with their jaws slightly ajar. I set the revolver next to the bullet.

"I never intended to shoot you, Dylan." My poor cousin's brow was drenched with sweat and his face was white as a sheet. "However, there is one more matter we must go over and that's where your loyalties lie." Dylan's head jerked up, eyes pleading. He opened his mouth to speak, but I stopped him with the shake of my head. "Put the bullet in the gun and line it up with the barrel," I ordered him. His eyes dropped to the gun and bullet in front of him.

The sound of a chair scraping the floor was followed by Jamie growling, "Maura!"

I ignored him as I watched Dylan's hand hover over the gun, apprehensively. "I won't ask again, Dylan," I said firmly and that seemed to be the push he needed. He scooped up the gun and bullet and once the cylinder was clicked back in place, I grabbed the barrel of the gun while Dylan still held the grip. When I pointed it to my chest, more chairs scraped across the floor as the men around me got to their feet.

"Maura, what are you doing?" Stefan demanded.

I could hear movement around me, but I kept my focus solely on Dylan. He tried to pull the gun away from my chest, but my hold was firm. I cupped his chin, making his eyes lock with mine. "Dylan, I know you were just following your father's lead. I know you wouldn't have betrayed the family if it wasn't for him."

"I'm so sorry, Maura. He said we were protecting the family. He said we had to make the deal with De Luca to stop the war and if it worked, over time he would tell Stefan. We haven't touched the money. It's all sitting in a safe. We were going to give it back. We took it as insurance to make sure Stefan wouldn't kill us until my father could calm him down and make him see reason, that the peace between us and the De Lucas was working."

"Shh...shh. I know." I comforted him by caressing his cheek. Samuel had fed him nothing but lies and manipulation. My poor senseless cousin, who idolized his father, had believed him without question. "I'm going to give you an opportunity to redeem yourself." Dylan's eyes widened as hope filled them. I moved the gun away from my chest and made Dylan point it at Samuel. "You can shoot your father."

"You stupid bitch! You think you can make my own son shoot me?!" Samuel roared, standing from his chair. Dean moved quickly by shoving Samuel back down into his seat while aiming his gun at Samuel's enforcer. Jamie stepped into my peripheral, gun also out and pointed at the enforcer, who now held his hands up in surrender.

"Or...you can take me hostage," I said, pulling the gun back to my chest. "You can try to give you and your father a chance of getting out of here."

"Maura!" Stefan yelled.

I gave Dylan a little smirk and shrugged. He needed to be faced with temptation if he was going to prove himself. Stefan wouldn't let him live otherwise.

"What's it going to be?" I asked, releasing the gun, leaving the decision up to Dylan. "If you shoot your father, we will spare your life. You can look after your mother and sister in your father's stead. Or you could try to save both of your asses by taking me hostage. The front door isn't that far from here and I highly doubt Stefan will risk my life to try and stop you."

"Maura, stop trying to convince him," Jamie admonished.

Dylan glanced back and forth between me and Samuel. He looked completely torn.

"What's it going to be, cousin? The clock is ticking."

"Dylan?" Samuel said, trying to get his son's attention.

"I'm growing impatient. I'm going to give you until the count of three. If you don't decide by then, we will all know where your loyalties lie...one!"

I could feel Dylan shaking through the gun still pressed to my chest. His eyes were cast down, lost in thought.

"Dylan, look at me," Samuel demanded, but it was as if his voice didn't reach him.

"Two!"

"Damnit, Dylan!" Samuel yelled.

My eyes met with Jamie's as I took in a breath to say three. Before the word could leave my mouth, the gun moved from my chest. Dylan aimed it at his father with detached yet determined eyes.

"I'm sorry," he whispered, cocking the gun.

As his finger curled around the trigger, I chuckled. Dylan froze, eyes darting to me. Everyone stared at me like I'd gone mad as I struggled to contain myself.

"Wow!" I grinned like a loon. "That was fun." I reached out and took the gun from Dylan's hand. I gave his cheek a little pat. "Thanks for playing. You did excellent." I hopped off the table and turned to face the rest of the room. They all looked stunned. Stefan was the exception. He looked like he wanted to string me up by my toes in the basement.

"If you decide to spare him, I'll take the responsibility," I said.

Stefan held my eyes for what seemed like forever but was really about thirty seconds. "Do you understand the consequence that will fall on you?"

I arched a brow. "And what consequence will that be, Stefan?"

"If he destroys this family, I will kill you both."

My darkness had always seen Stefan as a formidable opponent and the thought of going against him in a bloody fight formed a dark, twisted smile across my face. "Let's see what happens, shall we?"

Stefan's features hardened at the challenge. I, on the other hand, was becoming bored. My job here was done.

I sighed. "Can you take over? I'm hungry." I hadn't eaten all day because I'd been hungover. It was almost dinner time and my stomach knew it. Stefan nodded slightly. "I wonder what Jeana has planned for dinner. I hope it's tacos. I'd kill for some tacos," I rambled, holding my gun out to Dean. He took it from me as I stepped past him, making my way to the door.

"Holy shit," I heard Rourke say just before the door closed behind me.

CHAPTER THIRTY-SEVEN

With a shuddering breath, I relaxed. Allowing the darkest part of myself to take the reins by suppressing everything else that made up my soul took a lot out of a girl. Sure, it made things a lot easier, definitely more enjoyable when toying with the enemy. In fact, I fucking loved every minute of it, but the aftermath...when my emotions surfaced, I became unsettled.

The meeting was over. The job Stefan had tasked me with was completed. I'd succeeded. I should have been proud or celebrating that my sexist, nefarious uncle was about to meet karma. *Did he know karma is female and a bitch?* I should have been laughing at the irony, but I could barely muster a smile. Dylan's life had been spared—a mercy I hoped I wouldn't regret. There was no changing Samuel's fate, though. He had to die. That wasn't my issue, but yet it was.

This betrayal was gutting Stefan. He wasn't outwardly showing it, but I could still tell. Samuel was his brother—his twin. They had come into this world together, born with a bond —an assurance that they'd always have each other. Having walked the dark path of a Quinn alone, I was almost jealous. Even though I'd had Jamie growing up, he still was older and male. We'd learned at different stages and Stefan had had different expectations of us.

It was no wonder Samuel had been allowed to run amok for two years. There was no doubt in my soul that Stefan had sensed Samuel was up to no good from the very beginning. He'd have to have been dense not to and Stefan was anything but. Denial was a seductive asshole but now it was time for acceptance. Justice needed to be served. If I could have taken this burden from him, I would have.

"You need to eat more than two bites," Asher said from my left. I looked down at my barely touched plate. Glancing over at his next to mine and then to Dean's on my right, I saw both of their plates were clean. Jeana had made a pasta dish for dinner. I was equally bummed as I was relieved that she hadn't made tacos. The moment I'd begun to relax, I'd instantly lost my appetite. It would have been a crying shame if I'd let tacos go to waste.

The three of us were seated at the island in the kitchen. I'd come in here to join Dean and Asher when I'd realized I was going to be eating dinner alone. Stefan hadn't showed up, and neither had anyone else for that matter. They were all preparing for the execution by hunting down the rest of Samuel's and Dylan's enforcers and men in their inner circle.

Fixating on a glittery speck in the quartz countertop, I mumbled, "I can't eat." I felt strung tight with an abundant mix of bipolar emotions. I was sad for my father but happy my uncle was finally getting put in *his* place. I was tired yet wired, like the family meeting had given me a euphoric high I was relishing but crashing from at the same time. The memory of myself rubbing up against Mark like a cat in heat made my skin itch for a shower, yet I wanted to roll around, basking in the sweet scent of victory. Maybe I was having a stroke?

"What's wrong?" Dean grumbled. I blinked, breaking the staring contest I was having with the counter to face him. He was staring at me with a puckered brow. I couldn't tell if he was concerned or pissed off.

"I think I need to have sex..." I blurted with zero shame. I didn't have room for that particular emotion. Dean's brows shot up and Asher cleared his throat. "Or a cigarette. I'm feeling very contradictory at the moment and it's...unsettling."

"Uh..." Dean stammered, clearly at a loss.

"Why'd you take off your rubber bands? Didn't they help you when you were stressed?" Asher asked.

Stressed! I'll be damned, I guess I am. I usually got pissed when I was stressed. At the moment, though, I couldn't pin down one single emotion and just feel it.

A drink was definitely in order. Standing up, I made my way over to the pantry. Stepping into the temperature-controlled room, I scanned shelves with an array of unopened bottles. We were Irish, so it wasn't a surprise Stefan had enough whiskey to get an entire army sloshed. Thankfully, he also catered to those with other tastes. I sighed happily when I found a bottle of Patrón. It wasn't until I was walking out of the pantry with tequila in hand that I finally grasped everything Asher had said. My steps faltered. I stood there stunned as I locked my eyes on the giant sitting across the room. He was waiting, expectantly. *How'd he...?*

"How long did you spy on me?"

He smirked. Standing from his stool, he scooped up his empty plate. "The last two years," he replied as he made his way over to the sink. "And we weren't spying. We were there to protect you."

I fought hard not to scowl as I pulled a shot glass and salt from different cabinets around the kitchen. "Whatever you were doing, you were very *observant* if you knew why I wore rubber bands. Did you hack into the college to get my test scores, too? Tap my phone? Bug my house?" I grumbled as I set my collected items on the counter. I didn't return to my seat. Instead, I chose to stand on the other side of the island, across from Dean, who was watching as I uncorked the Patrón bottle and poured a shot. I preferred my tequila chilled when drinking it straight, but I didn't really have the patience to prepare it that way. Wetting the back of my hand with my tongue, I dashed some salt on the dampened skin. I licked the salt away and threw back the shot. *Damn, I needed that.*

Asher leaned against the sink with his arms folded over his chest after placing his plate in the basin. "You didn't answer my question."

I shrugged. "In case you haven't noticed, I'm not living among the sheep anymore. Showing weakness here is a death sentence."

"You're the boss's daughter," he said incredulously, like being Stefan's daughter gave me the entitlement to get away with whatever the fuck I wanted. That was true in some cases. No one could touch me without facing the wrath of Stefan. But that wasn't how I rolled. I wanted my enemies to hesitate to rise against me because of my own retribution.

"Aren't bodyguards supposed to stand in my shadow, silent while looking intimidating? Emphasis on the silent part." I pointedly eyed Dean because he too was an opinionated Chatty Cathy. I poured myself another shot, then repeated my salt regimen before tossing it back.

The sound of someone clearing their throat drew our attention. Louie was standing by the entrance leading in from the foyer. With his hands in his pockets, he looked apprehensive. "Can we talk?"

Without saying a word Asher pushed away from the sink. Dean stood from his stool and reached across the island to snag my tequila bottle. I glared at him as he and Asher left the kitchen, taking the Patrón bottle with them. *What a dick.* Once they were out of sight, I relented with a sigh. I guessed it was for the best. I needed to be clear headed later.

Looking back at Louie, I saw he hadn't moved from where he was standing. From what I could read in his eyes, I knew what he wanted to talk about. I'd been trying to avoid thinking about last night all day. Remembering it once right after waking up this morning had made me cringe. *Christ, I was such a hussy.* Only hours after ending whatever Jamie and I'd had together, I'd pounced on his best friend. What was worse was if Louie hadn't stopped us and Jamie hadn't shown up, I would have slept with him—I wanted to sleep with him. I could still feel his lips on mine, which was making my heart practically gallop out of my chest.

"What's up, Louie?"

My voice seemed to spark his resolve and he slowly made his way over to me. I'd never noticed how graceful he was when he walked or how his gray slacks stretched tight against his strong thighs with each step he took. He was a little on the leaner side but that didn't mean his body wasn't chiseled in all the right places. *Fucking hell. He's Jamie's best friend. He's Jamie's best friend! He's Jamie's best friend!*

A few golden strands of his medium length fringe that was normally slicked back escaped the rest and fell across his beautiful sapphire eyes. "We should talk about last night."

We should. Given how I was reacting with him just standing two feet away from me, though, I didn't know if I was ready. He was close enough now I could smell him. His warm earthy cologne caressed my nose, warming me from the inside out, making me want to slip off my suit jacket to help cool my flushed skin. Taking off any articles of clothing in front of him was a bad idea. I might find it hard to stop. So instead, I inched away from him, trying my hardest to be inconspicuous.

"We had a lot to drink..." I trailed off because I didn't know what else to say.

He nodded slightly, eyes boring into mine. "Is that all it was, a drunken mistake?"

Oh, hell. Floundering, my mouth opened and closed. I ripped my eyes from his, dropping them down to the counter. "No. I didn't intend for it to happen, but I don't regret it."

His sigh pulled my eyes back to him. His shoulders were sagged a little, as if relieved. "I don't regret it either," he said, slicking back the few escaped strands of sunlight colored hair. "Shockingly, Jameson's not pissed at me. I thought I was going to wake to find my dick cut off this morning, especially since he knows how I feel about you."

It was like someone had hit the pause button on my body. The act of blinking actually took thought.

He smiled sheepishly. "I shouldn't be surprised you've never noticed. It's always been Jameson for you and you for him." I was getting ready to argue with him because despite recent changes, Jamie and I had never felt more than friendship for each other, especially Jamie, but Louie beat me to the punch. "That story I told you last night...the reason Jameson was so pissed a year ago and why I took him out to get his mind off things was because he had just found out you were dating that brief, Tom. The security team watching over you sent over pictures of you and him getting it on in his car along with their weekly report. It set Jameson off. Fuck, it set him off for months. Everyone could barely stand to be around him." Louie shook his head while smiling.

"Why are you telling me about Jamie?" I was a little befuddled. I didn't want to talk about Jamie. He and I were done. He'd hurt me. I killed people who hurt me. But I couldn't kill him. I just couldn't because he was...because I... My thoughts and feelings were so scrambled, I barely heard Louie speak again.

"Do you love him?" The question was a loaded one.

"Why do you want to know? It doesn't matter anymore." He gave me an incredulous look, which pissed me off. "Are you wanting to know for him or for yourself? I'm getting mixed signals. One moment you're telling me you have feelings for me and the next you're campaigning for your best friend, which, frankly, you're wasting your breath. Whatever Jamie and I used to feel for each other doesn't mean I have to stop living my life because it's over." I could really use a shot of tequila right now. *Stupid Dean.* "I'm flattered you have feelings for me, Louie. I wish I could return those feelings. It's not like I'm not attracted to you. I was down to fuck last night and maybe I still am, but that's all it can be right now. Fucking. I can't give you more than that. All the men I've given more to have hurt me."

The defeated look he was wearing by the end of my angry rant told me I'd said more than I should have. He pulled his hand from his pocket and went to reach out to me, but movement behind him caught my eye. I think it was the look on my face that made Louie drop his hand before it could reach me and turn around.

"Someone needs to buy you a fucking bell," I snapped with a scowl. Jamie had snuck up on us again. I didn't know how long he had been standing there. By his unreadable expression and the way he was leaning against the archway leading into the kitchen from the foyer, I'd say long enough.

He ignored me by looking to Louie. "It's time to go."

Louie nodded, then turned back to me. I didn't want to talk anymore and if it was execution time, I'd take that as my excuse to bolt. Before he could say anything else, I started for the exit. My heels clacked on the tile floor with each step I took, piercing the awkward silence in the room as I passed Louie, then Jamie.

CHAPTER THIRTY-EIGHT

F ive black Escalades followed nose to bumper like a train traveling through the city, across the bridge towards East Haven. Our destination was the power plant that over-looked the water near the Port of New Haven. Asher drove with Dean riding shotgun while I sat in the back alone, texting Nicoli where to meet me for our *exchange*.

Security guards stationed at the front gate didn't even slow our party down. Instead, they had the gate already opened for us. We drove through, passing industrial buildings with dark smoke billowing from tall pipe-shaped chimneys, until we reached a dirt road that went up to the rocky shore. The five Escalades parked next to each other facing the water. The area chosen was in the far back corner of the plant's property hidden by tall trees. It was dark out, but slightly illuminated by the city lights coming from across the water.

Doors opened and everyone started to step out. Stefan and his personal security, who were dragging along Samuel, climbed out of the SUV next to mine. Jamie and a few of his goons were escorting Dylan in the next car. Louie and his squad were trans-porting three men who were part of Samuel's inner circle, with cloth bags over their heads and their hands zip-tied behind their backs. It was the same set up with three more guys tied up in Rourke and Conor's Escalade.

Dean hopped out and opened my door for me as I finished my conversation with the don. I scooted over the bench seat, but as I went to step out, Dean blocked my way. I arched a questioning brow at him. He reached into his coat pocket, pulling out a lighter and a joint.

"It's not sex, but it's better than a cigarette," he said in a low voice. I schooled my expression, hoping to look nonchalant. I didn't want to make a big deal of Grumpy's kind gesture. He'd known I was stressed and gone out of his way to help me. If I got all mushy and grateful, I might embarrass him, and he'd think twice before doing something like this again.

Cool as a cucumber, I took the joint and put it to my lips. Dean lit the end for me with the lighter. I inhaled and blew out slowly through pursed lips. *It's been a long time since I've had one of these.* A calmness took over almost instantly. It was euphoric and just what I needed. I gave Dean a small, grateful smile and he offered me his hand to climb out of the car.

The six tied up men were lined up and pushed down to their knees before our security ripped the cloth bags, which looked very similar to black pillowcases, off their heads and trained their guns on them. Jamie, Louie, Rourke, and Conor flanked Dylan, watching as Stefan, with a gun in hand, led Samuel towards the edge of the rocky shore.

My Louboutins crunched in the dirt, undoubtedly scuffing up the spiked heels. Jamie's head turned, eyes following me as I passed him to go stand in front of the men lined up on their knees. Samuel was placed to stand with his back to the water, facing Stefan. They talked amongst themselves quietly. Probably saying their goodbyes, not that anyone could hear them. I couldn't see Stefan's face, but Samuel, who had his hands tied behind his back, looked angry. Stefan said something to him because that anger slowly faded, and the tiniest hint of sadness took its place.

I took another puff of my joint, taking in all of the faces of Samuel and Dylan's inner circle. They were a mixture of enforcers and men trusted enough to help run the drug pillar of our family's empire. I had a file on each of them back at home from when I'd been researching, trying to find a lead on Samuel and Dylan's betrayal.

I watched all six of them while Stefan and Samuel conversed. Most held different expressions as they looked around at everyone. They clearly knew why they were here. As of right now they were guilty by association. The true question that needed to be answered was whether or not they'd known they'd been betraying the family or if they'd been just following orders. It would've been easier to just clean house and get rid of all of them, but I wasn't one to waste.

Holding the joint between my lips, I held my hand out to Asher and Dean expectantly. Asher pulled a pistol and silencer from inside his suit jacket. Taking them, I made quick work of screwing on the silencer.

Stefan stepped back from Samuel and everyone's attention was drawn in their direction, apart from mine. I didn't take my eyes off the six men kneeling before me. All were quiet as they watched the fate of their leader come to fruition. Two looked beyond frightened. One appeared remorseful. One's face was schooled, but his eyes betrayed him. They were full of anger as they looked from Samuel to Dylan. *Interesting.* The last two guys blatantly and defiantly glared at everyone, but mostly Stefan.

Stefan lifted his gun, already equipped with a silencer, and pointed it at Samuel. Stefan's jaw moved—saying his last words to his brother—before he pulled the trigger. A red mist formed behind my uncle's head just before his body crumpled to the dirt.

Dylan gasped loudly, drawing everyone's attention. His head was cast downward, eyes closed, and his hands were fisted at his sides. I held my emotions at bay by taking another puff, then turned back to the six kneeling men. Stefan handed over his gun to one of his goons and made his way over to me. I steeled my expression to match his. Now was a time for strength and I would be strong for him.

I took my joint from my lips and held it out to him. He needed it more than I did, even if he wasn't showing it. He eyed the joint, then cocked a brow. Nothing was said and no look was exchanged as I continued to hold it out to him. He eventually took it and took a drag. Satisfied, I stepped away from him, towards the six men, aimed my gun, and pulled the trigger twice.

Pop! Pop!

Down went the two who'd showed their obvious hatred towards Stefan. Taking a step to the right, so I was center with the remaining four, I looked between them, watching—waiting. The sound of tires crunching over dirt echoed in the distance.

I shot a look over my shoulder at Asher and Dean. They gave me an understanding nod and walked off to greet the approaching car.

"Are we expecting someone?" Stefan asked.

I kept my eyes fixed on the remaining four men as I answered, "I invited Nicoli De Luca. Our exchange was scheduled for tonight. I figured two birds, one stone, and all that jazz."

One of the four men's eyes widened slightly. *That's one.*

"What the fuck is he doing here?" I was surprised to hear my uncle Conor ask.

I turned around and found Conor and Jamie being held back by Louie and Rourke. If eyes could kill, the don would be dead twice over. Nicoli approached with Dean and Asher leading the way and four of his own men flanking him.

With the aura of confidence and maybe a tiny bit of arrogance,

Nicoli made his way over until he stood mere feet from Jamie, Louie, Conor, and Rourke. Nicoli looked between them with a smug smile, then noticed Dylan, who was standing a few feet back, defeated and with absent eyes. *Stop looking at him, Maura.*

"What is he doing here, Stefan?" Conor demanded.

"I invited him," I answered. I tsked as I circled around the group. "Such a display of testosterone. The air is making me want to gag." I chuckled and stepped between them. "You might as well whip out your dicks now and measure them. I have a ruler app on my phone." That seemed to draw everyone's attention. I received varying looks from amused to pissed off. I couldn't expect everyone to find me funny.

"Maura," Stefan said, tone displeased.

I sighed and looked to Louie. "You and Jamie need to take Dylan home. Be sure to remind him of the importance of family on the way there." Louie didn't look to Jamie for reassurance this time. He nodded and tried to herd Jamie away. I glanced at Rourke next. "You're no longer needed here. Take your father home before he does something I'll have to fix," I ordered, firmly. My uncle needed to go because he appeared to be seconds away from reaching for his gun.

Rourke nodded. "Come on, Da. You heard the Banphrionsa."

Rourke seemed to get through to Conor and he slowly backed up, then they started for their Escalade. It was taking a little more convincing on Louie's part to get Jamie to leave because he hadn't moved more than a few feet back.

Ignoring them, I turned to Nicoli and plastered a fake smile on my face. "Thank you for coming."

"It seems I've crashed a party," he said with amused eyes fixed on me.

"On the contrary, your presence here is very much needed. If you could please follow me?" I asked, graciously. Nicoli stepped away from his goons and followed me over to the four kneeling men. I gestured for him to stand next to me in front of them. "You would be doing me a favor by standing right here and looking pretty." He did as I'd asked before his eyes traveled to the kneeling men. I went back to watching them. Two stared at him, then me, clearly puzzled as to what was going on. The other two, however, which included the one guy whose eyes had widened at hearing the don's name, were both staring at the ground. I glanced back at Nicoli and found him staring at them and only them.

"You did perfect. Let me introduce you to my father, Stefan Quinn," I said, gesturing at my father standing to my other side. Nicoli stepped around me and the two most powerful men I knew greeted each other.

"Quinn," Nicoli said, nonchalant.

"De Luca," Stefan greeted back in an equally bland tone.

I rolled my eyes, but stepped away towards the two men, who had finally raised their gazes from the ground. Both of their eyes drifted to me as I lifted my gun and shot both of them. The remaining two men flinched as their comrades' bodies hit the ground.

"You can untie these two," I told the goons standing behind them.

"Maura?" Stefan sighed.

"Yes, Stefan?"

"Would you like to elaborate as to what you are doing?"

"I'm keeping these two, for now. The others were no good. Thanks to Nicky, I was able to weed out the remaining bad eggs."

"And how did you know they were bad? I just stood there and looked pretty," Nicoli asked with a shit-eating grin. I'd mistakenly fed his ego with that comment.

"Not to brag, but I'm pretty good at reading people. These two clearly hated you, Stefan, and did nothing to hide it," I explained as I pointed my gun at the first two guys I'd shot, then moved to point at the other two. "And these two...well, you did say it was lackeys who you'd exchanged with. No offense, Nicky, but it's no secret our families aren't friendly. If two of our men repeatedly met with you, a De Luca, and didn't tell us, it's obvious where their loyalties were."

"And you knew it was those two from just looking at them?" The don sounded skeptical.

I smiled. "Was I wrong?"

He shoved his hands in his pockets and the corners of his eyes squinted before his lip curled up on one side. *No, I wasn't wrong.*

I turned back to the two remaining men, who were now standing and rubbing at their free wrists. I closed the distance between us. "Congratulations, gentlemen. You've been promoted. You now work for me." The guy who'd given the evil eye to Dylan and Samuel turned his stink eye on me. I stepped even closer to him. "Careful," I warned him in a low voice. Thinking back to all the files I'd gone through on each of Samuel's and Dylan's men, I tried to put his face to a name. "Finnegan, is it?"

"Finn," he corrected in a gruff voice that could rival Dean's.

"Well, Finn, they were going to kill all of you. It would've been a hell of a lot easier, but I decided to spare you. You're alive right now because of me." My eyes locked with his dark ones. With it being nighttime, I couldn't make out the color. "You can glare at me and hate me all you want. I find defiance in a man entertaining. So if you're looking for attention, handsome, please continue. You have it. I should warn you; I may be a lot more tolerable of your prickly behavior than, say, Samuel, but even I can grow bored and I know everything there is to know about you. Like where your son lives with your ex-wife. Where he goes to school. What nursing home your father's in." I took a step back and glanced at the other guy, Gavin, I thought his name was, and let my threat sink in. "You're both on probation. I'd tread carefully. Really think about what it means to be part of this family and I'd mull over the definition of loyalty." I waved them off and a few goons escorted them to an Escalade.

I spun on my heel to rejoin Nicoli and my father, who had been quietly watching. Nicoli appeared to be slightly impressed where Stefan was proud. I scrunched my nose and glanced down as my heels sunk into the rocks. "Well, these shoes are ruined. You couldn't have picked somewhere with a flat solid surface?" I complained to Stefan.

"I'm sure we can get you another pair," he drawled.

I sniffed. "That's not the point. It should be a sin to ruin something so beautiful."

Stefan just blinked at me before his eyes shifted to Nicoli, who was wearing a bemused expression. "My daughter says she would like to set up a dinner for us. I think that would be a good opportunity to get to know each other and maybe settle some differences."

Nicoli nodded. "I agree. As long as your beautiful daughter can join us, that is?" The don phrased his response as a question. It was clear it wasn't.

Stefan gave him a fake smile. "Of course. Like she'd let me go without her. She's my heir, after all."

His revelation was like a punch to my stomach. Which I had to quickly recover from before anyone noticed. I had to put that on the back burner for now. Now was not the time to question or freak out on Stefan.

"Until then, De Luca," Stefan said and walked away with his goon squad following. Just before Stefan climbed into his Escalade, he whispered into the ear of a goon, who waved at another to join him. The two goons returned to our group, choosing to stand next to Dean. Stefan glanced back at me one more time before shutting his door and driving away.

Looking around, I found Louie had finally convinced Jamie to leave while I must have been busy, taking Dylan with them. The bodies had been cleaned up as well. This whole execution had been handled seamlessly. All who were left were Nicoli, his four men, Dean, Asher, Stefan's goons, and me. It was then that I realized that if Stefan hadn't left men behind, Nicoli and his men would have outnumbered me. This was why he was the boss.

"Shall we do this exchange?" I asked Nicoli, tilting my head towards my car. His fifty kilos were currently sitting in my trunk. The don held his hand out for me to walk ahead. I led the way to the back of my Escalade, where Asher opened the trunk, revealing six large duffel bags. I had to thank Rourke for retrieving the remaining fifty kilos from McLoughlin's for me.

Two of Nicoli's men returned from his car carrying a heavy bag each. We exchanged bags and took our time making sure everything was legit.

"This was definitely the most entertaining exchange," Nicoli stated.

"It was. I wound up owing you a favor."

A mischievous smile pulled at the corner of his mouth. "You do."

"A small favor," I added.

His smile only grew. "A small favor that I'd like now."

"Oh?"

He nodded. "I want a kiss."

I didn't fight my disbelief from showing. *Really?* "You're not going to offer to buy a girl a drink first, huh? You're just going to dive right into it?"

He chuckled. "Do you want me to buy you a drink first? I know a club I can take you to right now, but it won't count as the date you still owe me."

I shook my head because I couldn't believe I was going to agree to this. "Let's get this over with, Casanova," I said, flicking my fingers between us, but I cemented my feet where I stood. If he wanted me, he'd have to come and get me.

As if reading my mind, he gave me a knowing look. My stubbornness didn't seem to deter him. If anything, it amused him. He fluidly closed the space between us. His arms reached out, one circling around my back while the other sank into my hair and cupped the back of my head, pulling my body flush with his. A little flicker of panic fluttered in my chest. It wasn't enough to affect me outwardly, but it was enough to let me know it was there. I'd almost forgotten what it was like to feel that way when touched sexually. Jaime had been the exception.

"You know, most women would be a little more eager—show a little more enthusiasm when kissing me," he murmured softly, lips a few inches from mine.

My eyes locked with his gold ones. "I'm not most women. Killing turns me on. You're lucky you caught me at a good time or else I might not have been so agreeable."

"Turned on? I'd hate to leave you in such a state. Just say the word and I'd be more than willing to help with that."

I couldn't help myself. I laughed. "You're incorrigible."

He tightened his arms around me. "And you're beautiful. I must admit, I'm determined to have you."

"I'm not one to discourage someone's dreams."

My witty retort made his eyes darken and his lips pressed to mine. They were softer than I'd imagined. Not that I'd been imagining them. I just... *Damn*. He turned my brain to mush as he sucked my bottom lip between his. I found myself caving by kissing him back, molding to him more firmly. His tongue dove between my lips and I sucked and stroked it with mine, drawing forth a groan from him.

Hearing him cleared away some of the fog in my head. I became lucid enough to remember I didn't really want to do this. I flattened my hands on his chest and pushed. He broke our kiss. As his eyes bounced between mine, he seemed reluctant to let me go, but his arms unraveled, and I stepped away.

I fought the urge to lick my swollen lips. "A favor for a kiss. Transaction complete. Until next time, Nicky," I said, stepping backwards again, putting more space between us until I turned and walked to my vehicle where my security stood waiting. Asher opened the door for me to climb in. Like they were in sync, the rest of the guys hopped in and we drove away.

CHAPTER THIRTY-NINE

I t was late when I wandered downstairs. I couldn't sleep. The events of today kept replaying in my head like a movie, forbidding my mind a moment of peace. In nothing but a long red silk nightgown, courtesy of Angela, I padded through the dark and quiet house on my bare feet. I filled a crystal tumbler with some of Stefan's favorite whiskey and found myself standing outside the chamber.

I pushed open one of the heavy doors and flipped on the lights. It was eerily quiet. Mark's body and the evidence of today's meeting had been wiped away. But I could still see everyone sitting around the table, hear their voices, see the bullets I'd tossed around when trying to get Dylan's attention. I walked around the room, while sipping at my drink, until I was standing behind Stefan's chair. Resting my arms on the back of it, I stared at the Prionsa's chair—my chair.

I was Stefan's heir.

Was that something I wanted? It wasn't something I'd ever seen coming.

I felt lost, slowly drifting into limbo. The lack of control put me on edge. I'd set out on this path because I wanted change. I wanted equality and respect. My uncle had been taken out in the process and I'd been placed in a role I didn't aspire to.

My internal moping session got interrupted when the door on the other side of the room opened. Jamie stepped inside, eyes finding me instantly. By the lack of surprise, he'd already known I was in here. He quietly glided further into the room to stand behind my newly appointed chair. He mimicked my pose by resting his arms on the back of it. Dropping my eyes from his, I stared down at the crystal tumbler in my hands. There was a sip of whiskey left—a sad amount, if I was going to be in his presence.

"You were born to sit here," he said, gesturing down. "Today proved that."

"Why didn't you take it when Stefan offered it to you?" I asked, my eyes drifting back up to meet his.

"Because I knew it was always meant for you." There was no hesitation or resentment in his answer. Just pure honesty.

"Was I the only one who was oblivious the entire time? Was he really grooming me?"

Stefan had said that everything he'd done or put me through was to make me stronger. Had that just been more lies? I should have felt bitter. I was beyond fed up. Maybe I'd grown accustomed and that was why I couldn't feel anything other than numb.

Jamie dropped his arms from the chair to stuff his hands into his pockets. He was still dressed in black slacks and a burgundy button-down shirt he had worn to today's meeting. The shirt was untucked now, and the sleeves were rolled to his elbows, exposing his tattooed skin. His small smile was my answer. I had been the only one naive to Stefan's grand plan.

It was kind of nice talking to him without fighting. It was almost like the way we'd been before—friends. Then reality set in. I remembered the way he'd hurt me. My anger bubbled to the surface and I found myself hating him for making me miss him.

He must have noticed the change in me because his eyes narrowed. "How much longer is this shit going to carry on? I've tried to give you space. Yes, I fucked up, but how long are you going to punish me?"

"I'm not punishing you. Whatever it was we had is over."

"Stop acting like you don't know what we are to each other. I know I did a shitty thing, but it wasn't enough to call it quits. Punish me, fine, I deserve it, but you don't get to walk away from me. Not for that," he snapped, then shook his head. "There has to be something else going on. Something happened or changed that you're not telling me."

With a shuddering breath, I steeled myself. This was going somewhere I didn't want to venture. "You need to move on."

He reeled back and his eyes turned dark. "Like you are with Louie? Or is De Luca the one you want? It's hard to tell. You've kissed both of them in the past twenty-four hours." My surprise must have shown on my face because he smiled, cruelly. "I guess you were right about the security. They aren't so discreet."

It must have been Stefan's goons. Dean and Asher wouldn't have told him shit. Biting my tongue, I stopped myself from taking the bait. I didn't owe him an explanation and I was done fighting with him.

"I told you, you're mine," he said, calmness returning to his voice.

"I don't belong to you," I snapped, my control slipping.

"I love you."

I threw the crystal tumbler as hard as I could at him. He easily ducked. The glass smashed into the wall behind him, shattering into pieces that scattered on the wood floor. "Don't fucking say that to me," I bit out, jaw clenching. He was making things harder —to the point of unbearable. I needed to get away from him.

I turned and darted for the door. Just as I was pulling the heavy door open, Jamie's hands slammed it closed and his warm body pressed against me. "Stop running away from me," he growled. One of his hands dropped from the door and wrapped around my waist, lying flat on my stomach and pulling me close. His pelvis molded to my ass at the same time his nose brushed my ear, then burrowed into my hair.

"Let me go," I ordered, my words coming out strangled.

"I can't."

Trapped, I pushed on the door to try and shove him backwards to give me the tiniest bit of room to slip away, but my attempt was futile. It was like pushing against a cement wall. I only ended up rubbing my body along his, causing him to harden in his pants. His other hand, which was still holding the door closed, quickly dropped to grasp one of my wrists and pinned it above my head. His lips pressed where my neck curved into my shoulder, drawing forth a gasp.

My heart rate picked up speed. "Jamie, stop it." I didn't want him to know he was affecting me, but his touch, no matter how rough, and his lips made my body betray me.

He trailed open mouth kisses up my neck. My skin pebbled with goose bumps. When he sucked, then nipped with his teeth at the sensitive spot just below my ear, my whole body shuddered. "You want this," he said. His hand on my stomach slipped down over my thigh and his fingers began hiking up my nightgown until it bunched at my hips.

"Who are you trying to convince? Me or yourself?" I growled with zero oomph behind it.

He bit down hard on my sensitive spot, forcing a groan from me. "I know you want this, but you're fighting it," he whispered as he grazed my ear with his lips and his finger plucked at the band on my underwear. "If I slip my fingers into your panties right now, I'll find you wet and ready for me."

Why did the word *panties* falling from his lips seem to undo me? If I hadn't been wet before, I definitely was now. I ached to give in, beg him to fuck me. But I'd hate myself after.

His fingers slipped into the thin fabric protecting my core. I hadn't known I'd been holding my breath until he glided between my folds, brushing over my clit, making me gasp for air. "Fuck, baby, you're soaked," he groaned. His mouth began working my neck again, licking as he went. His strong fingers rubbed my bud of nerves into a frenzy. I was panting without even realizing it.

My body was desperate for him. My heart was scared of him. My mind was angry with him. I was short circuiting, unsure of what to do. In that moment nothing seemed right or wrong. I was just trying to exist.

When he circled my entrance before pushing a finger inside me, I whimpered. He finger fucked me slowly before adding a second while the heel of his palm ground against my clit. My restraint withered. I threw my head back on his shoulder, moaning.

"You're clenching around my fingers. Your pussy is begging me not to leave it. I wonder if my tongue would get the same response." My brain didn't even have time to process his dirty words because he tore his fingers away from my panties, spun me around, and slammed my back against the door. My night-gown was ripped off my shoulders, literally. The tearing of fabric barely registered to my lust subdued brain and before I knew it, I was standing before him completely naked. My protests bubbled in my chest but died in my throat when he kneeled and sucked my clit between his lips. I arched my back to give him better access. My leg was lifted and hooked over his shoulder. He worked my clit and probed my core with his tongue, forcing me to cry out. On one shaky leg, I rocked my hips as he got me to the edge. As I was about to fall from it and meet my climax, the bastard pulled away and got to his feet. His lustful eyes met mine while he wiped his wet mouth with the back of his hand.

"You want this," he said, flicking his fingers between us.

My lungs constricted. *He was playing with me.*

"I didn't want this. You made me want you!" I snapped and pushed off the wall. I slammed my fists down on his chest in a fit of rage. "I hate you! I hate you!" I repeated as I continued to slam my fists on his chest. He caught me by my wrists, but not before my fingers could snag ahold of his shirt. With my strength combined with his, we ripped it open, sending buttons flying.

His beautiful yet angry hazel eyes bored into mine as if they could read my every thought and every secret. With how perceptive he was, I wouldn't have doubted it. That was just another reason why I needed to stay away from him. I pulled at my wrists he still held tightly, to no avail.

"You don't hate me," he declared, stepping closer to me, invading my space, forcing me to step back. He did it again and again, walking me backwards. My hip bumped into a chair. He kicked it over and out of the way, pushing me even further until my bare ass touched the table. "You want to hate me, but you don't. The question is why?"

I pursed my lips in a tight line and tried to yank my hands free again. He surprised me by letting go. My freedom was short lived. As soon as he released me, his hands dropped to the back of my thighs and he hoisted me up onto the table. He stepped between my legs and pushed me back, not so gently until I was laying before him. He shrugged off his dress shirt, fluidly, then his hands pulled roughly at my hips until my ass was slightly hanging over the edge of the table. The distinct sound of a belt unbuckling reached my ears and I went to sit up, but his strong hand shoved me back down. "If you don't want to tell me right now, then fine. But I won't let this go, baby. I told you you were mine and I meant it," he bit out angrily. The sound of his zipper echoed in the room and my breathing picked up. I shouldn't have wanted him, but I did. I should have left, but I couldn't.

I felt him line up with my entrance and without warning or easing me into it, he slammed into me. I screamed out. "This is what you wanted," he grunted as he pounded into me with his hand locked on my hips. "You told everyone this was your fantasy. To be fucked on this table until you screamed." He was rough, angry, and unrelenting. It was the perfect mixture of punishing pleasure that I knew deep down I deserved. His hips rolled, changing the angle slightly so his pelvis was hitting my clit and I moaned out his name, begging him not to stop.

"That's it, baby. Come back to me." Without interrupting his rhythm, he reached up and cupped the back of my neck. Lifting me up into a sitting position, he touched his lips to mine. My legs locked around his waist and I held onto his shoulders. His fingers snaked into my hair, deepening our kiss as his cock continued to stretch my pussy and bumped into my cervix. I was so close. Between his passionate kiss where his tongue rivaled mine and the way his pelvis kept beating on my clit, I was hurtling towards the edge.

"Jamie! Oh fuck, Jamie!" I yelled out between kisses.

"I love the way you scream my name."

His deep and raspy voice did me in. I came so hard, spots took away my sight. My body locked around him, holding on for dear life. My nails scraped across his skin as my pussy contracted. He grunted and his hips began to jerk in short spurts as he found his own release, filling me with his warm essence.

Our ragged and labored breaths matched each other. My forehead was resting on his shoulder while I recovered. My legs and arms had fallen from around him like weak spaghetti. With how far my ass was hanging off the table, it was his body alone that prevented me from falling to the floor. His arms circled around me, hugging me tightly as if afraid to let me go. Lips pressed to my temple and a hand stroked my hair, showering me with affection.

The more I came down from my orgasm, the more lucid I became. My whole body tensed up. Just because we'd had sex didn't mean it had changed anything.

He stilled, hand mid stroke, sensing my change. Before he stepped away, he lowered me to the ground, being careful not to let me fall. When his face came into view, he was unreadable.

While he pulled up and buckled his pants, I went searching for my nightgown. It was practically ripped in half. *Great*, now I'd have to venture up to my room naked. There had to be twenty cameras between here and there.

A shirt was draped over my shoulders. By the burgundy color, I realized it was Jamie's dress shirt. Peeking over my shoulder, I found him in only his pants. Without saying a word, he leaned in, kissed my head and left.

CHAPTER FORTY

Z ombie-ing out of bed, I ran into Asher out in the hall.
The smell of coffee hit my nose and my eyes zeroed in on
the mug he was holding. He offered me the mug. I gratefully accepted it and brought the hot liquid up to my mouth,
blowing on it a few times before taking a sip. Internally, I wept for
joy. It was perfect.

"Thank you, Thor, god of coffee."

Going in for another sip, I glanced at him over my mug. The
corner of his mouth twitched as he took in my appearance. It was
another night of barely getting any sleep. My hair was in a
tangled knot on top of my head. I was wearing baggy and tatty
old sweats, because one: it had gotten cold last night. Winter was
starting to rear her ugly head. And two: Jamie had ripped my
nightgown apart.

"I know I look like shit. I feel like it too," I grumbled and
walked away, heading for the stairs. It was breakfast time; even
despite Asher's best efforts, I didn't eat breakfast, but I wanted to
check on Stefan. Not that I would outright ask him how he was
doing; I could still sit with him and see if I could pick up on
anything.

"Can you get me the names of the goons who accompanied us last night during the exchange with De Luca?" I asked over my shoulder. Asher's brows narrowed, but he nodded. "They don't know how to keep their fucking mouths shut. My little tryst with the don reached Jamie. This was the very thing I wanted to avoid. I would rather risk it on my own than surround myself with rats," I spewed angrily.

"Ah, that explains the mark on your neck."

I stopped walking once I reached the bottom of the stairs and peered back at him. "What?" My hand shot up to my neck, fingers grazing a tender area of skin. That bastard! Jamie had bitten hard enough to brand me.

"You might want to put your hair down before you head in there," he suggested, tilting his head towards the dining room. I made quick work of untying my hair and shaking it out. "I'll track down Dean and get those names. Make sure you eat something," he said before taking off in the opposite direction.

Jamie and Stefan were in the middle of eating their breakfast, looking ready to start their day. Conor, Rourke, and my aunt Kiara were also here. My aunt sat at the other end of the table, across from Stefan, with Conor and Rourke flanking her. Everyone glanced in my direction as I entered the room. Kiara's face was grief stricken, eyes red and puffy. She was the only one who didn't have a plate of food in front of her. Instead, her fingers were wrapped around a full mug of black coffee. Her eyes only met mine for a second before they dropped to stare absently at her mug. I looked from her to Stefan. Kiara's open display of emotion made me wonder if that was how Stefan looked internally. He eyed my appearance with disdain as I made my way towards my seat at his right.

"I thought we got you proper sleepwear?"

I smiled at Stefan's clear disapproval of my chosen ratty-tatty sweats. "Yes. Silky and skimpy sleepwear that would be perfect for summer or to entice a partner," I retorted and finished off my coffee before placing the empty mug on the table. "I got cold."

"You look like a homeless person," Rourke snickered next to me.

I gasped, mocking my outrage. "Rude."

He grinned. Fingers brushed my neck as my hair was pushed away. I stilled. Looking back at Stefan, I found him staring at my neck, or more specifically the hickey blemishing my skin. I hadn't seen it, but if my father's brows raising was any indication of how bad it was, it had to be ugly. Stefan's eyes shifted from my neck to Jamie, who surprise surprise was holding an unreadable expression. Stefan cocked a brow at him. Jamie made no comment and brushed him off by stabbing more eggs with his fork. Stefan sighed, releasing my hair, then returned to eating.

Ignoring them, I looked around the table. Aunt Kiara was still fixating on her coffee while Conor kept glancing at her, concerned, in between bites of food. I leaned closer to Rourke. "What's going on? Not that I don't like starting my day seeing your ugly mug, but what are you all doing here?" I whispered.

Rourke grimaced.

"Your auntie wanted to spend the morning with family," my uncle answered, clearly overhearing me. "Isn't that right, love?" He placed his hand on her arm gently. Kiara jumped, startled out of her daze.

"Wha—uh, yes," she stammered, and a single tear fell from her glossy eyes. "It's important to stick together—lean on each other in times of loss. Sam...he was flawed, but that doesn't mean we didn't love him," she sniffled.

I cast a concerned glance at Stefan. Shit, is he okay? I wondered if there was something I could do to help him through this. I was fine. Good riddance if you asked me, but that didn't mean Samuel's death hadn't hurt others. My family hurting affected me.

Stefan's brow puckered as he watched his sister. Sensing me staring at him, he looked at me. Reading my expression, he rolled his eyes. "Don't compare me to your aunt."

"Do you want to spend the day together? We could go some-where for lunch? Or we could go on vacation? Disneyland is known to be the happiest place on earth. Lord knows we need that particular feeling by the truck load. California has wonderful weather year-round. We can walk along the beach and—"

"Maura," Stefan said, interrupting my rambling by placing a hand over mine. "We're not going to Disneyland."

My shoulders slumped. "Talk about crushing a girl's dreams. Way to go, Stefan," I grumbled sourly.

He gave my hand a tiny squeeze, drawing my eyes to meet his. He gave me a quick reassuring look that told me he was fine, and I let it go.

"We couldn't do anything today, anyways. Rourke was about to invite you to tag along with him on his special errand," Stefan started.

"I—what?" Rourke stared at Stefan, confused, which Stefan returned with a pointed look. "Oh, yeah. Uh, I'm delivering a shipment to a buyer. Want to come?"

Real smooth, guys. Stefan was trying to pawn me off. The sad thing was, it was working. I was itching to know how we ran guns. "Sure."

An Escalade and an unmarked utility van were waiting for me in the driveway when Rourke came to pick me up. I didn't know what to wear to sell guns. Playing it safe, I went with business casual by choosing skin-tight black slacks, black peep-toe ankle boots, and a canary-yellow long sleeve blouse. I had no choice but to leave my hair down. There wasn't enough makeup in the world to cover the dark, huge hickey Jamie had given me. Asshole.

I slipped on a leather jacket as I rushed towards the door. Asher was already waiting outside. Dean had drawn the short straw and had been sent upstairs to get me once Rourke had arrived.

"Finally," Rourke griped. I flipped him off as I bounced down the steps leading to the cobblestone drive. Everyone started climbing into their assigned vehicle. Rourke hopped into the back of the Escalade. I slid in next to him and Dean sandwiched me between them, then shut the door. Asher rode shotgun, while Rourke's enforcer drove. Two other guys who worked under Rourke followed us in the utility van that was carrying our merchandise.

"Heard you kissed the don," Rourke said teasingly as we drove through downtown.

I was going to string up that goon by his toes and Stefan himself wouldn't be able to stop me. "If it matters, he kissed me. Not that I need to explain myself."

"How'd Jameson take it?"

"The fucker bit me," I grumbled.

"No shit? Let me see?" He turned his body expectantly. I sighed and lifted my hair. He hissed, then chuckled. "He went all caveman on you. Good for him."

"Hey!" I smacked him with the back of my hand on his shoulder. "I'm not—"

I didn't get to finish chastising him. Loud popping and glass shattering startled us all. Blood exploded from the front seat, spraying on my face. There was a split second where Rourke's green eyes met mine before hell ensued. His eyes moved from mine to look past me. Something made them widen and he went to reach for me, but a force slammed into the side of the car. Rourke's hand never reached me. Not that he could prevent what was to come.

Time slowed down. I was thrown from my seat. The car felt like it was flying, suspending me in the air as if I were weightless. Then gravity happened. My body was tossed around like a rag doll, hitting and smacking everything hard. I tried to grab onto anything. Headrests, seatbelts, they all slipped through my fingers. My head slammed against a side window, breaking it, then everything went black. For how long, I didn't know.

I came to face down on the ceiling in the trunk space. The Escalade was upside-down, windows shattered all around, leaving me lying on a bed of glass and debris. The whole world spun as my head redefined the word agony. The rest of me wasn't any better off. Every inch of my body felt battered and bruised. I didn't know where to start assessing the extent of my injuries.

"Maura!" someone called out to me.

A pathetic whimper was all I could respond with as words failed me.

"Damnit! Maura!" someone cursed. The sound of movement followed. I was rolled over, the pain forcing me to cry out. "It's okay, cuz. I got you." Rourke pulled my head and shoulders into his lap, eyes roaming over me in an assessing way. He looked like shit. Blood was splattered over his face. His cheek and ear were bleeding.

"Is she alive?!" Dean shouted, sounding panicked.

"Yeah!" Rourke yelled over his shoulder. "We've got to get out of here," he said, staring down at me.

Rustling and glass crunching was followed by footsteps echoing outside the car. "Maura, can you grab my hand?"

I turned my head as much as I could, finding both Dean and Asher kneeling outside the car. Dean reached inside, hand held out for me. Thank fuck, they were alright. Gritting my teeth, I lifted my arm and grabbed his hand. Before he could start to pull me out, more popping came. Gunfire. Rourke threw his body on top of mine and we all hunkered down. Bullets flew around us. Loud thunks made the car shake. Rourke's body jerked and he grunted above me. I knew I was hit when a sharp burning ignited on my side. I screamed into Rourke's shoulder.

The squealing of tires and the sound of more gunfire seemed to cease the firing on our car. It was like we were in the middle of a war zone. Dean never let go of my hand and the moment the fire was taken off of us, he wasted no time in pulling me out of the car. I was grateful I was wearing a leather jacket because I could feel glass scraping underneath me. Once I was out, Asher took me from Dean and sat me up against the car. He put a gun in my hand, then stood guard while Dean reached back into the car to retrieve Rourke.

Watching them, I was shocked they were still standing. They were cut up, banged up, and covered in enough blood to cause concern. Asher's nose was bleeding and he had a bunch of tiny cuts splashed across his face and neck. Blood was spilling like ribbons from a gash on Dean's scalp, just above his left temple.

Looking around, I found we had crash landed at the edge of a parking garage. Peeking out at where the gunfire continued to go off, I saw the two guys in the utility van were giving us cover from what looked like an army of men. Three SUVs, similar to ours, were lined up like a wall for about twenty men to use for cover to shoot from. Our two guys weren't going to be able to hold them off for long.

Dean dragged Rourke from the car, grunting from the exertion. Rourke wasn't moving. With adrenaline numbing my pain, I helped roll him over onto his back. "Shit! Shit! Shit!" I cursed. His shirt was soaked with blood. He groaned and put a hand to his stomach. I lifted up his shirt. Blood was pooling from a small hole a few inches from his belly button.

"We've got to move," Asher said and lifted Rourke to his feet. He took most of Rourke's weight by slinging his arm over his shoulder. Dean took my gun and yanked me up by my arm, making me grunt. His arm snaked around my waist after seeing how unsteady I was on my feet and the four of us ventured deeper into the parking garage.

We moved as fast as we could with me hobbling and Asher dragging Rourke. We were approaching the other side that exited into the street when tires screeched in the distance. Looking back, I saw one of our attacker's SUVs come into view. We weren't going to make it on foot. As I searched around frantically, an elevator by the exit caught my eye.

"Elevator," I pointed. Dean left me to run ahead and I limped on as quickly as I could without falling. He pressed the button to call the elevator about a million times. By the time we caught up to him, the doors opened, and we climbed in. Not really thinking, I pressed the button with the letter B that had a sticker next to it that read, Staff Only. The doors closed on the SUV coming to a screeching halt outside and the elevator made its descent.

The ride was short. Once the doors were open, I pushed the emergency stop button, preventing anyone from calling the elevator. We stepped into a mechanical room. On the far wall hung a bunch of electrical boxes with metal piping coming out of the top, traveling up the wall into the ceiling. On one side of the room there was a desk with a conference phone, walkie talkies, and a keyboard. The wall above it held six CCTVs, surveilling different areas of the parking garage. On the opposite wall was a couple bulletin boards, a mini fridge, a small table with a microwave on it, and a metal door with a tiny window that showed concrete stairs leading up.

Noticing a walkie talkie missing from the charging station, I could only assume the security guard had bolted the moment guns had started firing.

Eyeing the door leading to the stairs, I darted for it and turned the bolt, locking it. It wouldn't be enough, especially if they started shooting through the window. "We need to block off the door," I said out loud, looking around.

"We'll do that. Take care of Rourke," Asher ordered, laying Rourke on the floor. He was pale from losing too much blood. I looked around again for anything that might help stop his bleeding. A first aid kit hanging on the wall had me hobbling across the room.

Dean and Asher worked quickly, moving the large metal desk in front of the door, and as they were lifting the mini fridge on top of it to block the small window, Dean yelled out, "Incoming!"

"We need to call for help," I stated, ripping the white plastic first aid kit off the wall.

The door handle jiggled before the sound of loud banging. I could barely hear Asher talking on his cell as I kneeled next to Rourke and started sifting through the kit. I came across a few packets of gauze. Tearing the paper packaging, I stacked the pieces and pressed them firmly over Rourke's wound. He groaned loudly.

"If it hurts, it means you're alive," I said, reassuring him and myself. I released a shuddering breath. Now that I was finally sitting still, my aches and pains were quickly catching up to me. I wanted to throw up from the pounding pressure coming from my head. The side of my yellow shirt was soaked with blood and there was a sharpness intensifying on my side. With one hand, I lifted my shirt. Damnit. I'd been shot just above my hip. I was bleeding, but not as profusely as Rourke. Glancing back at the first aid kit, I saw Band-Aids, disinfectant, and an Ace bandage, all of which couldn't help me.

"Maura."

I quickly dropped my shirt. Asher stood behind me, holding out his phone.

I took it and put it to my ear, expecting it to be Stefan. "Hello?"

There was a sigh of relief on the other end. "Maura." Jamie's deep voice reached all the way to my soul, soothing it with relief.

Shots went off and bullets embedded in the metal door. Glass sprayed out as the small window shattered. Dean and Asher took cover against the concrete wall. They both released the clips on their guns, going over how much ammo they had left. It was obvious they didn't think the door was going to hold.

"Maura!" Jamie yelled, pulling my attention back to the phone.

"We can't hold them off," I said, voice strangely calm.

"I'm coming, baby." He tried to sound just as calm, but I could still hear his fear. He wasn't going to make it in time.

More shots rang out, cementing that realization. I did my best to tune them out as I let my feelings and regrets for the man on the phone come to the surface.

"I'm sorry," I blurted out.

"Maura—"

"You asked me what had changed—what was really keeping us apart and the truth is...I was scared." Tears I hadn't known were forming fell from my eyes. "I've loved you since we were kids and I haven't stopped loving you. It's only grown deeper. When I saw you with Angela, I realized you held my heart. You have the power to hurt me beyond repair and that scared me. I wish I could go back and yell at myself. Make me face my fear instead of running away from it because that would have meant I could have spent these last few days with you." I sniffled and closed my blurry eyes. The shooting had stopped, but there was banging and the sound of metal scraping. Dean and Asher were cursing and yelling as they fought to keep the door closed.

"I'm almost—" Jamie's words were cut off as shots went off from within the room, making me flinch.

Time was up.

"I love you, Jamie."

To Be Continued...

ASHLEY N. ROSTEK

ENDURE
The Pain

THE MAURA QUINN SERIES BOOK TWO

ABOUT THE AUTHOR

Ashley N. Rostek is a wife and mother by day and a writer by night. She survives on coffee, loves collecting offensive coffee mugs, and is an unashamed bibliophile.

To Ashley, there isn't a better pastime than letting your mind escape in a good book. Her favorite genre is romance and has the overflowing bookshelf to prove it. She is a lover of love. Be it a sweet YA or a dark and lusty novel, she must read it!

Ashley's passion is writing. She picked up the pen at seventeen and hasn't put it down. Her debut novel is Embrace the Darkness, the first book in the Maura Quinn series.

SOCIAL MEDIA

You can find out more about Ashley and her upcoming works on social media!

The Inner Circle ~ Ashley N. Rostek's Book Group
https://www.facebook.com/groups/arostektheinnercircle/
(THE BEST PLACE TO STAY UPDATED)

FACEBOOK
https://www.facebook.com/ashleynrostek/

INSTAGRAM

https://www.instagram.com/ashleynrostek/

<u>NEWSLETTER</u>

https://landing.mailerlite.com/webforms/landing/j7z0t1

Printed in Great Britain
by Amazon